Antimony

Antimony

by

Amy E. Richter

RESOURCE *Publications* · Eugene, Oregon

ANTIMONY

Resource Publications
An Imprint of Wipf and Stock Publishers
199 W. 8th Ave., Suite 3
Eugene, OR 97401

www.wipfandstock.com

PAPERBACK ISBN: 978-1-5326-8950-5
HARDCOVER ISBN: 978-1-5326-8951-2
EBOOK ISBN: 978-1-5326-8952-9

Manufactured in the U.S.A.   SEPTEMBER 13, 2019

To Joe

Contents

KAIA

SUMMER'S END

Blood

As I stroked the obsidian blade I had swiped from the museum's supply room, I practiced what I would say when I saw Dr. Vadim Grigori, when I would plunge the sleek black knife into the milky white skin of his neck and puncture his carotid artery. Just before the fluid would release its amoniac odor and stain his crisp white shirt and his silver-blue eyes would widen at me in surprise, I would make sure the last words he heard in this world were mine: "I hate the smell of Nephil blood, but sometimes it's unavoidable."

So much about me had changed during the four short weeks I had known him. Would Dr. Grigori congratulate himself for making me so much after his own image, even as I snuffed out his life? Would he note how well I had learned to lie, steal, hate, and now kill, under his tutelage? Would his last thought be: my darling progeny, my own creation? Was it the training I had received in the Grigori Young Scholars Program or the now-daily doses of antimony I needed for survival that bred these violent thoughts?

I started to wrap the blade in the pink GYSP T-shirt I thought made a fitting sheath, and caught my reflection in the knife's gleaming surface. I smiled at my newfound confidence.

Rats. A bead of spinach stuck in the gap between my right lateral incisor and cuspid.

Okay, my fierce avenger image still needed work. I rummaged the blob out with my pinky fingernail and checked my smile one more time in my dangerous mirror. I swaddled my weapon in the shirt and tucked it into my backpack. I pulled my locket from beneath my sweatshirt and the angel's wing engraved on the surface glinted as it caught the light. Snapping open the locket's lid, I tilted out one of the tiny gray pills, and gulped it down. The taste of metallic sand and its acrid sting grazed the back of my throat, warmth radiated from my solar plexus to my forehead and feet, and the scars on my back tingled. I recalled sounds and scents from far away: the thrush-thrushing of an angel unfolding its wings, the scraping against rock of chains stronger than titanium, and the pungent whiff of sulfur, and I knew it was time to go to work.

1

Two Months Earlier

Fresh Ink

The morning of my sixteenth birthday, my scars woke me up. Usually it was a smell that woke me: the scent, unique as a fingerprint, of someone already awake and walking around downstairs, releasing their particular combination of sweet and sour notes, stirring them into the molecules of morning before I could make adjustments in my breathing to tamp down the olfactory effect.

But that morning, it was my scars. In the stillness and dark, I felt them start to tingle and hum, as if they too were awaking, as if I might catch them aglow if I could crane my neck around far enough to see the twin vertical lines on either side of my spine. Lying on my back, I shimmied my left hand beneath me to run my fingertips across each of the two-inch long ridges that protruded like skinny twin caterpillars against my cotton nightshirt. My scars felt familiar to the touch, but on the inside a glimmer flickered, like I imagine a firefly feels before it turns on its light and blinks: *here I am, here I am.*

I glanced at my alarm clock. A couple of minutes remained before it would start its urgent buzzing. I flicked the switch to off, feeling gypped that today would be a few minutes longer than it had to be. I hauled myself out of bed and into the shower, got dressed, and checked my email before heading downstairs.

Just one message with the title, Fly Away. I didn't recognize the sender, GYSP, but, hey, at least someone was paying attention to me on what promised to be my worst birthday ever.

I clicked on the message and the screen turned sapphire blue, like the sky in November just before the first stars twinkle into view. A pencil-thin drawing of an angel's wing shimmered in silver on top of the blue. My name materialized on the wing's surface in a gossamer gold cursive script and pulsed gently.

I moved the cursor onto my name and became aware that the marker and my heart palpitated in concert. I hit enter and a video sprang to life. A man with jet black hair, but gray around the temples, straight white teeth, and warm olive skin, looked directly into the camera. He smiled as he said in a deep voice, "Hello Kaia." He paused, as if he knew I would need a moment while it sank in that this total stranger knew my name. "Pardon me for using your nickname. I prefer formal introductions, but I believe no one addresses you by your given name, Malachi."

"Malachi Catriona Smith!" came a hoarse hollering from downstairs. No one, that is, except my Aunt Alina the morning after she's been on a bender.

"Breakfast!" she yelled up the stairs. By which she meant, Get your butt down here and make me some.

"I'll be there in a minute!" I called in reply.

I turned back to the screen and the distinguished-looking man continued, "I am Dr. Vadim Grigori. It is my pleasure to tell you that you have been selected for participation in the Grigori Young Scholars Program. An exclusive group of promising students like yourself has been selected from all over the globe to attend a special summer study program at Harvard Divinity School. All expenses will be paid. This program will open doors you cannot yet imagine."

This had to be some kind of joke. Why would I be chosen for any kind of 'Scholars Program'? Who calls B minus students 'promising'?

"Kaia!" Aunt Alina shouted again. "Stop making me yell! My head hurts."

Her alcohol- and nicotine-laced breath streamed up toward me. I was sure she wanted me to whip up some Aunt Alina's Can't Fail Hangover Cure.

"Just a minute," I answered, trying to keep my volume down and a cheerful note in my voice.

"Kaia," the man said in his voice like dark oak, "you are a very special young woman. You have gifts that cannot be measured by SATs and GPAs."

I stifled a snort laugh.

"The Board of the Grigori Young Scholars Program has become aware of you and your hyperosmia. Some people, no doubt, find your heightened olfactory acuity strange, even unattractive. But we recognize it for what it is: a rare and important asset."

I swallowed hard. How did he know about my crazy sense of smell? He was right though. The fact that I could smell particular people coming from fifty feet away, detect who was in the room next door based on their body odor, or tell who they had kissed, or had to beat a hasty retreat when members of the football team decided not to change their lucky socks was not endearing. People thought I was nosy, no pun intended, or stand-offish, or just plain weird. When I was little, I would just sniff and let my thoughts show on my face. I quickly earned the nicknames Snuffleupagus and Snort. Once I learned to monitor my breathing to dampen my sense of smell, Mouthbreather got added to the list. Nice.

My condition has a name: hyperosmia, an over-active sense of smell. My parents had me checked out because there's another condition called parosmia, when you misidentify an odor, and another called phantosmia, a smell hallucination, when you smell things that aren't there. Either of these can be symptoms of schizophrenia or a brain hemorrhage. I checked out fine, just super sensitive.

Over time, I've gotten used to the fact that I experience the world in a different way from everyone around me, that it's really possible to smell when someone is afraid, that your friend's mother is trying to cover up her morning gin and tonic but it clings to your friend when she hugs him before school, that a person at the next table in the cafeteria has just eaten a bologna sandwich two days past expiration and they probably won't be making it to school for the algebra test tomorrow. I learned to keep my mouth shut, except when breathing through it, of course.

The man on the screen intoned, "We are offering you a rare opportunity to study with other young people who are like you. Imagine fitting in for the first time in your life."

He smiled and tilted his head slightly toward me. His eyes were silver-blue and sparkled as he inclined his chin.

"Join us."

He was looking directly at me. It was unsettling. And exciting.

"Soon a letter will arrive in the post—a traditional paper invitation. Show it to your aunt. I am certain she will agree this is just what you need to secure your future."

I was certain she wouldn't mind getting rid of me for the summer.

"And, you have no need for concern. We will keep your secret."

My secret? I gulped, a pang of guilt rising in my throat as I patted my jeans pocket to make sure the little plastic container of pills was there. How could he know about that?

"I look forward to meeting you in person, Kaia. Happy birthday."

The video contracted to a pinpoint, then the whole screen went blank. I right-clicked, panicking that my computer had crashed. The screen brightened. My inbox was there, with a few pathetic emails, notices from the library about overdue books and reminders from the school counselor about finding constructive things to do over the summer, but the GYSP email had vanished. I clicked Send/Receive Mail. I checked the trash. Nothing. Like it never existed.

Aunt Alina's whine broke the silence. "Kaia, please! It's almost time for school. Stop torturing me!"

I blew out a sigh and headed downstairs, the mysterious Dr. Grigori's words still in my head: "Join us. We will keep your secret." His voice was so smooth, but he held his s's just a little too long, like hisses.

Aunt Alina was sitting at the kitchen table, head in her hands. She was wearing her feathered mules and leopard print robe, but the gold lame scoop neck shirt she loved to wear dancing peaked out where her robe gaped open.

"Hangover cure?" I asked.

She nodded. "Honey pie, I'm sorry, I was just having such a great time with that adorable policeman. And," she leaned in close, "Officer Friendly gave me some dynamite pictures from the accident."

I cringed. How she could talk that way about anything related to the event that killed my parents was beyond me. I started breaking eggs into the blender and smelled the bleachy odor of freshly printed photographs. I looked over my shoulder and saw Aunt Alina spreading pictures out on the table behind me. I turned back to the blender, added the prescribed shot of Tabasco and emptied a can of Sprite into the mix while I pushed Pulse a few times. I sniffed back an angry tear.

"Oh sweet cakes, I heard that," she said. "I know it's a sore subject and I understand. I just wanted something to help you put this whole horrible thing behind you and move forward. Don't you think it's what your parents would want?"

I sloshed the slimy mass into a glass, stuck in a plastic straw and slapped it down in front of Aunt Alina.

She looked up at me and smiled weakly. The mascara she hadn't removed from last night had smudged, and she looked like a bedraggled raccoon. "Okay, honey buns, that's enough. Have a seat and give your Auntie a break." She patted the chair next to her. I sat but kept my face turned away from the photos on the table.

"There's nothing gruesome here," she said. "Just pictures of the car, or what's left of it. The pictures were taken after they took your mom and dad away."

I still couldn't look. Mom and Dad had died in a fiery crash on a country road three months earlier. They had gotten a call from a family friend who had invited the three of us to come for dinner. She said she had something important to discuss with my parents. I had a lot of homework, so I stayed home.

The phone rang two hours after my parents left. It was the friend, wondering if my parents had forgotten.

When I told her they had left hours ago, she told me to call my Aunt Alina and tell her to come be with me immediately. My heart started pounding. Aunt Alina had never spent much time with our family, but she was my only relative and her number was written down by the phone: In case of emergency—Aunt Alina. I barely knew her, so I was surprised the friend even knew her name.

A police officer and my aunt arrived about the same time a few hours later. I could smell burned metal, wire, and flesh, and knew before the officer opened his mouth that there had been an accident. After taking off his hat, the officer told us that my parents were both dead, probably died instantly, before their car was engulfed in fire. The car had gone off the road in a wooded area, flipped over onto its roof, and burst into flames.

No one was able to say why the crash had happened. There was no evidence of their car braking hard or swerving to avoid something on the road.

The police had received a call from a driver who happened to be passing the location of the accident. Said he had just driven past when he heard an explosion and thought the police ought to take a look.

My aunt suggested I go to my room while the officer provided more details, but I heard enough:

"Bodies too damaged to test for blood-alcohol or other substances . . . scorch marks on the vehicle abnormally dense and widespread . . . interior consumed . . . fortunate the caller happened to be driving past since there's never much traffic out that way . . . should be grateful for the kindness of strangers."

My aunt spoke up, "The caller was a kind of a guardian angel."

"Yes, Ma'am, I suppose he was."

I was stunned. Guardian angel? If this was the best a guardian angel could do, he, or she, or it, or whatever, was the worst ever. I thought angels were supposed to help, not just bring you really terrible news. My aunt was seriously off.

"But maybe he *was* your guardian angel," Aunt Alina insisted after the officer left and I shared my cynical thoughts. "Someone's watching out for you. Remember, you were supposed to be in that car."

§

Three months later, we were here at the breakfast table, and Aunt Alina was trying to get my attention. She took a drag on her cigarette and blew it out the side of her mouth.

"Come on, honey, just take a look," she said, and tapped one manicured finger on the corner of a picture.

All right, already, I thought. I turned my head slowly, gritted my teeth, and followed her candy apple red talon. The photo showed the tail end of the car, blackened and upside down, and something on the scorched earth beside it. I inhaled sharply.

"What is it, sweetheart? What do you see?"

"It's . . ." I started. "That looks like . . ." I gaped at Aunt Alina, who was staring at me. "I know it's just twigs and leaves, but doesn't it look like . . .?" I didn't finish out loud. Something in how Aunt Alina was studying me made me uncomfortable. But so did what I saw in the photo. Someone had placed sticks and twigs on the ground right next to the burned out car in exactly the same shape as I had just seen in my email from the Grigori Young Scholars Program—an angel's wing. If I hadn't just seen the shimmering wing on my laptop, I wouldn't have noticed it. Leaves and sticks in the woods—so what? But it was definitely the same design. I clasped my hands to keep them from shaking.

"Come on, honey, tell me what gave you such a start. Give me a hint. I want to see it too," Aunt Alina pleaded. But she was looking at me, not the photo. She reminded me of a detective in a TV show probing a suspect for information in an interview room, fluorescent bulbs overhead turning everyone's skin tone green, while some unseen presence watches through a one-way mirror. The detective shows the photo to break the suspect, not illuminate something that's happened.

"It's nothing," I said, trying to sound calm, "It's just a shock to see how wrecked everything is. But you're right, it's good that I looked. I should get to school." My chair scraped against the linoleum as I stood. "See you later," I yelled over my shoulder as I grabbed my book bag. I double-checked my pants pocket for my pill container and hurried outside.

§

That night Aunt Alina watched television and answered astrological queries on her laptop ("Astrology by Alina" was her online business) while I worked on my Spanish homework. I tried to resist the urge to copy the answer key from the back of the textbook, but gave in more frequently than I knew was good for me. *Yo soy the birthday girl, after all. Feliz cumpleanos a mi, or something like that.*

At about ten o'clock, I put on my pajamas and found Aunt Alina had shifted to the kitchen. She was sitting at the table, hunched over her magnifying mirror, redoing her makeup. "More drama for the evening hours," she told me as she swiped mascara onto her eyelashes. She'd had her lashes extended so far it looked like she had trapped spiders under her eyelids. "Remember," she said, "there are no ugly women. Just lazy ones."

Aunt Alina's dream was to be a makeup expert to the stars and provide them with expert astrological advice. "Cosmetologist and Cosmic-ologist to the A-Listers!" she'd told me. "Remember, 'if you can dream it, you can achieve it.'" She actually thought a good summer project for me would be entering a beauty pageant. "You know the Franksville Sauerkraut Fest Queen pageant has a 'Most Improved' category. With my help, you could place in that." Aunt Alina and I weren't exactly on the same wavelength when it came to aspirations. But at least she had some. I didn't really, other than getting away from my sadness, not entering a beauty pageant, and now, finding out what happened to my parents.

"I have a date," Aunt Alina said. "Officer Friendly again. I hope he doesn't think I'm getting too clingy."

I screwed up my courage and asked her if she knew the lullaby my mother used to sing to me, and hummed a couple of notes. I really wanted to hear it tonight.

"Sure. My mother—your mother's mother—used to sing it to us."

"You mean, my grandmother," I said, wondering at the distance of her phrasing.

"I guess, technically." She dropped the mascara wand from her eyes and looked at me, curiosity creasing her botox-smoothed brow.

"Technically?" I asked. I didn't know my grandmother. She had died before I was born. "What do you mean, 'technically'?"

"You mean your mother never told you? Well then, my bad. She had this thing about making you wait until you were old enough to tell you where you came from. I suppose now I'll have to be the one."

I grimaced. Did she really think I didn't know about sex? Just because I wasn't with someone didn't mean I was completely in the dark.

"Don't do that to your face," Aunt Alina said, and flapped her hand at my forehead. "Correction is expensive." I tried to pull my face back into neutral and switch the topic, but she beat me to it.

"Well, you're going to have to hold on a little longer. Don't want to keep Officer Handsome waiting. But here," she said, pulling a small object from the pocket of her lounge coat and handing it to me. It was a red velvet jewelry box tied with a gold ribbon. "Happy birthday, sweetheart. Go on, open it."

I untied the ribbon and opened the box. A small gold oval on a long chain was nestled on the satin interior. I lifted it from the box and noticed an engraving on one side. I caught my breath. For the third time today I saw the same disembodied angel wing. I held it closer, while I stared. No, this was slightly different—the mirror image of the other two.

"Let me help you with that," Aunt Alina said, seeing me hesitate. She pushed on the delicate clasp and the top popped open. Inside were two tiny photographs, one on each side of the locket. Two young girls smiled out at me.

"Do you recognize us?" Aunt Alina asked.

I looked closer at the miniscule photos.

"It's your mother and me, when we were about your age. Your mother got this locket from our mother as a birthday gift when she turned sixteen. Seems like you should have it now. Here," Aunt Alina said, and motioned for me to hold my hair out of the way so she could put the necklace on me. "I looked for a small photo of you to replace the one of me, but I couldn't find any pictures that fit. You can put whatever you like in there."

My eyes welled with tears of grief for my parents and at this act of kindness from my aunt who was now scooping make-up back into her kit.

"The lullaby," I started again. "Could you sing it to me before you go? It would make me feel a little better hearing it tonight."

"Aw, that's sweet. But honey, lullabies are for babies, and it's time for you to grow up."

That night, under the covers, I sang the lullaby to myself. My voice quavered and thickened with tears.

> *Angels watching ever round thee,*
> *all through the night,*
> *in thy slumbers close surround thee,*
> *all through the night.*

They should of all fears disarm thee,
 no forebodings should alarm thee,
 they will let no peril harm thee,
 all through the night.

I thought the lullaby would soothe me, but it didn't. Its mentions of "fears" and "forebodings" sent a shudder through me. I found myself wondering why my mother had sung it to me almost every night that I could remember. What did she think I needed protection from? I thought again of Aunt Alina's strange comment the night of the accident about the caller being my guardian angel. I shivered and closed my eyes, hoping I would fall asleep quickly. At least I hadn't needed one of my pills today.

By the end of the summer I would understand that the caller was an angel of sorts, but what he was guarding definitely wasn't me.

2

ANCIENT DAYS

The Temptation of Samya

Samya inhaled deeply, expecting the morning's customary aromas of jasmine and oleander. The stench that assaulted her was not only dreadful, it was impossible. Was her impeccable sense of smell yet another casualty of the Ordeal?

Since the waters had receded and life had begun its resurgence, daybreak usually smelled of bud and blossom, germination and sprout. She scoffed at this pathetic cosmic apology: the dead and decayed turned into fertile soil, lush greenery springing up in abundance. As if new life could absolve the Creator of the destruction of her world and the annihilation of everyone she held dear. But this morning, Samya's nostrils tingled at a disturbing combination: a mix of bright florals and the pungent tang of vomit and rotted meat.

Her mother had been a perfumer and cosmetics dealer, and Samya had learned in her shop to identify a multitude of scents. Her name, Samya, meant "exalted," reflecting her mother's belief that scent was the queen of the senses. She had taught Samya how to distinguish lemon from saffron, agarwood from ginger, peat from charcoal, the quick from the dead.

"The heart responds without hesitation to aroma, Samya. Here," her mother had said, removing a small pouch from a box of fragrance samples and passing it under Samya's nose. "What do you smell?"

"Daybreak," Samya answered. "New beginnings."

"This is essence of nard, artemesia, and acacia," her mother explained. "Notice, you did not list ingredients; you named their effect: daybreak. Yes." She reached for another tiny cloth bag.

"And this?"

Samya recoiled after sniffing. "It's terrible. Dangerous. Unearthly. What is it?"

"Unearthly. Good," said her mother, quickly cinching the strings of the pouch. She wrapped the strings around the neck of the sack several times and tucked it back into the wooden box where she kept these examples for teaching her daughter. "This is dried Nephil blood. While Nephilim live, their blood smells of the immortelle, or Everlasting Flower, with a fragrance like burnt sugar and dry straw; orris, like violets; and opoponax, with sweet balsam and lavender notes. But when Nephilim die their blood becomes putrid."

"How does it change from something exquisite to something so awful?" Samya had asked.

"When Nephilim die, their human elements decay and are released back into the earth, as happens with all humans," she answered, waving an elegant arm downward, gold bracelets on her wrist chiming as she gestured. "But their heavenly elements stay trapped in the earthly realm, where they were never meant to be. So they do not merely decay. They become rank, protesting their sublunary cage."

"Surely you never use this in perfume!" Samya exclaimed. A warm glow of excitement had begun to fill her stomach as she started to consider how and why her mother might know such things.

"All things have their uses. Educate your senses, dear Samya. One day you will find use for your knowledge."

As horrible as it was, the reek she detected as she walked farther along the path was bringing back some sweet memories, and Samya felt a pang of longing for her mother, who, like everyone else outside of Noah's immediate family, had drowned in the deluge. Samya had this same rush of memories of her mother whenever she opened her wooden box of pouches, which Samya had smuggled aboard the ark, her one memento of her life before the flood.

She wiped away a tear and at the same time felt a stab of resentment for her father-in-law Noah. Her marriage to his son Japheth was what saved her life, but Noah had called everyone else unrighteous, and she blamed him for their deaths.

She stopped walking and inhaled again, trying to focus on this morning's peculiar scent. If not for the flood, she would swear it was dead Nephil. But how could that be?

A lump of panic rose in her throat. Had someone stolen her box? That particular pouch? Had they emptied it here in this cedar grove? She looked around wildly, half hoping that someone had stolen her treasure because the alternative explanation was terrible to consider. But, if terrible, why did she feel a tingle of excitement as her nostrils widened at the smell?

No, it was absurd. All the dead had decomposed by now, surely. Yet, as she took another deep inhalation, she knew she had to consider the possibility that she was near the remains of an actual Nephil.

She winced. The smell was like vomit and meat left in the sun before maggots do their obliterating work. She thought she should just turn around, walk back home, retrieve the fragrance box from its shelf, open its lid, and reassure herself by the wonderful combination of smells that everything was in its place. She could put her nose into the container and find them all: sweet, floral, sharp, musty, herbal, grassy, woody, smoky, mossy, ammoniac, leathery, peppery, marine, nutty, animalic, and indolic. She could breathe deeply and be transported, at least in her mind, to the days before the Ordeal.

What days those were! Her mother's cosmetics and perfumes had brought her family great wealth. When she came of age, she would have taken up her mother's mantle as most sought-after purveyor of fine perfumes and cosmetics. Instead, she was the wife of Japheth. Their circumstances fell far short of the lifestyle Samya had once enjoyed. It was customary for a girl of her age to be married to a man so old, but did her mother have to consent to someone so dull?

At least she had not yet been burdened with a child by Japheth. "Be fruitful and multiply!" Noah incessantly intoned, as if her only purpose was to help replace the people he and his beloved Creator had watched struggle and drown. The thought nauseated her. Thankfully, her mother had taught her some ways to prevent Japheth's seed from taking root.

The stench's source was close by. A soaring royal empress tree stood to her right. Sunlight transformed the drops of dew on its blossoms into pink crystalline bells. Her eyes followed the sunbeams that filtered down through its branches until they rested on the mossy ground around the roots that ran like thin fingers from the base of its trunk. Then she saw the pale legs and feet, the size of a child's, protruding from behind the tree. The skin had a gray opaline translucence that reminded Samya of the wiry fungus called Ghost Flower or Eyebright.

Samya sucked in her breath. She had never encountered another person on her walks through this glade, and why would a child be out here so early in the morning and alone? She stepped quietly around the tree, walking a wide circle so that she wouldn't startle or awaken the child.

But the child, a little girl, was not sleeping. Her head was propped against the base of the tree, meeting her neck at an unnatural angle, her body limp, her legs splayed, her arms twisted like the limbs of a tiny fig tree. Her blond curls were dirty and matted. She was clad in a linen tunic, the kind parents placed on children they knew were marked for death, by famine, or plague or, in this case, flood. The wanness of her skin showed even through a film of soil, like she had been dug up and dragged to this verdant resting place and propped against the tree like a pale question mark.

The child was dead, but what was she doing here? She hadn't been here yesterday, Samya was certain of it. Who had moved her here, and why?

Covering her nose, Samya came a little closer. She could see that the girl's right hand was mangled. Probably one of the wolves that frequented the glade had uncovered her and pulled her to the tree. The girl's stench most likely kept her from becoming the wolf's dinner.

Samya gazed at the dead girl's face. Her skin was pallid, but otherwise perfect, alabaster smooth. The tiny blond lashes that rimmed the girl's closed eyes rested against her cheeks that had not yet lost their plumpness, despite the absence of life. Were it not for the strange angles of her body and the stink, Samya would think the child had simply lain down for a nap under the cedar that towered like a sentinel above her.

Was Samya's sense of smell correct? Was this a dead Nephil? She had never seen one so young.

Samya had seen living Nephilim, of course. She had even wondered if her own mother was of Nephil stock because of how skilled she was at the cosmetic arts and how comfortable she seemed selling to the Nephilim, her wealthiest clients. Nephilim usually stood out, although her mother had told her appearances could be deceiving.

"There is a luminescence to their skin. Dark- or fair-skinned, a light seems to emanate from within. This effulgence makes their skin a pleasure to enhance because the powders and ointments don't have to reflect light from the outside of the body alone. Nephilim covet my face powder because it refracts the light that comes from inside them as well."

Samya's mother had cocked her head toward the tall, handsome man who had come into the shop and was examining a box of eye-kohl. The man had lustrous black hair that hung in waves to his shoulders. His tailored silk robe clung taut against a well-muscled back. She had said in a soft voice, "Nephil, certainly. When he turns to face us, his olive skin will have a bronzy glow. I can see it even in his hands as he holds the box."

The man turned toward them. Her mother's eyes lit up in recognition.

"Mr. Turiel! Such a pleasure to see you! Such an honor to have you once again in my humble shop." She bowed low before the man who nodded.

"You merchandise the finest cosmetics, Madam Rukmin. It is appropriate to entrust my enhancements to such a talented artist." He took her hand gently but kissed his own thumb instead of her flesh. "What can you offer me today? I want my eyes to look even more commanding, if such a feat is possible."

Samya was surprised to see her confident mother duck her head demurely and look at the ground as she said, "You do me an honor by pretending I could enhance your already imposing appearance." She tittered and the man looked pleased.

"True, true," he sighed. "It will be a challenge, even for one as accomplished as yourself."

The man noticed Samya who had gone to the back of the shop and stood behind a table laden with minerals to be ground. "And who is the darling girl?" His voice sounded like warm goat's milk butter. She heard a slight purr as he said "darling girl."

Samya's mother motioned to her to come forward and stood Samya between herself and the man. "May I present my daughter, Samya," she said, and pushed down on Samya's shoulders to make sure she realized this was someone to whom she should bow.

"Charming," the man exclaimed. He stroked the top of Samya's head, passing his hand over her glossy black hair. It felt to her like her head might now glow or the roots of her hair sparkle.

"I am teaching her the arts," Samya's mother said. "She will inherit my abilities and my shop. Someday it will be her honor to serve you."

"I look forward to that day," the man said, then hooked his long index finger under Samya's chin and lifted it so he could look directly into her face. She felt the thick gold ring on his finger press into her flesh. Samya inhaled his scent. He smelled clean and new, not like a baby, but like possibility. There was something else too, a faint whiff of decay. He smiled broadly, then patted her on the head again. Samya felt both excited and scared to have the man look so intently at her and to know her name.

"May I send her back to work, Mr. Turiel? We have a shipment of antimony to be ground. The sooner we do it, the more potent the ointment will be."

"Of course."

Samya went back to the table, her head still tingling, proud that her mother would tell a stranger of her intentions for her but nervous to be in the presence of someone who elicited such an attitude of lowliness in her mother.

After Mr. Turiel left the shop, Samya's mother put his payment for eye powders and cologne into the moneybox. She motioned Samya over to watch as she sorted the coins and put them into the proper compartments in the container.

"He must be pure Nephil, equal parts Watcher and human," her mother had said. "His glow is so intense, and did you notice the size of his eyes?" She rubbed some ointment of fenugreek onto her hands to soften her skin after handling money.

She had looked at Samya to make sure she had Samya's full attention. Samya was wide-eyed, eager to hear more about the handsome man and why her mother had seemed different when waiting on him.

"You must be deferential and polite to everyone who comes into the shop. It's good business, even when you're serving someone unworthy of your time and attention. But take special care if you think the client is a Nephil." Her mother's voice took on a new seriousness. "They can be especially cruel to those they think have insulted them." She dropped her voice almost to a whisper. "Mr. Aruk, the tailor, was found with both hands cut off and his tongue sliced in half after he suggested to Mrs. Aziel, an Egregore Nephil, that it was she who had gained weight since her fitting, not he who had cut the fabric too small."

Samya had wanted to giggle, picturing the pudgy Mrs. Aziel, chin lifted, sniffing in affront at Mr. Aruk's comment. But then she imagined Mr. Aruk's cloven tongue, flicking like a serpent's. She shuddered.

"But loyal Nephilim customers will reward you handsomely." Samya's mother had patted the lid of the moneybox. "It is they who control your destiny in this world, dear Samya."

Samya looked now at the dead child, who must have been a young Nephil girl. The eradication of the Nephilim was one of the reasons for the flood, she knew. The official proclamation, from Noah's own lips as the rain began, was that Nephil evil and brutality were so widespread and ingrained that a new beginning was possible only if the Nephilim were wiped from the earth. Nephilim were terrified of water and the flood proved they were right in their fear. Their capacious lungs sucked in great quantities of water. They sank like rocks to the bottom of water-swollen valleys. Samya had seen what looked like opalescent scales shimmering on the water's surface, pooling and lapping against the bloated carcasses and limbs of humans and animals. She pointed, curious, and Noah had said, "the underside of Nephil flesh."

Samya felt a pang of grief for the girl. She looked so innocent lying against the tree. Should she really be held responsible for the sins of her Nephilim parents, whoever they had been?

She knelt down by the girl's side. She lifted the girl's delicate arms and crossed them on her chest. She brought the girl's legs together and straightened her head. The body was still pliable, not stiff, as happens soon after human death.

Samya stood and looked around. She could at least put flowers around the girl, offer some dignity to the dead. Maybe she could find something fragrant that would counteract the rank odor of her lifeless body.

Samya spied a few things that would do. She held her tunic out with one hand, making a nest for her gleanings, and with her other hand broke off some stems of acacia—child-like, soft and sweet. She gathered some lilies of the valley and added them to her cache. She thought the little white bells, with their clean and strong but fleeting scent, would not only provide a fragrance boost to the acacia but also described the young girl's life, over too soon. Samya pulled some Halliana vine, smelling of honey, from the base of a cedar sapling. She would wind this around the girl's head like a wreath or a crown.

Samya felt buoyant as she gathered her bundle of plants in her tunic basket. She realized this was the happiest she had been since the flood. She was putting her knowledge to use, doing what she was trained to do, perhaps made for, her purpose. Japheth tolerated her morning walks, but his eyes glazed over when she described the nuances of the notes she smelled. And he had erupted one morning when she started to tell him the effects of the saffron flower.

"You will not practice the arts of the Watchers!"

Samya was surprised. Japheth was usually so spineless.

"That was your old life," he had said urgently. "Don't you understand?" She could see tears forming in his eyes. He grabbed her hands. "We have to start again. We *all* have to start again."

She had opened her mouth to protest. It was the intentions of the practitioners, not the arts themselves that caused trouble. But she had nodded and then hugged Japheth, who suddenly seemed like a weak and scared boy, more to soothe him than to signal her submission. She realized this now as she stood with her tunic full of fragrant blossoms and vines, happy, content, even excited to tend to the young Nephil's body. She recognized that her excitement outweighed the resentment for Japheth and his edict that had been rising in her like a lump of fetid dough.

She arranged the flowers around the girl and was pleased with her work. But there was something missing, something she might find if she looked. The immortelle.

Her mother had told her the theory, one she had never been able to substantiate, that this plant had the power to quicken the blood. As Samya looked near the rocks where it liked to take root, she wondered if this rumor sparked her search more than did her desire to add the scent to the girl's bouquet. She paused and allowed a feeling of danger and power to surge through her and had her answer.

The thin stalk with its glowing white flowers was still dew-covered when Samya saw it. It was playing hide-and-seek, bowing out from behind a moss-covered rock, then tucking itself out of view in the morning's light breeze. Samya stroked the stem before cutting it near its root and carrying it like a baby to where the girl's body reclined, bedecked with flowers.

She knelt by the girl and lay the flower across the girl's hands. She looked at the girl's face.

The girl's eyes blinked open.

Then they focused on Samya, and Samya heard her say in a voice smooth as caramel, "Let us get the others."

3

KAIA

Chanel No. Five

The invitation arrived in the mail the next day.

"Something special came for you, honey buns," Aunt Alina called to me when she heard me come home from school. "Come on in and open it."

She had propped the large ivory-colored envelope on the table, resting it against a candleholder shaped like a crescent moon. She was sitting at the table fingering a golden facial powder compact with her astrological sign on it, Leo (*Your hair is your mane. Use it to stalk your prey*). She tapped the chair beside her with an open palm. "Come on, come on," she said impatiently, as if the envelope held something for her.

I picked it up. The paper felt creamy and soft. My name and address were written in the same italic script I had seen in the email. The back flap was embossed with the initials GYSP and the angel wing.

I slid my finger under the flap and the packet opened, releasing a complex scent—lemon, bergamot, rose, lily of the valley, riding undertones of vanilla and amber. I extracted a thick ivory card with this message engraved in turquoise ink:

> The Grigori Family Foundation
> is pleased to extend an invitation to
> Malachi Catriona Smith
> to join the Grigori Young Scholars Program

commencing the First of June.
The favor of your reply is requested within twenty-four
hours.
www.GYSP.ds.org

Along with the card were two smaller envelopes. One had my name on it, and one had my aunt's. I handed hers to her.

She turned it over, then raised it to her nose and inhaled. "Nice," she said. Her eyes were closed, as if she wanted nothing to interfere with the experience. "Like Chanel No. 5, the original." She pulled out a folded piece of paper and opened it carefully. She held it close to her as she regarded it, like she didn't want me to catch even a glimpse of its contents. "Handwritten," she said. "Classy." She read the letter quietly, her mouth moving slightly as she read.

She looked at me. "I hope missing the pageant season won't be disappointing for you. This letter asks for my permission. I'm giving it. What does your letter say?"

I opened it up and gave it to her. Mine had only one line:

As promised: Grasp Knowledge and Fly.

"As promised?" Her eyebrows knit together. She whipped her hand to her forehead to smooth the crease. "Doesn't matter. You have to do this."

"What does yours say?" I asked, curious about what wording had won over Aunt Alina so quickly to this plan for my future.

"Never you mind, darling. Just enough information to let me know this is exactly the right thing for you." She tucked the letter into her left bra cup, then stood. "Don't you have homework to do?" she asked. "Don't want these Grigori Foundation folks to think they've made a mistake."

What wouldn't she show me? What secret was she keeping?

4

Odorless

Aunt Alina wasn't the only one with a secret. However he knew about it, Dr. Grigori was right. A few weeks ago I had started taking little gray pills. A high schooler surreptitiously taking pills wasn't that unusual, but I wasn't taking them to get high, lose weight, or cram for exams. I was taking them for relief from headaches. The secret part was that I had no idea what the pills were and knew nothing about the person who had given them to me, other than that she had told me not to tell anyone. So far I hadn't.

The headaches started a couple of weeks before Mom and Dad were killed. When I got them three days in a row and over the counter medication didn't help, my mom took me for an eye exam just in case they had something to do with my vision.

The exam started out normal enough. I sat in the chair in the little windowless room and looked at the doctor's diplomas while I waited for her to arrive. After a few minutes, she stepped into the room and introduced herself.

"Dr. Uriel." She extended her hand. "Thanks for coming in today, Kaia. Let's see if there's something we can do to help you with those headaches," she said, looking at the sheet I had filled out explaining why I was there. She was slim and pretty and wore small rectangular glasses with bright red statement frames. Her velvety voice and scent of ginger crossed with vanilla put me more at ease. "We'll start with the standard tests and move on from there if we need to. Your records say you are hyperosmic, but that doesn't seem to be related to headaches."

I nodded, grateful that she mentioned my condition as a fact and didn't get all weirded out. Sometimes when people hear about my sensitivity to smell, they start trying to casually sniff their armpits or catch their breath in their hands for a quick whiff, just in case.

Dr. Uriel swung the apparatus with its gigantic spectacles of lenses and dials in front of my face. I focused on my breath to keep calm. We did the test with the lenses that spin and click into place making the letters on the wall chart clear, blur, sharpen, and soften again. The doctor's "Which is better? This one or this one? This one or this one? Now, this or this?" were like the tick-tock of a clock.

She pushed the contraption out of the way and pronounced confidently, "Nothing's wrong with your vision. I'll have Dr. Focalor come in to do a retina scan. If everything is normal, it will help us rule out any major problems."

"Major problems?" I asked, trying to sound calm.

She hesitated, inspecting me as though gauging what I could take. "Like a brain tumor. But it's probably nothing." She patted my arm lightly. Heat radiated from her hand through my sleeve and a wave of calm swept through me. "Dr. Focalor will be right with you." She closed the door behind her, taking her comforting scent with her and leaving me alone in the dimly lit room. No air moved and the only sound I could hear was my own heartbeat, *lub-dub, lub-dub.*

After a moment, another doctor in a white lab coat entered and identified himself. Dr. Focalor had a friendly, open face and did not wear glasses. His scent told me he had played racquetball at lunch and hadn't taken time to shower.

"This shouldn't take long. Let me know if you feel any discomfort," he said in a reassuring tone.

I put my chin on the white plastic chin rest and opened my eyes wide. Dr. Focalor shone bright light at me and turned some knobs. A weak current of air wafted toward my eyes like you feel when you lean in close to a sleeping baby, checking for air to make sure she's still breathing.

"It's taking a little longer to locate the right spot," he said apologetically.

He was fiddling with some knobs, making concerned-sounding humming noises when he said, "Ah, here we are . . ." then paused. He yanked the machine away from my eyes and looked at me. "Don't go anywhere," he said, all traces of reassurance gone. "Stay right here." He rushed out of the room, tugging the door shut behind him, leaving me alone again.

Brain tumor, I thought. Rats.

I wondered what would happen next. Surgery? Chemotherapy? Would I lose my hair? Did I have time to get on one of those 'grant a dying child her wish' lists and go on some fabulous, but final, trip? It would be my luck that they only slot they would have would be for swimming with the dolphins since I hated water. I was composing my 'I have always dreamed of traveling to Iceland to ride one of those beautiful little horses, so for my dying wish . . .' letter when Dr. Focalor strode back in with Dr. Uriel close behind him.

"I apologize for leaving so abruptly," he said. "I want to get Dr. Uriel's opinion about this. You have," he searched for the right words, "an unusual . . ." still uncertain of what label to give whatever he saw in my eyeballs.

"Brain tumor?" I tried, finishing his sentence so he wouldn't have to deliver the bad news.

"Oh, no!" he said. "I don't think so. It's just, I've never seen anything like it."

Dr. Uriel adjusted the machine in front of me, motioned for me to put my chin in the chin rest again and took a look. "Hmmm," she muttered. More puffs of air. "Ahhh. Hmmmm. Yes." She sat back, but kept the machine in place. I counted my breaths again, willing myself to stay calm.

The doctors conferred so quietly they must have been mouthing the words. All I heard was "gold," "reflective," "brilliant."

One of them swung the machine away. Dr. Uriel handed me some disposable sunglasses, giant cardboard frames with dark green plastic lenses and turned the lights up in the room.

Dr. Focalor sounded a little breathless as he said, "I don't know if this has anything to do with your headaches, but your retinas are very unusual. Rather than what we expect to see, a dark green or brown or red, your retinas are golden. They actually reflect light back when the right frequency of light is shone into them. It doesn't seem dangerous—you show no signs of cancer or illness—but this is highly unusual."

Dr. Uriel looked non-committal, like this wasn't such a big deal. Dr. Focalor clearly thought I was a freak of nature.

Dr. Focalor continued, "I wonder if you would be willing to participate in a study, so we can learn more about your unusual condition, what caused it, what it means. It could be very important as we learn more about eye health."

I didn't say anything, still catching up with the fact that I wasn't going to die, but I wasn't getting my dream trip to Iceland either.

"I'll just go get some paperwork for you to take with you. You can think about whether you would like to participate or not." He practically skipped out of the room, and I could hear the squeak of his rubber-soled shoes receding in the hallway.

Dr. Uriel shut the door, then immediately sat down on a padded stool and scooted it in front of me. She took my hand and squeezed it so tightly it hurt. "Do not let them study you," she whispered. "Don't. I'm sure Dr. Focalor means no harm and genuinely wants to help, but he doesn't know there are others. If they find out about your eyes, about what we have seen today, it will be terrible. For you, for everyone close to you. Say no."

I drew back, surprised and alarmed by her words. What was she talking about? What did she mean by 'there are others'?

"He'll be back soon." She spun around on the stool and yanked open a drawer. She took a small key from a chain around her neck and fitted it into a lock on a compartment within the drawer. She brought out two prescription containers full of small pills and pressed them into my hand. "Put these in your backpack. Now."

I glanced at the labels. Blank except for a phone number.

"Your headaches aren't caused by your eyes, but they're related. I can't say any more right now. Take one pill, but only when it's really bad. These are hard to get and dangerous if you overdo it. You have enough for a couple of months. Got it?"

I nodded, trying to take in what she had said. I jammed the plastic bottles into my bag.

She hurriedly locked the compartment and was shoving the drawer closed as the door swung open, and Dr. Focalor stepped back in. He took a seat on another stool.

"I want to emphasize that I've seen nothing today that causes me any concern for your health," the smile back on his face. "You concur, Dr. Uriel?"

"Oh yes," she responded, looking at Dr. Focalor. But when she swiveled back to face me, her eyes widened, as if reminding me of the seriousness of what she had said.

"Here's the paperwork. Read it over with your parents and decide if you are willing to help us. This could be quite an exciting research opportunity," Dr. Focalor said, but Dr. Uriel widened her eyes at me again in warning.

"Uh, thank you," I said. "Thank you both," I repeated, looking at Dr. Uriel.

"Someone will be in touch about the study," Dr. Focalor said as he opened the door and went ahead of us into the hallway.

"Tell no one. Anything," Dr. Uriel whispered close to my ear, ushering me out of the exam room. "Call my number, the one on the bottles, from a payphone. Wait a few days. And be careful." Then at a normal volume, "See the receptionist on your way out and schedule another appointment for a six-month check up. Have a nice day."

§

I tried the number three days later. It was hard to find a payphone, but they still had a couple of them at the bus station downtown. I heard the phone ring three times before a crisp click, and a grainy voice: "The number you are calling is no longer in service." Then the line went dead.

§

The pills worked brilliantly. But bizarrely, whatever they were, they had no scent whatsoever. I figured I should start with half a pill, since Dr. Uriel had said they were so valuable, and I had no idea what she meant by "dangerous if you overdo it." I tried to reach her at her office but was told she no longer worked there. I felt strange putting a mystery substance into my mouth that was given to me by someone I had met only once and then had disappeared without a trace, but I was grateful for the relief. The minute I took a dose, the pain vanished. For this, it was totally worth keeping a secret.

§

"We will keep your secret," Dr. Grigori had said. The pills were mine. What was Aunt Alina's?

When Aunt Alina went out to karaoke that night, I snuck into her room. I wanted to know what her note from the GYSP said and why she was keeping it from me.

I was in luck—I saw the note on Aunt Alina's dresser where it rested amongst a collection of cut glass perfume bottles. The paper was folded, and a little crinkled from its earlier hiding place, which I preferred to think of as next to Aunt Alina's heart rather than inside her miracle bra.

I paid attention to its placement so I could put it back in exactly the right place, and eased it out from amongst the forest of bottles and atomizers. I opened it carefully. The elegant blue script had only one line.

As promised: rewards await.

As promised? Rewards? Goosebumps rose on my arms. I knew in that moment it was possible to feel two contradictory things at the same time: alarm, signaling that I shouldn't go to this program if I valued my safety, and intense curiosity, announcing the fact that I absolutely had to go.

I went back to my room, fired up my computer, went to the address on the invitation. My name popped up with a box next to it. I clicked yes.

§

Aunt Alina saw me off at the bus station. "Have a great time, sweetheart. If this doesn't work out, I'm sure we can find something else for you to do. Maybe the Miss Dairyland Pageant or volunteering. Someone will want you."

Thanks for the vote of confidence, I thought, followed by, *If this doesn't work out will you get to keep whatever you're getting for putting me on this bus?*

"You have your locket, right?" she asked.

I pulled it up from under my T-shirt. "Yes, thanks," I replied. I had started carrying some of my pills in it and wore it all the time.

"Good. Take this too." She handed me one of my mother's art history books, a paperback full of glossy colored prints. "You never know when this might come in handy. You're going off to summer school, right? See, just holding it makes you look smarter."

I blinked at her, confused once again by her ability to mix thoughtfulness and insult in a single gesture.

"And here's one more thing. It will make you think of me." She rummaged in her bag and brought out a small sequined zippered pouch. She pressed it into my hands. "I know it's not really your thing, but here are some supplies," she said as she saw my quizzical look. "Just the essentials—mascara, tweezers, concealer, nail polish . . ."

I cut her off with a hug.

"Thanks for everything, Aunt Alina," I said, tearing up even though I didn't trust her. I said, "I know I have to do this, and you'll have a great summer."

"You know it, honeycakes. It's Bikini Season, and I am bikini-ready."

"Um, great," I said, resisting my urge to indulge in an eye roll. I climbed on the bus, and said goodbye to my life before the Grigori Young Scholars Program, the life I could never get back.

5

ANCIENT DAYS

Samya's Trap

Samya gazed at the mirror and ran her fingers over her cheek. Skin still taut, although with none of the blemishes she battled in her youth. As a reward for revivifying the twelve, they gave her what they called elixir. "Nephil blood," she thought. It tasted like her own blood, but it was silver in color. They told her that by drinking it she would develop Nephil traits, although the effect on her, a mere human, would be temporary.

These three hundred years since she found and revivified the Nephilim, her fool husband Japheth had taken pride in her youthful appearance. But she saw the way her father-in-law eyed her with suspicion, as if Noah knew Nephilim must be behind what she publicly attributed to good nutrition, her knowledge of cosmetics and unguents, and daily exercise of walks through the glade.

Of course, everyone but Samya, and Noah perhaps, believed that all the Nephilim had drowned in the flood. She knew that twelve remained, thanks to her, and had plans for domination over humans.

Her mother had been right: Nephilim were cocky. Samya found it annoying that they referred to themselves as the Peerless and to humans as the Merely. But she could understand why. Nephilim were superior to humans. Part human, Nephilim couldn't live forever, but their lifespan was much longer. They didn't show age the way humans did. They radiated confidence that matched their taller stature and stronger build. They toned down some of their traits when among the Merely, pulling down the corneal layer that masked the metallic sheen of their eyes, and never, ever, showed their wings.

To the ignorant, Nephilim were simply more compelling, more powerful, more charismatic people. Humans' belief that Nephilim no longer existed prevented people from seeing what was right in front of them: twelve Peerless Nephilim already in positions of power, about to take the next step in their plan. Samya had heard them say that the tower they were building at Babel would guarantee them supremacy and even immortality. "So long as they remember that they owe me," Samya thought.

She enjoyed being close to such power, but the downside to working for Nephilim was their self-absorption and ruthlessness. They gave her elixir, but she knew if they found her expendable, they would stop. So, beyond what she had already done for them, she had to find new ways to please them.

She had even known one called Gadreel hoping that she could produce an heir Nephil-enough to pass as one of them, to increase their numbers. Not that it was a hardship to be with someone so stunning. But every time she bore a child, it looked completely human, no different than the children she eventually had with Japheth. This was fortunate, since, on finding each child to be apparently Merely, Gadreel ordered her to dispose of it. Their inferior status, with not even enough Nephil blood to make them appear anything but human, made them detestable to the Nephilim. They called such offspring "Elioud." The name meant "the hand of God," a slap in the face from the Enemy who had tried to destroy them. Samya talked Gadreel into sparing her children and convinced naïve Japheth they were his own.

The Peerless were also fixated on Noah. His refusal to be intimidated by them led them to believe he had something over them, perhaps had something they needed. They had debated torturing him to find out what, but he was revered amongst the Merely and a revolt by humans would not be helpful. The Nephilim needed their labor, and, for now, there were far more humans than Nephilim to control them.

So, despite the fact that Samya despised Noah, she spent time with him and tried to appear interested in his ridiculous stories to see if she could discover what secret he kept.

6

KAIA

Linseed Oil and Rotting Fish

The Grigori Young Scholars assembled in the Divinity School Common Room for introductions. There were twenty of us from all over the world. Food smells from home still clung to many of us like olfactory passports. The room was redolent with the tang of curry, fermenting kimchi, citrus, and garlicky spaghetti sauce.

The scent that stood out in the mix and pierced me with homesickness was varnish and linseed oil. My mother had been an art conservator and that was how she smelled when she came home from her lab. I noticed some paintings hanging on the back wall of the room. Even though two people dressed in tough guy black stood nearby like they were guarding them, I could see they were all paintings of the Madonna and Christ Child. In each of them, angels flanked the mother and child and gazed intently into the baby's eyes. The child on his mother's lap and the smell I associated with my own mom made my heart ache, and I told myself now would be a really bad time to cry.

Luckily, a well-dressed woman gestured for us to take our seats in the upholstered chairs arranged in a semi-circle around a gleaming mahogany podium. As the woman waved her arm, though, what flooded my nostrils was an odd combination—meadow flowers, fresh rain, and fish that had turned to rot. I stopped myself from exploring the smell further so I didn't look odd sniffing in her direction.

A bell chimed and Dr. Grigori entered the room. He was even more distinguished in person than in his video. His silver-tinged hair was more lustrous, his white teeth brighter, blue eyes more dazzling. His perfectly fitting pin-stripe suit made him look more like a wealthy banker than a school administrator, at least any school administrator I had even seen. Aunt Alina would have been all over him.

Dr. Grigori announced that every one of us was here by special invitation, chosen because we had an extraordinary ability, talent, or aptitude that had come to the attention of the Grigori Family Foundation and made us suited for this program.

"Our program of work together this summer will unlock and bring to flourishment abilities yet untried or dormant. Discoveries in this program will create a legacy for generations to come," he said. We would be instructed by the finest professors, have access to first-rate scientific facilities, rarely viewed manuscripts, and precious artifacts, and acquire information "of which those outside this program can only dream."

Looking around the circle, taking the time for his gaze to rest on each one of us, he smiled slightly and continued, "GYSP participants become a team and achieve more than could any individual on his or her own. This analogy is appropriate—we attain the cohesion of a family . . ." Longing for my parents clobbered me again.

". . . although the Grigori Foundation has actualized an efficiency and influence greater than any family has ever achieved."

We waited in silence as Dr. Grigori paused to straighten his shirt cuffs, the pinky of each hand extended as his thumb and index finger adjusted his jeweled cufflinks. A large gold signet ring glinted on his right hand as it caught the sunlight streaming through the large windows of the room.

"Much will be demanded of each of you. This is an intensive summer program of study, not summer camp. We believe that you are worthy of this rare opportunity and expect no less than your full attention and cooperation. You will, no doubt, experience trials and obstacles that you must overcome in order to prove successful. If you feel anything but the strongest commitment to this program, then today, this very afternoon, is the time to leave." He paused, allowing his caveat to sink in.

"However," he continued, warm resonance flooding his voice, "if you do your part and give the Grigori Young Scholars Program your entire dedication, even devotion, you will receive rewards beyond your wildest imaginations—even the imaginations of such young, creative, and bright participants as yourselves." He smiled, eyes twinkling, which took the edge off the harsh promise of "trials" and "obstacles."

"And now, important business demands my attention and calls me to another assemblage," he said.

Assemblage? Anyone else talking like that would have sounded pretentious. Dr. Grigori sounded elegant.

"I anticipate with delectation getting to know each and every one of you better during these next weeks. I leave you in the capable hands of one of my assistants, the dean of students, Mr. Argyros, who will guide you through introductions and other administrative details."

Mr. Argyros was buff, tanned, blond, and smiley. His job appeared to be to restore some of the summer camp atmosphere Dr. Grigori's address had dispelled. His impeccable dress was preppy—pink and cream v-neck sweater, white button-down cotton shirt, and green and pink polka-dotted bowtie. He held an electronic tablet in one hand, which he glanced at over the round tortoise shell glasses perched at the end of his nose. He addressed us with a warm, "Well, hello there!" as if welcoming us all aboard a cruise ship and needing only to point out a few safety features before we set sail.

Despite his cheery demeanor, something was off about Mr. Argyros. Even someone with only normal olfactory capacity must have been able to smell the overwhelming amount of cologne he had doused himself with. I breathed through my mouth and hoped the nickname I had left at home wouldn't catch up with me here.

Mr. Argyros paused momentarily after his jaunty greeting to frown at something crawling up the leg of his crisply pleated khakis. With his free hand he swiftly plucked off a small winged insect, some kind of fly. He set down his tablet, pulled a fresh white linen handkerchief from his pants pocket, crushed the bug in it, walked over to a trashcan, and, grimacing, deposited the wad in the can. He shook his head as if clearing an unpleasant thought and turned back toward our group.

"Shall we get started?" Mr. Argyros asked, the jovial smile back in place. He led us through introductions, starting with some safe questions to put us at ease—no wrong answers, no big revelations: name, hometown, favorite flavor of ice cream, favorite subject in school, favorite color, if you were an animal, what would you be?

I missed a lot of what people said as I rehearsed my answers in my head. To my left, a boy named Neith finished talking. Silence. Too much silence. Oops. My turn. Trying to keep the quaking out of my voice I said, far too quickly, "Kaia, Racine, Wisconsin, mint chocolate chip, um, history I guess, turquoise, platypus."

A couple of students snickered.

Why did I say platypus? I wasn't even sure what a platypus is. Is it dangerous? Ugly?

The girl to my right said, "I love duck-billed platypodes. Some people say 'platypi,' but that's incorrect." She had a friendly way about her, informative, not arrogant. She smiled at me, and, still turned in my direction, said, "Platypodes are the only mammal, other than the spiny anteater, whose REM sleep patterns may be similar to those of human babies. I wonder what platypodes dream about." She stopped herself, aware that she had gotten way off the assignment. "So, anyway, Dilani, Chennai, India . . . what else? I know my animal, but what else do you want to know?" I envied the ease with which she spoke.

"Favorite ice cream flavor, subject in school, color, then wannabe animal," a blond girl interjected, smiling and nodding at Mr. Argyros as she repeated his list. She had introduced herself as Xanthe (Stellenbosch, South Africa, lavender glacee, political science, coral, lynx). She smelled like one of Aunt Alina's special occasion perfumes, Mantrap.

"Oh, yeah," Dilani said. "Thanks. Tiger stripe, biology, orange, spiny anteater."

"Tiger stripe?" I asked Dilani in a whisper as the person to her right started to identify himself.

"Orange sherbet, vanilla, and chocolate fudge stripes. Delicious!"

After the non-threatening questions, Mr. Argyros moved to the more serious topics you always know are coming after the warm up and asked us to tell a little about our families of origin. He nodded encouragingly as each of us spoke. It turned out that all of us were either adopted or had lost one or both of our parents.

"GYSP participants tend to come from families others label 'broken' or 'no longer intact,'" Mr. Argyros said sympathetically. "We find, however, that belonging to the GYSP family more than compensates for our individual losses."

He told us to share something about our hopes and goals for our time in the program this summer. My fellow students in the GYSP were brainiacs in search of answers to life's big questions. They came here with 4.0's and published scientific experiments. They had spent summers cataloguing previously undiscovered species of beetle in Amazonian rainforests, identified possible genetic codes that would help in the treatment of childhood leukemia, and given up spots to try out for the Olympic archery team to do this program instead.

Listening to their lists of academic, athletic, and extra-curricular achievements, I fully expected Dr. Grigori to step back into the room, ask me to join him in the hallway, and quietly inform me that the GYSP had made an unfortunate mistake. They thought they were admitting some other Kaia Smith.

Why was I here and what could I say that wouldn't make me sound like a complete loser or paranoid crazy person? That my parents had been killed and accident photos showed the same angel's wing that appeared in the GYSP invitation, which made me think coming here might help me find some answers? That there was something my aunt didn't tell me about her communication with the GYSP that made me suspicious about both her and the GYSP? Even what Dr. Grigori seemed to know about me sounded more like weirdness than talent: I can smell things others can't, but it's not like it's useful to be able to tell the difference from a hundred yards between stinky feet and Frito-Lay corn chips. I wasn't about to say those things out loud.

Truth be told, beyond curiosity, or paranoia, I was attracted by the lure of "fitting in," as Dr. Grigori had said, feeling like I belonged, although, hearing the answers around the circle, I had yet to see how that could possibly be true. We definitely didn't have academic prowess in common. So, as other amazing students spoke, my plan crystallized: use the time to see if I could at least find out the significance of the matching angel wings on the GYSP invitation, at my parents' crash scene, and on my locket until I was discovered as a fake, or flunked out, whichever came first.

"Miss Smith," Mr. Argyros said, calling me back to reality. "What are your hopes and dreams for your participation in the program?"

"I, I, uh, I just think it will be interesting to be here," I spluttered.

Oh great. I'm a stammering duck-billed platypus.

Mr. Argyros let my lame comment dangle in the ether a moment, then moved on to Dilani, who was hoping she would learn something that could help humans better understand ecological shifts during the last half a century and achieve universal harmony between bipedal and quadrupedal mammals, or something like that.

At the conclusion of our get to know each other conversation, Mr. Argyros nodded toward the door and a man strode into the room, pushing a wooden cart stacked with white rectangular boxes.

"These will prove invaluable tools and are yours to keep," Mr. Argyros said jovially, as he and the man went around the circle and gave us each one of the boxes. "You may open them now, if you like."

I slid the top off the box. Its fitted lid made a swooshing sound as I lifted it, like the sound of thick cream being poured into a pitcher. Inside was an electronic tablet, like the one Mr. Argyros held, and a stylus.

"When you turn yours on, you will see the names and locations of your classes and information about the special research project designated for you. If a research project has not been assigned yet, rest assured that your professors are paying particular attention to you and your progress in the program and an appropriate project will be found for you."

"Oh, interesting!" said Dilani. "I'm going to be working on cavitation." She looked like I should know what that meant." I shrugged.

Mr. Argyros held his tablet up and said, "Use yours for your homework, correspondence, personal journal, anything. In fact, you will use your new tablets instead of any personal communication devices you brought from home, which we will now collect from you." A trim woman appeared, holding an open wicker picnic hamper in both hands. "Smart phones into the basket," he said. "You will get them back at the end of the program."

Some of the participants started to make sounds of protest and disbelief.

"Now, now, no need for worry," Mr. Argyros soothed, like a coach wanting his athletes to know they were heading toward certain victory. "The tablets you have been given are far superior to anything you have brought with you. Superior to anything on the market actually. The GYSP has found that participants are more successful without the distraction of social media or contacting texting friends and family from home. Think of it as a small sacrifice for huge rewards."

Students dutifully put their devices into the basket as the smiling woman came around. At least we were all in this together.

"Now, you can leave your tablets here while we repair to the courtyard for some refreshments," said Mr. Argyos. "It just so happens that we have each of your favorite ice cream flavors on offer."

I looked at my tablet and pushed the On button. The screen brightened, my name appeared. But next to Research Project was a blank. Oh good, particular attention for peculiar me.

7

Downy and Crayolas

After snarfing some frosty mint chocolate chip deliciousness, I decided to check out the library. I wanted a little time alone. Our first class tomorrow would be soon enough for my next round of feeling inadequate. Plus, I liked the dried grass and vanilla scent of old books and running my fingers down their spines, wondering what other hands had held them.

When I walked through the front doors, I saw one of my fellow GYSP students sitting behind the front desk. Josh: Trenton, New Jersey, butter pecan, philosophy, blue, North American hare. He was tall and slim. His thick black hair was cut in a longish shag that reached the collar of his button-down shirt. He smelled like Downy fabric softener and crayons, two of my favorites. He was leaning over a book, engrossed, from the look of it, while kneading something in his right hand. Each squeeze of the lump released a plaskticky smell. His eyelashes were so thick I could see them from a distance. I paused, hoping I could watch him blink.

Josh looked up at me and flashed a killer smile. I almost looked away. Instead I went up to the desk, but I focused on what he was massaging in hopes of keeping my heart from racing.

"Silly Putty. Keeps the mind nimble," he said. "Not joining the others for a post-ice cream party in the dorm?"

"I thought I would check this place out," I said. I glanced around and tried to sound nonchalant, but couldn't keep from tugging at my locket and clearing my throat.

"Do you want a tour?" he asked. "Working in the library is my 'enrichment option.' Some people do chemistry. Some people play piano. I read books." He smiled. "They have some really important works in comparative religion. Working behind the desk will let me see what people are interested in right now too."

He had a faint birthmark the size of a dime on his right cheek that looked like a light brown version of those old-fashioned silhouette portraits.

"So what do you think it looks like?" he asked.

"What what looks like?" I said, my face flushing as I looked away from the mark and up toward his sparkling eyes.

"My mark. I saw you looking. What do you think? I usually get old lady or policeman. My personal favorite is the great state of New Jersey."

"Old lady," I said, laughing.

The rest of the evening sped by. I found out he was raised by his father since his mom had died when he was a baby. He had come to the GYSP hoping to study the work of mostly long-dead scholars who worried about the nature of God and existentialism and things that mainly made my eyes glaze over but sounded more appealing when Josh described them. He was especially interested in creation myths, stories of the origins of the universe from different cultures.

"What are you hoping to learn?" I asked.

"Oh, you know, the meaning of life, the universe, everything." He laughed. "Okay, I don't really think you can learn all that in any school, but this seems like a good place to get some bearings. There's a lot about life, and my life in particular, that I don't understand."

I nodded. "Me too." I bit my lip, then found myself confiding, "You know, I really feel like I'm supposed to be here, but not for the reasons the school thinks. I keep wondering how I got in, if the admissions office made some kind of mistake. Do you ever feel that way?"

"No. Not really," he said. "I'm not just handsome, I'm also smart and hardworking. I can't relate." He laughed again. "Don't worry," he said, looking me right in the eyes. "If you're supposed to be here, you're supposed to be here. The admissions department isn't God, you know. And you won't get all your answers from professors and doing the homework assignments."

At 8:45 PM, the bell in the Divinity School tower chimed, signaling fifteen minutes until curfew. "Time to go," I said.

"I have to put a couple things away. I'll see you tomorrow," he replied. "In fact, do you want to go to the main library with me? I have some things to look up and if you haven't been there yet I can show you around."

"Absolutely," I said. "After lunch?"

When he said yes, I blurted, "That's great!" I wondered if anyone had ever sounded so happy to go to a library.

§

We were given an early bedtime by our dorm proctor, Miss Liora, a plump, genial woman who smelled like hot cocoa. If I had to make up a grand-mother, she would be it. She told us to get a good night's sleep because our first class and "grand adventure" got underway the next day. We each had our own room, and she would be around to make sure everyone had lights out and was tucked in on time. "Pleasant dreams," she said, and sent us off to our rooms.

Her warmth cheered me. I still wasn't sure what I was doing here, al-though meeting Josh was definitely a bright spot, and Dilani seemed really nice. I was struck by how many of us had broken families or had lost people dear to us. Maybe that's what "fitting in" meant. This was like one of those camps they send children to who have experienced terrible loss, where they can be open about their feelings and don't have to keep answering questions that make the asker regretful and the answerer destitute: "What do your parents do?" "What do your parents think about that?" "Are your parents still together?"

But as far as being in a study program, I was definitely a misfit. *Grasp Knowledge and Fly* the GYSP invitation said. I hoped my grip would be strong enough, or that Knowledge would be obvious to me when it passed by. I closed my eyes and said a silent prayer that my first class would be all right and that I wouldn't flunk out or be discovered as an imposter before I had at least some answers to the questions that tugged at me. Starting with, why was I really here?

As I sank into sleep, strains of my mom's lullaby drifted toward me.

> *Sleep my child and peace attend thee . . .*
> *Guardian angels, God will send thee . . .*

But this time someone else was singing it, the most beautiful singing I had ever heard, a female voice, crystal clear. I started to review the student introductions I had heard. Who was the singer and how did she know the lullaby? But then I stopped. I let the sound envelop me and take me deeper into the comforting darkness of unconsciousness. With any luck, I wouldn't dream much either.

8

Resin and Rock Dust

The man lay on his side, in fetal position. His arms were crossed over his chest, wrist over wrist as if guarding himself too late from a shot to the sternum. Brown skin stretched taut over his cheekbones and brow line, and pulled his mahogany lips back to reveal a set of grinning bright white teeth. His eyes were shut and thick dark lashes rested against the lower edge of his eye sockets. His hair was jet black, tinged with red. His body was wrapped from the waist down in beige linen bandages and silver bracelets hung from both wrists.

The label on the glass that encased him said: *Mummified Man. Gerasene region, [Modern day Jerash, Jordan] ca. 1st Century CE. Extensive care was taken to apply makeup post mortem to the man's eyes and cheeks. His skin also bears the residue of aromatic oil, perhaps myrrh, often used in burial rituals. Gift of Gadriel Grigori to the Harvard Archaeology Museum, 1865.*

I leaned down to get a closer look. Sure enough, a thin line of black eyeliner rimmed the man's closed eyes and his eyelashes looked like they had a coat of mascara. A faint tint of azure blue adorned the man's eyelids, and his cheeks looked faintly rosy. On the Egyptian mummies I had seen, the image on the outer sarcophagi was often painted to show the use of eye-makeup, but as far as I knew, the mummy itself was always just natural, not made up. I inhaled and let the smell of the resin in which the man had been mummified filled my nostrils. It reminded me of car trips with my mom and dad in the summer, driving on just-oiled roads, before construction crews put down a layer of asphalt. The thought of my mom and dad made me tear up.

I wiped my eyes with the back of my hand and glanced at the clock on the wall. Five more minutes before I had to find my class, Ancient Artifacts. The class blurb said we would "learn how to analyze ancient objects using scientific and unconventional technologies."

Despite the fact that I wasn't on the genius track with my fellow students, I was actually looking forward to this class. I loved museums and seeing old things up close. My problems faded when I could wonder about someone else's life for a while, instead of focusing on the issues of my own.

I always felt sad for the mummies, though, especially the unwrapped ones, lying exposed, all burnt umber and dried out skin, with their un-trimmed hair that continued to grow even after life stopped, sprouting from noses and ears and untrimmed eyebrows. After so much effort was put into the wrapping and layering for their migration to the next world, to have it all undone seemed wrong. Whoever mummies were in life, the one thing we knew for certain about them is they wanted to be covered with bandages and sarcophagi, tucked into the center of an elaborate package, like a pres-ent to be opened on some god's birthday.

Instead here this guy lay exposed, grin frozen in place, hair matted, all the signs and symbols of the journey he never took catalogued, analyzed, and on exhibition, with a label that said only where he was from, that he wore makeup, and the name of the donor of his remains to the museum. Actually, that seemed macabre. How could a person donate another person to a museum?

"Back up," a guard ordered as I leaned in a little too close to the case. I straightened up as I wondered what harm I could do. What could I see that wasn't already on display to the whole world?

I wrenched my attention away from the Gerasene mummy and scanned the room for a sign to the seminar room. Leaving the warm hues and dim light of the Mummies and Funerary Arts exhibit, I walked down a bright corridor. Floor-to-ceiling windows gave views into a classroom with white walls and stainless steel tables, each with a pair of stools. A stand with a large illuminating magnifying glass and a stack of white cotton gloves sat neatly on each table alongside a microscope. The pristine environment seemed more like a hospital than a classroom. I managed to forget for a moment that this was school and that school was not my strong suit. I stepped into the room and saw the familiar faces of some of the other GYSP students.

"Let us commence. Promptness will be important for your success in this class and in life," the professor said. She was a middle aged, white woman, with hair the color of champagne swept up and pinned back in a chignon. She wore tasteful makeup that accentuated her large blue eyes. She had the same fresh scent tinged with acridity I had noticed in the Common

Room during orientation, some floral perfume, roses and lilacs, laid over a base of decaying meat. I opened my mouth just slightly and shifted my focus back to her appearance. Her manicured nails, painted pale pink, quickly disappeared as she stretched white cotton gloves over her long graceful hands.

"Choose a seat, two to a table. Now."

For someone who worked with things that hadn't seen daylight for millennia, she seemed overly anxious about punctuality. I plopped down at the table closest to me and was happy to find Dilani there.

"Hi," I said. "Kaia," in case she had forgotten.

"I remember. Platypus, mint chocolate chip. I'm Dilani. Here," she said, smiling cheerfully and handing me a pair of gloves.

A man wearing a lab coat appeared from a room at the rear of the classroom. With gloved hands he wheeled a stainless steel trolley holding small objects over to the teacher and stood next to her, facing us.

She spoke. "My name is Dr. Calleo, and it is my job to introduce you to the world of ancient artifacts and archaeology. You are about to see for yourselves how a small token can hold volumes of information, how one small object can open an entire world to you."

She picked one of the items off the tray and placed it in her open palm. It was hard to see any detail from my table three rows back. It looked like a lumpy pink cylinder, not an ancient treasure. I guessed they were starting us on the beginner's tray.

"This small object is one of thousands from the ancient world. Museums all over the world hold drawers full of these items."

Definitely the beginner's tray.

"Made of fine, but not precious, stone, these votives have been found in ancient burial and worship sites in locations as diverse as what is now Russia, China, Iraq, Iran, and parts of Europe.

"As you will see in a moment, each stone has been carved to resemble an animal. Some are crudely fashioned, lines scratched into the surface to suggest features. Others are exquisite. My assistant will bring you each a specimen to examine. For now, look, but do not touch. Allow him to place yours on the table in front of you. I repeat: use your eyes, not your hands."

The man in the lab coat pushed the cart and placed an object in front of each student.

Dr. Calleo resumed her presentation as she walked toward the back of the room. "Scholars are not sure of the purpose of these votives. The ancients may have believed they warded off evil spirits or brought good fortune. Perhaps they were offerings to be left at the altars of gods or goddesses. It would be much more convenient for a devotee to bring a small stone pig on pilgrimage to a holy site as a symbolic offering than to drag the real thing, grunting and squealing."

Dr. Calleo shuddered slightly when pronouncing the words, "grunting and squealing."

She stopped, pivoted on her heels and started to walk back toward the front of the room.

"Look, each of you, at your votive. What do you see? What animal does yours represent? Make a note of its color, texture, and whether you see any marks or lines on it."

I looked at mine. Pig, definitely. Some kind of pink stone. Uniform in color and a smooth texture, except where it was carved and the stone looked lighter and matte. Its rectangular body had shallow cut grooves that suggested four legs folded up underneath, as if the pig were lying down, resting on its stomach. One end came to a short little snout. Two pin-hole eyes were carved into its face, and small triangular ears were outlined by engraved lines. Cute.

I leaned in close and sniffed for good measure. Petrichor: the scent that hangs in the air just before rain falls sizzling onto hot rocks.

Dr. Calleo arrived at the front of the room. She stood with her back to us, placed her hands on her hips, and spoke. "Now, carefully, pick up your votive, and look again. What do you notice now?"

I picked up the pig and placed it on the palm of my left hand.

"Pay close attention to your votive . . ."

The teacher's voice faded as I looked down. My pig started to glow.

I curled my hands around it and looked up. Had anyone noticed?

I glanced around quickly. No one was staring at me. Everyone seemed attentive to their own little animals.

But then I noticed: a couple other hands too had started to close, white gloves like tulips reverse-blooming, petals closing in over the stamen and life-giving pollen inside.

I snapped back to my own hands. The stone had started to feel warm, heating up from within. I slapped the votive pig down on the table, relieved to see that the glowing stopped when I released it.

I glanced at Dilani. Her eyes were wide. She was staring at the animal she had placed back on the table. Her hands were folded in her lap, her shoulders hunched, and her breath was shallow.

"Yours too?" I asked quietly.

"Yup," she replied still staring at the votive. She turned her head toward me. "I don't know . . ."

"Kaia. Dilani. Please remain after class," Dr. Calleo said.

I gulped. She was facing the front of the room, away from us.

What did she know? How did she know?

The rest of the class went by in a blur. I took notes as Dr. Calleo described the various scientific tests—Oxygen Isotope Chronostratigraphy, X-Ray Diffractometry, other –graphies and –metries we would subject our little stone creatures to next class meeting.

At the end of the class, Dilani and I dutifully approached Dr. Calleo.

"Already in this first class, you both show great potential. It usually takes longer to see the stirrings you witnessed today." she said. "Come to my office tomorrow, ten AM. Do not be late. You will find the room number on the directory out front."

"Yes, Professor," Dilani said.

"Thank you," I echoed.

We walked out together, holding our breath until we were in the hallway.

"What just happened?" I asked. "That thing with the glowing stones?"

"No idea," Dilani replied, "but I can't wait to see what Dr. Calleo wants to show us."

I admired her courage. I felt rattled, but, like her, I was curious.

"Come by my room tonight before lights out, if you want," she said.

"Great. Thanks," I said, happy to think that maybe I was making a friend.

"I've got to run back to my room before lunch," she said, and waved goodbye, hurrying out ahead of me.

As I walked back through the museum, I passed the Gerasene mummy's case again, approaching him from behind, his spine curved away from me as he lay tucked in on himself. Then I noticed a detail I had not seen on my first encounter. Two thin vertical scars, each about two inches long, rested on either side of his bony spine. Startled, I absentmindedly raised a hand over my shoulder and felt for my own. I stood there, just for a moment, elbow crooked around my neck, fingers running along my scars, when I noticed the security guard looking at me. I pretended to scratch an itch, and made my feet start moving again past the mummy's case and toward the door. I glanced back and saw the security guard speaking into his walkie-talkie. I looked down again toward the mummy. I think he was smiling.

9

ANCIENT DAYS

Noah's Sense of Harmony

The old man gripped her arm so hard she feared his gnarled fingernails would permanently inscribe her skin with half-moon crescents thick as the rim of her drinking cup. Samya flinched but did not pull away even though she detested Noah, now more than ever since odors of age hung about him like flies swarmed the corpses of those worn out by working on the tower. He often held on like this while he scavenged for words, as if by squeezing tightly he could wring the phrase he was searching for from his toothless mouth.

Noah was old, nine hundred and fifty, one of the last of the super-annuated, born before his God declared that human beings would no longer see much more than a century. Samya was super-annuated too, although, thanks to elixir, did not show her age.

Samya didn't know how much Noah saw through his cloudy eyes or how well he could hear through ears that sprouted hair and earwax in equal measure. He could talk, and did so in rambling stories he had told a thousand times, now with words missing and phrases that didn't follow. He smacked his lips, then produced some meaningless syllable, and his eyes welled up in frustration when no one understood his non sequiturs. Sometimes a thin crust formed at the corners of his mouth. Samya found him disgusting.

He could often be found sitting alone and polishing little animals he carved from some of the Tower building stone. When he ran his hands through his tufts of thinning hair, he left stone dust behind. She stayed near him in case she got something useful to the Nephilim. He seemed to mistake her proximity for kindness.

If she forced herself to focus, Samya found that she could put pieces of his past together and that his gleaning of what was going on in the present was uncannily accurate for someone so obviously failing.

His favorite subject was the flood. She had been there, of course, and her main concern as the waters rose was keeping herself alive. Noah, however, had been absorbed with paying attention to others. He couldn't simply appreciate that he had been spared. His memories were peppered with grief, and he still shed tears these many years later.

"Not even when faced with tra-tra-tragedy," he stuttered, "could they treat one another with compassion. Mothers held infants to the . . . up, clouds . . ." He let go of Samya's arm and lifted both hands.

"Sky?" Samya offered, anxious for him to get on with it.

"Sky. Not to lift them above the surging waters, but as offerings to false gods. 'I sacrifice this child to you! Spare my life!' mothers said—mothers!"

Samya winced. Her own children were now dead; she had outlived them. Her memories of them were bittersweet. She preferred the ones fathered by Nephilim, and although their angelic blood gave them longer lives, they had died in excruciating pain. She had considered giving them some elixir to see if that would help, but knew there wouldn't be enough for both them and her.

Noah droned on, "Waters choked with bloated carcasses and sewage. Air full of birds hunting for a place to rest, plummeting exhausted to watery exertion."

"Extinction?"

"Extinction. Yes. You understand, dear Samya. You remember carrion gorging themselves to flightlessness, falling off the corpses at which they picked, to drown." He held a small carving of a horse up to his face and squinted at it, as if checking it for something.

"Why can't he just move on?" Samya thought. She detected nothing of value to her here. She prompted him, "And after the flood? What did you notice? Anything important?"

"Everything was washed away, cleansed by the deluge. Even my anger at people's hatefulness could not survive the flood. I was left with only pity and sorrow. C-c-c-compassion."

"Weak emotions," Samya thought and held back a sigh. *Anger motivates. Hate stimulates.* She had heard the Peerless repeat that mantra.

"The Creator was faithful. The rain stopped. Land became fertile. Waters spawned life. A fresh start. I thought humanity would learn kindness at last."

The old man looked wistful. With his free hand, he gave Samya's arm another squeeze and looked at her directly, his eyes suddenly clear. "Humanity must learn kindness," he said. Tears began to well and rim his eyes and they fogged over again. He looked like a seer, gazing into the future. She didn't like it.

Noah went on, "The Creator will never again cleanse the earth. Never again will we have this kind of second chance. When disaster next comes, it will arise from the . . . down . . ." He pointed the stone pony toward the dirt.

"Ground? Earth?" Samya asked. She hated this game.

"Earth!" Noah said, and breathed a sigh of relief. He looked at the rock in his hand and nodded.

"From the earth? You mean humans will do something?" Was this finally the information she was hunting for?

"Humans?" Noah sounded incredulous, like a frustrated teacher who couldn't believe his student hadn't been paying attention. "No. No." He shook his head. "No—Neph . . . Neph . . ." Now he looked frantic, as if beseeching her help. Should she say it? she wondered.

"You . . . you . . ." he stammered.

"He knows," Samya thought. How could he not? He had known Nephilim before the flood. He had to notice now that some beings amongst them were superior, even if they had cloaked their more obvious traits in order to escape detection at present. But did he know she was responsible for their survival?

"You can hear it too," he finally said, his words tumbling out in a stream.

"Hear what?" she asked, holding her breath.

"How the sound has changed." He looked plaintive. "The harmony is disintegrating because of the Tower. We are in grave danger. All of us. Even you." He put a hand on hers, but not to grip her. She realized it was a gesture of pity. "Even you," he repeated quietly. "But don't worry, dear Samya. This will save us," and he waved the little stone horse.

Samya leapt to her feet. "You old fool," she spat. "You worthless old Merely." He was clearly demented, and she would no longer waste her time listening to his nonsense. She stormed away while Noah set down the horse and picked up a fresh piece of rock, examining it to decide what animal he would carve next.

10

KAIA

Caramel and Leather

"**B**roccoli and ice cream—what a random combination," Josh said as we reached the top of the broad granite stairs outside the Widener Library.

"Sounds disgusting. What are you talking about?"

"You haven't heard about that?" Josh pointed up at the imposing marble plaque on the brick wall of the Widener Library portico. "Mrs. Widener and her legacy for Harvard students."

I read the inscription:

In Memory of Harry Elkins Widener
A Graduate of This University Born January 3, 1885
Died at Sea April 15, 1912
Upon the Foundering of the Steamship Titanic

"That's really sad," I said, pulling my hoodie tightly around me. The thought of drowning made me shiver.

Water was my number one phobia. I hated it. Had bad dreams about it as long as I could remember. In these dreams I was drowning, or someone else was drowning and I couldn't save them. I would wake up panting and coughing and covered with sweat.

"Harry graduated from here and went to Europe for the summer," Josh explained. "He was on his way home when the ship went down. His mom wanted to do something in his memory. She left enough money so that broccoli and ice cream would be served every day at the student cafeterias in perpetuity."

"The Div School has great mint chocolate chip."

"Not so fast. Have you passed your test?"

"The ice cream comes with strings attached? Is someone monitoring my broccoli intake?"

"Your swim test."

I stopped, my hand resting on the large brass handle of the library door. "Swim test?"

"Yes." Josh looked at me, his right eyebrow arched high, and a stupid crooked grin on his face. It wasn't bad enough I felt like a fraud. Now one of the few people I might actually get along with was acting like I was the only person not in on the basics. He said slowly, like he was questioning a child, "You really don't know about the swim test?"

I gulped. "No."

"Mrs. Widener left the broccoli and ice cream money, and the requirement that every student pass a swim test." Josh shook his head, his thick black hair swinging across his forehead. He swept his hair out of his face with his hand. "Not that swimming would have saved her son. You can be the smartest student here, win a Nobel prize for a class project, write the great American novel, but if you can't swim one hundred yards, no diploma."

I started to get the pre-faint feeling I sometimes got when I thought about being in water, where the edges of my vision get cloudy, and my hearing gets muffled. I bent over, my hands on my thighs.

"Are you all right?" I could hear Josh ask, although he was sounding far away.

I launched into my mantra: *I am fine. I can breathe. I will not drown. I am fine. I can breathe. I will not drown.* I tilted my head up toward Josh's face. His brown eyes were wide. He had bent over, his face close to mine, his forehead creased like he was concerned.

"Kaia, are you okay?" He put his hand on my back, lightly, but I could feel it rest on my scars. I jolted out of my faint, and his hand snapped back to his side.

"I'm fine!" I said. "Fine. Just a little dizzy."

"You were leaving me. You did not look fine."

"Must have been something I ate. Or the disgusting thought of broccoli with ice cream." I forced a smile. *Crum. One more reason I don't belong here.*

"If you say so." Josh started toward the door.

"I say so." I swung the door open and we stepped inside.

How on earth was I going to pass a swim test if I couldn't even think about it without passing out?

I looked back at Josh, who gave me a really sweet smile. I breathed deeply and the caramel smell of leather bound books and Josh's smile made me feel hopeful. I thought I might as well make the most of today, especially if I would get kicked out—or drowned out—soon. I remembered the make-up wearing mummy whose scars matched mine, and a research topic came to me.

"So," I said, exhaling. "Where can I find out more about Gerasenes?"

Most of the references to "Gerasene" I could find were to stories in the Bible where Jesus casts demons out of a man from a place called Gerasa. Jesus commands the demons to leave the man, but they beg Jesus to send them into a herd of pigs, which he does, and the whole herd runs off the side of a cliff and drowns. The man wanted to follow Jesus, but Jesus doesn't let him and instead tells him to go home and tell others what Jesus did for him.

I wondered what the chances were that the Gerasene mummy in the museum and the man in the story were one and the same. The mummy came from the right time, the first century. How many notable Gerasenes could there be?

Was it just a coincidence that my day so far had included a glowing pig votive and a mummy with the same scars as me, who came from a place remembered for a porcine mass suicide? I thought of the pigs hurling themselves over the cliff and pictured one lone pig running the other direction.

11

Jasmine and Dog Dander

That night, Dilani and I drank tea in her room, sitting next to each other on her bed. Dilani was beautiful. Her long hair was so dark it reflected light, and set off her sorrel-colored skin. She smiled easily. I was happy to be in her company.

"So how do you know so much about platypuses?" I asked her. "Or, platypodes," correcting myself, wanting not to seem stupid to her.

"Platypuses works too. Just don't say 'platypi.' It sounds right, but it's not, although it's easy to see why someone would make that mistake," she said. "Since I was little, I've just loved animals, felt close to them. All kinds. I love learning about them. It feels like a calling to me, you know, what I'm supposed to be doing."

I felt a stab of longing, or maybe envy, at her sense of having a purpose. "Do you want to be a vet?" I asked.

"Maybe," she said. "I'm not sure I want to do operations or anything medical. I definitely couldn't euthanize an animal, even though sometimes it's the best thing to do under the circumstances. So, probably not a vet, although I want to do something to help animals, the ones in trouble, for sure." She hesitated then looked at me, appraising, I could tell, trying to decide whether she should say more. "Can I show you something?" she asked.

"Sure," I said.

She got a scrapbook out from under her bed and opened it across her lap. Inside were articles cut out of newspapers and printouts of online news reports. "Frogs Close Greek Highway," one headline read. The story was about how on one otherwise completely normal sunny afternoon outside of

Athens, Greece, an army of about one hundred thousand frogs had emerged from a field and started across a busy thoroughfare. Stunned drivers, repelled by the gross and dangerous reality of driving over the mashed carcasses of the amphibians, skidded to a stop, causing a massive pile-up of vehicles that stretched for eight miles. It took thirty minutes for the surviving frogs to cross the highway and ten hours for all the accidents to be cleared.

"That's what a group of frogs is called, an 'army,'" Dilani explained, as if that were the noteworthy part of the article. "A group of toads is a 'knot.'"

"One hundred thousand frogs, out of nowhere? All needing to cross the road just then?" I said. "That does seem odd."

"Look at this one," she said, pointing to another clipping.

"Great White Sharks Heading North in Huge Numbers." The story was about the increase of great white sharks appearing off the shores of Canada, much farther north than they usually go. I noticed that a group of sharks is called a "shiver." Seemed appropriate.

"Is this some kind of global warming thing?" I asked.

"Maybe. Sometimes human actions create disturbances. A subdivision gets built in the middle of a cougar migration route and suddenly big cats are loitering in supermarket parking lots. But sometimes, there's no obvious explanation," Dilani answered.

We flipped the pages of the scrapbook. "Asian Carp Breach Electric Fences in the Great Lakes;" "Spangled Perch Fall from Sky over Remote Town in Australia."

"Of course, fish fall from the sky more often than you might think," Dilani informed me.

She had stories about individual animals involved in unusual events as well. "Dog Shoots Owner in the Bottom," was my favorite. A dog stepped on a loaded shotgun a man had left lying on the seat of the fishing boat they were in. The man survived the incident.

"How would you like to be him in the emergency room?" I asked.

"Embarrassing," she said.

"No, really, it was my *dog*." I smirked. "Now take the bullet out, please."

"I'm sure it was humiliating for the man, but think about the dog," she said, a solemn tone in her voice that stopped my giggling. "The dog must have felt very bad about it."

"Oh sure," I said sarcastically. "The dog was thinking, next time I'll just bark to get his attention."

"No, I'm serious," Dilani said. "This may sound crazy, but I know dogs can feel a tremendous sense of guilt, especially over accidents they cause."

"That doesn't sound crazy," I said carefully, afraid I had offended her with my joking. "I'm sure dogs have a rich emotional life," I added, trying to sound encouraging.

"Oh, good," Dilani said, relief flooding her voice. "Usually when I say I know what dogs are feeling, people think I'm a little nuts. My father does anyway. I don't tell many people. I'm glad I can trust you."

"Wait a moment," I said. "I mean, thank you. You *know* what dogs are thinking?" I was genuinely interested and touched by her confidence in me. I hoped I hadn't blown it.

"Dogs, cats, gerbils, hamsters, you name it. Not all of them, of course. A walk in the woods, if I could understand all the birds, for instance, would be chaos. A trip to the zoo, torture. But, some of them." She stopped, checking for my response.

"I believe you," I said.

"I've always felt an affinity for animals, like I said, but over time I realized I could actually sense their thoughts. It was kind of disturbing at first. I thought I was hallucinating or making it up because, of course, I would love to know what animals are thinking."

I nodded, stunned and excited. I knew exactly what she meant about having an odd ability, although I didn't blurt out that my own weirdness involved smelling pastrami from one hundred paces or the dander that still lingered on Dilani even though she was thousands of miles away from her family pet.

Dilani continued, "It's not like I have direct communication with them. I can't suddenly speak in their language or hear my dog barking and translate it to, 'No more of this terrible dry dog food,' or 'Don't worry, I'll protect you from the UPS delivery person' or anything. It's more like something comes on a wavelength, a sensitivity to sound vibration, that gives me a sense of what she's thinking."

"Did you test it? I mean, is there some way to prove you're not making it up?" I looked at her in a way I hoped was reassuring. "I'm not saying you are making it up, but there must be a way, if it's real, right?"

"The clearest examples are when I've encountered an animal with something wrong, especially when it's not something visible or obvious, like a bird with a broken wing would be. More like when the cat seems fine, but I know that the cat can tell an earthquake is coming and wants me to know too. I know a dog who can detect diseases in people, but has no way of communicating it other than a low-frequency whine. It's hard to hear, but I can hear, and I understand it. So far, he detected early stage breast cancer in his owner and an operable congenital heart disease in the little boy who lives next door. The people were so grateful when I told them they might want to have these things checked out and they turned out to be true. But it's not me. I'm just hearing what the dog is telling me. Weird, I know."

"Maybe not so weird," I said. "Maybe it's a gift."

"Maybe," she said. "But all these stories," she gestured to the scrapbook, "make me concerned, especially the ones about large groups of animals being in strange places, or like they're trying to get somewhere they don't belong or haven't been before. Something is out of whack. Boundaries are getting crossed, or lines are becoming blurred, and they can't go back. I wish I knew what, exactly, so I could do something about it."

She paused.

"I'm so glad I can tell you about it," she said, relief relaxing her face. "When I tried to explain it to my father, especially the part about being able to communicate with animals, he got really alarmed. Like he thought something is seriously wrong with me. He was actually ready to send me somewhere for psychological help. I came into the kitchen one morning and he had the brochures all fanned out on the table: a serene treatment center for girls in Switzerland, nestled in snowy mountains, long walks with matron through wildflowers blooming in the meadow; a sleek, hyper-clean steel and glass institute in France, racquetball courts and fencing for recreation; a gray gabled estate in Scotland specializing in therapeutic caber-tossing. At least that one offered falconry, and I could still communicate with the birds," she joked. "He thought sending me off to a place with girls who had suffered severe head trauma would be the best option. When the invitation came to join the GYSP, I leapt at the chance, even though I really miss my animals."

"My aunt said if I couldn't find anything to do this summer, she would enter me in beauty pageants. She said she could get me 'most improved.'" I said.

Dilani burst out laughing.

"I know, funny, eh? Someone as plain as me," I said, a little hurt that she couldn't imagine it either.

"Oh, not because you couldn't win. Everyone knows most of that stuff is faked anyway."

"*Most* of that stuff," I said, laughing. "What do you think it would take in my case? Eighty percent fakery?"

She laughed again. "No! I just think it's funny that you're a beauty pageant refugee, and I'm an insane asylum refugee."

I wanted to tell her about my parents and my suspicions about their death, about the angel wing symbol by their car that matched the one on the GYSP invitation, but didn't dare, in case she thought I sounded paranoid and told me she knew a good asylum in Switzerland where I'd fit right in.

Instead, I asked her if she'd noticed the Gerasene mummy in the museum and if she knew about the story about the demons and the pigs. It sounded right up her alley.

"I hated that story the first time I heard it. All those pigs drowning," she replied. "But over time, I've come to think the pigs knew something had to be done to get the demons into the water. Think about it," she said. "Angels, demons, you never hear about them being in water. Their realms seem to be heaven, air, or land. I don't think they can survive under water."

"I hate water," I said. "I'm terrified of it."

"I bet pigs aren't fond of it either," she said, "but they found a way to destroy a legion of demons. I admire them."

"If the story is true," I said cautiously.

"Sure. Too bad the mummy can't talk. I bet he could tell us."

The bedtime chime sounded. "See you tomorrow for Ethics class," I said, and made my way to my room.

I fell asleep with my mind a swirl, wondering what Jesus had said to release the demons, what the pigs would say to Dilani, and how the Gerasene mummy got his scars.

12

ANCIENT DAYS

What Noah Noticed

Noah held the little loaf-shaped stone close to his face. His vision had dimmed so he looked for a long time at each stone before he began carving, sometimes asking the stone what animal it held within it.

Noah often spoke aloud to himself, no longer caring what others thought, doubting anyone even noticed. He considered it an advantage of his age to be largely invisible to those around him. They assumed he was hard of hearing, so they didn't bother to shield their speech in his presence. It was, as his great-grandfather Enoch had once told him, both a gift and a sadness to be an elder. One can observe unobserved, but it is a particular loneliness to have no one with whom to wonder at the observations.

That's why he welcomed Samya's company, even though he knew she was in league with the Nephilim, and he suspected from the way they favored her that she had something to do with their survival after the flood. "No matter," he thought. He had his great-grandfather Enoch's word that the Watchers couldn't be rescued from their prison. The world was safe from ultimate catastrophe, no matter what schemes the Nephilim devised. Noah's job now was only to do what he could to help after the coming dispersion.

"What do you want to become, little stone?" Noah said. "What do you want to release?"

He held the stone up to his ear and listened, then chuckled to himself. His hearing was still quite good for someone his age. He had been trying to pay attention to the sounds around him because he was certain they held the key to what would happen soon—the Creator's unfolding plan and the part he might play in it.

He thought back to the flood. Once the rains stopped, there were the quiet schlumpfs and gurgles of decomposing bodies and swollen stumps as they finally slipped beneath the surface of the waters. Then, a hush so encompassing it was a presence that buoyed the ark as much as the waters did.

The silence lasted days. He lost track of how long the quiet hung around them, but he remembered the advent of a sound. He recognized it instantly—the crystal clear hum of the great celestial hymn, the music of the spheres. Noah had heard it as a boy, although his great-grandfather told him it had dimmed by then. It was the sound of pure joy, harmony. To hear it and feel it reverberate through the sky above was wonderful— peaceful and invigorating. Noah remembered the sound as transcendent, unreachable, yet it resonated within you as well, as if it needed you as its carrier, as if it would be diminished if it could not resound through your being. The sound rang out above the waters, over the floating sanctuary, and filled those within with hope.

When had the harmonic sound started to dim again? He hadn't noticed at the time. Perhaps he had been too busy tending to daily life. Not until the Tower began to rise into the sky did Noah notice the change in the sound. It was becoming faint, but it wasn't just the volume, it was the sound itself. It had become hesitant, mournful, as if tuning its own lament, preparing the dirge for its own funeral. The higher the Tower went, the more desolate the song became.

He was sure the Tower was the cause. One of the few who loathed the Tower, he saw it as a sign of disobedience rather than the bringer of fame the Egregores promised. After the flood, the Creator told people to multiply and fill the earth, a command that was also a blessing, an affirmation that the world was good again—all of it. The Creator had given it to people to explore and inhabit. "We should have spread out over the earth," Noah thought, "not gather all in one place, where resources would be depleted and skirmishes over property would break out. All but a few stayed here on the Plains of Shinar, preferring the security of the familiar to exploration of the unknown. We began to grow discontented, to scheme and wheedle and grow suspicious of one another."

That's when the Egregore family announced their plan, Noah recalled. "Together, we would build a tower, the Tower, the height of which had never before been seen. Even now, still unfinished, a three-day's walk does not obscure it from view."

The brilliance of the plan was that it brought people together. It put an end to bickering between neighbors and squabbling in the marketplace for the last of the skinny chickens and under-ripe melons. Everyone was united in a common task, creating something, the Egregores promised, worth sacrificing for.

Of course not everyone would be involved in the hewing of stones or setting them into place. But a construction project of this magnitude meant that if one weren't hauling or lifting, truing or squaring, one's labor was necessary to feed those who were. People were needed to keep fires and ovens roaring, to tend to the tired, or aid the wounded when accidents inevitably happened. Only Noah and some others who had grown too feeble to be deemed useful were excused from working in some fashion on the project.

"Ha!" Noah exclaimed aloud. "The price we've paid." A passerby glanced at him, then threw him a coin and hurried along.

Noah shook his head. If only people would see what was going on right in front of them: people valued only according to what they could do for the Tower. Builders were more prized than Boulder-bringers. Stone Masons more valuable than Mortar Mixers. Supervisors more important than Measurers. Anyone working directly on the Tower more esteemed than those who supported laborers, so Farmers, Herders, and Cooks less laudable than Sawyers, Carvers, and Scaffold Builders. Those bearing and teaching children were valuable only in so far as they were producing future workers for the Tower.

Such a great number of people were needed to transport stone from quarries and bricks from fire pits that the largest group of workers was the Haulers. Although their work was crucial, the Egregore regarded them as drones, less important to them than animals. The Egregore wanted the Tower built as quickly as possible so Haulers were worked to exhaustion. As they died from exhaustion and accidents, they were thrown into unmarked pits and replaced with new Haulers. The Egregore allowed, then cajoled, then forced younger and weaker Haulers to work. The lowest of all in the Tower hierarchy of dominance were those who filled the burial pits with, dead Haulers. The Egregore called them Refuse Removers.

The naming of people according to their occupations, their usefulness to the Tower, rather than some other attribute or honorific of the divine, was a Nephil innovation. Noah was 'bringer of rest,' by name. In Tower terms, he was 'useless.' Were he not known as the grandfather of all the living, he was certain he would be regarded only as a consumer of food that could be fuel for a worker. Already some of his elderly neighbors had disappeared and a young man born with a palsied limb had died unexpectedly.

The Egregore needed replacements, more laborers of all sorts. What frightened Noah most were rumors he heard whispered in the marketplace that the Egregore were impregnating women, trying to increase the population, not by encouraging love to flourish and families to grow, but by using women as breeders. Some families were approached to allow their daughters to serve the Tower by going to a plantation a two-days' walk from Shinar. They were told their daughters would be trained to work with children. Their training would be so intensive, they must be removed from the community to a place where they could devote all their energies to the program. But some of the young women had escaped and told of being made to produce, not teach, children. Some people did not believe them; others said they should consider it an honor if that's what the Egregore deemed necessary.

"How quickly we have been swept up in the schemes of the Nephilim," thought Noah. "Surely the Creator has a plan."

"I hope you will be of some help," Noah said out loud to the rock from which he was now certain he could release a rather handsome little pig.

13

KAIA

Patchouli and Putrefaction

"What, exactly, are we supposed to be learning here?" Kiran asked. Kiran (Mumbai, rum raisin, physics, purple, elephant), as well as being a physics whiz, was an award-winning painter. Among other achievements, he had figured out a way to duplicate the oil painting technique Leonardo da Vinci had used in his portrait of Ginevra de' Benci to make the young woman's skin look like porcelain. But his primary goal in life was to save the world from environmental disaster. During his junior year, he had developed a way to make solar panels more efficient and cheaper to produce, so it wasn't surprising that he was a vocal critic of what he called the "excesses" in the GYSP program. He waved his tablet and referred to the list he was keeping there: "No recycling. No renewable energy sources. Immoderate use of paper products. An endangered species of fish was on the cafeteria menu last night."

Some students were getting tired of Kiran's lists.

"I didn't come here to learn about composting," Aranka said.

"This is *ethics* class," Kiran rebutted, palms up, pleading with us to be reasonable. "The whole point of ethics is how we should live."

Dr. Eder was our ethics professor. "Call me Azar," he said at the beginning of our class. I was confused for a moment, until I realized he was inviting us to call him by his first name. I bristled. "Dr. Eder" was fine with me, especially since he had that cheesy 'don't think of me as your professor;

think of me as your friend' vibe going. He wore his long sandy hair pulled back in a thick ponytail, and his broad shoulders and muscular build made him look like a Hollister catalog model. He wore exactly the right colors to accentuate the glow of his flawless cedar skin. A perfectly even growth of stubble adorned his square jaw and dimpled chin. Thick lashes framed his large dark eyes. His ponytail holder was ornamented with chunky multi-colored beads and two small white feathers. It was hard to look at him and not wish he were a friend instead of someone who held the power of grades and promotion over our heads. But he, too, emitted the now familiar, yet still puzzling combination of pleasant and putrid scents—fresh-cut meadow flowers and foul fish. He was wearing a patchouli-based cologne, but it didn't quite do the trick of masking his underlying stink.

"There is a limit," Kiran opined, "to everything. Someday, important resources will run out if we don't pay attention. And it's poor people who pay the price first, living among our refuse, bearing the brunt of the conse-quences of deforestation, drought, rising sea levels."

"What if you are mistaken, Kiran, about the notion that something running out is a bad thing?" Professor Eder proposed. "Dinosaurs were eliminated, for instance. But human life and dinosaur life could not be sus-tained simultaneously for the long term."

Kiran looked uncomfortable with Dr. Eder's idea that extinction might not be problematic. Dr. Eder continued, "What you say is correct. The poor are the first affected when there is a global shift, but you can see that the poor are quite resilient by the fact that the poor survive."

"As a class of people, the poor survive," Kiran interjected. "Individual poor people often do not."

Dr. Eder replied, "Yes, as a group, the poor continue to exist. No one has ever succeeded in eradicating them all."

Kiran's jaw dropped. I could see him searching for a response.

Dr. Eder continued, "Should we not learn from their fortitude, their creativity? Rather than pity the poor, should we not emulate them in some ways? Not by adopting their circumstances, of course."

"I wasn't saying we should treat them with pity," Kiran objected. "I was saying that we shouldn't do things that affect poor people negatively, especially when they don't even get a say in it."

"Like handbags," the gorgeous student named Xanthe piped up as she ran her hand through her mane of blond hair. "There are cooperatives in Ghana where poor women are making stunning handbags from the plastic grocery bags that wash up on beaches."

"Handbags? Cooperatives?" Kiran asked, clearly unable to follow her argument.

"Yes. As I believe Azar is saying," she paused and looked at Dr. Eder—did she seriously wink at him?—"is that if these women weren't motivated by their poverty, they would be denied the opportunity to contribute to the world and the world's economy. And the resources just wash ashore for them—a gift!"

Kiran blinked. "An example of recycling, perhaps, and something good resulting from something bad, but shouldn't we look at what caused the bad situation in the first place?"

"You raise an interesting subject, Kiran," Professor Eder said, resuming control of his lecture. "A subject we will address in this class: the origin of evil." He stroked his ponytail with the fingertips of his left hand. "You have heard of creation myths, stories of the origin of the world. Every culture has one, sometimes more than one."

I looked over at Josh who looked suddenly very excited about ethics class. Okay, Josh's special area of interest belonged in the GYSP curriculum. When would something about me find a fit?

Dr. Eder continued, "There are myths for the origins of evil as well. It is important to study them and understand what they are saying, and not saying, about the reality of good and evil in the world. So, for next class meeting, read *1 Enoch* chapters one through sixteen, found in your reading packet. This is an ancient story, about twenty-three hundred years old. However, we shall find that it still has contemporary relevance."

Contemporary relevance. It was a gross understatement, but our ethics professor was, in this matter at least, being brutally honest.

14

Old Books and Garlic

I decided to do my ethics homework in the library, mainly for the chance to spend more time with Josh. When I arrived, he was sitting behind the counter, but strained forward, like he wanted to leap over it. He pushed aside a pile of books as I came over to say hello.

"Come with me," Josh said. "Let's go now. I have to show you something."

"Come with you where?" I asked. "Are you allowed to leave the desk unattended?"

"It'll just take a sec."

"Wait," I said. I scribbled a note on a piece of paper: 'Back in 5 Minutes' and left it on the counter.

"I guess you're one of those rule followers. Can't be trusted to figure things out on your own?" Ouch.

"Where are we going?" I asked.

He was already disappearing into the stairwell that led up to the stacks.

As much as I loved looking through the books, I found the stacks in this library unnerving. The lighting was kept at a low level. The floors were made of thick translucent glass, so you could make out the shadowy features of people on the floors above and below each level. You could see the soles of shoes, for instance, or make out the top of someone's head and maybe their arms as they reached to pull a book off one of the shelves. The fogged glass, darkened stacks, and quiet made me feel like I was trapped between layers of wax, as though I had wandered into a giant beehive during hibernation. If I weren't careful I might awaken the queen and her squadron of drones.

I followed Josh as he bounded up the stairs. We reached the fifth story, and he ducked in between two bookshelves. I tried to remember what section we were in. Transcendentalism? Chinese Buddhist meditation? Journals of missionaries in the American West?

"What are you looking for?" I asked, a little out of breath after the climb. I glanced at the call letters on the end of the shelf nearest me: BF1404-2055. Occult and Paranormal Phenomena. Was he one of those Ouija board, magic 8-ball types? I spotted him midway down the row.

"It's not a book," he whispered. He glanced behind him and past me. "It's me. I have something you'll want to see."

He started unbuttoning his shirt.

Wow. He was confident. "What are you doing?" I whispered loudly, although heat was rising to my face and my heart rate picked up.

"I'm not getting fresh," he shot back. "I just need to show you. Trust me."

He stuffed his button-down shirt on top of some books and started on the T-shirt he was wearing underneath, releasing a strong whiff of Downy. I breathed in deeply as he crossed his arms, grabbed his shirt at his waist and raised it half-way up his back. He turned and stood with his back toward me.

Two scars, identical to my own.

I gasped. He dropped his shirt and turned around.

"How . . . ?" I started. "When . . . ?"

"I thought that would get your attention," he smiled.

"I'm all ears," I said.

"Don't want to rush back to the desk? I'm sure my five minutes is up," he teased as he put his shirt back on.

"Stop it!" I said. "Talk. Quickly." His reminder about the five minutes brought me back to reality.

"You have them too, right?" he asked.

I nodded.

"I figured by the way you reacted when I touched your back at the main library. I checked out that Gerasene mummy," he said very quietly. "You noticed his scars as well."

"Yes."

He went on, "I'm not sure exactly what my scars are from. Do you know?"

I shook my head.

"Do you get the feeling that things here don't seem quite right?"

I shrugged.

"I think there may be things the people running the GYSP are working on, things that may concern people like us." He dropped his voice even lower as someone walked overhead.

"What do you mean, people like us?"

"I don't know. I know part of the picture—you do too. The obvious part. All the GYSP students are gifted, but not necessarily in the normal sense of 'giftedness.' At least two of us have identical scarring on our backs that also happens to match the scars on a mummy donated to the museum by a member of the family that has the same name as the program we're in. By the way, there's about a ninety-five chance that the mummy is the person in the Bible called the Gerasene demoniac."

"What?"

"Based on the population at the time and the number of people in the region using mummification."

"So?"

"So, I don't know exactly, but if it's him, the Gerasene demoniac had demons expelled from him and somehow ended up mummified and on display in the museum here. Do you think we've been collected by the Grigoris too?"

"I'm pretty sure I'm not demon possessed."

"It's not just the mummy and the scars. It's the conversation I overheard during orientation," Josh said. "Did you see the secret service wannabes at the back of the room?"

"In front of the paintings?"

"Yes. They were taking bets about how many of us would survive—that was the word they used—and who is the special recruit."

"Special recruit? Are you sure you heard right?"

"I have unusual hearing. I can hear really well from really far away."

I cocked my head, thinking about my own hyper-sensitivity. He must have thought I wanted more details, which I did.

"It's called 'hyperacousis.' It doesn't work all the time. It depends on the frequency of the sounds. Sometimes it's more like picking up the sound waves than getting actual words. But that I definitely heard correctly."

I told him about my sense of smell.

"What do I smell like?" Josh asked.

I wanted to tell him about all the things I associate with Downy and crayons—sunshine and comfort and being completely relaxed and at ease and that I wanted to kiss him, but I stopped at Downy and crayons.

He smiled. "I like that," he said.

"Go back to the special recruit," I said, not wanting to forget that, like me, Josh thought this place was kind of mysterious. "Who did they think it was?"

"They think it's Xanthe, you know, the pretty blond girl."

"Mantrap," I blurted.

"Wow," he said. "Jealous much?"

"Her scent." I blushed. "It's the name of a perfume."

Someone was approaching on this floor. Whoever it was had eaten a lot of the garlic bread served at dinner.

"I've got to get back," Josh said.

Neith, a GYSP student, came around the corner and saw Josh and me together.

"Uh, hi," he said, like he didn't want to interrupt.

"Hi Neith!" I said, too loudly for a library. "Can Josh help you find something?" I asked but noticed Josh had already gone.

"Maybe I can help," I offered, a little perturbed that Josh had taken off.

"I'm looking for this book about love potions?" It came out as a question, and he pushed his wire rim glasses onto the bridge of his nose as he held out a paper with the call letters on it.

"Love potions?" I asked.

"Yes. Or related enchantments. Haven't you done your ethics homework yet?"

I shook my head no.

"The Watchers, from our 1 *Enoch* reading, give humans various kinds of forbidden knowledge, including spells and how to undo them. I also think part of what they taught humans was pharmacopeia."

I looked at him blankly.

He explained, "Making medicines and drugs. The reading refers to knowledge about plants and roots. I thought I would do a little more research and find out if anyone knows specifically what it is they taught."

I tried not to smile as I wondered if Neith's interest in love potions was not just academic. During class he had been watching Zia, the singer, with big round eyes and a dreamy expression. Neith was sweet and seemed a little shy. His copper skin had a sprinkling of freckles. He was the only boy in our class who wore glasses.

I found the book with the call letters on Neith's slip of paper, *Ancient Enchantments and Incantations in Folklore and Fiction*. "There may be some other related titles in this area," I said, gesturing to the couple of shelves above and below where his book had come from. "Good luck!"

"Thanks," Neith said.

I decided to do my homework in my room, but I had to walk past the desk where Josh was.

"Sorry," he said. "I shouldn't have just left you like that." He dropped his voice. "I'm just nervous about things here. And I can't tell if I'm relieved you have the scars too, or whether that just confirms that I—we—should be nervous."

I looked at him. He smiled. "I won't do it again," he said.

"Okay. Rule number one," I said, "no leaving me in the creepy stacks, especially after a mysterious self-disclosure."

"I can follow that rule."

"To be continued?" I asked.

"Soon," he said.

I walked back to my room wondering how hard it would be to keep my mind on my homework, or whether, like Neith, I might go in search of info about love potions.

§

When I settled down to do my homework, here's what I learned. The book of *1 Enoch* was supposedly written by Enoch, great-grandfather of Noah, of "and the Ark" fame. It told the story of a group of angels called Watchers who were supposed to watch over humans, in the sense of looking after their best interests, like the guardian angels in my mother's lullaby. But these ones had different ideas.

When the Watchers looked at humans, what really caught their eyes were the females of the species. They swooped down to earth and mated with women (Watchers evidently were all males). Their babies turned out to be half-human and half-angel creatures called Nephilim. The next generation, the children of Nephilim, were called Elioud. So, part-angel and part-human creatures inhabited the earth.

This was not good. For one thing, the Nephilim believed humans should be their slaves. Their greed and desire for excess of everything— food, possessions, land ownership—caused environmental degradation on a huge scale. The Watchers also taught their wives secret knowledge, including magic spells and astrology, and how to make weapons, makeup, jewelry, and stuff with plants and roots. If *1 Enoch* were true, Aunt Alina was an expert on at least two of the forbidden subjects.

The story ended with God sending archangels to imprison the disobedient Watchers until a great judgment at the end of time. Also, because there was so much evil on the earth, God was going to send a great flood, and Noah would go down in history for the whole floating zoo thing.

Ethics class was going to be fascinating!

When I did fall asleep, I dreamed of winged creatures, leering and swooping down on toga-clad women, and the same women, wearing brilliant eye shadow and spangled bracelets, their slim arms raised toward heaven, whether in self-defense or supplication, I couldn't tell. Nearby, a group of men sharpened swords around a campfire and looked to the sky for a sign that it was time to go to war.

15

CIRCA 32 CE

Samya and the Gerasene Demoniac

"They came when I was eight, the voices at the fringes of my skull," the man told Samya. "Quiet at first, almost polite, humming a nearly sweet sound around the periphery of my brain. Like playmates wanting entry, not frightening, just new."

Samya was intrigued by this assignment, the latest the Peerless had given her. One of her own grandchildren, a descendent of hers with Gadreel, had been demon-possessed. It had been horrible to watch him succumb. Too horrible, in fact. The boy was taken from the village so no one would have to see him undergo such torture. Whether he was simply left on his own to die or was drowned, as she had heard they sometimes did to the possessed, she didn't know.

The young man before her now, the Gerasene, had been cured, and cured so completely that he hadn't needed any of her salves or ointments, the desire for which she assumed would provide her access to his story. He had declined and simply offered to tell her whatever she wanted to know. Having spent so much time with the Peerless, she was unused to someone offering her something for nothing.

What the Peerless wanted was information. How had the man been healed? Who had the power to exorcise the demons when others were unable to drive them out?

The young man continued, "Within months the sound grew more insistent, until I could feel it—a breach of my cranium, the way a rodent squeezes through a crevice in a rock wall, violating the tiniest flaw, contorting itself, altering matter to get where it wants to go. On the other side of the barrier, it expands to its original shape and girth, and takes up residence. I could hear clearly, inside my own head, a voice not my own, then several slipping in through the same fissure, then more than I could count. Like a swarm of birds, each with its own claws and caws, razor bills and screeches, straining to get my attention, ordering me to act or else suffer the stabs and shrieks of their horrible serrated beaks.

"At first I could not understand. I could only feel the stinging whine of their clawing and steely voices. My head throbbed and there was no way to relieve the pain. Only my screaming more loudly than the voices numbed me. As I howled, a red veil descended over my vision, so that everything I saw looked awash with blood.

"As I grew, these bouts of torture worsened. My parents referred to them as 'episodes,' and spoke of them in hushed tones. At first I took comfort in that name. It reminded me that calm would descend again and the voices would quiet until the next outburst. But as the interludes shortened, the label frightened me because it meant they would be back. With each return the voices were more numerous and their screeching more insistent.

"Once when I was twelve, during an episode, I ran from our house into the field behind our village. Although my body was small—it had been hard for me to eat enough and grow well with my condition—the presence of all these screechers inside me meant the open air was the only place I felt there was sufficient room for me. As their shrieking continued, and the red film descended, I collapsed to the ground. I pawed for a stone, and when I found one with a sharp edge I gouged myself. It was one way I could feel something that was me, mine, amidst the sense that what was inside me was not. This is my skin, my blood, my pain. The cutting did not quiet the voices, but it let me strike back. At a high cost. I would eventually collapse, exhausted, unconscious."

Samya shook her head, a compassionate gesture, as she remembered times she had seen wounds and scars, evidence of the self-harm of the possessed. The preferred targets of demons, according to the Peerless, were those with a high percentage of Nephil blood. Demons were the disembodied spirits that went loose when Nephilim bodies ruptured. Not allowed by the Enemy into heaven and not consigned before the final judgment to hell, demons had to stay in the earthly realm where they needed bodies to inhabit. But when demons took over a new body they caused chaos. They needed to be in control, to unseat the person whose body they had taken over.

Samya had asked Gadreel, "But why do they hurt their hosts? If they destroy them, they'll only need to move on to another body."

Gadreel had answered, "Demons loathe the physical body. They take pleasure in destruction. There will always be another host to destroy."

The man continued, "It was night when I awoke. I pulled myself up from the dirt and staggered back toward our house. I could see that the oil lamp still burned in the main room. My parents were awake.

"I was caked with blood and dirt. I paused outside the entrance to see if I could wipe some of the grime away without disrupting my wounds. I ran my hands through my matted hair and closed my eyes so the falling grit would not sting my eyes. The door was slightly ajar, and I could hear my parents' voices. My father spoke, 'We cannot continue this way. He needs to go now, before they destroy him, gain strength, and seek lodging in his siblings. It is hopeless, and too dangerous, for him to remain.'"

Samya swallowed and tried to push aside the genuine pity she felt for him and his parents. "What did they do?" she asked him.

He said that his father told him to say goodbye to his mother, then led him to the cemetery at the outskirts of the village. It was high on the cliffs above the lake.

"As we neared the cemetery edge, where the first tombs point up like teeth, Father sighed heavily. He put his hand on my shoulder and guided me through the gap in the low wall surrounding the graveyard and gestured for me to sit down on a stone bench next to a tall alabaster marker. The marker was shaped like an obelisk and glowed a purplish white in the moonlight. I looked at the name engraved in the base of the monument: Egregore. I didn't recognize it."

Samya swallowed and repeated the name to make sure she had heard him correctly.

"Yes," he said, then paused. "You know this name?" he asked her.

"I have heard of it," she demurred, hoping this wouldn't stop the story pouring out of him.

"My father told me, 'This is our family's monument.'

"'But our graves are over there.' I pointed to a row of small, plain stones farther into the cemetery. 'I remember where Grandfather was laid,' I told him, concerned that my father seemed to have forgotten where his own father's remains were buried.

"'You are correct, but this is our family's monument,' he told me, pointing at the gleaming alabaster. 'Here, with the Egregores, is where our family truly belongs.'"

Samya couldn't hold back, "Then it's true, you're part Nephil! That's why you were possessed!"

The man looked surprised. "You know about this? Not many people do." He paused again. Samya could see a look of indecision cross his face. Would her familiarity with the subject make him feel more comfortable about sharing, or wary?

She tried to encourage him. "Please go on," she said softly. "It's just that I've wondered if Nephilim exist. And if it's true that demon possession is more of a threat to them, what I might do to be helpful, as a healer," she added and gave her sweetest smile.

He looked relieved. He said, "It is true. We exist and because the demons come from Nephilim, it's to Nephilim they prefer to return. My father explained this to me as we stood by the alabaster monument in the moonlight. I felt terribly guilty, as if I were responsible for my own suffering and the suffering of my parents.

"My father told me there was nothing I had done to cause this. But he also told me there was nothing he or my mother could do but try to protect others. 'There is no cure,' he told me. 'And once they destroy you, they will look for others to inhabit.'"

"Others with Nephil blood," Samya said.

He nodded. "They would go first to those nearby, my brothers and sisters, most likely. They seem drawn to children. Then I understood why my father had brought me to the graveyard. It was a place where few people came. He could leave me there. The evil spirits could do what they would do with me and no one else would be harmed. I asked him how long until I would die. He said he didn't know.

"My father reached down to the bag of provisions he had carried from home. 'I am sorry to do this,' he said as he wiped tears from his eyes. He pulled out a length of chain and a shackle. I was stunned. Must I be restrained?

"He put the shackle around my foot while I still sat on the bench, trying to take everything in. 'There is food enough here for a week. I will come and bring more. If you are in your right mind, you will know I am here, and we can talk as before. But I will lose you soon, so we should say goodbye now.'

"He embraced me. I wept and clung to him. I felt his hands pry mine away. A wave of panic swept through me.

"'Don't leave me alone, Father!'

"Tears slipped down his face. He turned away from me, and the red veil began to descend."

"How long were you there?" Samya asked.

"I do not know. I noticed the passing of time not by sunrises or the changes in the night sky, but in how broken, bruised, and bloodied my body became. Each period of consciousness, when I felt in my right mind again, brought a new awareness of my torn flesh, new welts, yellow and green contusions. My clothing was in shreds, then gone. I had no energy even to feel shame at my nakedness. My ribs stood out like ridges in sand. My arms and legs became battered sticks. I stopped eating and I had no memory of human contact. I was in too much pain to be lonely. I wished only for an end. I tried to throw myself from the high cliff, but my shackle prevented it. I tried to strangle myself with my chain, but each time I was about to lose consciousness, it was as if I awakened the demons and they tormented me again. They would not let me kill myself. They would use me for their shelter for as long as my body could withstand it.

"Then he arrived."

"Who?" Samya asked.

"The man who rescued me."

"And who was that?" Samya wanted to know, both because she was getting to the information she had come for, and because she was intrigued.

"The one who released the demons."

Samya's throat was dry. "Yes?"

"He must have been very strong, because he gripped me while I was still in the midst of a visitation. The screechers raged, the red veil smothered me. Yet, even through the torture I could feel two strong hands on either side of my face. "Father?" I thought, then the demons prevented another articulate cognition. They slashed at me from inside, trying to reach the man who had me in his grip. The screeching congealed and formed words that burst from my mouth: 'What have you to do with me, Jesus, Son of the Most High God? I adjure you by God, do not torment me!'

"'What is your name?' the man demanded.

"It was the demons, not I, who replied: 'My name is Legion, for we are many.'

"His face came into focus. His eyes looked directly into mine. His grip on my head was firm. He opened his mouth and spoke. One word. Just one word and it was over.

"My body heaved, as if my entire body, not just my stomach, was expelling its contents. The man held my head firmly as a stream of red and black, like thick and milky smoke rushed from my mouth, and flew past him to somewhere beyond. I shuddered as the stream came to an end. The red veil lifted. My vision cleared. I could hear pigs squealing, then I watched as they hurtled themselves over the cliff and into the water below. I heard birdsong, and felt the breeze, then saw the man smiling as he said my name, 'Abhati.'

"He helped me to sit and gave me water and bread. He spoke again, 'Abhati, you are freed now from the intruders. You may do as you like. Only first go back to your village and show them you are freed and in your right mind.'

"'The word . . . your voice . . .' I was not sure what to say to this remarkable man, but I wanted to acknowledge what he had done."

Abhati paused and smiled a peaceful, beatific smile. He looked like the meaning of his name, "splendor, magnificence, light." Samya had never seen such peace. For just a moment she wanted this peace for herself. She thought about asking him how she could know it. Then she remembered her errand, what she had actually come for.

"The word—what was the word the man said, the word that released the demons?"

Abhati looked at her, maintaining a silence that seemed born of contentment. Finally he spoke.

"The healer told me, 'The word I spoke is important, yes. Others will pursue it, thinking it has power in its own right, like a spell. Do not give it to them. Its truest power comes only when spoken in love, for love, by love.'"

"But you can tell me, surely?" Samya replied, but she could hear the desperation in her voice, a sycophantic lilt she knew gave her away. "Please?" she tried.

"I have promised to protect the word. In gratitude to the healer, I obey him and safeguard the word."

"But if the word can set others free, why not share it? Aren't you being selfish?"

Abhati paused, as if considering, then spoke, "I will not."

"I know people who would reward you," Samya said, then added, "your own flesh and blood. Other Nephilim."

"Those who would offer me reward for forsaking trust are not worthy of my trust."

Abhati smiled again, this time a wistful smile. He said, "I wish you well, and I wish you peace." He bowed and walked away, leaving Samya alone. She considered going after him, to go with him, wherever he was going. But she stood still instead.

When she returned to the Peerless, she told them, "He knows nothing."

Gadreel replied, "You have failed, Samya. We will send someone more persuasive. And we will withhold your next dose of elixir. Perhaps you will try harder next time."

16

KAIA

Honey and Tar

I met Dilani in front of the Museum to go to our appointment with Dr. Calleo. Her office was on the museum's Lower Level. On our way there, we saw a door marked "Exhibit Material—Authorized Access Only." The door was slightly ajar and a dim light shone from within the room. I paused. Dilani looked at me, then at the door. "We're five minutes early," she said quietly, with raised eyebrows and a shrug of her shoulders. "Dr. Calleo isn't expecting us until ten."

I looked both ways in the hall. No one else was around. We tried to peer through the open crack. "I can't see anything," Dilani said.

"Me neither."

She pushed the door open wide enough to stick her head in. "There's no one in here. Let's take a look."

My heart was pounding. I was certain neither of us qualified for "Authorized Access," but Josh's remark about me being a "rule follower" still stung. Maybe this would be a safe way to prove him wrong and come back with some information about what was going on around here. We stepped inside, and I pushed the door back to the hand-width crack we had started with. The room smelled of honey and tar.

The overhead lights were off and there were no windows, but light emanated from a quart size jar sitting on a long stainless steel table in front of a stack of wooden crates. The jar seemed to glow brighter as we approached

74

and illuminated the objects spread out next to it on the table—a syringe, a petri dish, a magnifying glass, a flat black knife, a desk lamp, and a crow bar.

"What's that?" I whispered, pointing at the jar. "Fireflies?"

Dilani pointed at the petri dish. A large black housefly was walking across the bottom of the dish. "Gross," she said. "Flies are disgusting. Especially those big ones." She swatted at it, and it took off.

"Its feet . . ." I started.

"Wow," Dilani said in a hushed voice. The fly's feet glowed—tiny pin-pricks of light against our dim surroundings, like the fly had walked through glowing paint. It buzzed over to the crates and landed on the end of one of them.

"What's *that*?" Dilani whispered back. She pointed to where the fly had landed. Stenciled on the end of each three foot-by two-foot crate was "*Specimens. Duophysite. 4 mos-8 yrs. Abbysinia.*" There must have been at least a dozen boxes. Some were open and packing material—it looked like straw—stuck out from the top.

I felt around on the desk lamp for the switch. My hand was trembling, and my throat felt tight, but I found a round knob near the light bulb and turned. I heard a click and the bulb blinked twice then crackled to life. The lamp cast a wide ring of light that reached another table off to our right.

Dilani gasped. I followed her gaze. "Are those what I think they are?" She pointed toward the table. "They look like babies . . ." Her voice trailed off. She grabbed my hand, and we walked slowly toward them, careful not to block the light from the lamp behind us.

On the table were three clear glass domes about two feet high and about a foot and a half in diameter. The glass coverings rested on wooden bases. Under each dome was a small, seated figure. I looked down at the one closest to me, in the middle of the three. The left half of its body was encased in wrappings, beige linen strips pressed closely around its skin. The wrappings had been removed on its right side and folded back to expose the child beneath. I couldn't tell if it was a boy or a girl. Its skin was dark, almost black, leathery, and drawn tight to the withered muscles and sinews that still clad its bones and skull. Its mouth was half-open like it was trying to breathe, and tiny teeth showed beneath its taut lips. Its hair was thick and matted, curly and black, tinged with a rusty red. Its little arm rested on its outstretched leg and was adorned with a small tarnished silver beaded bracelet.

"A toddler," I stammered. "It looks real. Like an actual human toddler."

"A mummified human toddler," Dilani said hoarsely. "Another." She pointed to the one on the left. It was completely wrapped in bandages, tight enough to show the outline of its open mouth. A string of colorful feathers and large silver beads was wrapped around the torso. A hammered silver circle was pushed down onto its head. A crown? The circle was about an inch wide, thin, and embossed with tiny stars.

Slowly we stepped in front of the third glass dome. The child inside was completely unwrapped, no bandages, just draped with a beige linen cloth around its waist. It too was adorned with silver bracelets, one on each wrist. A silver necklace hung around its neck with a small circle pendant hanging in the middle of its chest. I looked at its face, its head slightly tilted back, its mouth open, its rows of small white teeth, parted, yearning for food or breath. Its eye sockets were empty, but its eyelashes were intact and, like the hair on its head, thick and black with a hint of red. As I moved my head to get a view from the side, something glittered on the small child's face.

"Dilani," I whispered, pointing at the toddler's head. "Is that gold? Gold dust?"

"Looks like makeup. See, there's a swoosh of it on each cheekbone. It's faint but it's there. And here!" she said, pointing at the rim above each eye. "Gold eye shadow." We leaned in closer. Dilani looked at me, "It's wearing eyeliner too. See? Just below the eyelashes."

"Just like the Gerasene mummy in the museum," I said.

"Who did this?" Dilani asked, looking down at the children. She turned back toward the stack of crates in the middle of the room. "They're marked 'Specimens,'" she said with disgust. "'Duophysite Specimens'—specimens with two natures."

"Two natures? Like half human-half angel?" I said. "Like in the Enoch story?"

"Like in the Enoch story, where makeup and jewelry are really important."

We looked at each other, neither of us wanting to believe it could be true. It sounded too crazy.

"Where's Abbysinia?" I asked, and then, too late, caught a whiff of a scent I remembered—roses, lilacs, rotting meat.

"Today we call it Ethiopia," a woman's smooth voice said behind us. The overhead lights went on. Dr. Calleo stood in the open doorway, her manicured hand on the light switch.

"You are late for our appointment," she said, her voice clipped. "I see you have found the material for our next special exhibit. It's this I wanted to talk with you about, a rare opportunity for you, if you can be trusted. And prompt."

My face flushed with embarrassment at being caught. And late. I wanted to make a good impression. Josh was right. I am a rule keeper. Following rules keeps you from looking like an idiot.

Dr. Calleo seemed unfazed. "Can you be trusted? And prompt?" she asked, looking first at Dilani, then at me. We both nodded. My shoulders relaxed as relief surged through me that Dr. Calleo seemed more worried about the clock than the fact that Dilani and I were trespassing.

"Fine," she said crisply. "Good." She shut the door behind her and walked toward the three mummified children, her taupe high heels clicking on the linoleum floor. We followed.

Gesturing toward the crates and then the three glass containers, she said, with admiration in her voice, "The Abyssinian Collection. A precious find. These specimens were presumed lost during the Second World War, but recently rediscovered in a vault in Budapest."

The way she referred to the children as "specimens" made my stomach tighten.

"We assume the Nazis had stored them, anxious as the Nazis were to study those they regarded as aberrations."

Aberrations?

Dilani spoke up. "Are they true mummies? Did people other than the Egyptians mummify?"

"Yes," Dr. Calleo responded. "These are the mummified remains of children prepared in Ethiopia. There are fifteen in all, of various ages, although none reached the age of nine."

She waved a hand over the glass domes. "These Victorian cloche bell jars date from when the mummies were first prepared for examination and display. Of course, our methods for scientific investigation have advanced tremendously since the late 1800s."

Wait, I thought. *You got them from curious Nazis, and now you're going to study them? How is this different?*

"Ethiopia was a prime source of materials used in Egyptian mummification. Natron salt, frankincense, myrrh, were all available in ample supply in Ethiopia. It's the source of very fine frankincense, the milky white resin from the tree, genus *Boswellia*. Ethiopians also used an exquisite white honey and asphalt or bitumen, called *mummiya* in Arabic, to preserve the dead. You can still smell it, can't you?" She inhaled deeply. A look of pleasure spread across her face. The acrid tar smell was making me queasy.

She continued, "Ethiopians may have begun mummifying those deemed worthy of special treatment even earlier than the Egyptians did." She walked to the other table and pointed at the stubby flat knife. "A necrotome." She picked it up and rested the pad of her thumb against the sharp edge of the blade. She pushed against it until she winced, then relaxed her grip, smiled, and said, "A knife used to examine the desiccated flesh of the deceased. Ethiopian obsidian. Sharper than surgical steel."

I glanced at the syringe next to the knife. I didn't want to know what that was for. Needles were just below water and just above public speaking on the list of things that made me feel faint.

"I imagine you have more questions," Dr. Calleo said. "We have no more time today."

"But, Dr. Calleo," Dilani began.

"I will leave you with this," Dr. Calleo said. "You may be witness to the most interesting and exciting inquiry ever undertaken in our institution." She paused. "These specimens . . ."

That word again. I swallowed the bile rising in my throat.

". . . were once considered to be gifts given by an immortal power. Now we have the power to ask: can they, even in death, give life?" Her perfectly groomed eyebrows rose with the question and hovered high on her forehead.

An intercom buzzed from near the doorway. "Dr. Calleo, your presence is required in Room 102," a male voice said.

"I'm sorry," she spoke in our direction, but like she was inconvenienced, not apologetic. "Our appointment will have to be postponed until next week. I will see you in class."

And then, although I had no idea why at the time, I reached back to the table behind me, grabbed the necrotome, and tucked the blade into my back pocket, pulling the hem of my hoodie down to make sure it didn't show.

"Now," Dr. Calleo said when we hadn't yet moved.

She ushered us out of the room ahead of her and switched off the lamp and the overhead lights. I turned back toward the room and could see the glass jar glowing as Dr. Calleo shut, then locked the door.

17

Charred Marshmallow

"Okay," Dr. Eder began, "What is our reading from *1 Enoch* about? Anyone—just call it out."

"Hybrid creatures who destroy the world."

"Fallen angels."

"Where weapons came from."

"How people started wearing jewelry."

"And makeup."

"And doing horoscopes."

"Magical spells and sorcery. And how to undo spells."

Dr. Eder gave an encouraging uh-huh after each response. "Anything else?"

"I'm wondering about the Elioud," Neith said, "the offspring of the Nephilim. *First Enoch* doesn't say what happened to them."

I saw Dr. Eder's eyes flash with excitement, like Neith had stumbled on some piece of treasure. Even more, I smelled his thrill. He emitted a burst of scent like the blackened outer crust of a marshmallow allowed to catch fire, then extinguished.

"What do you think?" Dr. Eder asked Neith.

"Well, their name is interesting to me, for one thing."

Dr. Eder invited Neith to continue.

"In Hebrew the name Elioud could mean 'Hand of God,' or 'Power of God.' But, if the Elioud are offspring of the Nephilim, and the Nephilim are the offspring of rebellious angels, how would Elioud be useful to God?"

"How indeed?" Dr. Eder spat back. He regained his composure and said, "Perhaps, if they make the right decision, they can be useful to their Nephilim parents." He paused as if wondering how much to say. "That is, perhaps the Elioud have some attributes that can help the Nephilim." He paused again.

Dr. Eder was using the present tense.

"I have a question," a boy named Fintan said. Fintan's thing was genetic research. He was working on a cure for childhood leukemia. Dr. Eder nodded at him. "Would Elioud be born only to two Nephilim parents or could Elioud also be the children of a Nephilim parent and a human parent?"

Dr. Eder looked revolted by the suggestion, but answered, "The purest form of existence would be a Nephil, born of a Watcher father and a human mother. Two Nephilim parents, ideally, could have an Elioud child who is just like them, carrying their best traits. It is also possible that the child could be burdened by the traits of the humanity within each of his or her parents. But, enough genetics for now. Let us return to ethics."

He seated himself on the edge of his desk and asked, "Now, how would you describe what this story is trying to do? What is its purpose?"

I was feeling brave and put up my hand. Dr. Eder looked at me but couldn't recall my name. He consulted his class seating chart. "Ah, Kaia, thank you. What do you think?"

"I think, like you said last time, it's a story about how evil got into the world. It's trying to explain where a number of things that cause us problems came from—weapons, wealth," I faltered. Those were the obvious bad things the Watchers taught, although probably sorcery wasn't great either. "And sorcery," I added quickly.

"Nothing else?" Dr. Eder prodded.

"Well, the other things must be negative too," I offered, my courage wobbling a bit, "because the outcome is so bad—violence, destruction, and the Watchers get locked up forever for sharing the information."

"Yes," Dr. Eder said. "This story is a classic example of an explanation for how evil got into the world. It is a little different from the one with which most of you are already familiar, the one in which the snake tempts Eve in the Garden of Eden and then Eve and Adam eat the forbidden fruit. In that story, the humans make a choice that displeases their maker, with a little help from the serpent. In this story from Enoch, a group of angels initiates the action."

"What's wrong with eye makeup and jewelry?" Xanthe asked. I swear she batted her eyelashes at Dr. Eder.

"Indeed, what is wrong with eye makeup and jewelry?" Dr. Eder said, smiling back at Xanthe.

"Like the other things—astrology and magic spells and weapons, they are meant to give one person power over another," Zia, our resident opera star, said.

"Oh," said Xanthe coyly, "Like how some people go all weak in the knees when a gorgeous, well made-up woman walks through the room?" She turned in her seat as she said this, so that all eyes could be on her. With one finger she twisted a pendant on a delicate chain around her neck, and I saw some knees losing strength.

"Well, yes, actually," Zia responded. "Especially if the purpose is to manipulate something natural to make it prettier or flashier. I'm not against makeup or anything, but I can see the danger, where someone might have ulterior motives, more than just wanting to look pretty. And jewelry can decorate, but it can also show how rich you are, or at least that you have more money than someone else."

I thought that Zia had a point.

"It's odd, though, isn't it," a girl named a Miyako offered, "that some of the things they taught are really vague, like 'the signs of the moon' and 'knowledge of plants,' while some are more specific, like 'gold,' 'silver,' and 'antimony.' We would have to guess at what the moon signs are, and I have no idea what plants they're talking about, but we all know about gold, silver, and antimony."

I had no idea what antimony was. Thankfully, Dr. Eder asked Miyako to say more.

"Antimony," said Miyako, putting her brilliance in chemistry on display, "is a really important element. On the periodic table it's number 51 and goes by 'Sb,' for Stibium, its Latin name. In ancient times, it was used by Egyptians to make kohl, the black eyeliner worn by both men and women. In modern times it has all kinds of applications: batteries, bullets, microelectronics, flame retardants, and fire-starters. It's used in camouflage paints and to prepare glass for television screens and computer monitors."

"Thank you, Miyako," Dr. Eder said.

Dilani spoke up. "It's also used in a treatment for dogs and cats who catch a disease from sandflies."

Dr. Eder nodded his approval at Dilani and said lightly, "It has been used to treat various ailments in humans as well. Evidently, even this one small lesson from the Watchers had a big impact," he said. "Imagine what we might find out if we did know more specifically what the Watchers taught about the things Miyako correctly identified as vague—the spells, use of plants, and signs of the various astronomical bodies."

I found myself nodding in appreciation of what Dr. Eder had said. There was so much to learn.

"But wait," I blurted, to my own surprise. I swallowed and continued, "Isn't this just a myth? Didn't you say this is just a way that ancient people tried to explain how things got messed up? How evil started?"

"Anyone care to address Kaia's question? That this is just a myth?"

"Myth doesn't mean untrue," Josh said, "It means so true it can't be reported just like any regular story. There's a truth in it so deep that only a story with such fantastical characters can begin to get at it. It's not like it has to be taken literally."

"Good," said Dr. Eder. "But can a myth also be taken literally?"

"They are sometimes," said Josh. "I know people who think there really was a snake in the Garden of Eden who could talk and that two people ate an apple and the world has been messed up ever since. There probably are people who believe that angels mated with humans and made bizarre babies too."

"There very well may be," Dr. Eder said, without a trace of judgment in his voice. "But let us consider Kaia's other point, that this is a story about the origin of evil. Is it?"

"Yes," several people said at once.

"Can someone say specifically why?" asked Dr. Eder.

"Kaia said it," Neith said kindly. "The outcome is really bad—death, destruction, violence, and judgment."

"So it is," said Dr. Eder, a melancholy tone in his voice. He stood up from where he had been sitting on his desk. A moment passed while we waited for his next words.

"But what if," he said slowly and distinctly, "this is just one side of the story? What if this is merely the way the winners told it?" He paused again to let his question sink in. He took off his glasses and said, "There are two sides to every story, are there not?"

He walked along the row of desks until he stood in front of Xanthe. He ran his finger slowly along the front edge of her desk. I heard a few of the students sitting nearby take a quick gulp of air.

"What if," he continued, "there is another version of this story with the same basic details, but rather than the Watchers being villains who unleash terrors and trouble into the world, the Watchers are the heroes who give birth to a bold new direction for life on planet earth? What if, rather than calling them by the biased name *fallen* angels, we were to think of them as angels who descended to earth bearing gifts?"

"You mean put a positive spin on the story?" Josh asked, clearly skeptical.

Dr. Eder turned and faced Josh.

"The scribe Enoch was giving only one point of view, the biased point of view that supports the side with which he was allied. What if the Watchers also had a scribe?"

"Is there another version of the story?" Zia asked.

"There are variants on the same judgmental, that is, negative, theme. For instance, later in *1 Enoch*, there is an allegorical version in which the Watchers are brilliant stars who fall to earth and land amidst the inhabitants, mate with them, and noteworthy creatures are produced. The passage states, 'Behold, a star fell, and it arose, and began to live and eat among those creatures . . .'" Dr. Eder looked as if he were remembering the event rather than quoting a line from a book.

"But, alas, no," he sighed. "We are aware of no extant version open to the possibility that something good began when the Watchers descended." Dr. Eder said, wistfully, and returned his glasses to his face. "It is up to bright young scholars such as yourselves to surmise what such a document would contain were it to exist."

"Well, in my version makeup would be a gift and jewelry would be a blessing," Xanthe said lightly, flipping shut the copy of *1 Enoch* on her desk.

Dr. Eder flashed her another smile.

"For next class," Dr. Eder said, I want you all to imagine an appropriate rebuttal to Enoch's interpretation. Imagine you are the scribe of the Watchers, and it is your job to write the story from their point of view. Make it not longer than two pages, double-spaced. Be creative."

§

"This is going to be a challenge," Neith said quietly to me as we made our way into the hall. "The story is pretty clear that what they did was wrong."

I nodded and said, "Yeah. I get Dr. Eder's point about there being different sides to a story, but it seems like he wants us to think this story is about something good." I felt uneasy, like I was being asked to do something against the rules, just considering the possibility.

"He sure seems to think Enoch got it wrong," Miyako said, catching up with us. "The antimony reference is pretty interesting, though. I'm going to take it from that starting point."

"Antimony," Neith said. "Interesting name. It comes from the Greek words for 'not alone,' or 'against aloneness.'"

How did he know that? I must have looked at him funny.

"Sorry," he said. "Can't help myself. I'm a logologist. Uh," he said to my blank stare, "Logologist: a person who is crazy about words and word puzzles. Anyway, maybe we can work on this together."

We decided we would meet at the library in the evening and share ideas.

§

Dilani, Miyako, Neith, Josh, and I found a table in the corner of the reading room.

"This sounds more like creative writing than an ethics assignment," Miyako said. "Eder's basically just asking us to make something up, right?"

"I think so," Neith said. "But I'm not sure why."

Dilani pitched in. "Well, if ethics is in part about vision, being able to see the right thing, or imagine what would make the world a better place, then doing a little creative writing may stretch our imaginations. Maybe that's what he's trying to get us to do."

"Sounds good," Josh said, "except that I don't see how this story can be retold so that it has a happy ending, if we're supposed to keep all the basic parts, which include a lot of people dying and environmental disaster."

We were all silent for a moment.

"Well," Neith said, "maybe we just start from what Eder said about switching up the point of view, leaving aside the mayhem and tragedy for now. Let's start with the Watchers aren't falling, they're descending with gifts. Where does that take us?"

Miyako spoke up first. "I think we're back to the interesting detail about how other things on the list of what they taught are vague and general, more like categories, no specifics, with the exception of gold, silver, and antimony. The gold and silver are explained as having a specific purpose. They're made into bracelets and other jewelry. But antimony is different. It says," she read from 1 *Enoch*, "'he showed them concerning antimony.' Do you see? It's a specific material—antimony—but what did the Watchers show them? What if it's saying that the Watchers taught them a whole bunch of things they could use antimony for?"

"Like the things you mentioned in class? Microelectronics and tv monitors? That seems a little unlikely given that electricity hadn't even yet been discovered," Dilani said.

Miyako replied, "Of course, but what if the idea is that the Watchers gave them enough information to get their knowledge of antimony's uses underway, like they got the ball rolling? It's quite a versatile element, and it seems like in every age through history, when one use of antimony goes out of use or style, another one comes in."

"For example?" Dilani asked.

"For example, it was used to make moveable type, for printing presses. That would be a bummer if you produced antimony and everyone goes digital, but great if it also can be used in computer monitors and micro-electronics. Antimony keeps coming in handy. If you know what to do with it, you have a huge resource at your disposal."

"And a lot of people's lives depend on you," Josh said. "In Britain, they keep something called a 'Risk List.' It names the basic substances we've become the most dependent on for our standard of living and economy. So if suddenly no more of the substance were available, it would be really catastrophic to our daily lives. Gold and silver are way down the list, but antimony is at the top."

"Is caffeine on the list?" I asked, slightly serious.

"These are chemical elements," Josh said, definitely serious. "Right now the biggest producer of antimony is China, followed by Russia, Bolivia, and South Africa."

"What's even more interesting," Neith chimed in, swinging his tablet around so we could all see the screen, "is that the mines that produce anti-mony are all owned by the GFH Corporation. GFH's most recent acquisi-tion is in Iceland, where antimony mining increased ten times over what it was before GFH got there. Guess what GFH stands for."

We shook our heads.

"Grigori Family Holdings," Neith said.

"So that's where the GYSP money comes from," Dilani said. "Hooray for antimony!" she said enthusiastically and did a fist pump. People around us shot dirty looks at Dilani's non-library demeanor.

"I think it's strange, don't you?" Neith said, his voice at library volume. "We're reading this story about Watchers whose actions result in chaos and mayhem, the point of which seems to be, here's why were in the mess we're in, you know—wars, some people rich, others poor, beauty for the sake of power. I'm not even sure what all the magic and astrology stuff is about—and the ethics professor of the GYSP is asking us to imagine it from the Watchers' point of view. Maybe it's a little self-serving, that's all."

Josh looked at me with a *See—I'm not crazy* look.

Miyako said, "I have time in the chemistry lab next week. I'm going to do some experiments with antimony. Come along if you want."

We all agreed to be there.

Dilani added, "I would also love to know more about the medical uses of antimony, for more than animals. Dr. Eder mentioned something about humans using it too, right?"

"Fintan might know how it's used for humans," I said, leaning my head toward the table where another group of students had gathered. Fintan, who already had medical schools fighting over him, was sitting opposite Xanthe and her equally glamorous new BFF, Aranka.

"Perfect!" Dilani said. "We'll give him an opportunity to show off in front of Xanthe and Aranka. I'm sure he will be happy to tell us more than we want to know."

We trooped over to the other table.

"Sorry to bother you," Neith said, "but we are wondering, Fintan, if you can tell us about medical applications for antimony, ancient as well as contemporary."

"If you happen to know anything about that," Miyako added.

Xanthe put her elbows on the table and rested her chin on her crossed fingers and looked at him. She pouted slightly as she said, "Please, Fintan, I would love to know what you know."

He turned toward us and said, "Antimony has been used for various medicinal purposes since ancient times. It was taken orally to stop bleeding in the brain and applied topically to treat ulcerations of the eyes, dog bites, and burns. People liked putting it around their eyes because it contracted the eyelids and made their eyes look bigger. Currently it's used to treat infections from parasitic protozoa and worms." He glanced at Xanthe and Aranka, as if what he was saying might offend their delicate ears. Seeing no signs of distress, he went on, his voice gaining in enthusiasm, "The most fascinating use, certainly from a medical forensics standpoint, is its former use as an emetic," he stopped to see if we knew what that meant. Everyone but Neith shook our heads no.

Neith spoke. "Vomit inducer."

"Yes," said Fintan. "In the 1600s people had antimony cups made for the purpose. Put a little wine in the cup, let it sit for a while. The wine soaks up part of the antimony. Drink it and purge whatever irritant was in the stomach." He glanced again at Aranka and Xanthe, who looked intrigued but not grossed out.

"It also worked as a laxative. In the nineteenth century it was popular in pill form. It was called the 'Everlasting Pill,' because you would swallow it, the pill would do its work, you would retrieve it, clean it off, and return it to its bottle, ready for the next use." He turned his head quickly back to his preferred audience, again looking fearful that he had crossed a line. Assured of their continued interest in his knowledge, he continued.

"Antimony may in fact be what killed the composer Mozart. In his day, it was touted as an effective sweat inducer, and his doctor had prescribed it to him. Mozart may have overdone it. It's very harmful if taken in anything but a tiny dose. But if you want to poison someone, antimony could help you get away with it because the symptoms of overdose look so much like common gastric disorders."

Aranka and Xanthe were still fine, but I was nauseated.

"Thanks," I said quickly, hoping my partners also felt like that was all the info we needed.

"Happy to help," said Fintan.

I wobbled back to our table.

"Fascinating," Dilani said.

"Definitely," Miyako agreed.

"Does anyone know what antimony looks like?" I asked, the question just occurring to me.

Miyako pulled up a page on her tablet and showed us. "In its powder form, it looks like this," and pointed to a picture of dull gray dust. "In its metallic form it's really very pretty." She pulled up another picture, this one of a beautiful, sparkly silvery chunk with long spiky crystals emanating from it, like something precious had frozen mid-explosion. "If you break up the metallic form into little pieces, it looks like this."

And there it was. Tiny, glittery morsels that looked a lot like my headache pills. Exactly like my headache pills.

She added, "It's one of the few elements that is completely odorless."

I gulped. Was I taking antimony? It would make sense of why the eye doctor said to keep the dose so small. I tried to remember what Fintan had said about taking it orally. I think I would know if I had parasitic worms. What else was it used for? Bleeding of the brain. Is that what was causing my headaches? My head swirled with new questions.

"See you all tomorrow in class," Neith said, collecting his things. "I've got to get to work. Good luck with the assignment."

Apparently, I needed luck with a lot more than just the assignment.

18

Onions and Anchovies

"**I** am not collecting your assignments," Dr. Eder said. "I am confident you have all worked hard on them and deserve top marks."

I wasn't the only one whose sigh of relief was audible.

"Instead, you will read yours aloud to the class, and then we will have some conversation about your work." He took a seat in one of the empty desks in the front row.

Dang. I could feel my throat tighten. Soon I would start to perspire. By itself sweat doesn't smell like much. But I did a quick review of last night's cafeteria meal to see what odors mine might carry: onions and anchovies. Not good. I shouldn't have gone back for a second helping of the steak with Italian salsa verde.

Xanthe, not surprisingly, wrote hers about the Watchers bringing the gifts of makeup and jewelry, two art forms that not only brought pleasure to the eyes but allowed artists to alter their own appearance, or someone else's, for the better. She titled her paper, "The Gift of Self-Expression."

"Nice way to get us started, Xanthe," Dr. Eder said, "although I hope others will be a little more creative in their interpretations." Xanthe looked stung, but then smiled when Dr. Eder winked at her.

Zia's was also along the lines of turning the secrets the Watchers exposed into some great gift to humankind, although it was trickier in her case. She had chosen to focus on the statement that the Watchers "taught men how to make swords of iron and weapons and shields and breastplates and every instrument of war." Her positive spin was that, although they had introduced armed combat, mass destruction, and the horrors of war to humanity, they had introduced a vibrant industry. "They didn't just arm one side and watch them kill off the other. They showed them how to make shields and breastplates, as well as swords, for example. The global military industrial complex employs many people all over the world, and job creation is a good thing."

She sat down, clearly not proud of her work. "I tried," she mouthed to me, shrugging her shoulders. But Dr. Eder looked pleased. "Thank you, Zia," he said. "Your putting the Watchers' pedagogy into the bigger picture is enlightening and proves that what the Watchers did can be interpreted in a positive light. The Watchers would be pleased with your paper."

Zia looked puzzled but was happy for the chance to bask in Dr. Eder's praise.

Neith went next. He too looked pessimistic about his efforts. "I chose to focus on the interesting detail that all the Watchers swear an oath that they will all participate in descending and producing children with the women." He cleared his throat and continued. "They're in it together, so my paper is about loyalty and being true to your friends." He read his two pages and then said, "I wanted to add that it helps if your friends are doing something good and not something wrong, but I wasn't sure if that fit in the assignment."

"No, Neith, it does not," Dr. Eder said, taking his familiar perch on the corner of his desk. "However, your interpretation of the Watchers demonstrating loyalty to one another no matter what is very insightful. Well done."

When it was my turn I stood at the front of the class, cleared my throat and said, "I decided to focus on what Dr. Eder said about the Watchers giving birth to a bold new direction for life on earth. He—you," I looked quickly at Dr. Eder, then back at a spot on the rear wall of the classroom, "said this had to be a positive spin that the Watchers would appreciate, not that it had to be good for humans." I gripped my paper with both hands, put my face down and read:

A Bold New Way of Being

The Watchers gave birth to a bold new direction for life on earth when they created a new race of creatures, the Nephilim. Because the Nephilim would have the attributes of both their angelic fathers and their human mothers, they would be a super race, perhaps superior to both their angelic and human parents. Although we usually think of angels as creatures capable of many great things and possessing extraordinary abilities humans lack, the combination of angelic and human might be even more powerful.

For example, focusing on the Nephilim's angelic nature, someone who was half-angel could be extraordinarily strong and exquisitely beautiful. Maybe they would even be able to fly. Because angels are immortal, Nephilim could live a very long time and might not be susceptible to the same kinds of disease and illness that humans are. If Nephilim wanted something enough, it would be difficult to stop them from acquiring it or achieving their goals.

Focusing on their humanness also leads to interesting results. Humans grow and develop. They aren't like angels because humans have to be born, learn things, and grow up. So the human side of Nephilim could make it possible for them to learn more and develop over time, instead of just being static. Humans also need each other, so Nephilim could learn to cooperate in order to achieve their goals.

When I picture the Nephilim, what comes to mind are beautiful creatures who glow with an inner light. They are strong, powerful, and persistent. They want to learn more, do more, and have more, because they strive to reach their potential. I imagine the Nephilim flying, wings unfurled, radiating light from within and looking for their next adventure.

I sat down. Okay, "looking for their next adventure" was laying it on a little thick, but Dr. Eder asked us to be creative.

"Very good, Kaia. Impressive," he said, standing up and coming to the side of my desk. "Kaia," he said, looking me directly in the eyes, "you understand."

His eyes were warm and large. I felt like I was being drawn into his dark, deep eyes that somehow were growing larger, his pupils dilating, and I was falling into a pool of warmth. Something was welling up to meet me as I began to tumble into his gaze. I snapped back to myself and realized the something shimmered like gold.

"May I take your copy?" He gestured to my paper. "This one is worth saving."

I gave him my pages, the edges damp from my sweaty hands.

He returned to the front of the class. "Next week we begin a discussion of when it is okay to do something to someone else without their permission."

19

Ripening Corn and Burnt Sugar

After class I went into the Div School courtyard and sat on one of the wooden benches. It was placed among planters overflowing with bright geraniums, impatiens, petunias, and flowing green vines. I thought about what we had just discussed, about the angels' rebellion and the unleashing of chaos and in the world and our strange assignment to rewrite the story from the Watchers' point of view. I recalled Dr. Eder's melodious voice reciting *Behold, a star fell, and it arose, and began to live and eat among those creatures* . . .

With a pang of homesickness and grief, I remembered how on hot summer nights in August, Dad would wake me up in the middle of the night to watch the Perseid meteor showers.

"Wake up, it's time," he would say softly as he sat the edge of my bed and put his hand gently on my shoulder. "It's time. Let's go." I was thinking of the summer I was ten.

I slipped on tennis shoes but stayed in my pajamas as I padded downstairs, carrying the quilt from my bed. Dad held the red Coleman cooler. I could hear the bottles of orange Fanta clinking against each other inside.

We loaded into the Camry and drove out of town, out beyond Six Mile Road where the houses and streetlights ended and the cornfields began. We pulled onto the gravel shoulder and Dad turned off the car.

I spread the quilt over the hood of the car and we lied back. The quilt slightly softened the pinchy feeling of vertebrae pressing on metal. The car's engine clicked beneath us as it cooled.

The air was warm, even in the middle of the night, moist and sweet-smelling with the scent of ripening corn—lush, rich, musky, like cotton candy overheated. A slight breeze riffled the corn leaves and they fluttered against each other like papery wind chimes, but it was no match for the humidity. The muggy air weighed down on us. I breathed in deeply and imagined the heavy air was the breath of God, warm, life-giving, expectant.

The sky was alive with bright white lights. It took a moment to adjust to night vision and take in details rather than just be overwhelmed by the wonder of more stars than I had ever seen and the realization that I was awake and outside in my pajamas and with one of the people I loved most in the world, supported by a warm, solid, clicking metal hand and blanketed by God's own breath.

We took turns shouting, "There!" and pointing in the direction of a streaking white light.

I thought about how safe I felt watching this show made by meteoroids beyond earth's atmosphere, compelled to join us, but unable to cross the boundary between us. They burn up trying. And we watch and point and shout.

Then I thought of Enoch's story and imagined the stars, not streaking sideways across the sky and being extinguished, but intruding—storming the barrier. I imagined one star swelling in size, and I realize, it's coming closer. It plummets to earth and lands nearby in the cornfield. As it makes contact, the ripe sugar smell blossoms and it's hard to breathe. Soon other stars join the first, raining down, and it seems the whole sky has come unhinged. The glowing light from the field is like no light I've ever seen, bright white, but somehow all the colors in the spectrum are visible too, shimmering, like the northern lights. The glowing lights rise, and I realize they're not just spheres of light—they are beings. They stand, straighten, their bodies rising high above the corn stalks. I am simultaneously drawn and repelled, fascinated and scared. I want to see them and I am terrified to.

I was snapped from my daydream as I realized I was no longer alone in the courtyard. I heard the clip of leather soles on the flagstone and turned my head to see Dr. Grigori coming from the archway that led to the library. I expected him to walk straight across to the doorway that went to his office. But he strode toward me, the sunlight glinting off his silver hair and flashing in his aqua blue eyes.

"Kaia, follow me. It is time we had a conversation in private."

I caught a whiff of burnt sugar in the air and swallowed hard.

20

Mahogany and Leather

D r. Grigori turned the brass doorknob and gestured for me to enter in front of him. I stepped into a room paneled in mahogany. Large leaded glass windows with small stained glass shields lined the side of the room opposite the doorway. Outside, clouds were forming, and the sky had turned ashen gray.

On the left side of the room, a woman with large blue eyes and thick blond hair sat at an oak desk, gazing at a large computer monitor. On the wall above her hung another painting of angels gazing into the eyes of the baby Jesus on Mary's lap. I allowed myself a little sniff and got, in addition to mahogany and aged linseed oil, toluene (had to be the woman's nail polish), perfume—something by Hermes I think, and, yup, there it was again, an underlying note of something rotten. I checked my shoes to make sure I hadn't tracked in something from the courtyard.

"Miss Hermani, meet Kaia, one of this year's most promising Grigori Young Scholars," Dr. Grigori said.

Miss Hermani stood and smoothed her red pencil skirt with her hands. Her nails were painted deep purple and on each of her long fingers she wore a gold band encrusted with purple gems that caught the glow from her desk lamp, sending sparks of light dancing into the room. She tucked an errant blond wisp behind her ear, where a large diamond adorned her earlobe, then shook my hand.

"Bring Kaia a refreshment," Dr Grigori said to her. Then to me, "Perrier? Skyvolt?"

I hesitated.

"Oh, you have not tried it," Dr. Grigori said. "Yes, bring her a Skyvolt."

Miss Hermani teetered on black stiletto heels to a panel by the door that turned out to be a refrigerator camouflaged in the same paneling as the room.

"Skyvolt is made of the melting icebergs off the coasts of Arctic Canada. The Grigori family owns the business—has for generations. It used to be quite difficult to melt the icebergs *in situ*. With global warming, we have only to capture the runoff. One of the advantages of climate change."

Miss Hermani pressed a crystal tumbler of water into my hand. Her rings glistened as she drew her hand away, and I felt my eyes widen.

"Oh, not real," she said and shook her head slightly. "They do get attention, though," she said as she flexed her hands in front of her, the way a cat stretches its paws, and wiggled her fingers. The gems in the rings flashed and dazzled. She returned to her desk. "Is there anything else, Dr. Grigori?"

"Yes, Miss Hermani. Kaia was no doubt gazing at your rings, not your fingernails."

"Oh!" she said, as she brought her hands to her mouth in surprise. She dropped her hands down to her desk and leaned slightly forward toward me. "The Musgravite gems are real." Then in a half-whisper, "The nails are fake." She turned her head toward Dr. Grigori and smiled. "These young ones are so adorable."

"Hold my calls," Dr. Grigori said as he opened a large door past Miss Hermani's desk. Again, he motioned for me to enter first as he held open the door, then shut it behind us. The door closed with a slight sucking sound, like a tight seal was made, and all ambient noise from the outer office was hushed.

The room we stepped into had no windows, and a crystal chandelier hung from the center of the ceiling. An oriental rug woven in pomegranate red, twilight blue, and roasted coffee bean brown covered the floor. The walls were covered in red velvet. The room felt airless, like we had entered a vault, or a tomb. A large desk filled the far end of the room. The wall behind the desk had a large flat screen and several large, framed diplomas. The left hand side of the room was filled with floor-to-ceiling bookshelves holding leather-bound volumes and small glass cases with objects inside that appeared to be statuettes and small metallic cups. On the wall to the right of the doorway stood a large fireplace with a creamy marble mantel. A large painting hung above the fireplace. It looked familiar to me.

"You recognize it?" Dr. Grigori asked, turning toward the painting and nodding at it appreciatively.

In the painting, two men wearing suits, ties, and hats recline on the grass in the midst of a lush wooded area. Behind them, a woman wearing a loose white gown stoops while bathing in a stream. I shuddered slightly at the sight of the water up to her knees. One of the men gestures toward a woman who sits with them, her head resting on her hand, and turned to face the viewer. This woman is naked, her right leg bent, her elbow resting on her knee, shielding part of her breasts and her private parts from view. Loaves of bread, grapes, and a tipped over picnic basket, spilling its contents onto a disheveled picnic blanket dominate the left foreground of the picture.

"It's by Manet," I said. "It's in the Musée D'Orsay in Paris," although the smell of the artist's materials seemed genuine. If this were a copy, it must be from about the same time as the original.

"And yet, you see it on the wall here. What shall we make of that fact, do you suppose?" He paused. "And the subject?"

"Well, it's, it's . . ." What should I say? It's two fully clothed men and a naked woman. It's a picnic blanket that looks more like a rumpled bedspread. It makes me feel like I've stumbled into a scene I shouldn't be part of, like I'm interrupting a party I wasn't invited to. What did he want me to say?

"My dear, I do hope your time here in the scholars program is, shall I say, rounding out your education. You must learn to articulate your thoughts, even if you find them new, or shocking, or, dare I say, exciting in some way."

A queasy feeling rose in my stomach.

Dr. Grigori continued. "It is Manet's *Le Dejeuner sur L'herbe*, Luncheon on the Grass, his interpretation of the judgment of Paris, in which the mortal Paris judges amongst three goddesses, Hera, Athena, and Aphrodite."

"I know the story," I said, trying to make up for my earlier stuttering. "The goddesses each appear before Paris, and he is supposed to decide who is the most beautiful. Each of the goddesses tries to bribe Paris, though, by promising him something if he chooses her. Hera offers to make him king over Europe and Asia. Athena promises him wisdom and skill in war. Aphrodite offers him a human woman as his prize, Helen of Troy. Paris chooses Aphrodite—and Helen—and starts the whole Trojan War."

"Well done, Kaia. That is correct. One wonders how much the promise of beautiful, warm, female, human flesh persuaded Paris in his choice."

My queasiness stepped up a notch.

"And this masterpiece? Do you recognize it?" He took me by the elbow and pivoted me around to come face to face with a white marble statue about three and a half feet tall, standing on a rectangular marble base. I had seen this one before too, at least in art history class. I was pretty sure this was the Varvakeion *Athena Parthenos* and that she belonged in Greece, in the Archaeological Museum in Athens.

The statue in front of me was a small version of the statue of the goddess Athena that originally towered over her worshippers in the Parthenon. The original was twelve times the size of this one and must have been stunning. The uncovered parts of the goddess's body were portrayed in gleaming white ivory, and gold leaf coated her flowing garment and the shield she held in her left hand.

But even the small statue in front of us was impressive. Wearing an ornate helmet adorned with a sphinx and two winged horses, the goddess stood with perfectly erect posture, a look of determination on her face. Draped over her neck and shoulders was a breastplate with a Gorgon, a snake-haired female monster, in the center, and coiled snakes all around the edges.

"One glance at the Gorgon," said Dr. Grigori appreciatively, "and one would be turned to stone. A perfect protector against the men and gods who desired her for her beauty and her virginity. She is Athena *Parthenos*, the virgin, the unobtainable, but, oh, so desirable," he said as he nodded toward the goddess. "She could protect the city and herself against would-be invaders. Ironic, do you not think, my dear, that her followers chose the snake as her protection against the male member?"

I felt my cheeks burn red.

"You must not be embarrassed. As a scholar your mind needs to be open to all the ways people have experienced the divine."

He looked at me, then licked his lips, his narrow tongue quickly circling his mouth. "I have made you self-conscious, and that is quite ungentlemanly. I apologize."

I was uncomfortable and embarrassed, but was also determined not to seem weak or immature in front of the head of the Scholars Program. I set my yet undrunk Skyvolt down on a nearby end table and tried to think of something to say that wouldn't make me sound stupid or naïve.

He picked up my glass. Beads of condensation were rolling down the crystal and had formed a ring where the glass met the table. He pulled a red silk handkerchief from his suit pocket, shook it open, and wiped up the ring. He wrapped the glass in the handkerchief and handed it to me.

"Take a drink. Refreshing and restorative, I assure you. In fact, why not take a seat here, next to me, on this sofa?" He motioned to a dark brown leather couch in front of the fireplace.

"I prefer to stand," I said, trying to maintain my composure and some physical distance between us. I gripped the crystal glass tightly, and took a sip, relieved to feel the cold water in my mouth.

"If you must, Kaia, but I was hoping we could have a talk. Not all of my students hold such interest for me." He tilted his head slightly to one side.

"You do stand out in a crowd, Kaia, although I know you try not to. Your innocence and inexperience are enticing. There are many things I can teach you."

My stomach did a somersault. I took another quick sip of water, while I tried to think of what to say. I wished Miss Hermani were in the room with us. Would he talk this way in front of her?

"Dr. Grigori," I began, summoning my courage, "I am very uncomfortable with the way you are speaking to me . . ."

"No, no," he interrupted. "You quite misunderstand me. I have no interest in any sort of physical intimacy with you. I assure you that if I were interested in physical pleasure, I could have my choice of far more interesting and experienced specimens than you." He drew his index finger down my cheek. I shuddered and drew my neck back. I felt sick and stuck in place. There was that word again, *specimens*.

"Kaia, it is your special abilities that are valuable to me. Doctors Eder and Calleo have reported that your performance this week has been exceptional. Your physical self holds no interest beyond a mere curiosity of how such abilities came to be housed in such a container.

"But I have made you uncomfortable, and need to let you go. We will continue this conversation at another time. And I would advise you to tell no one about it. The other Scholars might become envious."

He pushed the door open and I was relieved to step back into the outer office. Miss Hermani glanced up at me and then became engrossed again in whatever was on her computer monitor. As I passed I could see it showed a screen saver with parakeets flying back and forth in a large cage.

"Until next time, Kaia," Dr. Grigori said. "Remember to leave the glass, if you please."

Stunned, I placed the glass on Miss Hermani's desk. She unwrapped the silk handkerchief and tucked it into my hand.

"He means for you to keep this," she said quietly. "He always tells students to keep the handkerchief."

"Uh, thanks," I said. I turned around and walked quickly through the large door into the hallway. I stopped and realized I was shaking. What should I do now? First thing, get away from this office. Second thing, get rid of this feeling like I needed a shower. I hurried to the Common Room where I knew I would find a dispenser of hand sanitizer. I pitched the red handkerchief into the trashcan where Mr. Argyros had deposited his hanky at our orientation. I turned to the fireplace mantle to use the hand gel, but then stopped, and went back to the garbage pail. There were two other red handkerchiefs in the can in addition to mine. I wondered if I could find out who, besides me, wanted to get rid of the token of such a gross experience.

I was totally creeped out. I didn't like the way Dr. Grigori told me not to tell anyone about our conversation, although clearly, from Miss Hermani's comment and the garbage pail of cast off souvenirs, he had held meetings with other students. Had Dr. Eder already shown him my assignment? What had Dr. Calleo said to him?

But even though Dr. Grigori was so disturbing, I didn't want to leave the program. Josh was right. Something was going on, and I wanted to know what it was, something involving the Gerasenes, Nephilim, antimony . . .

Antimony. The word comforted me. Neith's definitions came to mind: *Not alone.* I liked the second one even more: *Against aloneness. Antimony,* I repeated, and touched my locket.

I needed to talk with the others. I would start with Dilani. I realized Dr. Grigori had been right about this: I actually had made some friends. Would our friendship survive whatever came next?

21

Vera Wang Princess

I was excited to have new friends, especially Dilani. I definitely wanted to know Josh better, even though he was sometimes annoying, and Neith, Zia, and Miyako too. They all seemed real, true to themselves with their special talents and ridiculous intelligence, but kind. They didn't make me feel like I wasn't keeping up or didn't belong.

Xanthe was a different story.

Xanthe had natural platinum blond hair that hung in waves to the middle of her back. Her flawless skin was slightly tanned, giving her a healthy, just came in off the beach glow. She had large green eyes and long thick dark lashes, but they didn't have the unnatural fullness or length of extensions. The arch of her perfectly groomed eyebrows mirrored the bow of her cherry-colored plump lips that, in turn, framed her super-white straight teeth. She was gorgeous. She even smelled good. Vera Wang—Princess, although I thought she overdid it on the application.

She was starting to collect a following and it was easy to see why. Everyone wanted to be close to her, be like her. Be her. Her beauty looked effortless. She hosted parties in her room, let others try on her beautiful clothes and jewelry. She even gave some of it away.

"Look," Zia said one morning over breakfast as she held up her right forearm and showed off a silver bracelet, engraved with a pattern of delicate wildflowers, on her wrist. "Xanthe gave it to me. Isn't it pretty?" It was.

"Why did she give it to you?" I asked, trying not to let the envy I felt seep into my question.

"She called it a 'friendship bracelet.' Funny, right? It's a long way from those braided thread things we exchanged at my summer camp." She pointed almost sheepishly at her ankle where a frayed colorful strip of woven embroidery floss was tied. "I should probably take that one off. It's getting a little old."

"I bet you have nice memories, though, of the person who gave it to you," I said, feeling badly the Do-It-Yourself anklet's life might be coming to an end.

"Yeah, I do," Zia said with a smile. "I guess I can keep it, at least for a while. She gave Aranka a tennis bracelet," she said nodding toward Aranka. Aranka was an equally magazine cover-ready ebony-skinned girl with lustrous wavy black hair, large umber eyes, full lips, and a toned body. Her ability to turn heads was on par with Xanthe's. She was showing the girls at her table a sparkling link of diamonds hanging around her graceful wrist.

"No way!" I said. "Do you think it's real?"

"Xanthe said it is. She said, 'Friendship is a precious gift,' then gave out the bracelets."

"Wow," I said, envy definitely infecting my voice.

If Xanthe wanted me in her collection of friends, she had an odd way of showing it. After class one morning, Xanthe invited me to get coffee with her. "My treat," she said cheerily.

When we sat down at a small café table by the window, Xanthe looked at my face appraisingly. Then she leaned in toward me, as if bringing me into her confidence.

"Why *are* you here?" she asked me, pouty glossed lips turned upwards at the corners of her mouth. "You're not smart. Your resume is boring. You're so average. So, I'm wondering what it is about you that got the Grigoris' attention." She leaned back and stuck a plastic stirrer between her perfect teeth, eyebrows raised, ready to hear my response.

I was taken aback, but actually found myself appreciative that she had initiated this conversation in private. I could totally imagine her saying it at one of her room parties, enjoying having an audience as I squirmed.

My surprised silence must have told her she had taken the wrong tack if she genuinely wanted an answer and didn't just want to put me in my place. She went on, smiling a little more warmly, "No, really, I want to know about you. You must be a very special person in some way that isn't apparent, and I just want to know what it is. Maybe I can help in some way, you know, let your light shine a bit. No one has to be average." She said it like it was a bad word, dirty somehow.

Actually, I thought, *a lot of people have to be average. Or even below average. If we weren't, people like Xanthe and Aranka wouldn't shine so brightly.* Should I say this? She might appreciate the compliment.

"Okay, don't tell me," she said. "Maybe you're shy." She took a careful sip of her nonfat soy latte, then set her cup gently back on the table. She looked into the cup as if trying to read the swirls of coffee-colored foam. "I will find out, though," she said, looking straight at me and no longer even feign-smiling. "People think my strength comes from my looks. But you and I both know that knowledge is power. I will find out what it is you know." A smile crept onto her face again as she winked a friendly hello to whomever was no doubt staring at her. "You probably have to study before your next class to be ready, right?"

She was dismissing me!

I stood up. My chair made a loud scraping noise as I backed it away from the table, and I could see people wrench their gaze away from Xanthe and focus on me. I could feel heat rising to my face. I mumbled thanks for the coffee, took my Styrofoam cup, picked my book bag up off the floor, slung it over my shoulder, and headed out, wishing it hadn't taken me so long to leave, or that I could have stormed out, or gracefully left, or something other than how I imagine us average people do it.

But as I schlumpfed away in my humiliation and outrage, I smelled something clawing its way up from beneath Xanthe's heavy dose of Vera Wang Princess, a stench so rank it made my nose crinkle and caused a gag reflex in my throat. It was worse than even the undertones I had detected amongst some of the GYSP professors and staff. I turned around to where Xanthe was rummaging in her Louis Vuitton clutch. She pulled out a small crystal bottle and gave her wrists another spritz of perfume. Then she shook a small pill out of a container and washed it down with the last of her latte.

What on earth was that horrible smell? I hurried away, curiosity mixing with my anger, dampening and diffusing it, like Xanthe's floral balm had made the smell of rotting diapers subside, but not disappear.

22

Sealing Wax

By the end of the first week, Kiran and four other students had been sent home. "Not a salutary fit," was the official explanation, but we all had heard the challenging questions they asked professors and administrators. Now they were gone, and we were down to fifteen.

Dr. Grigori addressed us. "Some students have demonstrated their inappropriateness for the GYSP. It is better that they leave before we enter more deeply into the discoveries and knowledge that will be shared with those who are more deserving."

I looked around our shrunken semi-circle. How long would I survive?

"It is beneficial," Dr. Grigori continued, "to belong to an elite cadre. More resources for fewer participants. Accept this bonus for your successful completion of the first week." He motioned to a handsome man wearing a white dinner jacket and black slacks holding a silver tray in his white-gloved hands. The man came over and presented an envelope to each of us, bowing slightly as he did. The envelopes had our names written in red calligraphy on the front and a glob of ruby red sealing wax on the back flap, with an impression of the now-familiar angel's wing.

"Open them," Dr. Grigori prompted when he saw us hesitate.

I unfastened the wax with my fingertip and pulled out a thick engraved card. It read:

*In Recognition
of Your Successful Completion
of GYSP Week One*

Under this heading was a photograph of Aunt Alina. She was smiling, wearing large sunglasses, the kind that make me think of Audrey Hepburn or
some other classic movie star, seated at a table in a sunny location on a stone
plaza surrounded by palm trees. Where was she? In front of her was a full
champagne flute. She had both elbows on the table. One hand gestured to
the wrist of her other upraised forearm, as if she were modeling a product.
On her wrist was a fancy gold watch with diamonds along the outer edge.
It was the kind she had drooled over in a magazine ad where it appeared on
the wrist of an otherwise nearly naked movie star. On the table in front of
her was a tablet. I could make out on its screen a website, "Cosmetology and
Cosmicology by Alina."

It took a second before the penny dropped. I completed the week;
Aunt Alina got a prize. A big prize. That meant two things. Probably more,
but two was all I could formulate at the moment: they knew what would
make Aunt Alina happy, and they had really deep pockets.

The pockets' depths became more apparent as I heard other students'
gasps turn to murmurs about what their envelopes contained: Dilani got a
photo showing an enormous check presented to her favorite blind cat rescue
organization. Josh got a note saying a first edition autographed copy of some
philosopher's book was on the desk for him in his room. Zia got a note saying she would have a private audience with the music director of La Scala
Opera in Milan. Xanthe got a gift certificate for Baccarat Les Larmes Sacree
de Thebes, "Second most expensive perfume in the world!" she squealed to
Aranka who hugged her. They were bouncing up and down like two Miss
America contestants who had just found out they were both in the top five.
"A vintage Tiffany dragonfly pin," Aranka bawled to Xanthe, both girls crying and dabbing at their mascara with handkerchiefs the man with the silver
tray had provided.

Once the elated sharing died down, Dr. Grigori said. "Make Week Two
profitable as well."

I wondered how Aunt Alina's reward was supposed to be a reward for
me. And while I wondered, I noticed the man who gave us our rewards was
watching us and taking notes. Was this part of our education? A test?

"Profitable for whom?" I mumbled quietly.

Josh heard, looked at me and raised his eyebrows.

"Let's find out," I whispered back.

23

Hoatzin

In the library that night, Neith motioned to me and Josh to come with him to the stairwell.

"Something is wrong here," he said holding his tablet in front of him. He stood like a waiter holding a tray, but the cook had sent him out to a table with a dish of doughnuts dusted with arsenic or a pizza with poison mushrooms.

"What is it?" Josh asked, looking down at the tablet, his eyebrows knitting together.

"Kiran didn't go home," Neith said, concern in his face.

"How do you know?" I asked.

"I got this email from his parents." He turned the tablet so we could see the screen.

> Dear Neith,
>
> We understand that you and Kiran have become friends. Since he has not responded to our email inquiring into his well-being, we are reaching out to you. Please tell him we hope he is enjoying his time in the GYSP, and we look forward to his return at the end of the program.

"Did you try his email?" I asked.

"I did," Neith responded, "but just got an auto-response saying he's away for the summer."

"Maybe he hasn't switched his auto-responder off," I offered, "or maybe he needs a new computer, or maybe the battery ran down in his phone after he put it in the basket at our orientation." I paused, having run out of possibilities for why Neith shouldn't worry.

"Wouldn't you check your messages as soon as you could? Especially if you thought you might be getting a big scholarship or an opportunity to show your invention to some big investor?" Neith responded.

I couldn't relate.

"And his room," Neith said, shaking his head, "It's already empty, like he was never here, like he evaporated."

"Maybe the cleaning staff is really quick," I said, but it sounded lame even to me.

Josh said, "There's something else, right? You look really anxious."

Josh was right. Neith was pale and his eyes were darting back and forth like he was worried someone might see us.

"I also got this—just now, as I was coming to find you. Your names are on it too." He showed us the message address line. There was a blank email with a video attachment. The sender's address was SPREE-Is.org.

"What is it?" Josh asked.

Dilani and Zia burst into the stairwell.

"We saw you come in here," Dilani said. "Have you seen it yet?"

I looked at Josh. We both shook our heads.

"Let's watch it together," Neith said. "It's addressed to all of us." He held his tablet up so we could gather around.

The video images were grainy and off-kilter, as if the camera taking the pictures was mounted askew, but the image was clear enough that we could see four children, maybe ten or twelve years old, speaking into the camera, while a dozen or so smaller children huddled nearby. They were all dressed for frigid temperatures, in parkas with fur-trimmed hoods pulled up around their heads. Their breath formed small bursts of cloud as they spoke. Their message was urgent, their eyes wide. They pointed repeatedly with mittened hands to the door visible behind them. One of the four was crying as she spoke, and she wiped at her eyes and nose with her lumpy mitten.

But what were they saying? The sound quality was poor. Only intermittent words and syllables were getting through. The rest was crackly static. We couldn't make out enough to know who they were, why or how they had contacted us, or what had made them so scared.

"We all got this, right?" Neith said. I checked my tablet. It was there. We all nodded.

"Five minutes ago?" Again we signaled our agreement.

"We should watch it again," Dilani said, "See if there are any clues about who they are, and what happened when the transmission stopped."

Neith pushed the refresh button, and the video repeated.

The room was nondescript, empty of anything personal. No signs. No pictures. No windows. Just a black steel door in one corner of the otherwise white room. The grainy image obscured other details, but it looked like it was made of cinder block.

"Maybe it's a storage room," I said. "It doesn't look like it's made to have people in it. There's no furniture and just one door that we can see."

"Anything about the kids stand out?" Neith asked, running the video in slow motion, so each frame was still for a second before jumping to the next. "Other than that they must be someplace cold?"

"It's a fairly multicultural group," Dilani said. "There's not much to go on, other than their faces and the bits of hair you can see under their hoods, but they're at least as diverse as we are."

"Can you make the sound any clearer?" Josh asked.

Neith adjusted some settings, but it didn't help much. Too much crackling.

"I can slow it down, but that's about it."

The whole video was only twenty seconds long. Neith slowed it to forty. We listened, twice.

"I'm not even sure it's in English," Zia said. "The first thing I can make out sounds like 'Danger.' Then 'Gri,' then static, then 'ee.' 'Grigori?' Of course, we're in the Grigori Young Scholars Program, but does 'Grigori' have something to do with them too?"

We listened to the next five seconds: something unintelligible then 'yood,' then something, 'mony.' We looked at each other, shrugged, went on. Again we heard 'yood' and 'mony.' Still no ideas, but clearly the children were in distress.

Then, in the last five seconds, all four of the kids were talking at once, repeating what sounded like, 'commen,' 'vien,' 'coming,' then, 'coma!' The last word was shouted, as all four turned toward the door. We could see the huddle of smaller children lift their heads and look in that direction too. A wisp of inky black smoke was curling up from beneath the bottom of the door.

Neith froze the screen. "I think they're saying that someone, or plural someones are coming." He opened a new screen and typed some words in the search box. "Yup. They're saying, 'kommen,' 'they're coming,' in German; then probably, 'viennent,' in French, then English. 'Coma' is third person plural for 'coming' in Icelandic. They're speaking Icelandic right when the black stuff starts to ooze into the room."

He touched the screen on his tablet and the video came to an end with a silver flash.

"We should message back," Dilani said. "Maybe someone there can tell us what's going on."

"You're right. We should try," Neith said.

He clicked on the reply key and wrote, 'Hello?' and pressed send.

The message bounced back immediately.

"Try it again," urged Zia.

Neith typed, 'Message received,' and pushed send.

Another immediate bounce back.

"What do we do now?" I asked.

"I don't know if there's anything we can do," Josh said. "We don't know how many people got the message and video. We don't know if we're the only ones who got it, or if everyone in the GYSP received it."

"Should we tell a professor?" I asked.

"Like who?" Josh replied. "Dr. Eder, who wants us to imagine evil angels are up to something good?"

"Or Dr. Calleo, who calls mummified children 'specimens'?" said Dilani.

"What?" said Josh and Neith in unison.

"We have to fill you in on that one," I replied. "But not right now." Dilani nodded her agreement.

"Okay, so we don't tell a professor," I concurred.

"Maybe this is some sort of weird test. Maybe this is part of the program, and they want to see how we respond," Dilani said.

"It would be a pretty disturbing test, don't you think?" said Josh. "I think those kids are really in trouble and somehow they've reached out to us." He paused. "What if the GYSP is monitoring our tablets? Why else take our personal devices away and tell us to use the ones they gave us for everything?"

We were all quiet as this idea sank in.

"Wait," I said, going back to the video. "What about the first words they say? I know we can't really make them out, but what if that's the message they want us to get? They know someone's coming, so they really want us to know about something before whoever gets there?"

"Or, whatever gets there. Got there," Josh said.

"Okay," Neith said, pushing the play arrow again, and slowing the playback down to one-quarter time. He turned the volume and brightness up. I focused as hard as I could on watching the children's faces as they spoke. The syllables we could hear were the same: *Danger . . . Gri . . . ee . . . youd . . . mony.*

"Oh wow," I said. "Think of all the new words we've learned since we've been here." I looked at word nerd Neith. "Okay, maybe not you. New to me, anyway. What if 'mony' is the end of 'antimony'?"

"Could be," Neith said. "It's hard to know where one word stops and the next word starts, but they could be saying a couple of syllables before. It could be 'antimony.'" We watched again. It was hard to tell. Would that be any more likely than any other words ending that way?

Neith was on the same page. "It looks more like they're saying 'anti-mony' than 'matrimony' or 'alimony.'"

"Or 'ceremony,'" Josh said.

"Or 'cinnamony,'" I said.

"They're scared," Dilani said. "I don't think it's 'cinnamony.'"

"What about 'youd'?" said Neith, going back to that place on the video.

"I don't know if this is right," I said, "but do you remember how the fallen angels story ended, I mean, besides death and destruction?"

"'Elioud,'" said Neith. "The Watchers and women give birth to Nephil-im. The Nephilim give birth to Elioud." We were all quiet.

"So the question is, who or what are Elioud?" Neith said.

"And if that's what the children are saying, why are they saying it, and why are they so scared?" Dilani added.

"And who came?" I asked, as my nostrils widened in response to a whiff of cedar, lime, and grapefruit over spoiled mayonnaise . . .

We all jumped, and Dilani let out a shriek when the stairwell door opened. Neith snapped his tablet down to his side.

"Am I interrupting something?" Dr. Dranoush, Curator of Historical Collections at the library and Josh's supervisor asked in his nasally voice. "Josh, you are needed at the front desk. You have been absent for some time. I should not need to come looking for you."

"Yes sir," Josh said. "That is, no, you shouldn't, sir. I'm sorry, Dr. Dranoush."

"And worktables and carrels are more conducive than stairwells for group study," Dr. Dranoush said gravely, looking at the rest of us. "Congre-gating in a stairwell might lead some to think you are examining suspect materials, rather than engaging in educative inquiry."

"Sorry, sir," I said, my face getting red.

We all exited into the reading room, and Josh went back to his stool behind the front desk. The rest of us waited until Dr. Dranoush went back into his office and then we hurried over to Josh. Dilani spoke. "Maybe our meeting with Miyako tomorrow about antimony will help us figure out if there's something we can do for those kids." She looked at me. "First, Kaia and I have our meeting with Dr. Calleo."

"And I'm going to test Josh's theory about our tablets being monitored," Zia said. "I'll let you know."

When the others walked away, I stuck a finger in Josh's chest and spat, "You didn't hear Dr. Dranoush coming? I thought you had super-power hearing or something." It was much easier to blame Josh than admit my own slowness to detect Dr. Dranoush's cologne and sewerage combo.

He took some cotton wads out of his ears. "Sorry," he said. "Sometimes I just need a break."

"Today you smell like a hoatzin," I whispered as quietly as I could and stomped off toward the door.

"A what?" Josh called out to me.

"You heard me," I said. Then, I thought, *Rats*. I turned around, stomped back to the desk and said, "A really stinky bird from South America. It reeks. Something to do with how it digests food. Makes it smell like manure. They brought one to the zoo when I was little."

He smiled, but I was determined to stay mad, at least for a while. I ran my fingernails along the pane of glass on the library door as I left, hoping it would make some terrible high-pitched squeal only he could hear.

24

Crushed Yellow Crazy Ants

Dilani knocked on the door to Dr. Calleo's office. Nothing. She knocked louder.

We heard Dr. Calleo say something to someone, then a door somewhere inside the office close. "Enter," she said.

"Dilani, Kaia," she said, and motioned for us to sit in sturdy leather chairs facing her spotless glass and steel desk. "Take a seat."

I glanced around her office as if the décor might hold a clue about why she wanted to see us. The wall behind her desk held several framed diplomas and glossy photographs of Dr. Calleo receiving awards and shaking hands with men and women in academic garb. A black and white photo showed her in a fitted sequined evening gown addressing a group of people seated at linen-covered banquet tables. The hairstyles and the people's clothing looked old fashioned but elegant. The tables bore the post-meal detritus of a fancy dinner: uncorked champagne bottles, half-filled crystal flutes, partially eaten slices of layered cake, and crumpled linen napkins. To Dr. Calleo's right, looking on with admiration, was Dr. Grigori. A brass plaque on the frame read, "London Duophysite Society Annual Meeting Awards." There was a date, but it looked like 1881. Maybe I needed to get my eyes checked again.

"I want to talk with you about your experience with the votives in class. Several members of your class had similar experiences, but the two of you may have gifts that make your interaction with the votives particularly valuable."

Dilani and I looked at each other. Dr. Calleo continued, "Both of you may be what we in the field refer to as 'Sensitives.'" She paused, as if to see if either of us were familiar with the term.

"Sensitives," she continued, "exhibit certain phenomena when they come in contact with materials that have been imbued with some form of communication. That is, if contact is made by a Sensitive, an object may convey information held within it." She paused again to see if we were following.

"For instance," she offered, "your votives began to glow when you touched them, correct?"

We nodded.

"This means," she said, "you may have the ability to unlock the message that has been trapped or embedded in the item."

Dilani spoke up, "Someone put a message into the rocks?" She sounded skeptical.

"All solids conduct sound," Dr. Calleo explained. "Some are better conductors than others and are frequently used for that purpose. Think of the copper wiring used in old-fashioned telephone landlines, for instance. Cork is an example of a substance that is a poor conductor of sound. But," she said, her eyes widening, "some materials absorb sound."

"Sure," Dilani said. "That's why you carpet wooden stairs, or why libraries can be so quiet with all those books soaking up the sound."

"Yes," Dr. Calleo nodded. "Good. And some materials," her eyes getting even larger, "absorb sound and hold it until it can be unlocked. By a Sensitive." She had delivered her punchline and stopped to see if we got it.

Dr. Calleo continued, "Sensitives are very important. If one could unlock the sound, say, of people talking, absorbed over time by an object, one could, with the help of an interpreter, begin to piece together the script and sounds that would help us recover the meaning of languages so far untranslatable, even very ancient languages now long-lost. Think of the contribution that would make to our understanding of the development of life and culture on earth."

I felt giddy. I wasn't sure how we would get from a glowing stone pig to translating ancient scrolls or tablets. But unusual sensations were welling up within me and they felt good. It took a moment for me to recognize them. They were happiness and hope. And pride.

"Of course, there is more for Kaia to do."

Pfffffffft went my pride balloon.

Dr. Calleo leaned back in her desk chair and retrieved a leather-bound folder and a gleaming black fountain pen from her desk drawer. "As I stated, it seems that the two of you are potential Sensitives. We are more certain about Dilani. Kaia, your potential must be honed. Are you willing to undergo discernment?"

"Discernment?" I asked.

Dr. Calleo looked at me and opened the folder. She passed the sheet of paper it held to me. "The discernment process will be described to you in more detail, but you must sign this release in order to be part of this important project. Your participation also voids the necessity of your having to pass the school's required swim test. GYSP will provide the necessary waiver."

I let out a weird little squeak of relief and joy.

Dr. Calleo looked embarrassed for me. She handed me a pen. Its weight surprised me.

"A masterpiece, amongst the first ink pens ever made," Dr. Calleo said. "From the year 970 CE. Crafted to the specifications of the caliph of Maghreb, in Northwest Africa. It should feel a pleasure to make your signature."

It was. The ink flowed smoothly. It had the pungent odor of formic acid, a scent shared by ink, the hairs of stinging nettles, and the crushed bodies of yellow crazy ants.

"So, Dr. Calleo," Dilani said, "there's nothing I need to do?"

"Dilani, your work on the Mantis shrimp is of the utmost importance, and we expect it will be where you make your greatest contribution. Discernment, in your case, is unnecessary. And, yes, we will provide the swim test waiver for you as well."

Dr. Calleo looked at me. She must have noticed the flash of envy on my face. Dilani had her special shrimp project, or whatever, and was all set, but I needed extra work?

Dr. Calleo spoke, "Kaia, focus on yourself. Do not let your perceptions of others get in the way of your own advancement."

She collected our forms and pushed a button on her desk. A door behind her opened. Xanthe walked in.

Dr. Calleo said to me, "Xanthe is my research assistant for this project, and she will be managing your process in the Dream Lab."

My jaw dropped.

"Platypus!" she said with a wide smile. "Looks like I'll be getting to know all about you after all."

25

Chlorine and Vinegar

"Goggles and gloves on," Miyako said as we walked into the lab. "Let's get to work."

We followed Miyako into her realm. One of the benefits of this program for her was lab time and materials to conduct her own experiments. She could help herself to anything in the supply cabinets as long as she promised not to blow up the building or set it on fire.

"Antimony gets its name, 'not alone,' from the fact that its pure form isn't found in nature. It's always combined with something else, like copper, lead, or silver. What's great is that here we have the pure stuff to play with."

She motioned to the counter where containers of various sizes held silvery crystals and pellets. I picked up a chunk of the glistening substance from a plate and held it between my thumb and forefinger. Pretty.

Miyako said, "To the naked eye, it mainly looks silver. Under intense microscopic imagery, it contains every color in the rainbow. Antimony's incredible stuff. We're going to do things to some samples and see what happens. Stand back for this one."

She shook a couple of small crystals from a vial into a stone bowl. "People in Enoch's time would use a mortar and pestle like this for grinding things. Let's see what happens when we crush some antimony." She took a long cylindrical stone and started pulverizing the crystals.

Bam! The crystals exploded with a flash of light and a loud crack. We all jumped back, covering our eyes and ears. When it seemed that no more explosions were coming, we dropped our hands and laughed with relief. I put the piece I was holding back onto the plate.

"Wow," Neith said. "Just that little bit made a big bang."

"Yeah," Miyako said, "And I was just grinding it by hand. Can you imagine what a large amount would do with some real pressure? Have you heard of Greek fire?"

"Yes," Josh said. "A weapon—liquid that burned, even on water. The Byzantines used it, fired it in pots from ships. Their enemies didn't stand a chance. It was so deadly people made a pact to stop using it so the human race would continue, and everyone who knew how to make it was sworn to secrecy."

"Modern chemists have guessed, though," Miyako said, "that it was probably some combination of antimony, crude oil, and potassium nitrate, which is used in fireworks. There's an ancient legend that says an angel showed the emperor Constantine how to make it around the year 305, just before he started to rule the Roman Empire."

"What if a fallen angel revealed it even earlier?" I wondered out loud.

"Next, let's see what happens if we heat it," Miyako said. We must have looked frightened because she reassured us, "No, we're not making Greek fire."

She went to a kiln in the corner and opened the door. A wave of heat flooded the room.

"It's been cooling for a while," she called over to us, "but the antimony will still be semi-liquid."

She pulled out a small dark metal container that looked like a pan for making tiny cakes for a doll's house. She brought it over to the counter and placed it on a hot pad.

"Let's see what happens as it becomes a solid again."

We watched a silvery scum form on the top. As it cooled, it made a tinkling sound, like fine silver bells being rung.

"Lovely," said Zia. "I imagine angels' wings making that sound when they flutter."

"So what do we know so far?" I asked.

"Well," Neith started, "antimony has been used for different things continuously since ancient times. It keeps replacing itself as a valuable commodity."

"It's decorative," Dilani said, "but it's also dangerous. You can paint your eyes, but you can also blow things up with it and start fires that are impossible to put out."

"It makes a beautiful sound," said Zia.

"It's mentioned as a heavenly secret revealed by fallen angels to humans, something they weren't supposed to find out about, but did. It's been used for some good purposes, but also for a lot of destructive things. And our ethics teacher wants us to think of that as a good thing for some reason," Dilani said.

"Don't forget," Josh said, "the GFH Corporation owns the majority of production in the world, and if they stop production, everyday life as we know it grinds to a halt."

Silence.

"Oh, and it's medicinal, in very small quantities, but too much can kill you," Dilani said. "Miyako, you mentioned the other day that you wanted to know more about that aspect."

I was interested in hearing more too, but it was Miyako who spoke up. "I should probably tell you the reason I'm interested in antimony as medicine. For about a year now, I've been taking small doses of it."

I looked at her. She looked down at the countertop and continued. "I was getting really bad headaches. A specialist my parents sent me to gave me these pills and told me to keep quiet about it. Of course, I didn't want to put some mystery substance from a stranger into my body without more information, so I ran some tests. It was antimony. I figured if I kept the doses small, I would be all right, and taking the pills makes me feel better instantly. So far, so good, but I've had to increase my dosage to keep the effects."

"You're not alone," I said.

"That's funny," Neith said.

"I'm not joking," I replied, then got my accidental pun. "I think I take it too." I opened my locket and took a couple of granules out and showed them to Miyako. "Headaches. A doctor gave them to me, then disappeared."

"My specialist vanished too."

We looked at the others. Everyone but Neith nodded.

Zia gave Miyako a hug. "I'm so relieved! I had no idea what it was, but it helps, you know?"

Dilani blew out a sigh. "Glad I don't have to keep it a secret anymore. And we know where we can get more."

While the others laughed with relief, I had a strange feeling about asking Miyako for more antimony. I was running low, but having to ask for her help felt like one more way I was inadequate around here. Was there some way I could sneak some now? With so much on the counter top, no one would miss it if I just took some.

I was just about to see if I could grab some undetected when Miyako started putting the various containers away with help from Josh and Zia. As they cleared the counter, Miyako said, "I have a personal interest in learning more about this element, but it's Dr. Grigori who told me working on antimony would be my special project during the program. Promised me some huge mysterious reward if I can figure out a way to synthesize it."

"Create it artificially?" Neith said. "Why, if they control all the mines?"

"I'm not sure. Maybe they think making it would be easier than mining it. Maybe they just want more of it."

"Maybe there's a reason they need more of it, beyond just wanting to make tons of money," Dilani said. "Think about it. All of us, except Neith, depend on it. That can't be a coincidence."

"What if it's not just some GYSP students, but GYSP faculty, including Dr. Grigori, who take it too?" I said. "They might be desperate to find ways to get more or make more."

"As well as wanting to control the world," Josh added.

I suddenly remembered Xanthe in the coffee shop, taking a pill after she reapplied her perfume. "I wonder if Xanthe takes it," I said. "Something is wrong with her."

"You mean her smell?" Zia asked. "I've noticed it too. Whatever is happening with her, it's bad." She paused. "When I was in her room, I did see a little cup, like one of those antimony cups Fintan told us about. I thought it was just an antique, an odd keepsake. Maybe she uses it to get antimony, to make herself feel better, not to make herself get sick."

Miyako got a small metal cup out of the cupboard and put it on the counter. It looked like a tiny gray chalice, enough for a couple of sips. "This was with the other antimony samples."

"Dr. Grigori has a collection of those in his office," I said.

Dilani said, "That's right! I saw them too."

I guess Dilani had a little tête-à-tête with Dr. Grigori as well.

"So, it makes some people sick, but other people well," Neith said.

"Yes," said Miyako. "That could have something to do with the dose, or maybe something to do with the person who takes it, and why they take it. I'm going to keep working on this. I don't know why the Grigoris are so interested but I know I won't always have access to this much antimony, and I can't imagine being without my pills. I should show you one more thing." She went back to the cupboard and pulled out a dark cylinder about a foot tall and four inches in diameter, wrapped in an old piece of paper.

Miyako removed the paper and showed it to us. A drawing of silver crystals like one of the samples Miyako had shown us was at the top of the page. A paragraph was written below, but I couldn't recognize the words, or even the letters.

"Do you know what this is?" Miyako asked Neith.

"I have no idea," he said.

I picked it up. "Looks like a page removed from an old book," I said. "The container it's wrapped around looks very new." I sniffed the paper and picked up the faintest odor of something like chlorine and vinegar.

Miyako set the cylinder down gingerly on the counter top and backed away from it slightly, "I can't believe they have this here and it's not under heavy security," she said. "This kind of cylinder was developed for holding super dangerous substances. Inside is fluoroantimonic acid. It's a superacid made with antimony." She paused, looking at the container like she was somewhere between awe and terror, like someone had given her the keys to a Nascar race car and said, 'Take it out for a spin, if you want. See what it will do.' Or maybe, 'Take it for a drive through a crowded parking lot.'

"It's the world's strongest known acid. This one cylinder holds enough to eat through the floor and the four floors beneath us and way down into the sewer system before we could call lab security for cleanup. Why on earth would the Grigoris leave this stuff lying around?"

We were quiet, each of us trying to put pieces together of a puzzle that we didn't have a picture for, but were seriously beginning to worry about what it might show.

26

Hot Chocolate and Lavender

My fingers trembled as I twisted the doorknob and shuffled into the Dream Lab. I was trying my best to follow the mantra, *if you can't get out of it, get into it,* but I was scared, especially since I didn't actually know what "it" was. Dr. Calleo said that undergoing the Dream Lab procedure, 'discernment,' would sharpen my gift, but I didn't like going into things blind, especially things that sounded medical and involved unconsciousness. Would it hurt? Worse—would it be embarrassing? Would they be able to tell what I was dreaming about?

"Oh, there you are," Xanthe said as I stepped into the pleasant room with sage-colored walls and soft warm lighting. My feet sunk into the Oriental carpet as I crossed over to the desk where Xanthe sat behind a computer monitor and a short stack of clipboards. She smiled slightly, exposing her perfect teeth. "Don't be nervous," she said, like she really meant it. "I'm sure nothing extraordinary will happen to you."

Oh, thanks.

"Have a seat and fill out the form." She handed me a clipboard with an intake form and a fountain pen. "They'll call you when they're ready for you. You'll love the snacks before the procedure, and the music they play is awesome. Nothing you've ever heard before, but you'll adore how calm it makes you feel."

Her perfume clung to the clipboard and pen. It smelled wonderful, even if a little overwhelming, like vanilla frosting with hints of mandarin and apricot. My stomach rumbled—I suddenly was hungry—until I caught Xanthe's underlying odor of old barbecue coals and ammonia. I put the clipboard to my nose for another shot of yummy dessert smell and took a seat in one of the red velvet wing-backed chairs.

I looked around the waiting room. Ilona, a quiet GYSP student from Hungary, was sitting down and hunched over her form, checking boxes. Her pen made a slight scratching sound on the paper. Light streamed in the window behind the desk where Xanthe sat. On the wall to my right was a large painting that covered most of the length of the small waiting room. The subject was the Annunciation, when the archangel Gabriel told Mary that God wanted her to give birth to Jesus. In the painting, an angel on bended knee holds a stem of white lilies and extends his hand in a gesture of blessing toward Mary who sits behind an ornate reading desk. The artist caught the angel on the cusp of motion. It looked like the angel was conjuring a blessing, making a physical object, rather than a wish he might throw across the distance separating himself from Mary. Mary holds a manuscript open with one hand; the other is raised and open, indicating surprise. Her open hand is poised at the same level as the angel's, as if Mary is ready either to receive his blessing or repel it. Her next action might be to cup her hand and look at what she caught from him, or to fling it back—"Thanks, but no thanks." A label affixed to the wall below the painting read, "*The Annunciation*, by Leonardo Da Vinci, from the Uffizi, Florence."

From the Uffizi?

I filled out my form. Standard stuff: name, age, birthdate, weight, allergies. Curious stuff: what and when I last ate, favorite smells. Stuff related to sleep: do I typically remember my dreams? Do I sleep on my stomach, side, or back? Ever sleepwalk?

A tall, slim woman in a white nurse's outfit, including white shoes, white hose, and an old fashioned white nurse's hat appeared in the open door near the reception desk. As she stood, framed in the darkened doorway, she looked like another painting, this one of a pale, wingless angel ready to summon people to some dark new world.

"Kaia? Ilona?" She said. We both looked up. "Come with me, both of you. Bring your things."

We went to the door. I looked back at Xanthe, who mouthed, 'Don't worry!' at me and shooed me with her hands toward the nurse. The nurse took our clipboards and looked them over quickly. "Okay, Kaia, you go through that door," she said, motioning toward a doorway to the left. "Ilona, you come with me this way."

I wondered why Ilona got an escort while I just got a wave. I pushed open the door and found myself in a changing room full of tall wooden lockers with plush bathrobes hanging from hooks.

"No, wait!" I heard a frantic voice exclaim. It was the nurse, who had rushed into the changing room behind me. "I am so sorry," she said. "Kaia, you come with me."

She sounded like she had made a mistake larger than a simple error. She pulled Ilona into the changing room and said to the attendant I hadn't yet had time to notice, "It is Ilona who is supposed to be in this program, not Kaia. So sorry."

She ushered me back out into the hallway and through another door, shaking her head. "That would have been awkward," she said, more to herself than me. "Very awkward indeed," she muttered.

"What would have been awkward?" I asked, hoping some conversation might make me less nervous.

"We have two programs underway right now. I'm assigned to the discernment process, the one you're in. I'm not assigned to the generating process so if I sent you there by mistake, they would be very upset with me." She widened her eyes, in a sort of 'you know what that's like' expression.

"What does 'generating process' mean?" I asked. "Like dream production?"

"That's quite enough, Nurse," a woman's stern voice said through a stiffened jaw. "Leave Kaia with me. I'll take it from here."

A brunette woman in a navy blue suit held out her arm to me. Given the sharpness of her voice, I was surprised how gently she put her arm around my shoulder, then guided me farther into a cozy room with a beautiful canopy bed, a small wooden table with a lamp burning a soft, warm light, and a coat tree with pretty nightgowns and flannel shirts and pants hanging on ornate hooks. A large, gold-framed mirror hung on one wall. I could smell chocolate and lavender, aromas that made me relax just a little.

My guide, Nurse Berith, Head of Dream Lab Services, had left her sternness behind with the mumbling nurse. In a voice like melting butterscotch she told me I could wear a nightgown or pajamas if I wanted, or I could stay in the jeans and sweatshirt I was wearing, however I would feel most at home. If I wanted to change, I should step behind the screen she pointed to because the mirror was actually a window where I would be watched during the night to make sure I was safe and comfortable. Nurse Berith's voice was honey sweet—like it had the strength to cover my anxieties and take their power away. She pointed out a mug of hot cocoa and some chocolate truffles on the bedside table. The small stone votive I had handled in Dr. Calleo's class was next to the mug.

"For good luck," Nurse Berith said, gesturing toward the little stone pig. Think of it as your talisman. The hot cocoa is made using Marie Antoinette's favorite recipe. 'Let her drink hot chocolate.'" She twittered a bit at her own joke and then told me with a wink, "You do not have to brush your teeth afterward if you do not feel like it. It will not hurt you to fall asleep with the pleasant taste of the world's most expensive chocolate in your mouth. Go ahead and change, or not, get under the covers, and I will be back in a moment to tell you all about the wonders in store for you tonight."

I decided I would go ahead and change into one of the beautiful pajama sets. I figured if I needed to make a run for it, at least I would be climbing out a window or racing down the hallway in better clothing than I was wearing when I got here. I plucked a navy blue pajama set off the coat tree and changed behind the screen, folding my own clothes into a tidy bundle I could grab in a hurry if necessary. I kept my socks on and tucked my shoes just under the bed.

The flannel was soft and cool. The sheets felt like smooth, silky soft liquid, like the powdery gloss of a butterfly's wing. I had touched one once, when a monarch had landed on my arm. I stroked its wing as it rested there, mistaking me for some safe perch, but I felt terribly guilty when the friend who was with me said, "Now it won't be able to fly. You've changed it forever."

I pulled the covers over myself and felt my anxiety melt away as my body started to feel the delicious heaviness of drifting off into sleep.

Nurse Berith returned. "Relaxing already? Good for you. You are in for a very good night's sleep."

I wanted to resist, even just a little bit, after working myself up into such a state of worry about what was turning out to be really quite pleasant. I grasped for something to protest or question.

"Music," I said, remembering Xanthe's comment that I would love it, and noticing that the room was silent. But just as I uttered the word, a woman's clear voice started a chant. I couldn't understand the words or be certain they weren't just syllables. Crystal clear bells or chimes accompanied the voice, ringing at the end of phrases. Xanthe was right. It was beautiful. It reminded me of a sound I had heard recently, but I couldn't quite place it, and it was receding into the background as I began to feel very drowsy.

"Is the volume all right?" Nurse Berith asked.

I nodded and covered my mouth as a deep yawn welled up in me. I was getting so sleepy I wasn't even going to get to drink the hot chocolate, which seemed like a huge waste.

"Now, before you drop off, I just have to attach a couple of small electrodes."

I jolted fully awake again.

"No need for concern." She held up three tiny circles, each no bigger around than the eraser on the end of a pencil, attached to small squares, like band-aids with little gray dot, in the middle. "These are wireless and will transmit information—no, not the content of your dreams," she said. She must have seen me twitch with nervousness at 'information.' "They simply allow us to monitor your vitals—pulse, breathing, blood-oxygen levels."

I felt a small wave of relief. The slight adrenaline surge I had felt a moment ago subsided, leaving me even more sleepy than before.

"Here, you can put them on yourself." She pointed to two spots, on the right and left of my ribcage and one on the top of my right hand.

I peeled the adhesive backing off the squares and stuck them in place.

"They do something for you too," she said. "Sensors in the electrodes allow you to change your dreams as you want to. If you are having a dream you do not like, the device heightens your brain's ability to alter your own experience. Like flipping the channel or changing to a different app."

"What does this have to do with . . ." I let out a gargantuan yawn. ". . . discernment?" I managed.

"We want to see if your brain has any additional resources to help you manage your dreams. You may have gifts that, if you can learn to tap into them at will, would be of great benefit to you. From the electrode monitoring, we will be able to tell if any changes you make in your dreams bring you positive feelings or not. And I promise, it will not hurt a bit. If you need anything, just ring this bell." She picked up a little brass bell off the nightstand. The room had already become a field of butterflies around me as I heard a faint bright chime and a woman's clear voice singing from a cloud that was passing overhead and growing fainter and fainter.

"Don't do it! Please don't!" Dilani said, putting her hands over her ears. "I can't stand it when someone tells me their dreams! It's always so boring, no matter what they dreamed about!"

She was right. It was sort of mysterious to me how to the dreamer these were the most amazing dreams ever, but the excitement never carried over to the person listening. Plus you could guess most of the content: The dreamer was flying or falling. They were naked or wearing only underwear and no one around them had noticed—yet. They were late for something really, really important and couldn't get there no matter how hard they tried.

"I know, I know," I said, pulling her hands away from her ears. "Just listen for a second. I promise I won't go through all the details. Aren't you even a little curious?"

"Okay, go ahead," she said. "Tell me about how real you thought everything was, but then you woke up and discovered it was all a dream."

"It's not that, although everything was really vivid."

I told her about the beautiful room, how comfortable everything was, how I was too sleepy to drink the hot cocoa, how I heard the most beautiful, ethereal, otherworldly music that lulled me to sleep. I told her that the only thing I knew they had done to me was have me put the little electrodes on, that they didn't hurt, and that I didn't notice anything weird. Nurse Berith seemed really nice, and I woke up this morning feeling refreshed and relaxed, like I had had the best night's sleep ever.

"Okay, what did you dream about?" Dilani asked. "Get it over with."

"I did have all those weird anxiety dreams—you know, in class and realizing I'm just wearing underwear and so far no one else seems to notice, late for class, can't find my paper, running but getting nowhere."

Dilani nodded and rotated her hand in a 'get on with it' motion.

"But here's what was different," I said. "Nurse Berith was telling the truth. I could change my dreams. Instead of just waking up in a cold sweat, while I was still dreaming, I was able to change what was going on." I stopped. Something about this was suddenly hanging out at the fringe of my memory, like the presence of a character I hadn't noticed was in the scene until just now.

"What do you mean?"

I went on. "I mean, I was standing in front of the class when I noticed I was pretty much naked. But instead of panicking, I thought 'I need clothes,' and suddenly I was fully clothed, and actually looked great." The little glimmer of something I had forgotten waved at me again, like a moth fluttering in front of a candle flame, making it flicker. What was it?

"Well, that is a little interesting," Dilani conceded. "Is that it?"

"Wait a second," I said. "There's something important I can't quite put my finger on—something else in my dream."

I tried to imagine the scene again, worried I would forget my dream before I captured whatever was hovering at the edge of my consciousness.

In the dream, I stood in front of my class at school. I noticed I am wearing only my plain white Hanes cotton briefs and bra—of course it would be something dumpy—even in my dreams I'm uninteresting. I am trying to explain something about volcanoes or something, and I suddenly realize I'm wearing only my boring underwear. A lump of panic rises in my throat, my ears start to burn, I try to cover myself with my hands. I want to run, but I know if I make any sudden moves, I'll only draw more attention to myself. Any second now, someone will notice and laughter will erupt. I think, I want to be dressed. Suddenly I'm wearing gorgeous jeans, a beautiful blouse, and fantastic stacked heels. I look around the room as I continue to talk about the formation of volcanoes—where is this stuff coming from?—and then I notice her. In the last desk, in the farthest row, a girl from my class is hunched over with her arms wrapped around herself, face red, wearing only her underwear. I've taken her clothes. Or transferred them to myself somehow.

"Okay, I should go study," Dilani said.

"No, wait. Please."

"What's wrong?"

"I know what happened, how it got fixed. In my dream, I take someone else's clothes. Not by force or anything. But when my problem is solved, it's at someone else's expense."

"Sounds like you're just working out some guilty conscience issues."

"Maybe. But if that's true, I feel worse now, not better."

"I really do need to go study. I'm glad the Dream Lab was okay, even if right now you're feeling weird about it."

"Thanks."

I watched Dilani walk away, while my mind went back to my dreams. What else had gotten fixed in my dreams, and how? I knew I had to remember fast, before things completely faded. Avoiding my tablet, I grabbed a piece of paper and jotted down what I could remember—what I had dreamt, what problem I had fixed, or situation I had changed. Each time, I had the feeling I had missed some person hovering at the edge, someone else involved whom I hadn't noticed at first glance. As I went over my dreams, I realized each one had the same disturbing feature: someone else took my place.

As I reviewed, I realized that with each dream, my complicity got worse. In the first, the underwear dream, I just wished for clothes and got someone else's. But in the second, I was being chased through a forest. I ran as fast as I could, barely steps ahead of my pursuer, an amorphous dark hooded shape I knew would kill me if it caught me. I came to a clearing, but the only way ahead was straight off a cliff into a whirlpool below. I faced death from the evil presence chasing me or by plunging into the chasm filled with swirling water. I teetered at the edge, terrified, but just then, I felt a small child's hand take mine. I looked down at her, a young girl with long blond hair. She looked up at me, then back at the thing chasing me. It was just about to reach us.

"Shall I go instead?" she asked.

"Yes!" I breathed, "You go! Not me!"

She leapt, arms outstretched, greeting her own certain extinction. The hooded presence stopped beside me, put an icy arm around me, and it felt refreshing. Together we watched her tiny body plummet into the water and get sucked down out of sight.

In the last dream, I was drowning. Somehow I was in deep water. I was thrashing, panicking, gasping for breath. Each time I plunged beneath the water, I was sure I wouldn't be able to surface again. My arms and legs were so tired, and I kept gulping salt water. Suddenly a life ring was extended to me. I grabbed hold. But someone else was holding on too. I couldn't see who it was and I didn't care. The small red rubber circle was half submerged, and I knew we couldn't both cling to it and stay on the surface of the water. So I reached out one arm and pushed against the other person, who must have been the one trying to save me, sharing this one hope of refuge.

With the last of my strength, I pushed the other person's head under water. I could feel the person's tangled locks in my hand, see how they spread as I held the struggling person's head beneath the water. Finally, no more fight, just two hands releasing their grip on the ring. The person's head tilted back for just one moment before sinking down into the water. It was Dilani.

I felt sick. I didn't want to be that person, not even in my dreams.

I thought back to what had happened when I woke up. Nurse Berith came in and asked how I felt. I told her I felt really good, refreshed. She told me I could take off the electrodes. But when I went to peel the little square off my right hand, I realized I was clutching the votive in my left. My fist was curled tightly around it.

"I can take that from you now," Nurse Berith said. "You may let go."

I gave the little stone object to her and felt a pang of loss. I didn't even remember picking it up and now I felt sad to part with it.

"How did I do?" I asked her, as I peeled off the little squares.

"You show great promise," she said. She showed me a printout on a clipboard. A line spiked three times. After each spike, the line sloped back down toward the bottom of the page. "You must have had three significant dream events. Each time, you resolved them in a way that brought you relaxation, even pleasure. Well done, Kaia. We want you to return next week for one more session."

What if I was that person?

I wanted to throw up.

I wanted to scrub off in a really hot shower.

I wanted to know if I really had to go back. And why I sort of wanted to.

The specifics of the return visit were slid under my door later that day on one of the now familiar creamy white GYSP note cards:

Dear Kaia,

Return to the Dream Lab Friday evening at 20:00 for your follow-up appointment and the opportunity to learn more about your family.

   Nurse Berith,
   GYSP Dream Lab Coordinator

If you can't get out of it, get into it. Do one thing every day that scares you. Whatever you are, be a good one. If you can dream it, you can achieve it. Whoever said stuff like this never lived my life, or they would know this was deadly advice.

27

Rose Petals and Vomit

That night Dilani, Josh, Neith, Zia, Miyako, and I met in the library to try to figure out more about the Elioud. It might provide a clue about what the kids in the video were so afraid of. Since our encounter with Dr. Dranoush in the library stairwell, we figured it was time to move out of the main reading room and onto an upstairs floor where fewer people might be around to overhear us. I really didn't like the dim lighting and translucent floors up there, and I wasn't sure we were completely alone.

"What do we know so far?" Dilani asked.

"We know that in this program they take that Enoch story very seriously, as if it's real, as in literally true, as in there are such things as Nephilim," I offered.

"Oh yeah," said Josh. "Dr. Eder was all over you taking the Nephilim seriously. He was all, 'Oh Kaia! You understand, Kaia!'"

Dilani joined in, "'Kaia, look deep into my crystal eyes, and see into my soul, you who understand the Nephilim.'"

"Dr. Eder does have weird eyes, though, don't you think?" I looked around at the others. They all nodded. "What if they are real? The Nephilim, I mean," I said quietly. "In the story, they don't get wiped out. They even have children, those 'Elioud,' whoever that is."

Josh started rummaging through his book bag. "Look at this," he said. "It fell out of a book Miss Hermani asked me to get for Dr. Grigori. The book was in the rare books and documents vault in the basement. It was a first edition called *Gregor Mendel: Experiments in Hybridization.*

Josh opened a manila folder and showed us a yellowed, hand-written letter. "I recognized the words 'Nephilim' and 'Elioud,'" Josh said. He looked at Neith. "It's written in German, so we'll need you to translate."

Neith looked it over, looked up a few words in a dictionary, scribbled some notes and read the letter to us:

Monastery of St. Peter
Budapest, Hungary
August 2, 1866

My Dear Brother Gregor,

I write this letter in haste, with sincere apologies for the lack of formality and imprecision that urgency necessitates. My fondest wish is that I am mistaken in my sense of the danger that drives me to put ink to paper and write to you now. I hope that some day we may once again sit in your garden, surrounded by your beloved snapdragons and sweet peas and discuss openly our experiments in the leisurely and patient manner with which scientific exploration is best conducted.

If there is one consolation in writing to you it is for the opportunity to assure you that your research has not gone unnoticed. I know that the melancholia to which you are inclined may have once again settled upon you following the reading of your brilliant paper at the Brno Society meetings last year. What an impact your research should have made! I expected your work to take root immediately, or to pollinate new research, in addition to your own. You must feel like a solitary gardener, who alone notices the growth and vibrancy of the plants you have so meticulously tended.

Ah, my dear Brother, you see how I long to converse with you and offer you encouragement, and how even the thought of such luxuries as face-to-face conversation with you puts my anxiety at bay and grants me the illusion of serenity and unlimited time. Illusion it is, alas!

To my task I return.

My consolation: someone is paying attention to the work you have done. Although I write of someone in the singular, he cannot be alone. The number of eyes I feel upon me and the manifold signs of being observed are too great for one individual. However, and this is my point, someone is aware of the implications of your work on hybridization.

You are aware, I believe, that I have now applied your work with plants, showing how the dominant and recessive traits of parents are passed to their hybrid offspring, to the mating of Watchers and humans recorded in 1 *Enoch*. We have long wondered what would happen to subsequent generations if Nephilim produced children with humans. Would Nephil traits become diluted? Could offspring appear to be human, yet have Nephil traits? If so, when would those traits become manifest?

When we last met in person you urged me not to embark upon such research due to its speculative nature. And speculative it was, my dear Gregor, at the time. I hope you will forgive me for saying so, but I am glad I did not listen to you, for since that time, I have been presented with the opportunity to examine actual remains of fourth generation angelic-human hybrids. (My dear brother, now I imagine you adding concern that I add desecration of the dead to my sin of speculation. However, I assure you that following my examinations I will entreat the abbot for permission to see that these unfortunate creatures receive proper burial. Although I do not know if they may be interred in consecrated ground, they are enabling me to further important research that touches on subjects related to Holy Scripture. Surely that fact will arouse some compassion in our abbot.) The point is, that I can now test to see if my speculation was in fact pointing to reality!

My preliminary work shows that in addition to noting your dominant and recessive traits, we must pursue the possibility that angelic and human traits may be blended in equal, or near equal proportion, creating beings of unusual beauty and powers, both deleterious and beneficent.

With the arrival of the hybrid creatures, about which I cannot say more here for fear of endangering your life as well, came also someone who watches me. Were we not in a monastery, I would swear to you that this person, a novice in the order, is a woman and that our monk's garb is keeping her identity a secret from others! What I am certain of is that this supposed novice shows more interest in my researches than in being formed in the way of the community, learning our prayers, and tending to the work the abbot requires. The novice goes by the name Brother Itzal. Itzal! The name means 'Shadow' and how fitting that is!

On more than one occasion I have spied this Shadow coming out of the laboratory in a furtive manner, the laboratory being quite off limits to him. I wondered if he had seen the hybrids or tampered with them in some way. They are kept under lock and key and only a few trusted brothers have access to them. Complaints to the abbot have not curtailed this man's surreptitious activity. The abbot, I fear, thinks I am developing the paranoia that sometimes comes with being too long cloistered and merely urged me to go attend another conference as soon as is convenient for the abbey schedule.

Yesterday I confronted Brother Itzal whom I found leaving my cell with my notebook in hand. In a voice too high for even a young man, this Shadow protested that he had taken it by accident, mistaking it for his own left in the chapel following the office of Terce.

"Why, then," I said, "it should be your notebook in your hand at this moment. But see, it is mine, *Brother*."

"Brother," he said, a steely hardness in his treble voice, "Do not monks hold all things in common? Surely your possessiveness is unbecoming to one in your position." He extended the notebook toward me but held on to it as I grasped it, a strange luminosity in his gray-blue eyes.

"Be careful, lest your research seem more valuable than your life," he said to me, then let go of the notebook at last, bowed slightly, turned on his heel and walked confidently down the hall.

I am afraid, Brother Gregor. This Shadow has been assigned to the infirmary for his occupation within the abbey. He will have access to dangerous substances. He is working for someone, Gregor, but I know not for whom or to what end, only that he is interested in hybridization and resorts to unseemly methods to learn more.

For this reason, I have kept my most important notations on my person at all times, until now, when I entrust them to you. You alone, Brother Gregor, understand the true import of what, through your tutelage, I study. I send my notations, praying you will receive them and that you will know what to do with them should something happen to me.

Clearly there is more to be learned following this line of inquiry, and, sadly, at present it seems dangerous to pursue it. I will do what I can, but do not want to risk the loss of what I have learned so far, or have it fall into the possession of those hands whose nefarious purposes I can only guess at.

Enclosed you will find the annotations I have made concerning *1 Enoch*. I send them by the hand of Brother Maurinus, loyal friend and co-laborer.

I entrust my life's work to you, my brother, and my soul to my Maker and Redeemer. If I am guilty of iniquity by my research and probing of unburied, unconsecrated hybrid creatures, I commend myself to the Lord's mercy. I have sought only to discover more about the wonders of this created world.

Pray for me,
Your faithful Brother Josef

"Wow!" Miyako exclaimed. "A letter to Gregor Mendel from another monk!"

"Something really weird was going on in his monastery," Dilani added.

"Read his notes, please," Josh said to Neith.

"The notes have two columns." Neith showed us the page again. On the left hand side was the story from *1 Enoch*. On the right were notes in German, which Neith translated after reading the heading written across the top:

Hybridization amongst Angelic-Human Generations.
Notes, Probabilities, and Questions for Further Study.

1 Enoch: "These and the others with them took for themselves wives from among them such as they chose. And they begin to go into them,

The Watchers mate with women

and to defile themselves through them,

This will weaken the angelic characteristics

and to teach them sorcery and charms, and to reveal to them the cutting of roots and plants.	Does 'the cutting of roots' refer to angelic revelation regarding hybridization or genetics?
And they conceived from them and bore to them the Nephilim.	Angelic traits and human traits are blended. Longevity of Nephilim is probable, but can human and angelic characteristics remain fused? Or will duophysite disintegration occur?
And to the Nephilim were born Elioud."	Necessitates further study. More Elioud remains or living subjects must be found. Some Elioud may demonstrate more human traits and some more nephilistic. If human traits dominate on both mother's and father's sides, child may appear human but carry nephilistic traits, which may manifest as a child grows. Duophysite disintegration a risk for some Elioud, as it is for Nephilim.

Engeln had written a note at the bottom as well:

"Concerning the Elioud: I found within the hybrids a high concentration of the element antimony. Whether this was the cause of their demise or a treatment for duophysite distintegration, I do not know. I believe it is possible that the cure for Angel-Human disintegration could be found within the Elioud themselves, some substance that could be harvested. Care would need to be taken in experimentation or extraction, lest the Elioud perish, and thus be unable to produce more of the curative or preventative substance."

That's where the letter ended.

"Engeln believed that Nephilim and Elioud actually existed," Josh said.

Dilani asked, "Do we know if Mendel did anything with Engeln's letter, or if he did any more research, or what happened to the hybrid creatures, or what they were?" The questions were pouring out of her. She looked at me and I knew exactly what she was thinking.

I said, "We know what happened to them. They're Dr. Calleo's 'specimens,' the mummified children we saw in the museum storage area. They came from Hungary, where Engeln's monastery was. Somehow they ended up with the Nazis, and now the Grigoris are studying them." I looked at Dilani. "What was it Dr. Calleo said?"

"Once given as gifts by an immortal power, can they, even in death, give life?" Dilani quoted.

"Engeln thought that maybe the Elioud contain something that can help fight against angel-human disintegration," I said. "What he calls 'duophysite disintegration.'"

"Duophysite: 'having two natures,'" Neith said.

"Yes," said Dilani, "that's how the mummified children were labeled."

"That same word was on a photograph in Dr. Calleo's office," I added. "She was addressing the London Duophysite Society Annual Meeting. Dr. Grigori is in the photo too. She was receiving some kind of award."

"Okay," Josh said, "Next assignment: find out what the London Duophysite Society is."

"What happened to Engeln?" Neith asked. "Does anyone know?"

"Poisoned," Miyako said soberly. "Apparently at the time, they thought it was just a severe stomach ailment, some kind of gastric distress. But Brother Maurinus, who delivered the letter to Mendel, demanded an autopsy. Large quantities of antimony were found in Engeln's system. It could have been delivered as a medicine, dispensed from the infirmary, or someone could have switched his cup for an antimony cup in the refectory. Pewter and antimony look alike."

"What about Mendel?" Dilani asked. "Did he carry on with the research?"

"We don't know what happened to him," Miyako answered, "because the abbot who succeeded Mendel after he died of kidney failure . . ."

I interrupted, "Mendel died of kidney failure? Can antimony do that too?"

Miyako shrugged and continued, "After Mendel died, the next abbot had Mendel's greenhouse demolished. Then he burned all of Mendel's papers in a huge bonfire where the greenhouse had stood. It could have been routine housekeeping, out with the old, in with the new kind of stuff, or it could have been jealousy since Mendel beat him out earlier for the abbot job."

I imagined a black-robed abbot ordering the brothers to throw into the flames everything they found in Mendel's cell and laboratory, watching as leather-bound journals hissed and crackled and papers turned to cinders and ash.

"But somehow this one survived," Dilani said.

Miyako asked, "What if this letter was what Dr. Grigori was really looking for, not the book he asked Miss Hermani to get from the library? What if he knew that the book would hold these papers? Who actually knows the letter exists?"

Josh shrugged. Then he quickly held his finger to his mouth. He pointed to the ceiling above us. "Someone is up there," he mouthed. Finally, he was using his hearing on our behalf.

"See you tomorrow!" Zia said brightly as she turned palms up in a "what should I do?" gesture.

"Yeah, good luck with your homework," Josh said with a similar motion. We each waved and grabbed our stuff to leave.

As we dispersed, I inhaled through my nose. Rose petals over vomit. I'm the one who should have been paying more attention. Two feet passed quickly along the floor overhead, taking the smell with them.

28

Maple Syrup and Immortelle

I made the same pajama choice as for my first Dream Lab experience and this time I scarfed down Marie Antoinette's hot chocolate before I got too sleepy. It was divine. I tried to stay focused on what I could learn by being here even as I began to fantasize about another trip back just so I could have some more of the hot cocoa prized by greedy French aristocrats. They should have just shared. They could have prevented the whole revolution. At least, they could have gotten suckers like me to pretty much do whatever they wanted for another cup of that steamy, hot, velvety deliciousness.

Nurse Berith smiled as she attached the tiny little sensors.

"This time, Kaia," she said, "We're going to try what we call a suggested dream. Rather than just see where your dreams take you, and if you can change them mid-course, we are provide you with a subject and ask you to try to dream about that."

"Okay," I said, trying to sound willing but not too enthusiastic.

"We want to see what happens when you dream about your family," she said, placing her hand gently over mine just in time to keep me from flinching. "I know that may be a sensitive subject since you have suffered so much loss."

I heard myself inhale. Did they want me to have a bad dream?

"We know you lost your parents. That must be very painful for you. But you may find some solace in your dreams. I know your departed parents are the first ones you think of when you think about your family, but perhaps tonight you will discover some other truth about who you are and where you come from."

I looked at her and tried to keep my forehead from creasing.

"Let your dreams be your guide, Kaia. And remember, like last time, you can always ring this bell," she gestured to the bell on the nightstand, "if you need anything at all."

I nodded.

"Kaia, you are one of our most promising students. We will not let anything disadvantageous occur." She smoothed a stray strand of hair away from my cheek. "Trust me."

"Thank you, Nurse Berith," I said, and covered my mouth as I yawned.

The beautiful music I had heard my first time started to fill the room. My eyelids grew heavy. I had that peaceful sinking feeling where my body felt heavier and heavier, and I jolted half-awake just for a moment, with that sensation like I've tripped over a tree root while walking on a path in the forest. Then everything went black.

§

I snatched at the electrodes, trying to yank them off as Nurse Berith woke me. "Calm down, Kaia," she said. She had taken both my hands in hers and had firmly pushed them down to my sides.

"Calm down," she repeated in a soothing voice. "You have done so very well. You have provided truly admirable results. Dr. Grigori will be very pleased."

I had stopped struggling and was fully awake. "What . . .?" I started.

"It is common to feel discombobulated when waking from such a revelatory dream," she said, and placed a cool hand on my forehead like she was checking to see if I had a fever. *Discombobulated?* Totally panicked was more accurate. Still, Nurse Berith spoke with such authority. Maybe she was right.

But as I became more awake, I became terrified—not at the dream's contents, but that it would slip away from me. My dream would become irretrievable, and I would just be left with a sense of emptiness. If I weren't careful I would lose a valuable piece of information, something basic I should know, like my home address, and something that if forgotten would prevent me ever finding my way home.

"Kaia," Nurse Berith said, "I can see you are trying to hold on to it. Here is your tablet, if you want to write it down." She handed me the tablet. "I can arrange for your breakfast to be brought here so you have plenty of time before your class, if you want to get your dream recorded. Some students find it interesting to go back to their dreams later. Keeping a dream journal can be very beneficial."

"Thanks," I said. I started to write everything I could remember.

"I will just go order you some cinnamon bun French toast and freshly squeezed orange juice," she said, and headed through the doorway to the adjacent office.

I typed as quickly as I could, wishing I had voice recognition software so I could get it down faster: the young woman named Samya walking in the glade and her longing for something more than life with her drab husband; her seething resentment of her father-in-law; the fresh, luxuriant earth following the receding of flood waters; the fragrances of loam and trees and petals and vines; the strange pale child and the flowers Samya laid on the girl's body, waking her from sleep or death—the immortelle; the ominous exhortation to get the others; Samya's rush of excitement, which I felt like a charge of electricity through my whole body. What did this have to do with my family?

The low battery warning light on my tablet came on. I pressed save, got out of bed, and went to the doorway to ask if Nurse Berith had a charger. She was still on the phone, her back to me, ordering my breakfast. But what I heard wasn't about maple syrup or bacon. It was, "Very promising. We will know in a moment. I will contact you when she is finished. Stand by."

What had I just done? What if Josh was right about somebody monitoring our tablets? I called over to Nurse Berith as if I didn't notice she was on the phone, "Um, Ma'am, I'm fine grabbing something from the cafeteria. I probably should be going."

"Are you sure?" she asked. "Did you get everything written down that you wanted?"

"Yes, Ma'am," I said. I stepped behind the changing screen, got into my jeans and T-shirt, pulled on my keds, tucking in the laces so I didn't have to tie them, stuffed my tablet into my backpack and headed into the hallway. A tall, slim, blond man in a white linen suit was rolling a cart toward me. On top of the cart was a dish with a silver dome, a large glass of orange juice, and a crystal vase with a single white bloom of immortelle. I blinked. Then my stomach growled.

"Wait a second," I said to the man. A sense of calm washed over me. Why was I running away? Apparently the Grigoris needed me for something. I was valuable to them.

"I believe this is mine." I raised the silver dome and took a piece of the French toast with my fingers. I dunked its corner into a steaming pitcher of maple syrup and took a bite. "Delicious," I said and swiped a linen napkin from the cart and stuffed it in my pocket. I grabbed the rest of the cinnamony treat with one hand and the pitcher of syrup with the other.

"I'll bring the pitcher back later," I called over my shoulder as I exited into the waiting area. I nodded at the GYSP students who were waiting for their appointments then stopped. My hands were full of breakfast food, and I couldn't get the doorknob.

"Grab that for me, would you?" I said to Aranka, whose eyes were wide. A smirk was forming on one corner of her mouth.

"You can tell Xanthe that the French toast is fantastic."

The sun was streaming in through the windows in the hallway. There was so much I didn't know. But one thing I did. I was the one with the power here. And I felt like having a great day for a change. So I would.

29

Bike Tires on a
Hot Country Road

But that would have to wait.

"Come on," Dilani said, grabbing me by the elbow and pulling me toward the Common Room as I stepped inside the dorm. "I've been waiting for you. For our end of Week Two assembly. Did you forget?" She stared hard at my mouth. "What's that?" she asked, pointing toward my bottom lip. "Ooh, gross. Sticky," she said as she accidentally touched me and then wiped her finger on her jeans.

"Maple syrup," I said, holding up the empty pitcher. "Delicious." I licked around the bottom of my mouth. "Probably the sap of some endangered hardwood from the rain forest. But, so tasty!" I remembered the linen napkin in my pocket and pulled it out with a flourish, holding my pinky in the air. I pulled my lips into a frown and dabbed at my chin. "Better, dahlink?" I said in my best swanky accent. Dilani rolled her eyes. "Just promise me you won't bore me with your dream," she said, rounding out her o's to sound as posh as possible.

"Wouldn't dream of it, my dear," I replied, raising the sticky pitcher up in a toast. "Here's to reality, whatever that is."

"Young ladies," Dr. Grigori's rich voice said from behind us. I could feel my face turn red. "Perhaps you will freshen up," he looked toward the washroom across the hall from the Common Room entrance, "and come join us when you are ready?"

Dilani looked at me wide-eyed when Dr. Grigori had gone ahead into the Common Room, and burst into giggles. We pushed our way into the washroom, turned on the taps, and washed our hands. I shrugged and tossed the linen napkin in the trashcan and left the pitcher by the sink.

We entered the Common Room and took our seats in the now quite diminished circle of chairs.

Now we were ten. Five more of us had been dismissed from the program to parts unknown. "No longer able to participate," was the extent of Dr. Grigori's explanation.

Ilona, with whom there was the mix up during my first visit to the Dream Lab, was one of them. A chill went up my spine when I heard Xanthe whisper to Aranka, "It took. She's pregnant."

The nurse had said "generation process" in the Dream Lab. Could she possibly have meant literally making new generations?

"A shame," Dr. Grigori tsk-tsked. "Not for you, however." The white-jacketed, white-gloved man with the silver tray had appeared again this week. We held our breaths, and you could feel the excitement in the room as he handed out the envelopes. No one waited for permission to open them this time. I heard gasps of joy and pleasure, but then nothing more as I gazed at my card:

In Recognition
of Your Successful Completion
of GYSP Week Two
For your exclusive use, plentiful antimony
Come alone to Dr. Grigori's office tomorrow

Did they know my pills were almost gone? That I didn't want to depend on Miyako to get me more? The Common Room was quiet as each of us looked at our cards, then furtively glanced at one another. No excited sharing this week. Had everyone received something personal, private? Something no one wanted anyone else to know about, but clearly the Grigoris must?

"Who knows what Week Three may bring?" Dr. Grigori said.

That night I dreamed of the merry-go-round in the school playground when I was little, a round flat metal disk, its white paint chipping, with raised red bars, handrails that radiated out from the center so there was something to hold onto. We took turns standing alongside and pushing, then hopping on to ride the spinning platter. Sometimes someone could be enticed or begged to push, faster, faster, while the riders rotate and zip past the pusher, over and over and over again, or look up and watch the blue sky whirl above. In my dream, though, the handholds had been removed and we riders had nothing to cling to but one another, as someone unseen spun the wheel harder and harder, trying to fling us off. Would we stay on? Or would vertigo and centrifugal force send us flying off the edge as one by one we could no longer hold on, or wanted to?

§

"I heard Ilona is pregnant and that's why she's not in the program anymore," Zia said that night when we gathered in her room.

"I think she was supposed to get pregnant," I said quietly, leaning over the table we were sitting at in the library reading room.

"What do you mean, 'supposed to'?" Dilani asked.

"I mean, she was in the Dream Lab with me, but the nurse said she was in the 'generating process' not the 'discernment process.'"

"And you think they mean 'generating,' like 'progeneration,' as in making progeny, the next generation, something like that?" Zia said.

"That's sick," Dilani said.

"The Watchers impregnated women." I said. "If Nephilim exist, wouldn't they try to make more Nephilim, or Elioud, or whatever?"

"You think there's a shortage of people with angelic DNA wandering around, and the GYSP is trying to do something about it?" Zia asked.

"I know it sounds far-fetched," I admitted.

"I wonder if I can get in on this Dream Lab thing," Zia said.

"Yeah, just make sure they send you in the right direction," I responded.

"I don't know," said Zia, "dreams about angels that are super realistic? Realistic enough that you end up pregnant? Could be amazing."

We looked at her.

"I'm just saying."

"Stop it," I said.

Zia responded, "But they are up to something weird. I know our tablets are being monitored." She explained that she sent a message to Dilani that she heard Xanthe say she was hoping to see Dr. Eder after class in the courtyard. She had some more creative responses to the assignment he might be interested in exploring with her.

"You're bad." I smiled at Zia, enjoying that she had used Xanthe as the bait in her experiment. "What happened?"

"Dr. Eder waited in the courtyard for twenty minutes for Xanthe to show up. He looked really disappointed when she didn't. He checked his phone a couple of times, as if he may have got the message wrong."

"Okay, no more tablet," I said, wondering what important information I had already given away. "What's next?"

"We had better keep using our tablets, or they'll get suspicious," Zia said. "We just need to be careful."

Dilani breathed a worried sigh.

I put my arm around her shoulder. "I'm glad we're together in this little world," I said, but a pang of longing shot through me, to be alone, riding my bike on the hot country roads outside my boring hometown, staring at nothing but cornfields.

30

White Camay Soap

I was about to get changed into my pajamas when I heard a quiet knock at my door. I thought it was Dilani, coming to say goodnight before the lights out bell.

"Come in," I said, around the ponytail holder I held in my mouth, while I ran a brush through my hair and tried to bunch it into something to keep me from looking like Medusa in the morning. My back was to the door, and I was surprised when I heard Miss Liora's voice. I should have known her by her clean scent of white Camay soap.

"Let me help you with that, dear," she said kindly, motioning for me to sit down in the desk chair and holding her hand out to take the brush. I gave her the ponytail holder too, hoping it wasn't too moist from my mouth. "How about a nice French braid?" she asked. "It will keep your hair tidy and if you leave it in overnight, you'll have beautiful waves tomorrow. All right, love?"

"Thanks, Miss Liora," I said. She brushed my hair and deftly arranged it into the braid. She pulled a hand mirror from her apron and told me to turn my back toward my wall mirror so I could see what the back of my head looked like.

"It's nice," I said. "Thank you."

She gestured toward the clasp of my locket at the back of my neck.

"Dear, where did you get that locket? Someone important to you?"

I gathered up the chain until the locket was at my neck. I pulled it out from under my neckline and held it out toward Miss Liora. "It was my mother's." I could feel myself avoiding looking at her in case I got teary.

"She's gone, isn't she?" she asked softly.

I looked at her and nodded. "My father too. An accident." I stopped talking, surprised I had said this much.

"Sit with me, dear," she said. She sat on my bed and patted the space next to her. "Do you know what the locket means?" she asked, very quietly.

"I know it was given to my mother by my grandmother. I got it when I turned sixteen."

"Dear, you must be very, very careful whom you show that locket to. You are safe with me. Here." She tugged at a chain around her neck and pulled an identical locket from beneath the collar of her blouse. "I'm one of them too, like your mother and her mother before her."

"Them? Who is them?" I asked, surprised.

"Your mother, and I, and many others, many now taken from us, sacrificed a great deal to raise children like you."

"What are you talking about?"

"You and the other GYSP students are very special. The Grigoris know this too. The question is, will you throw your lot in with the Grigoris or work for the side of the humans?"

"Miss Liora . . ."

She started speaking more quickly. "Those in charge, Dr. Grigori and his ilk, call the purely humans among us 'Merely.' You must remember that everyone is valuable and worthy of dignity, whether they are Nephilim, or human, or . . ."

"Elioud?" I finished.

"I knew you would figure it out!"

"Figure what out?" I said. "That was a guess, mostly. What exactly are Elioud?"

Miss Liora glanced quickly at her watch. "Put that away," she said, nodding at my locket, "but keep it with you at all times," she warned as she tucked hers back under her blouse. "Go see this person—another friend." She tucked a folded paper into my hand and stood up, reaching for the doorknob.

"Wait, Miss Liora," I said. "Elioud and Nephilim," I practically just mouthed the names, "they really exist?"

She nodded. "All around us."

"But how . . .?" She cut me off again, shaking her head and standing suddenly. "No more."

I looked up at Miss Liora. Her brow was furrowed. She reached for the doorknob.

"Miss Liora, who gave you yours?" I pressed on my locket now hidden under my shirt. She turned back toward me.

"My own mother, gone to her reward. A brave woman. I think of her every day and try to make her proud. I have no family of my own now, at least, no blood family. Watching over children like you—you're the family that matters now. Remember what I said. Little time remains, and you have more to learn than I thought."

Miss Liora looked both ways in the hall then stepped out and closed the door behind her, leaving me alone in my room, my questions swirling.

§

After classes the next day, we were all summoned to the Common Room to meet our new dorm proctor, Miss Rukmini. "Miss Liora had to leave. Family matters," she said. "I am your proctor now."

I blinked and tried not to reach for my locket, stuffing my hands into my pockets instead. I shuddered as my thoughts jelled and clarified, and my questions re-formed: What had happened to Miss Liora? What really happened to my parents? Who or what are the Elioud?

31

Rancid Meat

As we filed out toward the cafeteria, I felt an ice-cold hand on my shoulder. I instinctively jerked away, but turned to see who had touched me.

"I'm sorry, Miss Rukmini," I said when I saw the offended look on her face.

"Circulatory issues," she said in a crisp voice. "You are wanted in the Dean's office, immediately after you finish your lunch."

They must have found out about the syrup pitcher. It's not like I stole it, but I had promised to return it and hadn't. Or was it the knife from the museum? That would be hard to explain. Why didn't I just stick to the rules? The rush of confidence I had felt on my way out of the Dream Lab had been short-lived. Maybe the pitcher was still where I had left it in the bathroom, and I could drop it off in the cafeteria.

I pushed open the door to the washroom. Immediately a smell like rancid meat and sulfuric acid assaulted me. My eyes watered, and I ran to the sink, covering my mouth with my hand in case I didn't make it there before throwing up.

"Oh good, it's you." The voice was familiar, but strained and shaky. "In here."

I turned and saw Xanthe through the open door of a stall. She was crouched down against the back wall, holding her knees to her chest like she was protecting herself from a blow to the solar plexus. Her make-up had run, and her hair was disheveled.

"What's happened to you?" I asked and started toward her, but a wave of nausea hit, and I turned back toward the sink.

"Of course you think of yourself when I'm the one in distress."

"What?" I replied, confused. Thinking of myself?

I was, though. The stench was sickening. I got on tiptoe and pushed open one of the windows high in the wall and sucked in some fresh air. Fortified, and trying not to breathe through my nose, I went back to the open stall.

"Xanthe, what's wrong? What's happened?" I asked as I knelt down in front of her.

"I'm rotting," she said, fresh tears streaking her face. "I'm literally rotting. Look." She twisted away from me and pulled up her shirt. I was knocked backward from the stink. Silver-green pus oozed from a vertical gash along her spine. Her skin looked like it had pulled apart leaving a chasm of about two inches. I swallowed back another gulp of rising stomach acid. Although I had never seen anything like it, it looked like something I should know about, had heard about somewhere recently. Where?

"It's getting worse every day. I can't make it stop. You can help, though. I heard about you in the Dream Lab." She pulled her shirt back down and winced as the fluid-soaked fabric grazed the infected wound. "Help me."

"Has anyone else seen this?" I asked. "Have you been to a doctor?"

"When it first started, about a year ago, my mother gave me an old cup to drink from every morning and evening. Told me it had been passed down through generations of my family and had helped others. But it hasn't helped, and the infection, or whatever it is, is getting worse. Dr. Grigori sent me to see a specialist in Boston. He gave me these." She rummaged in her bag and pulled out a prescription bottle. She held it out to me.

Sb was hand-written on the label. "Antimony," I said.

"Whatever," she said, rolling her eyes and grimacing. "It's not working. He said it might be too late. I don't want it to be too late!" She buried her head in her hands and sobbed. "Do something!"

"What can I do? I mean, other than get you to a hospital right away?"

"They said you're the real thing, the one who can save us. A realm crosser. In the Dream Lab. I heard them." Her smeared and mascara-blackened eyes were wide, pleading. I had no idea what she was talking about.

She winced and went on, "I thought they must be wrong. It can't be you. But what if they're right? Do something!"

"Who are 'they' and what's a realm crosser?" I asked. "Maybe that will help me know what to do."

"I knew it. You're an imposter. Useless. I don't know why I even thought . . ." She arched her spine as she clawed at her back with one hand as a new streak of pain shot through her.

"I'm going for help, Xanthe," I said as I stood. I ran to Miss Rukmini's room and told her Xanthe was in pain in the bathroom and needed to go to the emergency room right away.

Miss Rukmini looked calm as she said, "Thank you, Kaia. Go eat your lunch, and I will take care of the situation." She nodded her dismissal as she reached for her phone.

I kept expecting to hear the wail of an ambulance's siren as I walked to the cafeteria, but the yard was silent except for the chirping of birds and the buzz of air conditioning units. Or was it flies?

§

I was still in a fog as I stood with my tray in front of a buffet offering a choice of Kobe beef burgers, lobster tails, or shark fin and caviar pizza. Nothing was remotely appetizing with the reek of Xanthe's rotting flesh still clinging to the inside of my nostrils.

I suddenly remembered: I was supposed to go see Dr. Grigori. The panic pinprick swelled to a drill bit. He would be wondering what was taking me so long. I asked for two pieces of dry toast, wrapped them in a napkin, and stuck them in my book bag for later. Rats. I had forgotten all about the syrup container. I hadn't noticed if it was still in the bathroom.

I started composing my apology as I walked. Would saying that I had tried to help Xanthe be a good explanation for why I hadn't returned it yet? Maybe I should just leave my apology vague and see what he said. The pitcher looked expensive, but I supposed I could pay it off somehow if they asked me to replace it.

Miss Hermani greeted me when I arrived. "Go in, they're expecting you," she said looking up from her screen and waving me toward Dr. Grigori's office door. A large black fly landed on the top of her monitor. With a lightening fast swipe Miss Hermani grabbed it, her red fingernails digging into the palm of her hand and holding it trapped. I stared at her.

"Go in," she insisted. "What are you waiting for?"

32

Woodchips and Cedar Moss

Nurse Berith and Dr. Grigori rose from the leather sofa as I entered the room. The room smelled like a fresh application of men's cologne, with buckskin, woodchips, and cedar moss. "FireIce," Aunt Alina had told me once, the men's scent that captures the fragrance of Iceland, after I told her I wanted to travel there some day. It was nice, but Dr. Grigori had laid it on thick.

"Come in, Kaia," Dr. Grigori said. "Be seated." He patted the back of one of the wingback chairs. One of his diamond cufflinks sparkled as it caught the light.

I perched on the edge of the chair, in case I needed to spring up and escape. Was Nurse Berith here as a witness to report my literally sticky fingered theft of the syrup pitcher? She and Dr. Grigori smiled at me. They were enjoying this.

Nurse Berith began after Dr. Grigori nodded at her. "Kaia," she purred, "I have shared the results of your Dream Lab visits with Dr. Grigori. We are pleased with your progress. You are, in fact, the most promising GYSP participant we have seen since the program began." She looked at Dr. Grigori who nodded. "Your score on the self-promotion diagnostic was perfect. Your ability to summon family history was remarkable."

I could feel my head cock slightly and my left eye squint as I tried to figure out what she was saying. What Aunt Alina called my "Skeptical Popeye" look. "Very unattractive," I could hear her say. I tried to make my face relax, but it was too late.

"Kaia," it was Dr. Grigori's turn to speak, "you are unused to being in the spotlight, even in such an intimate environment as this." He pivoted his hand, like a monarch waving at the luxurious room. "Your naiveté is charming." He glanced at Nurse Berith who smiled at me like I was a four year-old who had used a grown up word incorrectly or dressed herself inappropriately for school. "But it is time for you to realize your full potential. Realizing potential is, after all, the purpose of the GYSP. Tell us, Kaia, are you enjoying the program thus far?"

I sat quietly for a moment, wondering how I could answer his question, but get some of my own questions answered first.

"Dr. Grigori, Nurse Berith," I cleared my throat, "I am enjoying the program. Just like you promised," I looked at Dr. Grigori, "I have made some friends, people I care about."

"Splendid," he said.

"But I want to know more about the Dream Lab, about 'self-promotion diagnostic' and 'family history.'" And why I should be excited about nightmares.

"Of course. And you shall. Patience, Kaia, patience. Good things take time to come to pass. Generations, sometimes." Dr. Grigori leaned forward and put his hand on the mahogany table between us. He stroked the wood surface slightly. Somehow his gesture was soothing.

"Kaia," he leaned toward me, "You are owed an apology. The GYSP promised you the opportunity to fit in." He shook his head from side to side. "You will never fit in."

There it was: the truth. I didn't belong. Time to pack. I was torn between relief—my ticket out of this disturbing place, the relief of going home, even to my weird little life with Aunt Alina—and disappointment. I wanted to be part of figuring out what was going on here.

"Kaia, pay attention," Nurse Berith said sternly.

"Sorry," I said, snapping back into the conversation. Dr. Grigori was now nodding, apology over.

"You will never fit in," Dr. Grigori repeated. "Those capable of greatness can never remain with the rest of the pack."

Skeptical Popeye was back.

"Greatness?" I said

"Greatness," Dr. Grigori repeated while it was Nurse Berith's turn to nod.

He leaned closer. "You have an advanced aptitude for what we call 'anamnesis.' Smell is the most potent of the Merelys' senses connected with memory." He stopped himself, as if he had spoken a dirty word: "Merely."

But whether the word was distasteful to him or he had let it slip in front of someone who shouldn't hear it, I couldn't tell.

He continued, "Your olfactory abilities unlock powerful memories that go beyond your own direct experiences. That, combined with your capacity for self-regard, makes you potentially very powerful, an asset for the greater concerns of the consortium that developed and facilitates the Grigori Young Scholars Program."

My heart fluttered. Although I had no idea what they were talking about, the thought that I might be good at something was thrilling. I suddenly realized I was grinning—a big Most Improved Miss Sauerkraut Fest toothy smile. But my cheek muscles flattened into neutrality when I realized they were saying I was selfish, and they hadn't actually answered my questions about my dreams—nightmares.

"I don't understand what this has to do with bad dreams," I said.

"Appraisal is all relative. Is that not so?" Dr. Grigori said. Nurse Berith bobbleheaded agreement again.

"You demonstrated your awareness of the relativity of what is called 'good' and what is called 'evil' in your exemplary essay on the Nephilim in ethics class."

He paused, and I felt slightly ashamed of my paper.

"History will be written by the winners, Kaia," Dr. Grigori continued. "You have insights that will be useful for when the winners emerge. When it is time for the rightful interpretation of history to come to the fore, your insights and abilities will be most valuable."

"You think the Nephilim exist," I said, and just as quickly wished I hadn't said it out loud.

Dr. Grigori said somberly, "I could not be more certain."

"But how . . . what . . . ?" I wasn't sure what to ask, only that I should be asking something at this moment.

"The truth often perplexes at first. But your own propensity for anamnesis gives you evidence that what I am saying is true."

Nurse Berith broke in after first turning toward Dr. Grigori. She lowered her head and raised her eyebrows, silently asking his approval to speak. "What Dr. Grigori is trying to tell you is that you have the ability to make the past present in your dreams. That is the meaning of 'anamnesis.' It is the equivalent of 'un-forgetting,' 'un-amnesia-ing,' if you will, the past."

Is that what Xanthe called "realm crossing"?

Dr. Grigori elaborated, "Anamnesis is a way of bringing the past into the present you can experience it firsthand, keep it from being forgotten or lost. One with this gift can access the information as if one were there when it happened."

"Which of my dreams did that?"

"What does the name 'Samya' mean to you?" Nurse Berith responded. My throat dropped into my stomach. Then I could feel my nostrils flare.

"You said you couldn't tell the content of my dreams!"

"Does that matter if we have uncovered a gift?" Dr. Grigori said, his voice like hot fudge drizzling on ice cream. "Your emotional outburst shows your need for further work on control and detachment. Not allowing strong feelings to get the better of you in tense situations will help you obtain and maintain the upper hand." He paused and inhaled deeply as if to show me how to calm down. I breathed. It worked.

"We desire to say more, but you must be ready to hear it. Are you willing to sacrifice the pleasure of your new friendships in order to reach your full potential? To become what you truly are meant to be means that you will have to make some sacrifices now for a greater good later."

Something in his voice made me think he meant more than giving up friendships. I think he meant giving up the friends themselves—betrayal.

"Let us start with a rhetorical question," Dr. Grigori said when I didn't respond. "Would you ever choose one person over another?"

"I suppose so," I answered, even though I didn't like the way that sounded.

"Of course you would. Everyone does. You would, for example, choose to be friends with Dilani rather than Xanthe. Or rather, you did choose Dilani over Xanthe."

I didn't realize he would be aware of who my friends were. Suddenly the thought of Xanthe in the bathroom and her oozing wound made me gag. I put my hand to my mouth.

"Xanthe is now beyond your help."

I shuddered.

"She said I could do something," I said quietly into my lap.

"Not yet. You are not far enough along in your studies," said Nurse Berith. "She was correct, just premature."

There was a knock at the door. Dr. Grigori turned his head in the direction of the interruption.

"Come!" he said over his shoulder, and Miss Hermani stuck her head in.

"The board is gathering, Sir," she said meekly, "You said to let you know."

"I did." He stood. The meeting was over.

"Think carefully, Kaia, about with whom you share this information. Those you call friends may not have your best interest in mind." He smiled. "To achieve greatness, you must be willing to go it alone. Friends, more often than not, will hold you back." He motioned toward the door. I went out ahead of him and Nurse Berith.

"To be continued," he said.

When I was back in the hall, I stopped and leaned up against the wall. Too many things to sort out. I wanted help, and I wanted that help from Dilani, Neith, Josh, Miyako, and Zia. All of them.

But what if Dr. Grigori and Nurse Berith were even just a little bit right? What if they could see something about me that no one else could? What if I could accomplish some things on my own that would benefit my friends too? Would any harm come from going along with Dr. Grigori and Nurse Berith, even just to find out something more?

Something caught my eye. Through the window into the courtyard I saw several tall figures, maybe eight of them, all about the same height and build as Dr. Grigori. They all wore dark coats and hats, pulled down over their brows, and each held a single white flower in their black-gloved hands. A light mist was falling. I stepped back from the window and watched as they formed a line. Two people in hospital scrubs and masks carried a body on a stretcher, covered with a white sheet. They set the stretcher down at the feet of the dark-clad figures and walked out of view. I saw one of the dark clad figures cover his nose, then, as if making an effort, dropped his hand back to his side.

I winced. I knew who was under the sheet, a fact confirmed when the figure closest to the head end, folded the sheet back, exposing Xanthe's face, which now looked gray and drawn. Someone had arranged her hair, combing it back from her face, and piling its luxuriant waves so they spread around her head like a platinum lion's mane. Then each figure placed a flower into her hair as they filed past her and formed a circle around her.

Another person appeared, carrying a tray with small silvery goblets, and delivered one to each of the figures around the circle. He bowed and stepped out of my view. The figures raised their cups and drank, but none drained their cup. As one, they emptied the rest of the liquid onto Xanthe's body. Their cups were collected, and they joined hands, bowed their heads, and stood in apparent silence. Then one of them spoke. I could see his mouth moving and strained to hear what he said but couldn't. Their hands still clasped, they raised them toward the sky. A flash of blinding white light, a tongue of red flame that burned just for an instant, rose from the middle of their circle. I thought I saw a flock of small black birds take wing, but they were gone before I could follow their path of flight.

The circle dissolved. The figures departed, and on the grass where Xanthe had been laid was a fine covering of black ash.

I thought of what Josh had said happened after Mendel had died. The new abbot burned all of Mendel's papers in a bonfire. I pictured a ring of monks watching the flames and then spreading the ash when the fire died out.

But these ashes had been a living, breathing person.

It suddenly occurred to me what had been nagging at me since I saw Xanthe's oozing wound, why it felt like it meant something, something more than just the obvious fact that her life was in danger. What was it Josef Engeln had written to Mendel in his notes on *1 Enoch*? Something about 'disintegration' or 'rupture' happening to Nephilim if their angelic and human natures don't remain fused? Was Xanthe one of the Nephilim? Was that the bad smell many of the professors at the GYSP were trying to mask? Was antimony supposed to save them? Why didn't the pills Xanthe got from the doctor do her any good? Were the scars on her back that had ruptured like mine? Was this what was in store for me?

I found the nearest wastebasket and finally threw up.

33

Iron and Ashes

We had agreed to meet that evening, but the library no longer seemed safe.

"I have an idea," Josh said. "I know a place we can have all to ourselves."

Sounded off limits to me.

"The bell tower," Josh said.

"I'm sure that's kept locked," I replied.

"Of course it is," Josh said. "They can't let just anyone have access to the bell tower."

"So?" I said, already getting nervous.

"So, I know where the keys are kept in the vault in the library."

"They let you just walk off with a key?" Dilani asked.

"An impression of the key," Josh said. He held up a pinkish lump containing a key-shaped indentation. "Silly putty," he said. "All kinds of practical uses." He smushed the silly putty back into a wad and produced a freshly cut key with his other hand from his pocket.

"Let's go!" Miyako said.

"As long as we don't stay up there longer than fifteen minutes," I said, trying to sound relaxed. "Doesn't the bell chime every quarter hour?"

"So we'll have to be quick," Josh said.

"It will be fun," said Zia.

"Awesome," said Dilani.

Nothing from Neith, who had turned the color of wet cement. "What's wrong?" I asked.

"I'll be fine," he replied, "as long as I don't have to look down."

"Afraid of heights?" Zia asked.

"It's embarrassing," he said. "I was the only kid in my neighborhood who didn't want to climb to the top of the jungle gym, or look off observation decks, or ride a Ferris wheel."

"Sorry," Josh said. "We can go somewhere else."

"No," said Neith, "I've got to get over this sometime."

We walked to the wooden door that led to the bell tower. The door was marked "No Entrance—Danger."

Josh unlocked it and we stepped into a small, dim vestibule with winding wooden stairs. Josh had brought a flashlight and flicked it on. I was last in line and pulled the door closed behind us. The bell chimed once to signal quarter past. The sound reset my heartbeat. I wondered how Josh could stand it.

"Fifteen minutes!" Josh said. "Let's go."

As we climbed, I tried not to get dizzy. Each stair step was like a slim wedge of cheese in a circular wheel. I was looking forward to the trip down so I could unwind.

"This is odd," said Dilani.

"What? Us sneaking around in a place we're not supposed to be? No odder than whatever the Grigoris are up to," Josh said.

"No. What's odd is that this staircase isn't supposed to be used, but everything is clean."

She was right. The place was pristine, as if it were used on a regular basis.

"Maybe the person who rings the bells is allergic to dust," Neith said.

"The bells are automated. We passed a timing mechanism at the bottom of the stairs," Josh replied.

We kept winding our way up and up. It was hard to tell what level we were on, or how far up we had come.

"Wait," whispered Josh. He swung the flashlight around as he halted on the stairs. He put his finger to his lips and switched off his beam. We could make out a doorway just above us, and off to the side of the stairs. Light leaked out around the edges. We could hear voices from the other side of the door. The tone was serious, but calm, and very soft. I looked up toward Josh. He mouthed, "Can't understand."

But there was enough of the stench of GYSP faculty for me to know who was speaking.

Josh pointed up the stairs and shrugged his shoulders in a "keep going?" gesture.

It seemed risky. What if they heard us? What if they caught us in here? What if they were already in the only safe place to meet in the bell tower?

While I was going through my list of 'what ifs,' my fearless companions had already made the decision to keep climbing. I hurried to catch up, trying to step as softly as I could. As I ascended, a musty metallic odor of iron grew in strength and competed with the GYSP staff stink. Time to mouth-breathe some more.

We must have climbed another story or two when we reached the top. A large platform extended the width and length of the tower. An immense iron bell hung above us, along with the mechanism that would make it ring about twelve minutes from now. A vein in my temple bulged in anticipation.

On each wall was a large open window. Moonlight streamed in, giving us plenty of light to see by. Everyone except Neith went to the windows. The views over the campus were beautiful. Warm light shone out from dorm room windows, our fellow GYSP students getting a start on their homework, no doubt. Lights were on in the library. Farther off, the city square was lit with streetlamps and lights from restaurants and coffee shops.

"We should get started," said Neith. "We don't have long until Big Bertha rings the half past signal, and we all suffer major hearing loss."

We sat in a circle on the floor directly below the bell. Zia began. "Antimony. I've got some more information."

She passed us each a sheet of paper.

"Bible passages?" Josh asked.

"Bible passages that mention people who 'painted their eyes with antimony,'" she replied.

We looked at the page where she had highlighted specific verses: 2 Kings 9:30, Jeremiah 4:30, Ezekiel 23:40.

Zia said, "They could have just said, 'painted their eyes' or 'put on eye makeup.'" She patted her right eyelid with her forefinger as she spoke. "But they make a point to say 'with antimony,' as if that's significant."

I said, "Maybe it tells us something about the person using it."

"Like maybe they're not actually people," Dilani said. "They're Nephilim. Maybe it's a way to point that out without saying as much."

I scanned the page. "Yikes," I said. "In the Ezekiel passage, they're describing something pretty awful." I swallowed.

"Child sacrifice," Dilani said, frowning.

"Yes," I said. "The prophet is accusing the antimony-users of sacrificing their children."

"Wow," said Dilani. "It actually says in verse thirty-nine, 'they slaughtered the children they had borne for God.'"

"If they were Nephilim, those children were Elioud," Zia said.

"And this all takes place after the flood," Josh said. "If the flood was supposed to kill Nephilim, it didn't work. They're still around."

Suddenly my Dream Lab dream came to mind, the one with Samya and the Nephilim child. "Let us get the others," she had said. The Nephilim were definitely still around. I was starting to have some really bad feelings about why the GYSP was so interested in my dreams, and how close "around" might be. Dr. Grigori's claim to know personally that they existed made my stomach tingle with fear, but I also felt some excitement.

"I've got more information too," Miyako said. "Another place antimony shows up is in CFCs."

"CFCs?" I asked, annoyance in my voice because when people talk in alphabet soup, I'm usually the one who has no idea what they're talking about.

"Chloroflourocarbons. They used to be in aerosol cans, refrigerants, and fire extinguishers. Antimony was a catalyst in making them work. But they've been banned because they deplete the ozone layer."

"If they've been banned, what's the problem?" I asked.

"The problem is," Miyako responded, "scientists identified the problem about fifty years ago, but not everyone cooperates with the ban. CFCs are still in use and people still need antimony to go with them."

"So, the Grigoris benefit from CFC smuggling," Josh said, putting the pieces together.

Neith jumped in. "But if CFCs keep being used, it contributes to the deterioration of the ozone layer. Why would anyone participate in that? Who benefits from environmental disaster?"

"No one," Miyako said.

"No one," Josh said slowly, "except someone who thinks they won't be affected if there's no more ozone."

"Huh?" said Dilani.

We were all quiet.

I tried to see if I understood where Josh was going. "You mean someone on earth will survive, even if the ozone layer is destroyed, so they don't really care."

"That's what I mean."

"Humans won't survive, and a lot of animals won't," Dilani said.

"That's right," Josh said. "But what if the Grigoris can? Because what if Nephilim can?"

Was this part of their plan? I felt sick.

Dilani spoke. "We've only got a minute before the bell rings. We should go."

"Listen," Josh said.

Even I could hear the low sound coming from beneath us. Several voices, but unified, like a prayer or a pledge.

Josh put his ear to the floor.

"I can't understand it," Josh whispered. "It's like nonsense syllables."

A small trapdoor, just big enough for one person to shimmy through was cut in the floorboards. We got down on our stomachs and tried to peer through the slits around the edges of the door.

I could see maybe a dozen tall figures all dressed in black. The candle-light illuminating the room flickered, making the figures' shadows dance on the walls. They were sitting around a large wooden table. Manila folders and small bowls containing what looked like antimony were on the table in front of each figure. The chanting came to an end and at once each of them took a pinch of the substance from the bowl and put it to their faces. From above I couldn't see exactly what they were doing. Swallowing it? Snorting it?

One of them pointed up at the ceiling. They pushed back from the tables and stood.

Suddenly we understood what the gesture meant. We scrambled up from our bellies and covered our ears. "To the windows!" Josh yelled, as the bell was struck.

We scurried to the window that overlooked the quad, ears still covered as the first chime reverberated and the clapper struck again. Being near the window gave a little more room for the sound to escape, but it was still deafening. With his hands to both ears, Josh gestured with his elbows to a space below us where a dozen large black birds took flight as one. The moonlight glinted off their shiny sable wings as they wheeled around and flew up and away beyond our view. The air had become cold.

The bell's reverberation came to an end. The silence was beautiful and complete. I thought for a moment that I must have suffered serious hearing loss, but then Zia spoke.

"We should get out of here before they do." She gestured toward the floorboards.

But when we looked that direction, we noticed the light had gone out.

Dilani went back to the window and looked out. "I haven't seen black birds that large in this area before. In fact, I don't know of any that exist in this area."

Josh put his ear to the floor, then sat up. "They've gone," he said.

We headed down the stairs.

"Let's go in," said Dilani as we came to the room where the others had been. "This may be our only chance."

"I'm sure they locked it behind them," I said.

Dilani pushed the door open.

"Okay," I sighed.

"We should still be quick," Neith whispered. "That bell rings again in thirteen minutes."

Josh swung his flashlight around. On one wall hung portraits under a plaque that said "Peerless." Beneath each was a small shelf with a glass vial.

"This one's Vespasian," Josh said. He looked at me. "Vespasian was a Roman Emperor. Oversaw a military campaign in Gerasa . . ."

"Where the mummy's from," I said. "The Gerasene Demoniac."

Josh nodded. "About thirty or so years after he was healed."

"Look at the dates on these," Zia said. "Can't be birth and death dates. Way too long."

I pointed to the dates under someone named Maria Anthoni Josepha Johanna. "Could she really have lived seven hundred years?"

"That's Marie Antoinette," Miyako said.

"They serve her hot chocolate in the Dream Lab," I said. "And she would have lived longer if she hadn't been such a snob. Who is Heironymous Joseph Franz . . ." I waved at his picture, skipping his long list of names, but noting his ripe old age of nine hundred fifty-seven.

Zia knew. "One of Mozart's patrons. Didn't really appreciate him though. Mozart's rival Salieri got him to give Mozart bad reviews. Then he fired Mozart and Mozart died not long after."

"Fired him, or killed him?" Dilani asked. "Remember what Fintan said about Mozart overdosing on antimony."

Josh pointed to the portrait of Herod the Great. "He's the one who had all the babies killed in Bethlehem, hoping to kill Jesus in the process." Four hundred and thirty-five years old when he died. "Died of acute intestinal rupture," Josh said.

Like Xanthe?

Zia had gone ahead to the last picture. "Holy cow," she breathed. "It's Xanthe."

There she was. With this year as the final date. According to the plaque, she was four hundred sixteen.

We looked at each other. Neith pointed at the glass vial below her portrait. "Is that . . .?"

Miyako took a latex glove out of her jeans pocket, shook it out and put it on. She dipped her forefinger into the vial and rubbed the gray dust between her finger and thumb. "Ash," she said.

I told them about Xanthe and what I had seen in the courtyard.

We were silent until Josh shone the torch on the adjacent wall. Then we gasped.

Glass cases perched on shelves, containing cross-sectioned heads. We went closer.

"Larynxes," Neith said, pointing at the containers. He got very quiet. "This is my GYSP project, studying these things to learn how vocal sounds are made. The larynx is the part that makes speech possible. Each one of these is slightly different." He gestured as he walked along the wall. "The placement and size of the larynx changes."

"Like they're from different people?" Dilani asked.

"Like they're from different species," Neith said. "But close to humans."

"They're not apes," Dilani said. "Apes' larynxes are much higher. That's part of the reason they can't make speech like us, even though we think they can understand a lot of human language."

Josh shone the light on the table where a business card rested. Miyako picked it up and read it to us: "The Rev. Francis Canon, PhD, St. Hildegard of Bingen Church." The address was downtown.

Josh said, "Looks like we have a field trip next on our agenda."

"Wow," said Dilani, as she pointed to a glass case on a sideboard. The case held tubes of a glowing substance. It looked like what we had seen in the storage room where the mummified Ethiopian children were kept. She then pointed out a flat black case resting next to the glowing tubes. She opened it gingerly. Six hypodermic needles lay neatly inside the red velvet-lined case.

"Is someone injecting that stuff?" Zia asked.

"We have to go," Neith said softly. Everyone nodded, and we turned toward the door.

That's when I saw a marble plaque on the wall by the door. The heading said

> ADDRESS
> TO THE
> LONDON DUOPHYSITE SOCIETY;
> *Delivered at the Annual Meeting on the 21st June, 1881*
> By N. T. GRIGORI, Esq.,
> PRESIDENT

I called out to Josh, "Quick! Silly Putty!" He saw where I was pointing, and together we spread the substance as flat as we could to pick up as many of the words on the plaque as possible.

"This will have to do," Josh said. He rolled up our polymer scroll, and we hurried down the steps and out of the building. We gathered under a street lamp, unrolled the putty and saw what we had managed to get. Not much:

> DISTINGUISHED MEMBERS, I proceed to lay before
> you a statement of the progress made in Duophysitical sci-
> ence during the past year. I believe that you will agree with
> me when I say that—

Josh put the inscription into my hand and shrugged apologetically.
Together we turned back and looked up at the tower. About two stories beneath the tower bell level I saw one small opening I'd never noticed before.
It must have been a small window to that weird meeting room. It looked like
a tiny black eye looking back at us unblinking.

§

When I got back to my room, I spread out the now warped Silly Putty sheet
and read it over several times. I didn't want to go back into the tower, but I
wanted to know what else was in that address.

I popped my nightly dose of antimony and settled into a fitful sleep.
I dreamed I was sitting at one of the tables in the photograph I had seen in
Dr. Calleo's office, the one where she's receiving an award while Dr. Grigori
looks on adoringly.

In the dream, Dr. Grigori gives his address. When he concludes, the
members of the London Duophysite Society give him a standing ovation. I
join in their applause and shouts of "Bravo!" Dr. Grigori bows slightly to his
audience. Then, turns his head toward me, licks his lips with his skinny little
tongue and nods.

I woke up in a sweat, my heart pounding, and wrote down everything I
could remember. What I knew for certain is that the speech explained what
was at the heart of the GYSP. Nephilim existed. Some called themselves The
Peerless. Something was seriously wrong with them, something called "disintegrative discoinherence" that I would bet my life meant rotting from the
inside, like Xanthe did. I was here, and every other GYSP student was here
so they could figure out how to do something about it.

I had to get the rest of that address. I thought about asking Josh for
his key, but instead picked the lock with the necrotome I had stolen from
the museum storeroom. I snuck into the tower and wrote down the whole
address.

> DISTINGUISHED MEMBERS, I lay before you a statement
> of the progress made in Duophysitical science during the
> past year. I believe that you will agree with me when I say

that much has been accomplished of late which will add fresh laurels to those who have already distinguished themselves in our exploration.

But first, before I announce the magnificent development that heralds a New Epoch in our progress, I must detain you for a brief time, while I refer to those amongst our associates whose loss we lament since our last meeting.

OBITUARY

We must note the passing of three distinguished members of our Society—Count Grüçich of Lasbard, Major-General Arhmani of Sicily, and Professor Petrosnal of Copenhagen. We have, I regret to say, lost three of our most valued and useful correspondents. From them we were in the habit of regularly receiving identification of potential juvenile specimens for study. Regrettably, our colleagues have succumbed to the disintegration that is the plague of our otherwise glorious existence. We deplore their extinguishment, and I pledge that our society will continue the meritorious investigations of these agents now beyond our reach.

Having dispensed with the announcement of our losses, I now report on the Society's new program for the Identification and Collection of Subjects for our further research.

OUR LABOURS

It is time to dispense with our outmoded practice of relying on those with Hybrid tendencies to come to us. We begin in earnest the recruitment and identification of Subjects amongst the young. It is now imperative that we actively pursue, gather, and analyze those we believe will be assets to our cause. It is not only the advances of disintegrative disco-inherence amongst our noble and ancient line that make this action our obligation. We also now possess advanced means for experimentation that will aid us in our crucial endeavor to restore purity amongst our kind. In particular, we will pursue new work in the fields of Oneirology and Hybridization, thanks to the Friar Gregor Johannes Mendel, first published in the *Proceedings of the Natural History Society of Brünn* in 1865.

The time has come for more aggressive measures. The first and foundation of these is the commencement of the

Grigori Young Scholars Program, which will be housed under the auspices of The Harvard Divinity School, of Cambridge, Massachusetts, in which our Society has gained a foothold and the full cooperation and sponsorship of Dr. Vladimir Grigori, my cousin, a member of the Peerless long laboring on the North American Continent.

Therefore, on this day, I announce to you the beginning of a new Epoch as we begin the programme that will lead to our glorious goal.

I got out of there as fast as I could, but not before I noticed that Xanthe's ashes and portrait were gone. Where the painting had hung was a black rectangle, like it had been burned, leaving scorch marks behind.

I went straight to the library and looked up "Oneirology." The study of dreams.

34

Match Heads and Incense

The address on the business card led us to the large white wooden church that was literally in the center of town, built within a traffic circle from which streets radiated. The sun was setting as we arrived. Streetlights designed to look like old-fashioned lanterns stood around the circle and cast a warm yellow glow. The building's window frames and the arches of its bell tower were trimmed in black, its broad front double doors painted bright red. A sign next to the door read, "Saint Hildegard of Bingen Church," and listed the Sunday worship times. A grassy churchyard with a few large grave markers and leafy sycamore trees surrounded the church. A cross and the year 1692 marked the building's cornerstone.

The front doors were locked. We knocked. The sound of lumber clattered on tiled floor and the doors pushed open. The man who greeted us was dressed in a priest's shirt and collar and gray slacks. He had a trim build, dark hair, and smiling eyes, with deep-cut laugh lines. His pinched brow suggested wariness, but when he saw us, he grinned broadly.

"Usually, I leave everything unlocked, but with your arrival, I had to be cautious," he said as he ushered us inside.

"You thought we were coming, so you locked the door?" I asked.

"I knew I should expect visitors from the Divinity School. You are students there?"

We nodded but looked at each other. Was he expecting us, or other visitors from the GYSP?

He looked past us, out into the churchyard, his eyes sweeping the space as if to see whether we had been followed, then pulled the doors closed behind us. He swung a two-by-four across the double doors and dropped it into place across two waist-high metal brackets designed to hold it. "They didn't bother with complicated locks in the old days," he said. He turned to us and extended a slender hand. "I'm Dr. Francis Canon. Who are you?"

We introduced ourselves one at a time and shook hands. He repeated each of our names after we said it, as if going over a mental checklist.

"So, you're here about the job," he said. I couldn't tell if he was making a joke, attempting to make the situation a little lighter.

"What 'job'?" I asked, still wondering if coming here was the right thing to do and if it was safe to be locked in an old church with Dr. Canon, nice as he seemed. A two-by-four keeping someone locked out was scary. A two-by-four keeping us inside was creepy.

"You have work to do and you're here to discover part of it."

"Uh, I guess that's right," I said. "You're sure it's really us you were expecting?"

"Others are on their way, I know, but I also knew that sooner or later some of you would find your way here, and that when you did, I would be ready to share what I know. I wish I knew the whole plan," Dr. Canon said with a sigh. "But I don't. I only know the part that's been given to me. I simply trust, or attempt to, and hope you can too, that knowing the little bit ahead of you is enough. It has to be enough." He looked at me, and then at each of us. We nodded our assent.

"Okay, then. Onward. Come, I have something to show you."

He led us to the chancel area in the front of the church. "It's okay, come on up," he said, motioning to the few stairs that led up to the sanctuary, the area in front of the stone altar. In the wall above it were three large stained glass windows. The street lamps outside provided just enough light to il-luminate the subjects. The central panel showed the magi, three of them according to tradition, kings from the east who came to adore the Christ child. Their gifts for the baby—gold, frankincense, and myrrh in opulent containers—were already offered at the Madonna's feet. But these magi were clearly identified as astronomers as well. One held a golden astrolabe, a tool for locating and predicting the positions of the sun, moon, stars, and plan-ets. The second held a small brass telescope; the third a silver sextant, used to measure the angle between the horizon and a celestial object. Above the magi, their famous guiding star twinkled and shone a ray of light down on the baby cradled in his mother's arms, his small hand extended in a gesture of blessing over his exotic visitors, while Joseph looked on in wonder. In the upper right corner of the panel, a choir of minuscule angels burst into song above a faraway hill populated by shepherds and their flocks of sheep. The source of the magi story was written below: Matthew 2:1-12, and the verse,

"We observed his star at its rising." I thought immediately of the Enoch story, with its tale of angels moving in the opposite direction—falling: the advent of chaos. No wonder the magi were hopeful when they saw a bright star rise.

The panels on either side of the magi were divided in half vertically. Each held two of the four archangels, wings unfurled, each angel holding his identifying attributes, his name, and its meaning written below: Gabriel, 'Strong Man of God,' with a branch from Paradise and a scroll; Michael, 'Who is Like God?' treading on a dragon, holding weighing scales and a sword; Raphael, 'God Heals,' with his bottle and staff; Uriel, 'God is My Light,' with a flaming sword and a fire burning in the palm of his hand. The archangels looked like they were standing watch over the magi and the holy family, whose lives were about to be turned upside down when evil King Herod would decide the infant was a threat. The family would flee to Egypt, while innocent children would be massacred at home. Why couldn't the guardian angels intervene then? I wondered. Couldn't? Wouldn't? Didn't.

Dr. Canon saw us gazing at the windows, trying to make out the features in the dim light. "They're beautiful, aren't they? Raphael is the patron of those who suffer nightmares," he said. "And Uriel is the patron of young people, especially those who dedicate themselves to fight against evil. But what I really want you to see is up there." He pointed above us.

Although the overhead lights were low and just a few candles were lit, we could make out clearly the beautiful domed ceiling overhead. It was painted a magnificent deep blue, the color of the night sky. Stars of various sizes painted onto the dome glittered in gold and silver, twinkling and sparkling in the candlelight.

"Wow," Dilani said. "Beautiful." Her voice sounded clear and bright as she spoke.

"It's the dome, isn't it?" Zia asked, looking at Dr. Canon. "The acoustics in here are spectacular. Dilani's voice sounds like a bell. So does mine."

Zia's voice always sounded like a bell if that meant clear and melodious. You wanted it to ring forever.

"That's exactly right," Dr. Canon said. "It was built to convey sound in a special way. Neith, go over there," he said, motioning to the end of one of the choir stalls that lined both sides of the altar area. "Say something quietly. Anything. The rest of us won't look at you as you speak so you'll know we're not reading your lips."

Neith stepped into shadows across from us.

"Go ahead," Dr. Canon prompted.

"I'm afraid of heights," Neith said. He must have spoken very quietly, but we could hear him precisely, a small crystal voice, as if he were standing right next to us, but even brighter somehow.

"Perfect!" Zia said with delight. "Not that you're afraid of heights," she said softly, so Neith too could hear the clarity of her voice even from a distance.

"I don't like the dark much either," came Neith's reply. "Can I come back now?"

"Yes, yes," Dr. Canon said. "The dome amplifies perfectly. Very useful on Sunday mornings when the acolytes get fidgety during my sermons. 'I can hear you,' I say to them from the pulpit. Freaks them out a little the first time," he said with a smile. "But what it does for music is extraordinary. Okay, who's the singer in the bunch?"

Zia put her hand up.

"Try this," Dr. Canon said, handing her a sheet of paper with a hand written musical staff, notes, and words.

Zia held the paper close to her face, eyes scanning. "Got it," she said. She lowered the paper, closed her eyes and sang. Music soared, reverberated, swelled, and filled the church. I couldn't understand the words—they must have been written in another language—but they conveyed an otherworldly beauty that ascended high above me and also filled me, resonating inside me. I had the sensation of light streaming down on us, filling the dome. I didn't even try to stop them as tears of joy streamed down my face. Zia sang the last notes, long and sonorant. Then silence.

We all looked at Zia. She opened her eyes, a gentle smile on her face. "Thank you," she said to Dr. Canon and handed him the sheet of music.

"What was that?" Josh asked quietly.

"A song to the angels," Neith said. "Latin. May I?" he asked Dr. Canon, who nodded and handed him the sheet.

Neith read, translating as he went,

"O you angels who guard the peoples, whose form gleams in your face,
and O you archangels who receive the souls of the just,
O you cherubim and seraphim, seal of the secrets of God."

"Very good," said Dr. Canon. "It's by St. Hildegard of Bingen, the saint for whom this church is named. The sheet music you sang from," he looked at Zia, "is a very early copy of one of her musical compositions. An amazing person," he said, and bowed slightly as if Hildegard herself were present. He pointed to an icon hanging on the wall on the right side of the altar. A woman in a dark nun's habit was depicted sitting with her black-shoed feet resting on a small stool. In her left hand she held a book on her lap. With her right hand she held a writing tool, a pen or stylus. Tongues of flame like rosy tentacles descended from the archway above her, alighting on her head, her eyes, ears, and throat. She looked at peace, even as the flames touched her. "Hildegard received visions," Dr. Canon said. "Her visions gave her insight into the nature of creation and inspired her studies in theology, music, and science."

"What kind of science?" Miyako asked.

"The healing qualities of gemstones and metals. Her book *Physica* contains information about how to prepare and administer tinctures, powders, plasters, and other ways to treat a number of ailments and diseases."

"Anything on antimony?"

"She probably knew it as stibium but that entry was lost."

"Or stolen," Miyako said thoughtfully. She explained to Dr. Canon, "In the chemistry lab I found a page torn from an old book I can't decipher. It's about a crystal of some sort, like antimony, but I can't make out the writing."

"Does it look like that?" Dr. Canon said, pointing to the dome. Around its base were symbols of some sort.

"Exactly like that," Miyako said.

"Hildegard invented her own language, called *Lingua Ignota,* or 'Unknown Language,' with its own alphabet of twenty-three letters. People who study or invent conlangs—'Constructed Languages' or planned languages, languages that have not developed naturally over time—think of St. Hildegard as their medieval predecessor, their patron saint, if you will. She was the first person ever to create an artificial language."

"Do we know why she did it?" Zia asked.

"We're not sure, except that she believed it was something that came to her as a gift, another revelation." Dr. Canon said. "Why would you make up a language?" he asked us, as if curious about our ideas.

"If I were trying to keep something secret, I would make one up, like a code," Josh said.

"Yes," said Zia, "and without the key, you can't understand it. You could also make a language that isn't really secret but is meant for people in a particular group. Like Klingon. Klingon isn't a secret language, but you've got to be a Trekkie to know it, or want to."

"Or maybe she was working on a language for everyone," I offered. "You know, like Esperanto."

"Yes, a universal language," Dr. Canon said. "All good ideas. Well, if she wanted to keep it a secret, she didn't do a good job of it. She recorded the key. So, that's one piece of evidence that she may have been trying to construct a universal language, or uncover one. Here's a copy of her alphabet and the corresponding Roman alphabet letters." He reached for copies of a pamphlet off a pile on a small table by the chancel steps and gave us each one. "What you see in the dome is a line from her theory on harmony. Hildegard believed that when we sing we join the company of the angels and saints in heaven praising God, and also the celestial harmony, sometimes called the 'music of the spheres,' which she believed was a literal sound made by the revolutions of stars, moon, sun, and the planets. The celestial harmony is also what we feel and participate in when we act in accordance with our purpose given by God. She believed she could hear the sound of that harmony and put it into her musical compositions." He pointed at the letters on the ceiling. "This quotation says, 'Harmony in heaven and earth, through the joining of heaven and earth, in the alignment of the stars, in the vanquishing of discord and evil.'"

I looked at the stars again, above the words. "Are those constellations?" I asked, pointing up. I didn't see anything that looked familiar.

"I'm certain they are," Dr. Canon answered. "When the church was built, they took extravagant care to make sure every detail had meaning. Every aspect of the church's architecture and decoration was documented and explained. Nothing here was ever meant to be a secret—that's just not our way. We want to celebrate and expand our knowledge of all aspects of life—spiritual, temporal. That's why they never cared about locking up the church. At least until more recently, when knowledge seems to be a dangerous thing . . ." his voice trailed off. Then he started speaking as if he had a sense that our time together was running out. "However, the one place about which we have no information is the dome. All the details for the dome have disappeared. The sheet with the preliminary drawings, the pages that would have held the explanation of the stars and their placement all disappeared from our archives, like they never existed. Anyone who used to know is gone. In fact, anyone related to anyone who used to know has also died, moved away, is unreachable. I've tried."

I took a piece of paper and a pencil out of my bag and started sketching the design. "We should be able to figure it out," I said. "We can probably find out the date and the place where this sky would have appeared just like this." I was excited by this project.

Zia spoke again. "Dr. Canon, you said the quotation on the dome is about harmony, right?"

"Yes."

"Specifically about the harmony that comes 'through the joining of heaven and earth.'"

"Yes, 'in the vanquishing of discord and evil.'"

"We're trying to find out more about the Nephilim, right?" Zia looked around at all of us. "Nephilim are the product of 'the joining of heaven and earth.'"

"Yes," Josh said, "but they're a source of discord and evil, not the solution to it, at least according to the myth."

"I know. I just wonder if Hildegard was trying to tell us something about how the Nephilim operate, or what they're up to, or maybe what the solution is to defeat them. I can't put my finger on it. But there's a reason we found Dr. Canon's card. And it's not just so we can admire the church's acoustics and pretty stained glass. Can we try another sound experiment?"

"Of course," said Dr. Canon.

"What happens if the dome's effect is interrupted? Like this." She positioned us around in a circle at the base of the dome and sang quietly the first line of St. Hildegard's song again, "*O vos angeli.*" We heard her melodic voice clearly. "Now Josh, you're the tallest. Stand in the middle." He did.

"'*O vos angeli,*'" she sang. It sounded exactly the same as before, sweet, jewel-like, and clear. She frowned. "It should have changed, at least a little. Dr. Canon, do you have something Josh can stand on?"

"No problem," Dr. Canon said, curiosity making his eyes sparkle. I'll get a ladder. It's sacred space, but we still have to dust." He returned from the sacristy, the small room off to the side of the altar area, with a tall aluminum stepladder. "Here, try this," he said to Josh.

Josh stood on the ladder under the center of the dome. He held his arms up to make himself as tall as possible, his shins against the top rung.

"'*O vos angeli,*'" Zia sang quietly. I heard her sing it, because I was standing right next to her. But what we heard, all of us, by our shared reaction, was the opposite, a grating, screeching sound, that drove our hands to our ears and made us all take a step back from the circle. Josh tottered on the top of the ladder, but kept his balance.

Suddenly the lights flickered, the candles were blown out, and an icy breeze like fingers of fog filled the church.

"Quick!" Dr. Canon said. "Follow me! This way! Now!" He helped Josh off the ladder and ushered us all into the sacristy. He pointed at an Oriental rug. "Under there is a hatch. Lift it, go down the ladder. Go to the eastern wall," he pointed to our left, the same end of the church that the altar stood against. "Feel up the wall from the floor, five bricks up, and seven bricks from the north wall. There's a gap in the mortar. Use your fingers to push into the gap and you'll find the way out. Take this." He handed Dilani a flashlight. "Go quickly and do not look back. No matter what." He nodded at us, turned, walked through the door, and shut us into the sacristy. A deep booming sound swelled on the other side of the door and the smell of soot and tar flooded my nostrils. Josh yanked back the rug and opened the hatch. We scrambled down the ladder, Dilani leading the way. We were in some kind of storage room, dank, with dirt floors. Jugs of sacramental wine, wooden crates of candles cushioned in straw, and piles of moldering prayer books lined the walls. A rat scurried away from the eastern wall as Dilani swung the torch toward it. Zia counted the bricks while Dilani shone the light on the wall and mouthed a thank you to the departing rat. Zia pressed her fingers into the hollow in the mortar. A section of bricks fell into a small tunnel, just large enough for us to crawl through. "Go," said Josh. "I'll try to stack the bricks back in place."

"Don't take too long," Zia urged. I could feel the damp cold that had invaded the church coming into the tunnel behind us.

The light from the flashlight bounced off the sides of the tunnel. At least if we met any more rodents, Dilani was first in line for reasoning with them, or whatever you did to get them not to sink their teeth into you. I tried not to think about it and kept crawling. After about five minutes we stopped.

"I'm shutting off the torch," Dilani whispered. A warm light was coming from a space in front of us, and I caught the whiff of coffee, freshly brewed. The tunnel widened to where it was possible to crouch, then stand, then walk. We turned a corner, and found ourselves on one side of a metal gate. We could hear voices and music from a room beyond, just around another corner. We looked at one another, wondering where we were. We were covered in dust and our pants legs were filthy. Dilani pushed on the gate. It creaked slightly as it swung open. She looked at us and shrugged. We all nodded and tried to pat the dust off ourselves and each other. We walked through the gate, turned the corner and found ourselves in a softly lit room with a couch, a few armchairs, and some wooden tables and chairs. A young man wearing a dark knit cap was sitting in one of the armchairs, his back to us, listening to something on his laptop through his ear buds. As we walked by, he blew on the contents of the paper cup he held gingerly in both hands. He took a sip and looked at us blankly, apparently not interested or surprised that we had materialized from nowhere. Or maybe he knew about the tunnel. I turned around and saw a small sign mounted on the wall. "Around this corner a gate leads to a tunnel sealed since 1900. The tunnel was once used as part of the Underground Railway, connecting this building to the historic church of St. Hildegard of Bingen. During the Revolutionary War it may have been used by privateers working on the side of the British to smuggle goods out to ships waiting in the harbor."

I pictured Dr. Canon with a shovel and pick ax unblocking the tunnel so it could provide safe passage again.

We arrived in a larger room, where baristas made coffee drinks and customers chatted around tables or worked on laptops, a hipster coffee shop in the basement level of an old building. Seizing the opportunity for a caffeine fix, and trying to make it look like we fit in, Zia bought us all cappuccinos to go. We left the shop and climbed the stairs to the street level and saw the church on the other side of the traffic circle. All the stained glass windows were dark. Light no longer glowed from within. The soot and tar smell hung heavy in the air, now mixing with a tinge of gasoline, but no one else seemed to notice. I said a silent prayer for Dr. Canon's safety as we walked toward the T-station that would take us back to the school, I hoped, before the curfew.

As we descended the stairs to the subway station, a sharp noise cut into the quiet of the night. Was it the squeal of the subway train's brakes as it pulled to a stop? Or was it the sound of a stained glass window being shattered?

§

The next morning Dilani and I went straight to the astronomy lab. We had received a tour as part of our GYSP orientation from a cheerful research assistant named Fred. We found Fred sitting behind his huge computer monitor, squinting at something on the screen through his thick dark-rimmed engineer glasses.

"Hiya, Ladies," Fred said, looking up at us. "What's up?"

"We need your help," I said. "Can you tell us when and where a particular version of the night sky would appear?"

"Do you have a picture?"

I handed him my sketch.

"These X's are stars, right?"

"Yes," I said, a little stung. I wasn't an artist, but I thought it was obvious.

"I wasn't criticizing, just making sure. Precision is important for accuracy. Let's do this on the big screen."

We went through the double doors marked "Planetarium."

"Have a seat," Fred said. "Anywhere." He sat down at the desk near the door and turned on the computer. We took two seats nearby. We could hear him moving a mouse around and making clicking sounds.

"The larger the X, the larger the star, correct?" Fred called out.

"Uh huh," I called back over my shoulder from my tilted-back seat.

"This should just take a second," he said. "Enjoy your ride through the nocturnal stratosphere."

He turned the lights down. A bright, starry sky appeared on the dome above us. Near the bottom edge of the sky, today's date appeared, along with our longitude and latitude. Suddenly, the sky began to swirl. Lights of stars and planets flashed, grew, and disappeared. Streaks of light surged through the darkness. The date stamp was streaming backwards, but so quickly, I couldn't read it. The whirling sky picked up speed, then abruptly slowed until stars clicked into place. The date and location stamp read June 21, 3445 BCE. 32.5364° N, 44.4208° E.

Fred spoke, "We're in Iraq. Known as Babylon then, of course. More precisely, a place known as the Plains of Shinar. Where'd you get this?"

I didn't answer. Why did that place sound familiar? I noticed a little hourglass shape was blinking at the end of the line, just after the longitude and latitude notation. "Does that mean anything?" I asked, pointing toward the blinking hourglass, hoping to deflect Fred's question.

"It means the same configuration of constellations is going to happen again soon."

"When?" Dilani asked.

Fred put the cursor over the hourglass and clicked. "Exactly two weeks from now. It won't be in exactly the same place as the first time due to shifts in the earth's rotation. It will take a little longer to find out where. Where did you say you got this?"

Then I remembered. The Tower of Babel was built on the Plains of Shinar!

"Sorry, Fred," I said, getting up and pulling Dilani out of her seat. I grabbed my drawing from Fred's hand. "We've got to run, but we'll come back to see what you find as the next location."

"Uh, sure," said Fred. "What's the rush?"

"Don't want to be late to class," I lied. I wanted to get back to the others as soon as possible to tell them what we learned.

"Yeah, thanks, Fred! Great show!" Dilani said as we hustled out of the lab.

"What just happened?" Dilani asked when we got out to the sidewalk.

"The constellation was the sky over the Plains of Shinar."

"Shinar as in Babel? As in 'Tower of'? Where people built a high tower and tried to reach heaven?"

"But God got mad and scrambled their language and they had to stop building. Yup, that's the place. Zia was on to something with her experiment in dissonance. Somehow the dome at St. Hildegard's replicated the effect of the Tower of Babel, complete discord. The constellation on the ceiling is supposed to point people to that story. Babel was a place that went from harmony, or at least people working on a common project, to total discord and confusion."

"Do you think it's significant that the constellation is going to appear again soon?" Dilani asked.

"I don't know. Could there be another Tower of Babel? That sounds pretty far-fetched."

We hurried off to the refectory for breakfast, lost in our thoughts.

We got our trays and sat down next to Zia, Neith, Miyako, and Josh, anxious to tell them about our discovery. But before we could start, Josh asked in a harsh whisper, "Did you hear?"

"Hear what?" I asked, a little too loudly.

"Shh!" He looked around. "On the news this morning. St. Hildegard of Bingen Church burned to the ground last night, shortly after 10 PM."

Dilani gasped.

"Act normal," Neith said, placing his hand gently on Dilani's arm.

"The place was completely incinerated," Josh said. "Charred ash is all that's left. Even the cornerstone is gone."

"But how—" I stammered.

"Firefighters were called right away, but they couldn't put it out. Even once they chopped through the front doors and smashed in some of the windows to put fire hoses through, they couldn't extinguish the flames. Fire chief gave an interview this morning saying he'd never seen anything like it."

"Is Dr. Canon okay?" I asked.

"No one has been able to locate him," Neith replied.

"Greek fire," Miyako said, her voice somber. "I bet if they test the ash they'll find antimony and an accelerant."

"How long until the police come looking for us?" Zia asked. "We must have been the last ones in the church, other than Dr. Canon."

"And whoever came in when we did our little experiment," Dilani said.

"Or whatever came in," I said. "It felt like icy fog, but I didn't see anyone, did you?" I looked around at the others.

"What if someone knows we were in the church and thinks we had something to do with it?" Zia asked, panic edging her voice.

"We tell the truth," Josh said calmly.

"We were visiting the rector, we noticed something really weird about sound under the dome, a mysterious cold front came into the locked church, Dr. Canon escorted us to a tunnel that was blocked up in 1900, we got cappuccinos to go, and came back here." I reported, trying to sound calm. "We probably shouldn't mention that Miyako knows how to make Greek fire."

"Yeah, that sounds strange," Josh said.

"Let's hope Dr. Canon escaped," Zia said sadly.

We sat quietly for a moment until Neith asked, "What now?"

Dilani and I told them about what we found at the planetarium. "We should check back with Fred about the date of the next occurrence, but we need to be careful not to let anyone know where the sketch was made, especially now."

I looked at Zia, who exhaled, then said, "Okay, so we did an experiment under the dome. Without an obstruction, the acoustics were glorious, gorgeous, perfect. With an obstruction, in this case, Josh on a ladder, harmony turned to absolute ugliness, discord. Something painful even."

We all nodded.

She went on. "That's when we all felt the cold whatever it was, and Dr. Canon whisked us out. Just after the discordant sound, right?"

We all nodded again.

"It turns out, according to what Dilani and Kaia discovered, that the church's dome is a replica of the sky above the Plains of Shinar in just the right era when archaeologists say people first built ziggurats, ancient towers, like the Tower of Babel."

"That's right," I said, "and the sky will be like that again, exactly two weeks from now, but we don't know where yet."

"Josh on the step ladder was like a mini Tower of Babel under a mini Plains of Shinar sky," Zia said. "We discover that, and suddenly we have to stop the experiment. In fact, we can never recreate it, because the church is cinders and the dome is destroyed."

"So, whoever, or whatever that was that Dr. Canon saved us from, didn't want us to learn anything more," Neith said.

"Or, had gotten the information it needed and stopped the experiment before we tried anything else," Josh said.

Josh said, "Sounds like we have exactly two weeks, or until the arson squad drags us in for questioning, to figure out what's going on."

"Or, until Dr. Canon is found safe and sound," Zia said. We nodded, but none of us had much hope of that.

Josh said, "We really need to find out more about the Tower of Babel."

"Universal language, too," Neith said. "I'm curious about why St. Hildegard would try to invent one, and why a universal language and Babel are connected. Wait a second," he said and pointed to a notice on the refectory bulletin board. "Looks like this is our lucky day."

"Sure," said Zia, "if you don't count possibly being wanted by the arson squad, and the fact that a nice man who was trying to help us is probably dead, and that really creepy things are happening all around us, I'm sure this is a very lucky day."

"Okay, so it wasn't the best way to say it, but look. This is exactly what we need." Neith snatched a flyer off the bulletin board and held it in front of us. "Who's up for Conlang Con?"

35

AD 1538, MALMESBURY ABBEY, WILTSHIRE, ENGLAND

The Province of Birds and Angels

B rother Aylward tugged his gray wool cloak up around his shoulders and shook his hands, trying to release the knots from his fingers and get some more blood flowing into them. He reminded himself of one of the mistel thrushes who bathe in the horses' water trough outside the monastery's stable, then flap their wings dry before taking flight. He was wearing his writing gloves, the ash-colored ones with no fingertips, and his pudgy hands did resemble the little thrushes with their gray and white feathers and fat bellies. The monk would have been much happier wearing his felt mittens given the cold in the scriptorium, but they turned his deft hands into paws. His task as scriptor, copying the monastery's manuscripts, demanded a precision impossible if his fingers couldn't guide his quill pen and drag the ink exactly where he intended it to go.

The monk exhaled and saw his own breath. He chuckled, but it sounded more melancholy than cheerful. Brother Aylward tried to remain positive, despite the recent hardships, which included the monastery's being on a restricted supply of firewood since Henry the Eighth had begun dissolving the monasteries three years earlier. Rumors wheeled like a flock of swallows that the king had his eye on Malmesbury too, despite its importance as a center for learning and the skills of its copyists. If gossips had any purchase on the truth, King Henry planned to strip the monastery of its treasures and sell the entire property to one of his wealthy friends. Brother Aylward shook his head. Hadn't Jesus overturned the moneychangers' tables in the temple? And now here was the king planning to sell the temple itself. At least the monk had important work to do while they waited to see if the regal axe would indeed fall.

He put his spectacles on and gazed out the window next to him. He needed his glasses to see any distance beyond a few feet, but his near-sight was perfect. He was certain that his visual sharpness, at least at short range, contributed to the excellence of his work as a copyist.

He loved his work, but almost as much, he loved where he did his work. Abbot Geoffrey, about three hundred years before, had moved all the scriptors to where Aylward now served, in a room that shared a wall with the monastery kitchen on its west side, and the best windows in the abbey on the east. The light was ideal for their work, and during his brief breaks he put on his glasses and engaged in one of his great pleasures, watching the many birds who frequented the abbey grounds: the little olive-brown chiffchaffs who perched in the elms; the happy wrens who nested in the abbey stonework; the pipit meadows who sang as they took to the air and did not stop until they parachuted recklessly, with wings half-closed, back to terra firma. And, during times when the monastery knew plenty, the fires in the kitchen always burned, making the scriptorium delightfully warm. Aylward's work, the birds, the proximity to the kitchen, and the fact that the abbey's kitchener sometimes gave Brother Aylward extra food during the day contributed to the copyist's generous girth, and made this the perfect assignment. Thinking of the possibility that the monastery would be shut brought a cloud of downheartedness around the monk, despite his best efforts to trust in God's providence and hope that King Henry might yet relent.

Brother Aylward watched as a sleek black jackdaw flew past and light-ed on the gray stone tower that loomed over the abbey grounds to his right. The bird's silver head caught a glint of sunshine. It was from this tower that one of the abbey's most famous monks had once jumped, not to commit that tragic sin of which one has no opportunity to repent, but in order to fly.

Everyone knew about Brother Eilmer, who had lived five hundred years before, who somehow had the notion that he could master the art of flight, which, as anyone knew, was the province of birds and angels alone. "And also winged insects," Aylward thought. "And the flying squirrel and the Exocoetidae, the so-called flying fish, although theirs is not true flight," he mused, "but rather gliding." Brother Aylward found tales of flying unicorns and dragons far-fetched, and did not believe they continued to exist, at least since the time of Noah's flood.

Despite the absurdity of his project, Brother Eilmer constructed a pair of wings from leather and wood and climbed the tower stairs to the roof on a particularly windy day. Using leather straps, he affixed the wings to his hands and his feet. Judging a moment he thought to be propitious, he climbed over the crenellation, and flung himself off the tower, arms and legs extended—a great tonsured jackdaw, but with a gray woolen stomach of monk's robe and pinions of calf hide and knotty pine.

Brother Eilmer had flown just over a furlong before his experiment crashed to an end and broke both of his legs. He spent the rest of his life with a limp and a reputation for pushing the limits of what humans would be permitted by the divine.

Brother Aylward wondered what would possess a man to attempt flight. Was it an envy of birds? Or had something else given Eilmer the idea?

Aylward took off his spectacles, turned his head back to his desk, and got ready to begin his next task. He felt a small pang of regret that he had allowed himself even a short pause to shake his hands and gaze out the window. For the past year, monks in the scriptorium were assigned to work double shifts, excused from their routine chores in order to devote all their work time to copying. If Henry Rex did decide to sell off the contents of the monastery, the abbot did not want their collection to fall into the hands of people who would not respect the treasure of which the monks had been the stewards for nearly eight hundred years. The abbot knew it was possible that Henry or one of his abettors might allow the library to be ransacked, documents taken or burned for the thrill of mayhem or to provide warmth. So the monks copied and copied, trying to make sure they had duplicates of every manuscript, book, codex, and scroll for safekeeping. As the scriptor completed each copy, he took it to Brother Wystan, the armarius, head of the scriptorium, who alone knew whether the original or the copy was being sent out of the monastery for preservation and where the documents were being stored. Brother Aylward thought that to have both pieces of information could tempt even the most pious among them to commit the sin of fraud or larceny, but, being obedient, he kept his thoughts of the possibility of trespass to himself.

He looked at the next manuscript on the pile the librarian had left on his desk. Its label identified it as an acquisition from a sister Benedictine monastery in Disibodenberg, in the Rhineland. The monastery was well-known, even this far away. Their abbess had once been Hildegard, a woman, of course, yet a person of science, letters, music, and the arts.

The manuscript was brief. Just one page, front and back, with a splendid multi-colored illumination along the top of the front page. Aylward leaned close so he could see the details of the pictures. The three frames were exquisitely executed and showed three biblical stories. The first, Aylward had rarely seen, although he knew the story. Large winged beings swooped down from heaven toward women with arms raised as if to fend them off. Very tall men in gold and silver robes stood to the side. "Ah," thought Aylward. "Genesis 6:4, 'The Nephilim were on the earth in those days—and also afterwards—when the sons of God went into the daughters of humans, who bore children to them.'" He marveled at how effectively that the illuminator had portrayed a look of panic on the women's faces and the appearance of malice on the angels.' Such emotion in a miniscule space.

The next frame was easily identifiable: Genesis chapters 6 and 7, Noah and the ark. Tiny pairs of animals were lined up to board the ship, while storm clouds hung low overhead. Infinitesimal drops of rain were starting to fall. Aylward was cheered to see that the illuminator had included several pairs of birds hovering above the ark, ready to gain refuge from the incipient flood.

The third frame, like the first, was more rarely portrayed in Aylward's experience. Yet, he identified it immediately. It portrayed events of Genesis 9, the aftermath of Noah's drunkenness. Noah was the first man to plant vines and make wine, that substance so great a blessing and curse. The scene showed two moments. Noah's sons covering the unconscious Noah with a garment, and the subsequent cursing of Ham by Noah for Ham's having viewed his father's shame. Aylward nodded in appreciation of the illuminator's work and prepared to begin what he thought would be a simple manuscript containing Genesis chapters six through nine.

Aylward always began his work with a prayer, and also by smoothing the parchment gently with his fingertips as if connecting with his counterpart from centuries before who might reach out to him from the page. It was a way to remember he was part of a long chain of preservers of tradition, handing sacred texts from one generation to the next.

His fingertips felt something, even in his gentle graze. He touched the parchment again, just lightly, and was certain it bore something that he could feel but not see. As he brushed from left to right, his fingertips taking in a couple of lines of the Scriptural text, he could also feel a texture that did not match the elegant inked letters. He felt a pattern running vertically as well. He ran his fingers up and down the page and, indeed, felt the presence of another script written perpendicular to the one that appeared in the bold, black characters he was assigned to copy.

Closing his eyes so as not to be distracted by the visible script, he tried to detect with his fingers what might exist, invisibly, on the page. Was the page a palimpsest—a twice-used page?

Brother Aylward was familiar with palimpsests. It was a common practice to reuse vellum and parchment because of their dearness. A good goatskin parchment or calfskin vellum should certainly be used again if at all possible, rather than being thrown away simply because the words were no longer considered valuable. Brother Aylward had seen the parchmenter at Malmesbury scrape the ink from a lovely piece of vellum using a very sharp lunellum, its crescent shaped blade reflecting shards of light from the fire all over the walls of the chamber in which he worked.

But this was different. There were no signs of scraping. No one had tried to remove the writing he could feel but not see. Someone had inscribed lines of text over top of the horizontal lines of Genesis story in neat rows of some miniscule he could not identify. He turned the paper a quarter turn so the visible black lines were now sideways to him.

He squinted his eyes and held the paper so that sunlight raked across it to see if he could make out the letters. He could see shadowy raised letters, embossed onto the page, but they were very faint and indecipherable.

He scratched his head. The quickest and easiest thing to do would be to copy the writing he could see, be finished with his task, and move on to the next item in his pile. If this were a true palimpsest, the invisible writing was surely not the point of the manuscript. It served merely as an accidental backdrop for the text assigned to him.

But the hidden writing was precise and filled the page. What if the hidden writing was the reason the old page had been saved?

His first idea was to rub some graphite over the page and see if that revealed the hidden letters. He rejected the idea as quickly as it had come to him since he knew he would obscure the beautiful visible text. The graphite would be difficult to remove entirely, and he could not imagine taking the damaged page to Brother Wystan and explaining that it was he who had desecrated the biblical text. He decided to go quickly to Brother Kendrick who worked in the infirmary and engage his assistance.

Brother Kendrick was a man of slight build. If Brother Aylward was a mistel thrush, Brother Kendrick was a whinchat, small and darting, moving from perch to perch. Even as Brother Aylward entered the infirmary, he could see the busy monk hopping from where a paste bubbled in an iron pot hanging over the fire, to a low table on which strips of linen were waiting to be rolled for bandages, to a glass cylinder whose vaporous contents looked like the monk's breath in the chill room. Brother Kendrick looked up and waved Brother Aylward to join him by the cylinder.

"I haven't long," said Brother Aylward as he thrust the mysterious page under Brother Kendrick's pert nose and explained the problem.

"Try this," Brother Kendrick chirped and handed Brother Aylward two small glass containers. One contained a dozen tiny gray metallic pellets. The other contained a clear liquid. "When you are ready to proceed, dissolve the beads in the liquid. Use a fine brush and apply the solution carefully over where you feel each letter. If the letters were inscribed using an iron nib, the solution will stain any iron residue and bring the letters into full view. If nothing is there, you won't corrupt the beautiful apparent text."

Aylward thanked his friend and turned to go. Suddenly Brother Kendrick's delicate hand lighted on Aylward's shoulder, causing the tiny pellets in the container in Aylward's hand to rattle. "Whatever you do, do not ingest the beads or the solution. Use them carefully and do not eat or touch anything after handling them before you wash thoroughly. They are toxic and can be withstood inside the body in only very small doses. Bring everything you don't use back to me immediately."

"What are these?" Brother Aylward asked, holding up the pellets. He was grateful for the warning, but now a little nervous.

"Antimony," said Brother Kendrick.

But when Aylward examined the script, he drew back in surprise. Not Latin, as he expected, but the very script of Abbess Hildegard herself, her *Lingua Ignota*. Aylward clapped his hands together in delight. He had seen, but never been asked to copy something by the great Abbess, and here was a manuscript written in her own language, the one she had promoted as a universal language, a tongue that could be used and understood by all, a way to speak and write that would undo Babel.

Aylward cherished the idea of the universality of language, although even these five centuries hence, her idea had not caught on. Scholars debated its name, *Lingua Ignota*, or "Unknown Language." Was the name given by Hildegard claiming some divine or unknown source for its origin? Or was it rather a taunt, given later, when it had failed in Hildegard's purpose for it?

Aylward preferred the former interpretation. He had even taken the liberty of copying out her script and its grammar from a book in their library, and he stored this copy at his desk. Monks are supposed to own nothing as individuals, as he well knew. He considered this not a private copy, but rather a tool, should the need for it ever arise. Having his own copy would save him the time of having to go to the library to find and retrieve the book. What a gift of providence that he should find himself holding such a manuscript.

As he began to make the copy, he paused. Should he not allow himself the pleasure of not just copying, but also translating? Whenever else would he have the opportunity to read the words of Scripture in Abbess Hildegard's own language? Each translator brings something fresh, some small nuance. He promised himself only a verse, or possibly two, so that he did not spend too much precious time on this unrequired activity.

But as he began, he noticed not the familiar words of Holy Scripture. He was sure they did not come from Genesis chapter six, nor anywhere else he could remember.

What he found, instead, was this:

> *My Dear Noah,*
>
> *By now you have been given instructions you cannot comprehend for a purpose you cannot fathom. You fear that even if you comply, your efforts will ultimately be in vain. You must say yes.*

What was this document?

Brother Aylward sat with the deciphered page in his hand, his heart racing and head ringing. He was now sure that the point of the manuscript—what made it so valuable and worth saving for all these centuries in Malmesbury's library—was not the Genesis stories, but the hidden palimpsest text, recorded in the almost unknown *Lingua Ignota*. It was, in fact, a letter to Noah from his great-grandfather, the Patriarch and Scribe Enoch.

The monk wiped his brow. He grabbed both his translation and the original page and hurried to the armarius's room. Brother Wystan called out for Aylward to enter.

"I have found something that needs your immediate attention," Brother Aylward said, holding the parchments toward his superior.

Brother Wystan took them and looked at them, his eyebrows rising in apparent surprise as Brother Aylward relayed how he had discovered the hidden text. He brought it over to his desk where a candle was burning and held it close to the flame.

"Who else has seen this?" he asked Aylward.

"Brother Kendrick saw the page. It was he who provided the solution to reveal the hidden script."

"But did he see what was written?"

"No. I came directly to you as soon as I translated it. I realize that translation was beyond my task, but it seemed correct to me to attempt it. No one else has seen it," Brother Aylward said.

"You have done well, Brother Aylward," the armarius said.

"Shall I proceed to make a copy of the now-revealed text for safe keeping?" Brother Aylward inquired.

"You will leave these pages with me, Brother Aylward." Brother Wystan's voice had a sharp edge to it that seemed to surprise even Brother Wystan. He softened his face and voice and touched Aylward lightly on the arm. "You have done well and your attention to detail, as always, brings you credit. But your work on this page is finished. Continue with your next manuscript."

"Yes. Of course," said Brother Aylward, wishing he could take one more look at the mysterious text. Perhaps he should have made a copy before bringing it to the Brother Wystan. He could feel his face warm with shame for the doubt concerning his superior that was seeping in at the edges of his heart.

"Go now, Brother Aylward," Brother Wystan repeated, nodding at his fellow monk. Then he added, "Do not mention this to anyone. It could cause unnecessary excitement, and at this moment productivity is more important than intrigue. Do you understand?"

Now it was Aylward's turn to nod. "Yes, Brother," he said, fighting the urge to snatch the pages back from the other monk's hand, at least for one more look at what they contained.

"The angels will reward you for your work," the armarius said in a sober tone.

"Yes, Brother," Aylward said, but he thought it an odd remark, blasphemous even. Why would the angels, rather than the Almighty, reward him? He stepped back into the hall and felt suddenly cold again.

Brother Aylward sighed. The next manuscript was straightforward enough, a ninth century copy of the Gospel according to Matthew without illustration. He was well into the second chapter and the story of the visit of the Magi, guided by the star to the babe at Bethlehem, then warned by an angel in a dream to return home by another way, when he put his quill down.

Several hours had passed since he had given the Noah Letter manuscript and translation to Brother Wystan, yet his heart still felt heavy. He thought he should let go of his curiosity, which could lead to nothing good but only distraction from the task at hand. But every mention of an angel in his new assignment—the visitation of an angel to Joseph to tell him about Mary's pregnancy with the Christ child, the angel's appearance to the magi, another angelic visit to tell Joseph to take Mary and the baby to flee to Egypt to escape King Herod's wrath—brought Brother Wystan's strange benediction and dismissal to mind.

Brother Aylward straightened from his hunched copying position and rubbed the back of his neck, rolling his head from side to side to work out the stiffness. Through the window, he caught a glimpse of a slim dark shape moving toward the monastery entrance below. Donning his spectacles, he could see the shape was a person in a long black cloak. He presumed it would be a man coming to the monastery, but the figure moved like a woman and had the slight build of a woman. The cloak's hood was pulled high over the wearer's head so only a soft jawline showed. The person had a confident stride, and the black cloak stood out against the snow that had fallen during the night. Alyward saw the door open and the porter welcome the visitor inside. A rule of the Benedictine Order was to welcome everyone who arrived at the abbey. As the Epistle to the Hebrews had admonished, "Be not forgetful to entertain strangers: for thereby some have entertained angels unawares."

Brother Aylward sighed and chastised himself. *Return to your work.* A verse of Psalm 42 came to mind—*Why so restless, o my soul? Why so disquieted within me?* Then he immediately began to recite the entire Psalm aloud from the beginning:

> *Vindicate me, O God,*
> *And plead my cause against an ungodly nation;*
> *Oh, deliver me from the deceitful and unjust man!*

He stopped himself as the image of Brother Wystan came to mind. He removed his spectacles, said a brief prayer of rededication to his task and started to copy Matthew chapter three.

He looked up again when he heard voices coming from the armarius's chamber. One was Brother Wystan's, but the other was unfamiliar. In a monastery where every brother took a turn reading the scriptures aloud during the offices and reciting from an edifying text during meals, he knew well every monk's voice. It must be the visitor, and the visitor must be a woman, with such a high pitch. However, if smoke had a timbre, it would be this. Brother Aylward couldn't make out any of the words—*now he had been reduced to eavesdropping, may the Holy One forgive him!*—but he continued to try.

What caught his attention was the sound of elation. Both voices were excited, giddy. He listened again. This was not the solemn joy that under-girded every holy Mass. It was more like the scavenger magpie's chattering *chip-chip-chip* when she returns to her nest in triumph, clutching the broken body of the chick of another bird. He shuddered, and thought of the dread counting song he had learned as a child, numbering magpies as ill omens: *one for sorrow, two for still birth, three for dread, four for death, five for silver, six for gold, seven for a secret not to be told.*

The armarius's chamber was quiet again. Brother Aylward could see, even without his glasses, the cloaked figure heading back across the snow with something under her arm. A manuscript chest? When the figure reached the gate, Aylward gasped. He thought he saw the black creature take flight and pause atop the abbey tower. He fumbled to raise his glasses to the bridge of his nose just as he saw two glistening black wings unfurl and carry the creature out of sight. He must have his spectacles checked. Surely the lenses needed refitting to be playing such tricks of perspective. It must have been a raven.

A moment later Brother Wystan stood at Brother Aylward's desk.

"My brother," he said gravely. "I have not forgotten the promise of your reward."

The scriptor blinked up at the armarius. "I deserve no reward," he said, "for fulfilling my appointed tasks." His voice shook slightly, and he blinked nervously as he thought about how much he was not attending to his tasks.

"No, the angels await you," Brother Wystan said as his eyes alighted on the glass container of antimony solution still sitting on the desk. "But you must go greet them to inherit your reward."

Brother Aylward followed the armarius's gaze to the solution.

"Here is grace, Brother," Wystan said, a smile of satisfaction lighting his face. Aylward thought of a cat clutching a dead sparrow.

"Drinking this draught will bring you to the angels faster and with less pain than my dispatching you," he said into Aylward's ear, while he pressed the sharp tip of a lunellum into Aylward's side.

"But why?" Aylward stammered. "And the angels will not welcome me for drinking poison by my own hand, as you well know," he pleaded, tears of confusion rolling down his cheeks.

"I did not say which angels," Wystan sneered, and tilted the glass container into Aylward's parted lips.

36

KAIA

Lamination

The flyer had a logo at the top, a purple background with a stylized red ziggurat against a yellow sun. Whether the sun was rising or setting I couldn't tell. Beneath the logo, in large letters, was written:

> CONLANG CON
> Convention Center Downtown
> Friday and Saturday
> All Conlangers and Conlang-Curious are welcome!
> Registration $25.00—Includes Totebag!

"Perfect!" Neith said. "Let's go!" He sounded way too enthusiastic. But he was right, this would be exactly the right place to find out more about Constructed Languages and maybe what St. Hildegard was up to or why the Tower of Babel was so important.

We arrived at the convention center, paid our fee, collected our totebags, and hung our laminated participant badges on lanyards around our necks. The plastic smell of the badges was strong but calmed me. I had my badge. I belonged here, even if I had no aptitude for languages.

I examined my badge. Beneath "Paid Registrant" were the words *Pagis Aliganto.*

Neith looked at his badge. "That's 'Paid Registrant' in Esperanto, probably the most famous and widely-spoken conlang."

"You are going to have a great day, my geeky friend," Josh said, and poked Neith in the ribs.

We walked toward a signboard where the day's schedule was posted.

"Look," Zia pointed. A table to the right of the signboard was piled with T-Shirts that had the icon we had seen at the church of St. Hildegard receiving her visions with the words, "If you're a Conglanger, say" and then a bunch of squiggles. Neith got out St. Hildegard's *Lingua Ignota* alphabet key and deciphered. "It says, 'Thanks Hilda!'"

"I kind of want one," Zia said quietly.

A group of people walked past us all dressed in similar gear: black pants and tunics, overlaid with metallic gray armor vests and large shoulder pads. They all wore wigs with big, frizzy hair, and sported glued-on oversized, deeply grooved foreheads. Like us, they carried Conglang Con totebags. One of them dropped a piece of paper. Neith picked it up and said something to the man who dropped it. He took the paper and gurgled something back to Neith.

"No way!" Dilani said, "You speak Klingon?"

"Not fluently," he said, his cheeks reddening with embarrassment. "I had an uncle, a serious Trekkie who wanted me to learn Klingon, so for a while he spoke to me only in Klingon. 'Immersion Klingon,' he called it. It was fun. Drove my parents crazy, since my uncle and I could talk without anyone else knowing what we were saying. I never went as far as donning the rubber forehead. My aunt made him stop. She said the constant guttural noises ruined family gatherings."

We looked at the schedule. There were three tracks. Track One was "That's Conlangtainment!" and had talks about invented languages for games, television, and films.

"Bard Homer is here. That explains those Dothraki warriors." Neith pointed at a group of men, some wearing fake beards, dressed in leather loincloths, sandals, and necklaces made of enormous beads and feathers. "Bard invented the languages used in a couple of Sci-Fi Channel TV series, and a big one for HBO. That talk's going to be packed."

Track Two was "Conlang: the Journey Within." The talks in this section were about inventing your own language for self-expression. One of the talks was titled, "So What if No One Else Understands? My Own Private Conlang."

The third track, "Coming Together the Conlang Way," was about the merits of invented languages, that they were supposedly easier to understand or learn than languages that developed naturally. These people seemed to be in search of a universal language, something everyone could use. There were talks on Esperanto ("Why Doesn't It Catch On?"), Intralingua ("Not Just for Scientists Anymore"), and Mathematics as the true universal language ("It All Adds Up—Everyone Uses Numbers").

I wondered if people in the various tracks got along.

One presentation was listed all by itself at the bottom of the schedule. "Reconstructing the Unconstructed Construct: The Original Language," by Rowan LePlage, ABD. Room 311, 2:00 PM. 'The Original Language' caught my eye. Plus, his talk looked kind of lonely hanging out there all by itself.

It was just about two o'clock. We took the elevator to the third floor and followed the arrows toward Room 311. Room 310 was completely filled, and several people were sitting outside on the floor in the hall. We stepped over their outstretched legs and made our way into Room 311. It was small, airless, and had no windows. Its lighting came from those fluorescent bulbs that make everyone's skin look slightly green. Five folding chairs were set up in front of a podium to which a Conlang Con logo had been affixed.

Only one person was in the room when we arrived. Wearing a flannel shirt and jeans, he was sitting behind a folding table, his loafer-clad feet propped up on top of it. His thinning auburn hair was pulled back in a ponytail. He was reading a paperback, *Don Quixote*, through his rectangular framed glasses when he noticed us. He looked back down at his book and said, "You want room 310, next door. Follow the herd."

"Are you Mr. LePlage?" I asked.

He looked up, surprised.

"Yes," he said, pushing himself up to a full sitting position. His 'yes' came across as a question mark.

"What does 'ABD' stand for?" I asked.

"It means I have completed my PhD, except for my dissertation, 'All But Dissertation.' I'm in my nineteenth year of graduate work. Wait. Who sent you? Why are you here?" he asked, eyeing us suspiciously.

"Aren't you speaking on the original language?" I persisted, wondering why he seemed so surprised to see us.

He cleared his throat. "That is my topic. You want to stay?" he asked.

"We want to know more about the original language."

His face broke out in a smile. He took a thick sheaf of papers from a battered leather briefcase on the floor, stood up, smoothed his flannel shirt, and went to the podium. We sat in the folding chairs. He glanced at his watch, and said, "Somebody better close the door. They're going to get rowdy next door."

He riffled the pages he had set on the podium and straightened his glasses. *Oh no,* I thought, *he's not going to read all of that.*

"Reconstructing the Unconstructed Construct: The Original Language, by Rowan LePlage."

Mr. LePlage inhaled, as if he needed a lot of air for what he was about to read at us. Josh seized the opportunity to speak, "Since it's just us, can you just tell us about the original language?"

Mr. LePlage looked stunned. He clearly wasn't used to being interrupted. He didn't seem used to having an audience either.

"Just tell you?" he asked.

"Yes. Since you're the expert, can you just tell us?"

Mr. LePlage perked up at 'expert.'

"Well," he cleared his throat. "Here are all these people making up languages—making them up!—for games, navel-gazing, what-have-you," he said, his disdain for adherents to Tracks One and Two apparent. "One group of conlangers, call them 'universalists,' if you will, wants to do something actually noble—make up a universal language everyone can use—"

His voice was drowned out by laughter and cheers coming from the other side of the partition that separated the fully-subscribed Room 310 from Room 311, which, I now noticed as I looked around, might actually have been a snack alcove for Room 310.

"Next they'll start with the Valerian drinking songs," he said, rolling his eyes and shaking his head.

A rowdy and melodic chorus rose from next door, deep voices singing together.

"The Conlang Con program committee invites me to give a presentation every year, even though no one ever comes. But clearly," he yelled toward the partition, "they have no respect!"

The singing died down and Mr. LePlage continued, "I can respect what the universalists are trying to do, but they are completely misguided."

He sounded pretty sure of himself for someone addressing a broom closet of high schoolers.

"What's the problem with the 'universalists'?" Josh asked.

"They are wasting time inventing—*constructing*—something that already exists!" Mr. LePlage exclaimed. "That's one of the reasons I get no respect here. I'm the only one who believes we can recover the original, universal language."

"There already is a universal language?" Neith asked, genuinely interested.

"Well, was," Mr. LePlage said, slumping slightly and looking a little deflated, as if something important had gone missing and he were somehow responsible. But he looked up and saw us waiting for him to continue and brightened up, happy to find himself lecturing to real, live, students. "I'm sure you already know the story of the Tower of Babel?"

We nodded.

"That story was told to explain the diversity of peoples and languages. Why don't we all use the same words? Understand one another? The Tower of Babel incident takes place after the flood, right?" he paused to see if we were following. We nodded, encouraging him to go on.

"Now remember, people were commanded to fill the earth, go everywhere, see new things, spread out, multiply!" He blushed slightly at 'multiply,' pushed his glasses back up to the bridge of his nose and went on. "But did they? No. All the people of the world gathered on the Plains of Shinar and started to build a great tower that would reach the heavens. Why?"

"We may have an inkling," Zia said under her breath. I thought of the horrible noise under the dome in the church.

Mr. LePlage stuck to the biblical storyline: "To make a name for themselves!" He pressed his fingers against his chest. "Fame. Fortune. Reputation." He shook his head, as if despairing at the Babel construction workers' folly. He was turning out to be quite the showman. "Of course, humans' misguided pursuit of fame is just one of the theories for why God decided to thwart construction. Some ancient rabbis said the builders were trying to reach heaven to take it by force, or that they constructed an idol at the top of the Tower. Why exactly God was so affronted isn't explained definitively within the story itself.

"For whatever reason, God put an end to their plans. Stopped construction on their skyscraper. How?" Dramatic pause. "By scrambling their language. Suddenly, bricklayer number one can't understand what bricklayer number two, standing right next to him, is talking about. 'What did you bring for lunch today?' he says, but the other guy looks at him like he just told him his pants are on fire. The foreman is yelling, 'We need more mortar on the thirty-sixth floor!' and the confused guy at the bottom, loading supplies at ground level, fills the basket full of rocks. Everything screeches to a halt.

"But notice," his eyes grew wide, "before then, everyone was speaking the same language. One universal language. And that's not all. It was the same language used from the very beginning. Not just universal, but *original*." He paused again.

Neith put up his hand.

"Yes?" Mr. LePlage said, pointing to Neith.

"*Who* used it from the very beginning? And do you mean the very, very beginning?"

"I do. This was the language the first humans, Adam and Eve in the biblical story, used with each other and with the animals too. The serpent addressed Eve in this tongue. And if God spoke creation into being, this is the language God used."

"*O prima vox, perquam omnes create sunt . . .* O first voice, through whom all creation was summoned . . ." Zia sang softly.

"You know Hildegard of Bingen," Mr. LePlage said. His eyes were shining and his nose got a little red. "A lot of people around here know about the great abbess's constructed language," he dabbed at his eye with a hanky he pulled from his pocket, "but not many can sing her music, and certainly not as beautifully."

"So," Neith said carefully, "you think this language existed, and that it still exists? And you are trying to find this original universal language, instead of constructing a new one?"

"Exactly!" Mr. LePlage beamed, clearly pleased with his own ability to explain his theory to a willing student.

"So, where is it?" Neith asked.

A round of enthusiastic applause erupted next door.

"Hooligans!" Mr. LePlage shouted at the wall.

The sound tapered off and he continued. "I've seen it. That is, I've seen a document written in the original language, with my own eyes, so I know it exists."

"Where is it?" Neith tried again.

"I don't know. Gone. Maybe forever." Mr. LePlage's face crumpled and he looked at the floor.

"Please go on," Dilani said soothingly.

"It's called 'The Book of Noah.' My dissertation director, Dr. Sturgeon, had a copy, maybe the only copy. Got it from two people who approached him in the bar he was known to frequent, a dive. Cheap beer, sticky floors, dim lighting. Usually pretty empty. The day after he got it, he told me a man and a woman wearing dark suits, sunglasses, and leather gloves came in while he was having his nightly Pimm's cups. He glanced up at the mirror behind the bar and saw one of them bolt the door. They sat down, one on each side of him. They were alone in the place, except for the bartender who stepped down to the far end of the bar and started polishing glasses. One of the dark suits slid a briefcase up on the bar next to him. It was handcuffed to the man's wrist. 'Dr. Sturgeon,' the woman said, 'we have some manuscripts you will find interesting.'

"Dr. Sturgeon was in charge of a big translation project, Dead Sea Scrolls, ancient fragments from stone jars in caves in the desert, that sort of thing, so his interest was piqued. But lots of people approached him with lots of different things, many of them faked or forged, so he said to them, 'This isn't Antiques Roadshow. What have you got?'

"The woman unlocked the briefcase and pulled out a piece of papyrus in an archival folder and handed it to Dr. Sturgeon.

"Dr. Sturgeon took a look and knew he was staring at a section of the Book of Isaiah, really old, possibly 2500 years old. He was definitely interested.

"Next the woman took out a cylindrical clay container, about the size of a tube of toothpaste, stuck a gloved finger inside, and slid out a rolled-up scroll. She held it up so Dr. Sturgeon could see. Dr. Sturgeon gasped so loudly the bartender started over, bringing the baseball bat he kept behind the bar. 'No! No! We're fine,' Dr. Sturgeon assured him and waved him away. He said to the pair, 'A letter from the Queen of Sheba to King Solomon! Written with authentic Ethiopian charcoal ink!' He couldn't believe what these two dealers were offering. But it was the third document that intrigued him most, and, most likely, ruined his life.

"After seeing the genuineness of the first two manuscripts, Dr. Sturgeon knew they must have serious connections in the antiquities market. The third manuscript would likely prove to be genuine as well. The woman set out a soft paper mat. Then she pulled out a larger scroll, and carefully unrolled it on top of the mat in front of Dr. Sturgeon. 'What is it?' Dr. Sturgeon asked. He didn't recognize the script and couldn't make out any of the words.

"'The Book of Noah,' the woman said very quietly.

"'It exists?' Dr. Sturgeon gulped. 'A couple of ancient sources refer to it, but everyone in the scholarly community thinks it's been lost forever!'"

"'Before your very eyes,' the woman told him, tapping her gloved index finger on the corner of the opened scroll.

"'What do you want for it?' Sturgeon asked. The words rushed out too quickly, made him sound desperate, but he was afraid they would vanish with the scroll and he would never see it again, or, worse, they would offer it to someone else and he would lose his chance at unparalleled fame in the scholarly world.

"'Translate it. You translate it, it is yours. We will give you a year.'

"'That's it?' He couldn't believe his good fortune. He was one of the world's premiere translators of ancient languages and dialects.

"The quiet man unlocked the briefcase's handcuff from his own wrist, placed the bracelet onto Dr. Sturgeon's wrist, and snapped the ratchet into place. It was so tight it bit into Dr. Sturgeon's arm. He showed me the impression that still marked him the next afternoon. The woman put the scroll back in the briefcase and locked it. She put the other two items in her handbag and gave Dr. Sturgeon two keys, one for the briefcase and one for the handcuff.

"'One year,' the woman repeated. Then they left the bar.

"Dr. Sturgeon ordered another drink to celebrate. 'To Noah!' he said.

"The next day, when we met as usual in his office, he showed me his prize. 'This, my dear Rowan, is what will make me famous. You too, by the way: protégé of the great Dr. Sturgeon.' I asked him what the Book of Noah was about.

"He said no one knew all the details, but the scroll was apparently written by Enoch, of 1 Enoch fame. Ancient references to the Book of Noah indicate that it is a letter Enoch wrote to Noah to encourage him to accept the mission to build the ark and save the future of humanity and animal life on earth. 'You can understand Noah's reluctance,' Dr. Sturgeon told me. 'Noah wasn't sure how the plan would work, why the Watchers wouldn't just come back and mess everything up again. So Enoch wrote to his great-grandson with more details than he provided in 1 Enoch. What those details are, no one knows without reading the letter. Whatever Enoch wrote must have convinced Noah to go ahead with he plan."

"So, if someone could read it, it might tell them more about what happened to the Watchers, or maybe where they are?" I interrupted. Mr. LePlage eyed me like I had suggested we all go for a ride on my unicorn. "Right," he said, "if they actually existed."

He continued with his story.

"'The important thing for me,' Dr. Sturgeon had said, 'is that it's written in the original language. It may be the only surviving document we have in that language. Deciphering it will be an amazing milestone in human intellectual development. Who knows what doors it will unlock?'

"He showed me the three words he was sure of: Noah, book, and antimony."

We all gaped at each other.

Mr. LePlage gave us a quizzical look. "You know what antimony is?"

"Of course," said Miyako, covering for us. "Basic chemistry. It's right there in the periodic table. Go on, please."

Mr. LePlage grabbed a sheet from his stack on the podium. He turned it over, grabbed a ballpoint pen from the pocket protector in his shirt pocket and wrote the words.

"Like this. I still remember the look in Dr. Sturgeon's eyes when he showed me, a gleam, but with a tinge of mania. That's all he had to go on.

"Dr. Sturgeon became obsessed. He stayed in his office. Never went home. Ate only what he could get delivered to his office or what I brought him. Drank way too much caffeine, even more alcohol. Stopped showing up for the classes he was supposed to teach.

"When the year had almost passed, he stopped coming into the office at all.

"I checked everywhere I knew to look for him. Finally found him in that crummy bar, hat pulled down over his eyes, slumped in a corner booth, stubble on his face, beer stains on his raincoat. Empty bottles in front of him. He looked terrible.

"'Dr. Sturgeon, what are you doing?' I asked. 'Let's get you out of here.'

"He looked at me, panic in his eyes. 'I've done it. I've cracked it. To-morrow they come for it,' he said.

"'Congratulations, Dr. Sturgeon! I replied. 'Shouldn't you be happy? You look frightened. What's happened? Whatever it is, I can help.'

"'No one can help,' he shot back. 'I have to destroy it. I can't give it back to them, to those . . . those creatures! But I can't bear to have it lost to the world, and to me!'

"He broke down weeping. 'My chance for glory!' he wailed.

"I got his office key from his jacket pocket and helped him back to his office. I got him onto the sofa, opened his jacket, and took off his shoes. I locked his office behind me and slid the key under the door.

"It was the last time I ever saw him. He was found dead the next morn-ing by the cleaning staff. Massive heart attack during the night. After his body was taken away, I checked his office. The manuscript was gone."

"What a loss," said Neith. "Your professor, the language. What do you think happened?"

"Dr. Sturgeon was really scared. Like translating the manuscript got to him. But I don't know if he destroyed the scroll or if someone took it. I just know I've seen it, and the three words, 'Noah,' 'book,' and 'antimony.' It's not much to go on, but it's my life's work now, to reconstruct the original language."

I felt really sad for Mr. LePlage, and for Dr. Sturgeon too. My nose started to burn hot with anger as I thought about who the manuscript push-ers in the bar must have been and how they ruined one life and were now keeping Mr. LePlage lonely and stuck at conventions where no one appreci-ated him.

He brightened slightly, then said, "You might be interested in this, though, since you know about Hildegard." He reached into his briefcase, and handed a sheet of paper to Dilani, who was sitting closest to him. "I found it in Dr. Sturgeon's desk. It's the Book of Noah, translated into the *Lingua Ignota*."

"What?" said Neith. "You know what it says? I thought you said Dr. Sturgeon was frightened by what he found there."

Mr. LePlage replied, "If you think what it says is real, it would be frightening, but it's just a myth. I think he just cracked under pressure. He used to copy all sorts of things into Hildegard's language. It was a way to keep a copy that very few other people would ever pay attention to."

We all glanced at each other. Dilani said, "Can we keep this?"

Mr. LePlage nodded. "Sure. I wish I could give you the original language. I will keep working."

"Can I ask how you hope to go from three words to a whole language? Josh asked in a gentle tone. "Do you have any other clues?"

"Just a couple. I remember a couple of other letters that went with the name Noah, so those are probably prepositions. The other is that I assume that the original universal language had some connection to languages that developed and are still known. The story says God confused the language, not invented an entirely new way of communicating. So I've been playing with the meanings of 'Noah,' and 'book, and 'antimony' and words that sound like those words in other languages to see if that gets me anywhere. You know, like my last name, LePlage is the French word for 'beach.' And my first name, Rowan, sounds like 'Owen', although the meaning is different."

"Wait a second. Owen Beach?" said Neith, his eyes growing wide. "Are you *the* Owen Beach?"

A small smile broke out on Mr. LePlage's face and he blushed a little as if Neith had discovered a secret that delighted him. "That was my stage name. I was a child actor. Did a bunch of commercials, started with diapers, did some cereals . . ."

Neith interrupted, his voice trembling in excitement, "But your big role was playing Tommy Starnes in Season Three of the original Star Trek!"

"No way! You were Tommy Starnes? In 'The Children Shall Lead Them?'" Dilani jumped in.

"Tommy Starnes—that's me." He beamed, maybe happy to remember a simpler time, before the Book of Noah. He explained to the rest of us not familiar with every episode of the classic TV series, "I was the leader of a group of children possessed by the evil spirit Gorgan who killed our parents and got us to take over the Starship Enterprise, until Kirk, Spock, and Dr. Bones snapped us out of it, saving us and the universe."

"That was you," Neith said, appreciatively.

"It was." He opened his wallet and showed us a slightly crinkled 'Tommy Starnes' original autograph series Star Trek trading card. A young, fresh-faced, red-haired boy stared off to the right, wearing the green and white striped boat neck shirt he must have worn in the episode. I could see the resemblance.

"I made some money from my acting, my investments went well, and now I can devote all my time to my real passion, searching for the original language," Mr. LePlage, aka, Mr. Beach, aka, the exorcised and fully in his right mind Tommy Starnes, said.

From the raucous applause breaking out next door, it sounded like the session was over and it was time to go.

"Thanks, Mr. LePlage," Dilani said.

"Yes, good luck. Great presentation," Zia added.

I still wished we could do something for him.

We opened the door and started to step into the hallway when we noticed two tall men wearing dark designer suits, expensive-looking leather shoes, and Raybans, loitering outside the room. They were wearing the laminated "Paid Registrant" nametags and holding limp Conlang Con totebags, but they definitely did not fit in with the Conlang crowd. They looked like the bodyguards I had seen hovering anytime Dr. Grigori addressed us. We jumped quickly back into the room and shut the door.

Neith waved his tablet. "Mind if I take a picture?" he asked.

"Not at all," Rowan LePlage said. Neith stood next to him, held the camera out in front for a selfie, and snapped the picture.

"Thanks!" Neith said. "One more thing. Don't let your fame go to your head." He clicked a few things on the device and smiled.

Suddenly the door swung open and three men dressed like Captain James T. Kirk, four Spocks, and a bunch of Officer Uhuras in mini-skirts and go-go boots swarmed into Room 311, brandishing cell phone cameras and chanting, "Tom-my! Tom-my! Tom-my!" We squeezed past the crowd in the doorway and noticed the Armani-arrayed men crushed against the hallway wall, trying to escape being trampled by the swelling, chanting crowd.

We hurried in the opposite direction and made it into the stairwell.

"What did you do?" I asked Neith.

"I posted the selfie on the Conlang Con website, with 'Owen Beach signing autographs and posing for pictures in Room 311.'"

Later that night, we used a computer in the library to get onto the Conlang Con website. The big story on the homepage was the surprise guest appearance of Child Star, Owen Beach. It was accompanied by a photo of Rowan LePlage, ABD, surrounded by Uhuras, a huge grin on his boyish, shining face.

§

We got back to Harvard Commons and gathered around a café table in the square, listening as Neith read aloud:

My Dear Noah,

By now you have been given instructions you cannot comprehend for a purpose you cannot fathom. You fear that even if you comply, your efforts will ultimately be in vain. You must say yes.

The Archangels have instructed me to write this letter to you to convince you to agree to your difficult task. You must be the sprig from which the human race will once again grow, multiply, and fill the world.

You are afraid that even if you accept your unlikely mission, even if you bring your family to safety along with all the plants and animals needed for the flourishing of creation after the deluge, the Watchers will escape their prison, will once again wreak havoc upon the earth, causing violence and destruction.

My Dear One, fear not! Remember that I would not lead you astray, that I know truth straight from the mouths of angels, and that I share this with you at the behest of the Holy One. Would that I could take your task on myself and save you the ordeal you will undergo. But I cannot.

To you, and to you alone, I disclose this information so that you will know the wisdom of the Holy One, the strength of the chains which bind the Watchers, and the ingenuity of their place of capture, and be reassured that the plan will not go astray. The importance of what I share is also such that you must destroy this missive, tempted as you will be to keep it.

I disclosed in the book named for me that the Watchers are chained beyond the mountain of antimony, deep in a chasm filled with fire, they await their final destruction. To you alone, I disclose this additional detail: the location of the Watchers' imprisonment so that you may know that no one will ever find them.

Their prison is a rocky island surrounded by a fierce and cold ocean, a land of ice and fire. The Watchers are held in a chamber deep below columns of fire and dense mountains of ice. The island is uninhabited. Who would go to such a place? And, even if someone should visit its inhospitable shores, who would make it their home?

Only when the Great One signals the end of time, the time of judgment and recompense, will the Great One speak the word of release, the only word that will unbind them. Only at that time and by that word they will be unchained and led away to their final destruction.

It pains me to encourage you in this journey that you must make. I know you will suffer. Your heart will break as the floodwaters rise, and you will wonder if there is another way to begin again. You will long to hear a word of restraint by which the waters will cease their relentless fall and dry land will once again appear. But, my dear Noah, you must say yes.

I must stop now. Allow yourself one rereading, then destroy this. Share its contents with no one, and all shall be well.

Your loving Great-Grandpapa

The clink of cutlery and chatter of tourists at the surrounding tables suddenly seemed jarringly loud as we sat in silence.

"I understand something now," Josh said, pulling a small Bible out from his back pocket. He read aloud a passage from Genesis:

"Noah, a man of the soil, was the first to plant a vineyard. He drank some of the wine and became drunk, and he lay uncovered in his tent. And Ham, the father of Canaan, saw the nakedness of his father, and told his two brothers outside . . . When Noah awoke from his wine and knew what his youngest son had done to him, he said, 'Cursed be Canaan; lowest of slaves shall he be to his brothers.'"

"This is after the flood," Josh explained. "Noah gets drunk, and Ham sees Noah's 'nakedness,' and his whole family gets cursed for it. Seems kind of harsh, right?"

We agreed.

"Scholars have tried to figure out what it really means, why Noah would react so strongly to something that sounds embarrassing at worst. But 'nakedness,'" he looked at Neith, "can also mean 'shame,' right?"

"Yes."

"In other words," Dilani interrupted, suddenly seeing where Josh was going, "Ham saw what caused his father shame—that Noah kept the letter. Ham saw the letter! He must have read it and seen that Noah was supposed to destroy it."

"He could have realized this information would be very valuable. He could have sold it, or given it, I suppose, to one of the Nephilim," Neith said.

"But by this time, it's after Babel and no one knows the original language anymore. So the Grigoris or their agents give the manuscript to Dr. Sturgeon, who translates it," I tried. "They maybe even kill him once they know he's finished. So the Grigoris know what it says. But they may not have counted on there being a copy in the *Lingua Ignota*."

"And they were hovering outside the lecture room," said Dilani, "because they don't want anyone else to know what it says."

"Because the Grigoris don't want anyone to stop them," I added. "They want to release the Watchers and the Book of Noah gives them important information, information Noah was supposed to destroy."

"And what might have seemed vague when Enoch wrote it, isn't vague anymore," Josh chimed in. "The Book of Noah tells us where the Watchers are."

Dilani spoke quietly, "An island with columns of fire and dense ice."

"Columns of fire *under* dense ice," Josh said. I could tell by the way he was giving the clue that he had already figured it out.

"Oh no," I said, cluing in too. "An uninhabited island, 'nor will it ever be.' Enoch hadn't counted on the Vikings. It's Iceland, isn't it?"

"Where the transmission from those kids came from," Neith said.

"Where the Grigoris are mining more antimony." Dilani added.

"What does it say again about how to break the Watchers out of their prison?" Zia asked.

Neith pointed to the place in the letter. "Enoch says the Great One will 'speak the word of release, the only word that will unbind them.'"

"Do you think that's literal?" Josh asked. "*The only word that will unbind them*? Like he's saying there is one word, 'the word of release,' and that if that word is spoken, the chains will come off the Watchers."

"We better make sure no one says the word, whatever that is," Neith said.

"We had better keep this letter to ourselves," Josh said, looking around.

"And we had better get back to school before they notice we've been gone all day," said Zia.

I bent over to pick up my tote bag and found myself staring at the logo. I was fixated on *the word of release, the only word that will unbind them*. Where had I heard of a word of release? A word spoken that let something, or someone go? That set something free?

I was jerked back to my surroundings by the shouts of a young boy, a toddler, having a tantrum. His father was pulling him by the arm, trying to get him to stand up from where the boy had plunked down on the filthy sidewalk and was refusing to move.

"Please, let's go," the man said to the boy. "Stand up. Stop it," he tried to reason with the toddler who was wailing and beating his clenched fists against his father like a tiny crazed tyrant.

"Like he's possessed," a woman muttered to her companion as they passed.

The penny dropped. The Gerasene Demoniac. Jesus says a word and the demons leave the man's body. One word is spoken and the demons are released.

Could that be what Enoch was talking about? One single word that would set the Watchers free if spoken? What was the word? Did the Grigoris know it?

§

That night my tablet signaled that I had an email—a message from Fred. I had forgotten to tell him not to use my email in case it gave anything away to our monitor. Too late. I clicked it open.

Coordinates for the next appearance of your constellation: 25.2048 degrees N, 55.2708 degrees E.

I copied the coordinates, put them into a map app, and a location popped up: Dubai. Site of the world's tallest skyscraper.

37

Formaldehyde

Time to follow up on Miss Liora's lead. According to the paper she had given me, Dr. Ellis's office was in the Zoology Museum, down the street from where the other GYSP professors had their offices. Dilani wanted to see this museum and came along.

When she first suggested coming with me, I resisted. Miss Liora told me to go see Dr. Ellis. She didn't say anything about bringing Dilani. If Dr. Ellis found out she had tagged along, maybe he wouldn't like it and wouldn't give me crucial information. Maybe Dr. Ellis would also end up incinerated, like Dr. Canon probably was, if I didn't follow her instructions. But maybe I was trying out the idea Dr. Grigori had planted, that I might be too dependent on my new friends. If Dilani wanted to see the Zoology Museum, she didn't have to use my meeting as an excuse.

I was just about to tell her I wanted to go by myself, when she asked if she could have some of my antimony. Her supply was running low, and she hadn't had a chance to ask Miyako to get her some from the lab.

"I'm running low too," I lied. "I can't help you."

"Oh, okay," she replied. "No problem. I can get some from Miyako for you too. So, shouldn't we be leaving now for your appointment?"

When the lie first came out of my mouth, I felt a jolt of elation. Same when I first heard her response. She believed me. But just as quickly, a bloom of shame welled up inside me. Why did I do it? Was this another part of trying on Dr. Grigori's new identity for me? I had been mulling over Xanthe's comment about being a realm crosser. Dr. Grigori said it had to do with crossing boundaries between the past and the present, but suddenly I wondered if it also meant I had the potential to cross from truth to fiction easily. My face got hot as I thought about Dilani's kind offer to help me out in response to my falsehood.

"You're right, Dilani. It's time to go," I said, and tried to forget what I had just done.

§

While I scanned the list of names and office numbers on the wall by the museum's front desk, Dilani looked through the brochure of exhibits and museum map. I didn't see Dr. Ellis's name anywhere on the directory. In fact, it seemed that most of the offices in the building belonged not to professors, but to the cleaning staff.

The security guard at the front desk asked if she could help us find something, "an exhibit, perhaps? Or are you here about the taxidermy job?"

"Some*one*, actually," I said. "Dr. Ellis. Can you tell me how to get to his office?"

The security guard looked like a friendly pastry chef who would have been more at home in an apron than the uniform she was squished into. She spoke with an Irish brogue, her gray hair was pulled up in a bun, and her green eyes twinkled. I looked at her badge. "Ms. Mary Healey," it said. She seemed happy to help, and even more happy to chat.

"Basement level, get off the elevator, go straight to the end past the off-exhibit specimens. When you get to the giant squid, turn left. His door's the last one in the hall."

"Giant squid?" I asked, making sure I had heard correctly. Dilani put down the brochure. She came over and stood with me in front of the desk.

"Yes," Ms. Healey answered. "The lighting is terrible down there, but you'll recognize the long glass cylinder. Take a look. Actually, since you have a reason to be down there," she dropped her voice, "take a gander at what else is there, if you have a strong stomach. It's all stuff no longer on display. Items offensive to the public."

"What did the squid do? I mean, to offend the public?" Dilani asked.

"Oh, that one's just out of date. But most of the other stuff down there," she flung her hands back in an 'I give up' gesture, and widened her eyes, "that's what's offensive to the public. It's poor, monstrous creatures—experiments. None of them lived, of course, but they kept them just the same. Hybridization, they called it. I call it desecration."

"Hybridization? As in crossing two species?" I asked.

"Exactly. You know, mate a horse with a donkey and get a mule. That's one thing. Although even a mule isn't quite right—infertile, you know. But they were trying all kinds of strange things." She had dropped her voice to a whisper. She leaned toward us. We stepped closer so we could hear.

"Down there, there's a monkey they mated with a bird. You'll see it if you look. Poor little thing never came to term, but you can see the little nubs of wings on its back. There's a fish, too, they mated with a dog. Looks like a hairless puppy, with long ears, gills, and a fin on its back. What they were after with that one, heaven only knows. They were trying to mix things that don't even belong in the same realm, let alone making babies together. It's unnatural, it is."

I wasn't sure which I felt more strongly—the desire to see these things or the urge to grab Dilani's hand and run from the building right now. Curiosity won out.

"Who did the experiments?" I asked. "And why keep them if they didn't work?"

"Well, it was some time ago, my dear, back in the early 1900s, but you know, it was the Grigori Family, same folks running the program over at the Divinity School. Same program your Dr. Ellis is part of. Those poor abominations were on display in the museum gallery for a short time, but they were taken down to the basement when too many parents complained their children were having nightmares. Pathetic little monstrous creatures." She made a sympathetic clucking sound. "But do take a look, my dears. You've never seen anything like it."

She leaned even farther forward, her large bosom resting on the surface of the desk. She looked in both directions to see if we were alone.

"Now, what I want to know," she whispered, "is what Dr. Ellis did that they stuck him in the bowels of the building. That's where professors get sent right before they're booted or quit. When they've got tenure, it's hard to get rid of them, so they banish them to the belly of the basement and they're never heard from again, or they resign. So," she looked at us closely, "what do you know about Professor Ellis?"

I wasn't sure how to answer. The truth was I didn't know anything, but I wasn't sure what I should say to someone so eager to share what she knows with others.

"I've seen his picture," I said hesitatingly. That was true. He was in a photo of the GYSP faculty. "He seems kind of disheveled," I said, trying to give her something. "But I guess they wouldn't put you in the basement just for needing a makeover."

"Nay, it must be more than something a shave and a haircut would take care of. Run along to your meeting now, but do let me know if you find anything out, won't you, my child?" She winked and pointed in the direction of the elevator.

"I'm coming with you," Dilani said, leaving the museum brochure on the counter. I was so glad I hugged her.

The Zoological Museum was an old building with an elaborate brass and marble staircase that wound through its center. The elevator was a wrought iron cage that ran through the middle of the staircase. We got in, and the screen door screeched in protest, or warning, as I pulled it shut.

I pushed the B for basement button. The elevator started to move with a thunk and a bounce. Then it lurched downward. An arrow above the door indicated the levels as we passed them. B was actually down three levels. I could see the two lower levels below the ground floor through the mesh of the elevator cage, rows of shelves holding containers and file cabinets going past, lit by cold fluorescent lights. The staircase stopped at lower level two, so the only way to reach the basement was the cage in which we were riding. We landed on the basement level with a squeal and jerked to a stop. I yanked open the door and hoped no one would be calling the elevator to another floor in case we needed to beat a hasty retreat.

The corridor was about fifteen feet wide, lit by the same kind of fluorescents as the other lower levels, although some of the bulbs hissed and buzzed like they had a short or were just about to burn out. On either side of the hallway were steel shelves a few feet deep, holding glass containers of various sizes. I could make out a yellow liquid in the containers and the smell of formaldehyde. A mildewing mop in a bucket was leaned up against one of the walls. I could see shards of glass on the floor by the bucket. A jar with a jagged top was discarded in a metal waste paper can nearby. I didn't dare look to see what else the garbage can held.

Our chat with the security guard had already made me late for my appointment, but I lingered alongside Dilani as we peeked at some of the intact jars while we slowly made our way toward a huge glass tank at the end of the corridor.

The security guard was right. It was sad, this parade of strange creatures floating in their yellow-green jars, pale and lifeless, unfinished creations of juxtaposed species. We saw a container labeled "Hybrid Experiment 30145: *Pan Troglodytes* with *Pandion Haliaetus*, 3 months short of parturition. Extracted."

"That is a chimpanzee mated with an osprey," Dilani half-whispered, a horrible awe in her voice.

Dilani pointed at the next one, "Hybrid Experiment 30156: *Canis Lupus Familiarus* with *Gadus Morhua*, 4 days short of parturition. Extracted." Her voice was thick, swallowing tears. "A beagle with a cod."

There were also insects (millipede with honey bee; earthworm with dragonfly) and one that made me want to keep my head down and sprint toward the giant squid and Dr. Ellis's office: the "Hybrid Experiment 30267: *Theraphosa Blondi* with *Gymnogyps Californianus*, 36 days from parturition. Extracted." But Dilani paused in front of it, wonder stopping her.

"Even though it's nowhere near its full-grown size, you can probably already tell," Dilani said, gesturing toward the large jar, "that the *theraphosa blondi* is the world's largest spider. They live in Argentina. They eat birds, they don't mate with them." The fetus was already hairy, its wiry fuzz floating in the liquid. Bony wings were folded against its striped back. "The bird is a condor and was extinct in the wild, but it's starting to come back," Dilani said, a small note of hope in this otherwise bleak and bizarre place.

We walked toward the container holding the squid and paused at the end nearest the squid's gelatinous bulbous head. A milky eye the size of my face was open but unseeing. The tank filled the width of the hallway and was about six feet tall and four feet deep. The squid's stringy tentacles were looped and snarled into a mass like angel hair pasta.

"At least this one was already dead when they found it, unless they're not telling us something," Dilani said, ever the hopeful one.

"How can you tell?" I was speaking to Dilani, but I kept my eyes on the squid, making sure it wouldn't wink its pale glassy eye at me and start unfurling its tentacles.

"No living giant squid had ever been seen until just about ten years ago, off the coast of Newfoundland. A scientist there was obsessed about seeing one alive. He built a special lab so he would be ready when one finally showed its face. Or eye. Or even a tentacle or two. He got lucky, and one brave, or lost, giant squid swam past. One more showed up a few years later. Until these two, the only specimens humans have ever seen have been dead. They've floated to the surface or washed ashore." She bent down to look at the squid like she was looking at a friend. Actually, more like she was paying her respects to a friend lost too soon. "Still, it's an amazing creature, don't you think?" she said, rubbing her hand along the surface of the tank.

"I think this squid is one of the reasons I'm terrified of water." I imagined a fifty foot-long tentacle wrapping around my leg and pulling me down, down, down. I stopped myself. Sweat was starting to bead on my forehead.

"But," I said, trying to take my mind off of drowning by tentacle, "this one isn't a hybrid. Seems strange when everything else preserved down here is some failed, warped experiment."

"What if they're not failed?" Dilani said, disgust in her voice. "What if the experimenters didn't actually care about whether or not their creations were viable? What if they just wanted to see what the hybrid looked like, or what happened as it developed? The labels all say 'Extracted.' They were removed, not stillborn."

"Oh, wow. You're right." Forcing myself to look back at the jars on the shelves, I noticed jars behind the ones visible at the front of the shelving. I pulled my sweatshirt sleeve over my hand so I wouldn't have to make direct contact, and nudged the closest giant tarantula-giant bird a little to one side. Behind it was a row of jars, like sodas lined up in a see-through vending machine. Each one held a smaller and smaller specimen. The labels verified that each one was younger, slightly less developed, not as far along in its gestation. It was true for the other hybrid creatures as well.

Dilani and I looked at each other. She spoke first. "These jars hold progressions, not necessarily things that didn't work."

"You think a giant tarantula is out there somewhere that can fly?"

"I sure hope not."

Silence.

Dilani said, "The experimenters who did this were interested in watching the growth of creatures they made, to see how their hybrids developed."

"Hybrids," I offered, "between animals and insects that are earthborn, air-born, and water-born. Mary Healey was right. They cross realms. They never would be together naturally, even if they could mate in real life."

"The Grigoris put them together, then harvested them from whatever animals were carrying these weird offspring and preserved them. But why?"

"To study them?"

"For sure. That's why these are in a university museum. Just like those mummified babies in the archaeological museum. This isn't just some eccentric's collection of curiosities. It's a collection for study. But what are they trying to find out? And how do a bunch of circus-freak animals help them do that?"

We turned back to the giant squid.

Dilani gulped. "This one is a hybrid too. Look." She pointed to a place just below the squid's globular head. "Nubby proto-wings."

We looked for a label and found it along the bottom edge of the tank.

Dilani read it aloud: "Hybrid Experiment 30252: *Architeuthis* with *Pinguinus Impennis*, 3 weeks short of partuition. Extracted."

I swallowed. "That means they had a living giant squid to experiment on. Or more than one. And they killed it, or them, to do this."

"They crossed it with a great auk. Those birds have been extinct, at least as far as the rest of the world knows, since the mid-1800s."

I tried to puzzle things out. "So, the Grigoris, who we are pretty sure are Nephilim, are themselves hybrids, right?"

"Right," said Dilani. "Heavenly plus earthly."

"And they're making other hybrids. Or did in the past."

"Apparently."

"And harvested the fetuses at different points in their development and preserved them for study."

"Yes," Dilani said, encouraging me to continue.

"They were looking for something," I said, feeling like I was on the verge of insight. "It wasn't to see if they could do it, whether or not they could make a monkey-dog or a giant squid that could fly. What they were looking for was something else."

Dilani urged me on. "Which is . . .?"

A scrape of metal across concrete came from the other side of the door to the left of the squid's, or rather squid-bird's, tank. I had almost forgotten I was here to see Dr. Ellis.

We looked at the door. "Kendrick Ellis, Ph.D. Professor of Missions" was written with a ballpoint pen on a yellow sticky note on the door. On the wall to the side of the door was a proper room nameplate that read "Broom Closet LL3, #4." A felt-tip marker X was drawn over it.

"Please stay with me," I begged Dilani.

She nodded. I knocked on the door.

The door swung open. Dr. Ellis stood in the doorway. His gray hair puffed out like dust bunnies had settled on his head. His bushy eyebrows seemed to sprout even more wild hairs than I had noticed when looking at the faculty photo. They had joined forces, making one long hairy caterpillar that rested on his brow as he observed not just me, but also Dilani standing in front of him. His forehead relaxed and the caterpillar was bisected, each half finding a resting spot above a bright hazel eye. The unification and division of his eyebrows had knocked his wire rim glasses akilter, and he readjusted them so they sat evenly across the bridge of his nose. He wiped his right hand on the patched sleeve of his faded tweed jacket and extended it in a warm handshake to each of us and exclaimed in a lilting Welsh accent, "How fortuitous! Dilani, I am so glad you're here too! I was going to invite you for early tomorrow. I usually try to have these conversations one student at a time for reasons of confidentiality, but if the two of you are comfortable being in on this together, it will save us precious time. Are you?"

We nodded.

"Come in then, please." He looked back into his office, which did seem like it still was a broom closet. "Hmmm," Dr. Ellis murmured and ran a large hand through the right side of his moppy hair, making it look even more like a fluffed up Brillo pad. The scraping sound we heard must have been the one folding metal chair we could see crammed into the space between the wall and his desk. Behind his desk was an upside down milk crate with a pillow placed on top of it. He looked at his metal waste paper basket, which was heaped with crumpled papers. "Ah!" he said, raising an index finger to the side of his head like a light bulb had flicked on. He picked up the garbage pail and squeezed past us. Gently, he emptied the contents onto the floor in front of the squid. "Sorry for the mess, Herman," he said softly to the gummy hybrid. "Watch these for me, will you?"

"It's not alive, is it?" I asked Dr. Ellis tentatively.

"Oh no," he said. "But he was once. And they're my company down here," he pointed to the squid and the other contained creatures, "so I try to be respectful, even if the Grigoris weren't." He shook his head. "That they made new creatures isn't the problem—look at the Creator's sense of adventure and creativity in making animals. The rhinoceros! The aardvark! The duck-billed platypus!"

I smiled. "That's my favorite animal," I said.

"And a great choice that is," Dr. Ellis responded. "Lovely creature. But these," his arm sweeping across the corridor, "these were made just to be used. Tragic."

His words made me hopeful. Maybe he could tell us more about the strange creatures. But surely that wasn't why he wanted to see us.

"Come in, come in," he pointed to his office. "No, wait. I must go first. Please excuse my ungentlemanly behavior."

He set out the metal chair and the pillow-topped crate for us to sit on, squeezed behind the desk, and gestured for us to be seated before he took a seat on the overturned garbage pail. The room held cleaning supplies as well as some binders, manila file folders, stacks of papers, and books that Dr. Ellis must have brought into the room.

"Let me come to the point quickly," he said, tapping his fingertips together. "How much do you each know about your own backgrounds?"

"Backgrounds?" Dilani echoed. "Like ethnic identity?"

"I mean parentage," Dr. Ellis clarified. "Families of origin."

"I know my parents' names and my grandparents' names," I said. "Although they're all dead now," I added quietly.

"My condolences, of course. Your mother has passed as well, I believe," he said to Dilani in a sympathetic voice. She nodded.

"What I'm about to say may come as a surprise, but it's important that you each understand what I'm telling you. It may have everything to do with why you're here." He paused.

In a broom closet in the basement of a museum off a hallway filled with preserved hybrid animals?

"In the Grigori Young Scholars Program," he clarified. "And why your lives may be in danger," he said with sudden gravity. "Although the fact that you're still here in week number three leads me to believe that you're worth more to them alive than dead." He rested his chin on his fingers and looked off toward the upper corner of the miniscule room, ruminating, as if he had forgotten that we were still there and that our lives were in danger.

"Dr. Ellis?" I prompted.

"My apologies. There's just so much to consider." He wrestled himself back to this conversation, running both his hands through the sides of his hair, smoothing out the mop, and then straightening his glasses again. "These conversations get no easier, I'm afraid. But I must say, I'm hopeful. I remain hopeful."

"About what, Dr. Ellis?" I prompted again, hopeful myself that he would, in fact, get to the point.

"Why, about the abilities of young people such as yourselves," he said, evidently so moved by our potential that he took a handkerchief from his pocket and wiped a tear from his eyes. He repositioned his glasses, returned the handkerchief and began again.

"My work in Missions afforded me the opportunity to travel the world, not only to study the spread of the world's major religions, but also to pursue another quite crucial interest of mine concerning the adoption of infants and young children." He looked at each of us. "You were both adopted—I'm sure by parents who loved you very much and were very proud of you." He took two manila folders that were poking him in the shoulder down from the shelf next to him and put them in front of us on the desk. "I apologize for the abruptness of this announcement if this comes as news to you, and we will return to the subject of your adoptions in a moment. But first I must tell you more about my work so that you will understand the context in which we find ourselves."

"That makes sense," Dilani said. "Being adopted. My mother used to look at me sometimes like I was a complete stranger. I'd even catch her saying under her breath, 'where did you really come from?' My dad would tell her to be quiet."

My head was spinning with questions, and images flashed in my mind like photographs in a digital slideshow. Me as a young child blowing out birthday candles on a cake as my mom looks on from behind. My father pushing me in a stroller at the zoo, a helium balloon tied to my pudgy wrist. My mother, father, and I smiling at the camera in front of our Christmas tree, the last photo taken of us all together before my parents were killed. Dr. Ellis was talking, and I shook the images away, trying to focus on what he was saying. He was asking a question.

"Do you? Understand about the connection between the Grigoris and the Nephilim?"

I looked at Dilani.

"I understand your reticence," he said kindly. "The Grigoris are not to be trifled with. But now we find ourselves in a situation not of our own making, but perhaps one which we have been uniquely equipped to address. You do understand the Grigori-Nephilim connection?" One of his fuzzy eyebrows was raised inquiringly.

I paused, but realized we had to respond to this question if we were going to get any answers. I said, "We suspect that Dr. Grigori, his family, and perhaps several of those associated with the GYSP are Nephilim." He heard the hesitancy in my voice that must have signaled my unstated question to him: "Are you one of them?"

He reached into the pocket on the inside of his jacket, then opened his hand to reveal what he had withdrawn: a small silver token bearing the same angel as on Miss Liora's and my locket.

"This is mine. Given me by my father."

All three of us looked at the token in his open palm. He closed his hand over it and returned it to his pocket.

"I am a mere mortal," he said. "Happily so. Several of us regular human beings hold positions on the GYSP staff. We have our uses. As you can see by our present surroundings, I am not currently finding favor in Dr. Vadim Grigori's sight. I accidentally wandered into a meeting concerning archaeo-acoustics that Dr. Grigori was holding with some of the faculty members in a room near my old office. Although I overheard nothing of any utility on that occasion, I was informed that my office had been relocated. I'm being punished, but with only a slap on the wrist at this point. In characteristic Nephilistic style, they are keeping me close to see if they can get more information from me before disposing of me."

"Disposing of you?" Dilani interjected, horrified.

"It is a possibility. So I, too, am wary and cautious. But remember, although the Nephilim are powerful, they are not omniscient. They need to learn and gather information like the rest of us."

"What if they've bugged your office?" I said it in a whisper, although I realized that, if they were listening, it would be too late.

"I don't think so. But tomorrow may be different. A maintenance team is scheduled to do some wiring work, which I assume means installing cameras and listening devices. I've been down here two weeks, and, so far, I think the place is secure. The Nephilim are ruthless, but they still have to deal with the physical realm, and university bureaucracy and tedious work orders apply to them too."

I hoped he was right.

"The most powerful of the Nephilim are members of the Grigori family and its many tendrils, known by various cognate names—Egregore, Grigegore are a couple of them. My study of Missions traced the spread of religions but allowed me to monitor Nephilim activity as well. Nephilim are interested in all the major religious traditions—whatever works for good in the world, or, as the Nephilim would say, promotes the causes and goals of the one they call 'The Enemy': love, freedom, the betterment of others, justice, mercy. But they are extremely interested in Christianity, because, for a long time, they've thought that Jesus was one of them."

"Jesus—a Nephil?" I blurted.

"Think about it. Human mother, divine Father. And the Holy Spirit, the one 'by whom Mary is with child,' according to the Gospel of Matthew, has been imagined in different ways. Sometimes as a dove, as you've seen in so many paintings of the Annunciation, or as a spectacular light, or, and this is important, as an angel, or an angelic being."

"But there's a huge difference between the story of how Nephilim came into existence and how Jesus was born," I protested.

"Several differences, of course," Dr. Ellis said. "One striking difference is that no, uh," he grew red saying the words, "sexual, uh, congress took place between Mary and the Holy Spirit. The Bible is quite insistent upon that point. Nothing physical went on, although a physical pregnancy and baby resulted."

"And Mary had a say in it," Dilani said. "No angel just swooped in, taking her, like in the Watchers' story."

"Yes." He agreed. "She gives her consent. Free choice is involved. But there are two differences the Nephilim find most unnerving and fascinating.

"First, the results of the birth of baby Jesus are good, unlike the legacy of the Watchers. The Watchers cause the dissemination of violence, war, greed for wealth, control over others. Jesus brings a message of peace, forgiveness, second chances, new beginnings. This quite unnerved the Nephilim. It seemed to them that the One they call Enemy had used the very same tactics the Watchers had—joining with humans and creating a hybrid—but to the opposite effect, an effect which could ultimately defeat the Nephilim."

"But doesn't traditional Christian doctrine say that Jesus was completely human and completely divine, not half and half? He's not supposed to be just a mixture, right?"

"Correct," Dr. Ellis replied. "That's the other thing the Nephilim are obsessed with. Nephilim face a problem. The purest ones, the ones they call Peerless, are fifty percent human and fifty percent angelic. More angelic, and they tend to return to the side of the Holy One. More human, and they're not as strong as the half-and-half's. But you've heard how organ transplant recipients sometimes reject their new organs, even when they're a perfect match?"

"Oh," I said, my own lightbulb going off. "Nephilim were never meant to exist. Angels and humans weren't supposed to mix like that. So it doesn't work after a while." I thought with a shudder of Xanthe, her deteriorating flesh, the Duophysites' fear of disintegrative discoinherence and Brother Josef's research.

"That's right," Dr. Ellis said. "They can coinhere for a while, but with time and the stresses of earth's conditions on the angelic nature, the cohesion eventually breaks down. It literally tears Nephilim up. They rupture. It's one of the reasons they can't live forever, despite their angelic genes. That's partially why Jesus, divine and human in one being, is so interesting to them. Some Nephilim believe Jesus had some secret way he was able to keep his two natures together, some means of guaranteeing internal coinherence. Most Nephilim believe that the reason Jesus went to the cross was not the ultimate act of self-sacrificial love for others, as Christians teach, but a way to keep his secret. Take it with him to the tomb. Secrecy, subterfuge. The way a true Nephil would do it."

"That's what I would have learned in Nephilim Sunday School?" Dilani said quietly. "Fascinating. They must be looking for a cure."

"Antimony," I said, more light dawning on me. "No wonder it's so important to the Grigoris to control the world's supply. We've seen them snort it."

"You've seen it? They're getting sloppy, or else quite comfortable around you. Did you know Newton called antimony 'hermaphrodite'?" asked Dr. Ellis. "Can you guess why?"

"It's not about it somehow having both male and female qualities," I said. "He was describing its ability to help two different things stick together, remain unified."

Dr. Ellis nodded and said, "You probably also know that antimony is dangerous, poisonous if taken in too great a dose or for too long."

"So they're looking for something else too," I said, "some other way to cure themselves."

Dilani gulped, "That's why all these specimens are here!" She popped up off her milk crate and flung open the door. Dr. Ellis and I followed. Dilani inspected the labels on the jars again.

"Extracted. Extracted. Extracted," she read under her breath. She looked up. "I thought 'Extracted' on the labels meant they were extracted from the womb, or wherever they were made. But 'Extracted' means something was extracted *from them*. The Grigoris took something from them, something they hoped would shed light on how to keep two things not made to be together, together." Dilani looked back at me, "The mummified Elioud babies in the Archaeology Museum, and what Dr. Calleo said . . ."

We quoted together, "Can they, even in death, give life?"

"This is why my work with adoptions is so important," Dr. Ellis said, scooping us back into his office and closing the door. Nephilim aren't interested in just dead Elioud."

"What are you saying?" I asked.

"Based on modern genetic theory, we think that Elioud carry recessive and dominant traits from their Nephilim parents. This means Nephilim parents give birth to children, some of whom they can immediately tell are like them, look like them, will develop to be like them—are, for all intents and purposes, Nephilim." Dr. Ellis started pulling on one of his eyebrows. "They also give birth to offspring who look like regular human children, who show no signs of being Nephilim. These are the children Nephilim call 'Elioud' to distinguish them from the ones they call 'Nephilim.' We're not sure how they distinguished between the two categories with infants, since so much of what seems to be Nephilistic develops later. For example, wings—the most obvious—don't begin to develop until a child is about two."

As he spoke, I found myself thinking of the images I had seen around the Div School, in the Common Room, in the reception area to the dean's office, paintings of angels cradling newborns, staring into their eyes. I thought they were guardian angels gazing lovingly at the infants entrusted to their benevolent care. They weren't guardian angels. They were Nephilim examining their children for signs that they were either Nephilim or Elioud.

"I know how they do it," I said. "They look into their babies' eyes. Nephilim eyes are different, right? Not just slightly bigger, but more luminous. They must look into their newborn babies' eyes and be able to tell." I thought of my eye exam and started to shiver although the tiny office was stuffy and warm.

Dr. Ellis nodded and said, "We have had reports of Nephilim eyes actually emitting light, which could be reflected back at them if the retina of a newborn had a particular characteristic."

"Such as a metallic quality," I said, my voice squeaky and small. "Like being golden," That I had spoken aloud at all was verified by Dr. Ellis's nod.

He continued, "For centuries, Nephilim simply cast off their Elioud children. They were disgusted by offspring who appeared to be merely human. They saw them as a waste and a burden. They killed them outright or exposed them. Sometimes they sold them into slavery, figuring they could get something out of their misfortune to have produced a 'merely.'

"Some people, from early on, knew this was happening and tried to rescue the Elioud, sometimes finding the exposed ones and taking them, sometimes buying them back from the slavers."

"What did they do with the Elioud they rescued?" Dilani asked.

"Most of the time, we tried to resettle them with adoptive families who would mainstream them as much as possible. Treat them like normal human children. For those who developed Nephilistic traits later, they either had surgery performed, such as the removal of nascent wings, or tried to convince them to join our side, use their powers for good."

I felt a tingling sensation in my back. Is that what my scars were from? And Josh's?

"Our most successful efforts in Elioud rescue began in the 1860s. We founded *La Société Pour le Refuge des Enfants Elioudiques*, in Paris, which we called by its acronym, SPREE. The angel I showed you is our logo, although we don't show it to people outside the Society."

"SPREE—I've heard of that," Dilani said. "It's a Fresh Air Society, right? An organization that gets children out of the city and into nature. I went on one of their outings once. It was a day on a farm to learn more about animals. It's one of the reasons I love animals so much." She smiled at the memory. "I was pretty little, maybe four or five years old. I'm sure it was SPREE."

"SPREE was the perfect cover," Dr. Ellis said. "It started in Paris, but we opened offices in other cities and countries as well. Sometimes we took children just for enrichment, a time for them to enjoy nature, be with other children like themselves . . ." he looked at Dilani, raised an eyebrow slightly, knocking his glasses askew again.

"Sometimes that's how we connected them with their adoptive parents. Elioud children would be taken by SPREE out into a forest or to a park or a farm, where they would be given to their new families. We didn't have enough adoptive parents for all the Elioud, unfortunately, so we also founded what we call sanctuaries, group home facilities, where several Elioud children could live together in a secure and safe environment with some adult caretakers. Too many children, who may exhibit Nephilistic features, all living together in one place would certainly attract attention. Therefore sanctuaries are located in rather remote locations, where the children have relative freedom, so long as they remain in the sanctuary. Some of the adult caretakers themselves grew up in sanctuary and are able to give the children the gift of being raised by someone who knows firsthand what they're going through as they grow and discover their gifts."

He looked down toward his lap, then rubbed a hand through his hair. He said, "Unfortunately, we haven't received communications from any of the Sanctuaries recently, which worries me."

He sighed, then continued, "It was a brilliant cover for our work. People who had no clue about our true mission loved the idea of getting babies and toddlers out of the crowded cities, especially the highly industrialized ones, and no one paid close enough attention to notice if fewer children came back or if bundles of joy had been replaced by bundles of blankets.

"SPREE became essential after the 1880s and Gregor Mendel's work with recessive traits. The Grigoris became quite interested in this work and realized that they had been destroying or abandoning offspring who may be carrying recessive Nephilistic traits, traits that wouldn't show up until future generations. They leapt into action, trying to compile records of which Nephilim had reproduced, which offspring had been labeled 'Elioud,' and what had been done with them. They started trying to find and recover Elioud children and descendants. Sometimes they went on raids and used violence to try to get them back. We notice that several of our SPREE families are the victims of accidents in which parents are killed and children go missing, or are orphaned and are subsequently taken by Nephilim parents."

My flesh was cold. Is this what happened to my parents?

"But the Nephilim don't want normal human children, and some Elioud never exhibit Nephilim tendencies, right?" Dilani asked. "What do they do with the more human-seeming Elioud?" She looked like I felt, afraid to hear the answer to the question.

"We fear the Nephilim may still regard them as useful. Either for breeding, for study, or, more specifically, for 'extractions.' They may think there is something produced in the bodies of Elioud that they can harvest and use to prevent disintegration."

I felt nauseated.

And on fire. Like I suddenly had a sense of purpose. I felt ready to strike out—do something, act. Even if I had no idea what the something should be.

"The Nephilim use other methods in addition to violent ones to try to find and regain Elioud children," Dr. Ellis said slowly, waiting for us to finish the thought.

"The Grigori Young Scholars Program," I said.

"Yes. The fact that you are here means you have been identified by the Grigori as Elioud. They are testing you and cultivating you to see if and how you can be useful."

"Why don't they just do genetic testing or see if we've had surgery to remove wings or some other Nephilistic tendency?" I glanced at Dilani to see if the wing removal idea resonated with her too. I couldn't tell. She did respond, though, to my question.

"Maybe they're trying to be more subtle than just rounding us up and sticking cotton swabs in our mouths. If they did that, we would all figure out that they're looking for something and we might not be as cooperative. They're obviously trying to lure us in, woo us, with the extravagant prizes they're giving us, right?"

"Good point," I said. "I think I already know the answer," I looked at Dr. Ellis. "But, just to be sure, you think Dilani and I really are Elioud, right?"

"I will be happy to tell you for certain, but first I need your help."

My heart sank. Even Dr. Ellis was using us, bargaining with us. Just like the Grigoris. We were wrong to trust him after all. Suddenly I felt resolute. We can be manipulative too. Do what we need to get what we want.

"Okay," I said, pasting a smile on my face and trying to ooze cooperativeness, "What is it that Dilani and I can help you with?" I laid it on thick. "What would most change your life for the better right now?"

His eyebrows rose, as if surprised by the question.

"Well," he said, dropping his voice as if overcome by shyness, "that's much more than I had anticipated. I was going to ask for something simple, but if you really want to change my life, what would, or could, perhaps, help me with my heart's desire . . ." He paused, looking kind of pathetic, sad-puppy-like, "would be your help, with my . . . appearance." He dropped his eyes to his desk, embarrassed.

"Your appearance?" Really? We were talking about matters of life and death, about whether or not Dilani and I were some kind of genetic freaks, and Dr. Ellis was worried about what he looked like? Sheesh. No wonder Nephilim thought humans were ridiculous. And yet, if this is what it would take to get us what we needed, maybe I had better pay attention.

"You met Ms. Mary Healey when you came into the museum," he said, light and hope returning to his eyes. "She's a good woman, and one of the most beautiful creatures God ever put into shoe leather." He smiled wistfully. "But she won't give me the time of day. Just looks at me with pity."

"She thinks you're down here because you're either going to be fired or quit," Dilani said. "Maybe she does feel bad for you."

"She is definitely curious about you," I interjected. "She asked us to tell her about you. But, yes, a little makeover magic might help. Show her you're thinking of her, making an effort." Crikey. I sounded like Aunt Alina. There are no homely professors. Just lazy ones. Rats. I smiled weakly. He was in love, not mean. "Okay, so if we give you a makeover, you'll tell us if we're Elioud."

"Absolutely! Yes!" He sounded so excited. "And, of course, if you go get the files!"

"What are those?" I pointed to the manila file folders he had put on his desk.

"These aren't your files," he said, the blush blooming on his cheek again.

"What are they then?"

"In here?" He placed his hands gently on the folders. "Poetry I've been writing for Ms. Mary Healey. Want to hear some?" He opened the top folder and launched in.

> "Oh my sweet Mary,
>
> "I dare no longer tarry
>
> "For to you my love to carry,
>
> "But I grow wary . . ."

Because I am so hairy, I finished the poem in my frustrated little mind.

"Dr. Ellis," I spoke aloud, "I'm very sorry to interrupt, but please tell us what you mean by 'get the files.'"

"Yes, from my old office. I couldn't risk bringing them with me with those Armani-clad flying-monkey goons the Grigoris sent to watch over me. They came and told me that my office was being relocated. I grabbed the few books, binders, and file folders I could carry and was ushered down here."

"So your files—our files—are still in the other building?"

"Yes, thankfully I had the foresight to hide them. I never kept SPREE records with other files. They're in the acoustic panels above my old desk. Just get those and bring them here. I can tell you more about yourselves."

"And other GYSP students also," I said.

"All the SPREE children. I have the records going all the way back."

I looked at Dilani who nodded her consent.

"Okay, we get the files and some scissors, and, uh, makeover equipment, and come back. Where exactly is your old office?"

He told us and looked relieved, I think more about the makeover than anything else. Maybe Aunt Alina was right and beauty tips really could change lives.

But as Dilani and I got back into the rickety cage that would take us back up to daylight, I realized who now inhabited Dr. Ellis's old office: Dr. Beakley, Professor of Historical Philology, who gave us a lecture about ancient languages and was the most boring person I had ever heard drone on about anything. How were we going to get into his office? And how would we explain why we needed to get up into the acoustic tiles on the ceiling? We needed a plan and the help of our friends.

38

Air Freshener and Coffee

"This isn't going to be easy," I said, "but you can see why it's important we get in there and get the records."

Josh looked worried. "I'm not one hundred percent sure it's worth the risk," he replied.

We had gathered up in the bell tower. Dilani and I had explained what we had learned from Dr. Ellis. We left out the promise to give him a makeover and skipped right to our need to break into Dr. Beakley's office, somehow get up above the acoustical tiles, and retrieve the records.

"I'm scared too," Dilani said to Josh. "But we need to get those records."

"It's not that I'm scared," Josh shot back. "Okay, I'm scared. But I also don't know what we gain by taking the risk to get them. We all now know, thanks to the two of you, it's possible that all of us are Elioud. What difference does it make to know for sure?"

"I just found out I'm adopted!" I said, too loudly, then dropped my voice to a harsh whisper. "I just found out I'm adopted, and that I may in fact be not just randomly strange, but strange because my biological parents were part evil angel. Aren't you curious to know if that's the truth about you too?" I didn't add, and for all I know you are my brother, you knucklehead.

Josh responded calmly, "Of course I'm curious. I'm sure we're all curious, but if we're caught, if we can even get as far as rooting around in the ceiling of an office that may be inhabited by creepy biological relatives of yours, or ours—what do you think they will do to us then? Is it worth it, just to know for sure where your strangeness comes from?"

"Now who's being the rule follower?" was the best retort I could think of. Thankfully Neith spoke up. "There's another reason we have to get those records. Remember that transmission we got? Dilani and Kaia just told us what that was. It must have come from one of the Elioud sanctuaries."

I nodded. "Neith is right. Dr. Ellis said sanctuaries were founded all over the world but SPREE hadn't received any communications from them lately. The Grigoris, or someone, must have attacked the sanctuary, and the Elioud got through on our tablets somehow. You think the records might show us who the Elioud in the transmission are or where they transmitted from." I looked at Neith.

"I do," he said. "I wish I didn't, because otherwise I'm with Josh. Whether I'm Elioud or not doesn't matter at this moment. I'm here now. I may as well do what I can to survive and help others too if at all possible. But I'm not excited about the possibility of being caught and arrested by campus police if we're lucky or turned over to the Grigoris if we're not."

"All right," Josh said.

"First we need a plan for how to steal the records. Anybody got any ideas?" I asked.

"We could steal a key to Dr. Beakley's office, make a copy, and go in after hours," Miyako offered.

"We could distract Dr. Beakley. Get him out into the hall somehow, and sneak in while he's out," Dilani said.

"We could come in through the window instead of the door," I said. "Then we wouldn't need a key."

"Does one of us have spidey-powers?" Josh asked.

"We could pretend to be with the maintenance crew and say we're there to fix something important and that Dr. Beakley needs to leave us alone in his office while we take care of it," Neith said.

"The maintenance crew?" I asked. I could feel my forehead wrinkle and my eyebrows reach my hairline. "Do we get to wear uniforms and tool belts?"

I could tell Dilani actually liked this idea. "Why not?" she said. "We persuade some maintenance workers to lend us their uniforms and we figure out some problem in the ceiling that needs to be checked. HVAC or something."

"Who would lend us their uniforms?" I asked. "Maybe," I said sarcastically, "we could lure some crew members into the washroom, conk them on the head, switch clothes, duct tape their mouths shut, lock them in the washroom, go find the records, hope they're still unconscious when we get back . . ." I stopped. Everyone was staring at me like I had gone crazy. "I'm kidding!" I said, rolling my eyes. "We are not conking anyone on the head!"

My rant had not been helpful. We sat in silence for a moment.

Josh spoke again. "It doesn't have to be difficult. Dilani said we could distract Dr. Beakley. She's right."

"How?" she asked.

"You all know. What is the easiest way to distract a teacher?"

"Loud noises in the hall?" I asked.

"No, easier," Josh said.

"Pull a fire alarm," Zia said.

"Easier."

"Throw up in class," Neith said confidently.

"No!" Josh said. "Pretend you're really interested in what they're saying. If they think you're interested, they're putty in your hands!"

"That could work," Dilani said. "Plus, have you noticed how Dr. Beakley closes his eyes when he talks about something he finds fascinating?"

"Wow. You've stayed awake long enough to see him close his eyes?" Miyako asked admiringly. "Have any of us ever remained conscious through a whole Beakley lecture?"

We all shook our heads. She was right. Boring didn't begin to describe him. The most interesting thing about Dr. Beakley was the coffee mug he brought into class with him: yellow with a big smiley face on it. Its cheerfulness seemed really incongruous with the solemnity of Dr. Beakley's style. I never saw him drink from it, but I assumed a big mug of caffeine was what kept him awake during his own dull monologues.

"So who can pretend to be interested long enough to distract him to the point that he might even close his eyes, without losing consciousness themselves?" asked Dilani.

"We have to draw straws," Josh said. "It's the only fair way to decide. Plus, whoever doesn't have to go and fake fascination still has a hard job. The rest of us need to sneak in, get the files, and get out undetected."

"Do you have a plan for that too?" I asked, hoping he did.

§

Miyako drew the short straw. And Josh did have a plan. Thankfully, it included a detail that sounded more certain than relying on Dr. Beakley to keep his eyes shut while we rummaged around in the ceiling above his desk. However, the same detail was what made our plan even more dangerous.

Miyako would go in during Dr. Beakley's office hours, feign interest in something he taught, try to lull him into a state of rapture over the world's most mind-numbing topic so he would shut his eyes and wax eloquent.

Miyako would then slip a sleep aid she would make into Dr. Beakley's smiley face mug, wait for the drug to take effect, open the door, and let us in. We would get the files and exit the office before the soporific wore off. Miyako would stay long enough to thank Dr. Beakley for the stimulating information and probably even get brownie points from him for her rapt attention.

What could go wrong?

Okay, plenty, but dwelling on the possibilities seemed counterproductive, especially when the lives of Elioud children could be at stake.

Miyako knocked on Dr. Beakley's door.

"Come in?" we heard a dry voice rasp from inside the office. The invitation sounded more like a question, as if Dr. Beakley were surprised someone actually came to his office hours.

Miyako gave us a thumbs up as she pushed open the door and stepped inside.

"Good afternoon, Dr. Beakley," we heard her say. "I was wondering if you could tell me more about your theory of comparative genealogy."

"Ah, my dear! That is one of the most fascinating, yet strangely underappreciated topics in historic philology!"

Our Google search of Dr. Beakley's dissertation had paid off. But I didn't envy Miyako. I hope she had drunk a triple espresso with her lunch.

"Shoot!" I said, "Aranka's coming." I could smell the combination of her deodorant and the sharkfin sandwich I had seen her eat at lunch. She appeared at the end of the hallway and was digging in her Prada clutch as she walked. She didn't seem to have noticed us. "We can't just hang out here. A crowd outside Beakley's office will look suspicious."

"Let's duck in here," Neith said, already pushing open the door next to Boring Beakley's.

"You go. I'll distract Aranka and keep an eye out for Miyako's signal," Zia said.

Dilani, Josh, and I scurried after Neith. Too late I noticed the brass sign on the door: Male Faculty Restroom. Rats.

The others had already figured out where we were, based on the room's furnishings.

Neith was wide-eyed and beads of sweat were breaking out on his forehead. Dilani pressed her finger to her lips and checked under the stall doors to make sure we were alone. Her shoulders dropped as she relaxed and whispered, "All clear," but we all knew we couldn't just hang out here. Josh, however, had already gone over to the window on the far wall.

Josh tugged at the window frame, while Neith, Dilani and I ducked into a stall in case anyone came in. Dilani pushed Neith into the open room. "We can't have six legs poking out beneath one stall!" she whispered at him.

"Four isn't better!" He whispered back.

We exited the stall and watched Josh. The window groaned and shuddered open as Josh pushed it as high as it would go.

"Bingo!" Josh said. "A ledge. It goes the length of the building, including past Beakley's office next door. We're only three floors up," he said gently to Neith. "Can you handle it?"

We heard a low voice talking with someone right outside the bathroom door.

"I guess I'll have to," Neith said.

"The exam results look good so far," the deep voice said to someone. We could see the door start to swing into the room. One by one we scurried out onto the ledge. It was wide enough that we could step onto it and move toward Beakley's office window. We wouldn't be able to pass each other, but we had enough room to turn around, and the gray stone blocks of the building's façade had enough space between them to get a good handhold.

We were all out on the ledge when we heard the voice in the rest room. "The next stage should be interesting. We'll see who survives . . ." the voice was muffled as the speaker closed the window.

"Great," Neith murmured.

"Just keep your fingers on the wall, relax, and if you need to look at something, look at me," Dilani said in a soothing voice. She was good at this. She was very steady on her feet and barely using just one hand to keep her balance. She could see me staring at her.

"I've spent a lot of time watching cats," she said.

"They have nine lives. You don't. Please remember that," I said.

"Now what?" I asked Josh.

"Now we adapt and incorporate your idea," he replied.

"Conking maintenance workers on the head?" I asked nervously.

"Going in through the window."

Oh boy.

Josh and I were the first in our procession along the ledge and took our perches on either side of the window, holding onto the brick edging along the frame, so we could peer into the office. The window was large, with the slightly wavy glass you find in old buildings. Like the one in the washroom, the bottom pane would slide up and give just enough space for someone to step in.

The ripples in the glass distorted Miyako's face, as if we were looking at her in a carnival funhouse. But she was not having fun. We could see Dr. Beakley from the back. The top of his head was tilted slightly toward us. His wispy comb-over looked like strands of seaweed washed on the smooth shore of his pale head. We guessed that his eyes were closed, based on the contortions Miyako was going through to keep herself alert. She alternated between pulling at her cheeks, giving herself the wide grin of a circus clown, and sucking them in so she looked like a bored fish trapped in a glass bowl.

"He's still awake," Josh said to the others behind us. "The drug must not be working yet."

"Please hurry," Neith said, and I uttered my own prayer to whichever evil angel had given humans the secret of pharmacopeia.

We waited, our muscles tensed. The feeling of cool, gritty mortar at my fingertips was changing to warm, slippery moistness.

Josh and I jerked back in surprise as we saw Dr. Beakley suddenly stand and rush past Miyako to exit the room. Miyako sprang from her seat, suddenly very awake, and hoisted the window open.

"The drug isn't working! But he suddenly thought of a chart he had made showing the differences between Sumerian and Akkadian generational reckoning, or something like that." She winced. "Even my feet are asleep. Get in here quick before he comes back!"

Josh and I scrambled in the window, and Neith, and Dilani scooted along the ledge behind us so they could see in. Josh climbed on the desk and pushed up one of the acoustical tiles, easily dislodging it from the metal frame that held it in place. He handed the tile to me and his head disappeared up into the space above the dropped ceiling.

The tile was disgusting. Along with the random pattern in the fiberglass, grayish speckled spitballs were stuck to it like tiny hornets' nests, probably shot there by some earlier bored student trying to stay awake during one of Beakley's torturous discourses. The wads looked slightly damp.

"I don't see anything!" he said, his voice muffled by the remaining ceiling tiles. His head poked back down, a look of panic on his face. "It's just wires and dust, no files!"

"He's coming!" Miyako exclaimed. "Get out!"

I turned toward the window, the fiberglass board still in my hands. I thrust it at Dilani, who took it as I scrambled back onto the ledge, Josh following close behind. We heard the shoosh of the window closing. Josh waved us along the ledge back toward the window into the Faculty Men's Restroom. To my surprise, Zia's head popped out from the open window. She extended a hand to each of us and helped us back in.

"I came in here when Beakley's office door opened. I had to duck into a stall because two people were already in here. But get this, it was Dr. Eder and Dr. Calleo. They were talking about whom they would examine in the Dream Lab next." She looked at Neith. "It's you." His eyes widened, and he dug in his pants pocket.

"Are you okay?" Dilani asked him.

Neith pulled an inhaler from his pocket and took a deep pull. He breathed out slowly. "Asthma," he said. "Anxiety can bring it on. But I'm all right."

"Eder and Calleo are gone, but we should get out of here." Zia spoke quickly, then paused. "Why do you have that?" she pointed to the tile in Dilani's hand.

"I'm not exactly sure," Dilani replied, looking at me.

"Oh no!" I said. "What have I done? Beakley's going to notice that part of his ceiling is missing!"

"Maybe you did him a favor," Zia said, her lips curling in disgust. "That thing is gross."

"Leave it in here," I said to Dilani. "Stuff it in the garbage can."

"Wait!" Neith said. He grabbed it from Dilani, held it level with his eyes and rocked the panel slightly back and forth. Shoving the board under his arm, he pushed the door open and rushed into the hallway. He called back over his shoulder, "C'mon! Get Miyako and tell her we need her at the chemistry lab!"

I went to Beakley's office door and peered in the window just in time to see the professor, who had been standing behind his desk and using a stick to point at a graph on a large chart labeled "Frequency of 'Begat' Cognates in Proto-Northwest Semitic Dialects," suddenly drop the stick and chart. He swayed slightly forward, then slightly back, and forward again, and then dropped with a muffled thud face first onto the desk.

Miyako stood as I cautiously opened the office door.

"It's about time," she said, stretching and shaking herself to alertness.

"Maybe he just tuckered himself out," I said.

She smiled. She checked his pulse, then pulled gloves and a paper towel out of her bag. She slipped the gloves on and wiped his coffee mug inside and out. The cheery mug looked like it approved of what we had done.

"We need to go to the lab," I told Miyako. "Neith thinks we have something."

"Just a sec," she said, whipping out a notebook and a pen. She wrote, "Dear Dr. Beakley, Thank you for your lecture. I hope you had a pleasant nap. Sorry I wasn't a more engaging audience."

§

Neith and the others were waiting for us outside the lab when we arrived. Miyako let us in, and we gathered at her station. Neith grabbed a pair of tweezers and began to pry the spitballs away from the tile, dropping them onto a glass plate next to her microscope.

"Microdots," he said as he popped the last one off the board. "Dr. Ellis said the files were in the ceiling and we thought of paper files above the ceiling tile. But they're here." He pointed at the wads. "Microdots are tiny photographic images. Each one can have an entire page's worth of information. SPREE started in Paris, right?"

"Right," said Dilani.

"Microdots were invented there in the 1870s. It was a way people could give carrier pigeons a lot of information to carry all at once. SPREE must have used the technique to communicate with families outside the city. Ellis must have embedded the dots into moistened hunks of paper and thrown them at the ceiling when the security guards came to move him from his office. Can we look?" he asked Miyako.

She turned on the microscope and Neith stuck one of the gray masses under the lens. He looked through the eyepiece and poked at the lump with the tweezers until he dislodged a couple of the dots.

"Yes!" he said. "This one is a list of names, dates, and locations . . . This one too." He looked up from the microscope. This could take a while, but we've got names of Elioud. Maybe the dates are birthdates."

"Or dates SPREE rescued them," Dilani said. "Or dates they went to new families."

"I see a heading on this one," Neith said as he looked into the microscope again. "SPREE Norway 1920. This one is SPREE Denmark 1935. Each of these is a long list of names, all under one date and location. This is SPREE Ethiopia 1872. It has an end date. 1875."

"Where the mummified children came from," I said. "These are the sanctuaries and their start dates. And end dates," I added, my heart sinking. The Grigoris must have found that one.

"Here's 'SPREE Island 1945.'"

"SPREE Island?" Dilani repeated. "The others are countries."

Neith said, "In English it's Iceland. That must be where the transmission we received came from."

"And where the Grigoris are mining more antimony," Dilani added.

We were silent for a moment.

"Can you find us on one of those dots?" I asked.

"I'll do it," Miyako said. Neith slid her the microscope. "I don't actually need it," she said. "I have kind of freakish sight. I can see ridiculously small things." She looked sheepish. "Helps with doing chemistry," she said. She looked at a few dots briefly, then said, "Okay, this should be the right time period."

We sat in silence as she looked. Then slowly, as she found each one of us, she said our names aloud. She found everyone in the program but Neith.

She looked at him. "I'll keep looking if you want, but everyone else in the program is on here, even the ones already sent home."

"Except we know that Kiran, and maybe the others weren't really sent home."

"Extracted," Dilani said quietly.

"You don't think . . .?" Neith began.

"Why not?" Josh asked. "If we're not useful to the Grigoris one way, why not use us in some other way?"

"So, Xanthe was Elioud," I wondered aloud.

"She's listed here," Miyako replied.

Maybe that's why her portrait had been decimated and her ashes removed from the gallery in the Bell Tower.

"What do we do now?" Zia said.

"I'll transfer this information onto a thumb drive. We need to keep it safe," Miyako offered. "Who wants to hold on to it?"

Dilani raised her hand. "I'll do it. I've had extra pockets sewn into all my clothes. My homage to marsupials. I can keep it with me at all times."

"Okay," said Miyako. "What else?"

"Let's go see if Dr. Ellis can tell us anything more." I looked at Dilani. "Ready for the makeover?"

"Makeover?" Josh asked.

"Long story. Trust us."

We quickly packed a duffle with scissors, tweezers, a razor, shaving cream, towels and a hand mirror. I threw in an eyeliner, concealer, powder and blush, just for good measure. But when we got to the Zoology Museum, we found out that Dr. Ellis was gone. Ms. Healey too.

"Left together," said the new front desk security guard. "Sweet, really. I was coming off my rounds in the exhibit hall, and there he was, down on one knee in front of this very desk. Ms. Healey was saying, 'Yes, oh you adorable scruffy lamb of a man, yes!' He grabbed her hand and off they went."

Well, I thought. *At least theirs is a happy ending.*

I hoped.

"Are you Kaia and Dilani?" the security guard asked. We nodded.

"I should probably ask for ID," she said. We showed her our student cards, and she slid an envelope across the desk toward us. It was the GYSP's signature thick cream linen. Our names were written in the now familiar lavish calligraphy.

I took the envelope, my hand trembling slightly.

"Open it," Dilani said, her eyes wide.

I slid the thick card out and read, "Congratulations. You have both qualified for the GYSP Week Three Reward Expedition. Report at once to the Common Room."

39

Anticipation and Panic

"Congratulations," Dr. Grigori said to our once more diminished group.

We were down to eight. I was relieved to see that Dilani, Josh, Neith, Miyako, Zia, and I had survived. Aranka and Fintan rounded out the group.

"We are disappointed," said Dr. Grigori, "that not all of our participants are able to continue with us into Week Three's activities. However, let that be of no concern to you." No one mentioned why Xanthe wasn't with us anymore. It was like she had never existed. He went on, "Once again, the loss of the expelled is your gain. Call it the economy of the strong."

I felt a chill.

But I also felt my heart beat a little faster. Even though I was repulsed by Dr. Grigori's coldness, I was sure he was going to announce another weekly reward. What fabulous prize would I get this week? I had even day-dreamed about it during the week. I had always wanted a great road bicycle. A really expensive one, something titanium or lighter, and someone to do the maintenance on it, so all I had to concentrate on was riding. It wasn't my fault the others hadn't made it. Why shouldn't I benefit?

Dr. Grigori brought me out of my reverie with his announcement. "Personalized rewards have come to an end."

I could hear some intakes of breath around me. Even a soft whiny "Uhh?" At least I kept my pang of disappointment to myself. I think I did, anyway.

"However," said Dr. Grigori, "we move now to group rewards. This week you all continue your studies abroad."

Aranka brought her hands to her mouth as if she were an inflated balloon someone had forgotten to tie off and her fingers were keeping in the air. Or like she was Miss Ohio hearing that Miss Wisconsin was the first runner up, so it was she who would be the next Miss America. Dilani saw it too and rolled her eyes at me.

"Your next week will be a travel adventure. The course is called 'Sky-scrapers: Past, Present, and Future.' Our itinerary includes the site of the world's tallest skyscraper."

Dilani's eyeroll turned to eyes wide open. Dubai? And why in the week before the same constellation that had appeared over the Tower of Babel was going to spin into place over the city that held the world's tallest building?

Dr. Grigori said. "Meet the limos out in front in precisely half an hour. You are dismissed." He turned to leave.

"Dr. Grigori," Fintan said, as he shot his hand into the air. He trembled slightly, embarrassed, I'm sure, at calling after Dr. Grigori.

Dr. Grigori nodded at him and the excited talking that had started with the word 'dismissed,' suddenly stopped.

"I don't have my passport with me," he said. "I didn't think I would need it."

My heart sank too. At least he had a passport. I had never been anywhere a passport was required.

"No matter," Dr. Grigori said, opening his hands in a friendly and dismissive manner. "You will not require it."

Now Aranka looked crushed. "But we are going out of the country, right, Dr. Grigori?" Her forehead was wrinkled in confusion. Maybe she was thinking what I was, that Dr. Grigori must be taking us to Las Vegas or someplace where they had miniature versions of famous cities. Or was there another Dubai, maybe somewhere in the Midwest? I made a mental adjustment. It would still be a new adventure and it would solve the passport problem.

"Allow me to reiterate," Dr. Grigori said, his voice gaining a new gravitas, "and do me the courtesy of listening." He looked with an arched eyebrow first at Fintan, then at Aranka. "You will not need passports. The Grigori Young Scholars Program enjoys certain privileges that make passports irrelevant." He cleared his throat, then raised his eyebrows and widened his eyes when Aranka again raised her hand.

"Yes?"

"I'm not sure thirty minutes is enough time for me to pack."

"Ah." His eyes sparkled as if she had made a valid point and set him up for something he would enjoy saying. "My earlier comment seems to have been misperceived. This reward is quite personalized in one respect. A bag has been already been custom packed for each of you." He looked at Aranka, and she made the Miss America hand-to-mouth gesture again.

Honestly, even I felt like one of the fifty finalists when they're issued their personal competition-issued bathing suit and evening gown—special and swept up into something bigger than themselves. I inhaled through my nose, caught my own scent, and smelled one more feeling before I named it—utter panic.

40

Clover, Buttercups, and Stone

I awoke with a start as the plane fell, bounced, rose, dipped, jerked right, slid left, bounced again.

"Turbulence," said Dilani, who had turned cactus color. She held one of the little white paper bags stashed in our seat pockets below her chin. "Just turbulence."

A voice intoned over the loud speaker. "We have started our descent and will be landing shortly."

The plane dropped again. So did my stomach.

The voice soothed, "The wind over the Orkneys is always a factor in our landing. Have no worries. We have a very capable captain."

Out the window I saw flat moss green and storm cloud gray land below us. The plane lurched sideways, and my view suddenly included a stretch of steel blue water with whitecaps. The only Orkneys I had heard of were the Orkney Islands in the north of Scotland. Surely there were no skyscrapers there.

The plane jolted back to horizontal. I breathed deeply as we approached a landing strip at what appeared to be a normal angle. The thrill ride was almost over.

We came to a surprisingly smooth landing and a collective cheer went up. The wind outside howled, and the plane listed from side to side as we taxied to a stop. Heavy clouds sailed by overhead. Mr. Argyros gave us each a navy blue slicker and rain pants marked with the GYSP logo in white on the jacket front and across the back. The identification would come in handy if we got blown out to sea and someone had to identify our bodies. I imagined a person with a long hook hauling to shore a bloated corpse and saying in a thick Scottish brogue, "Aye, another one marked GYSP."

Two forest green Land Rovers rolled up to meet our jets. Mr. Argyros told us to leave our bags on the plane.

"This will not be a long visit," he said, "but it will be fascinating, especially for some of you." I thought he looked in my direction, but if he did, it was probably because I looked like a giant blueberry in my rain suit. I glanced over at Aranka. She had managed to tie hers at the waist somehow so it resembled a charming sailor's outfit.

We climbed into the vehicles and drove away from the landing strip and onto a single-track road marked, "Ring of Brodgar." Even from a distance I could see what we were aiming for. It wasn't a skyscraper, but if our tour started with something ancient, this would be it, and it definitely qualified as something reaching skyward.

On a grassy green plateau, a circle of standing stones, each about twelve feet tall, jutted into the sky. The stones were thin rectangles, though many of the tops looked broken off, like damaged teeth. The circle was immense, three hundred feet or more across. The stones looked like an immense color wheel in the spectrum of gray. This circle would be a giant's array of paint chips—porpoise fin, cinder, dove-in-flight, morning fog, city sidewalk, gullwing, steel wool. The stones stood out against the equally variegated charcoals, lead, and ash grays of the clouds overhead. I had no idea gray came in so many shades.

We got out of the Land Rovers at a gravel path (screen door gray) that led to the ring of stones. We had the place to ourselves. The wind flapped our rain jackets and pants, and I felt like an enormous navy blue and white flag. I wondered what I would mean in semaphore if I lifted my arms to the sky. I tried it. If the giant choosing amongst paint colors saw me, was I signaling wonder or distress? Aranka stared at me, baffled, I'm sure, by what I was doing. A gust of wind actually propelled me forward a step.

Dr. Calleo led our procession of blue flags to the standing stones and motioned for us all to keep up. The path crossed an earthen bridge over a deep ditch hewn from the rock beneath us. Almost ten feet deep and twenty feet across, the ditch encircled the stones. I looked down as we crossed the bridge and saw a trickle of water meandering along the bottom. If the ditch were full, it would have kept anyone frightened of water out of the circle. Although anyone who didn't like water wouldn't feel at home anywhere on this island. On two sides of us were lakes, the Lochs of Harray and Stenness, and we weren't far from the sea.

I looked around and tried to take in the whole vista. Stone, earth, water. Sky, land, sea. Paper, scissors, rock. Which would win if the elements went to war? Today my money was on rock. Even a puff of this wind would blow paper away. Scissors would rust in the misty air. These rocks had persevered a long time. But who had placed them here and why?

We stepped into the circle and Dr. Calleo gathered us close. The grass in the middle of the circle was dotted with fragrant buttercups and clover. I also smelled the same petrichor scent my votive emitted on our first day of classes. Odd, since that smell usually comes before it rains on dry stones and this terrain certainly wasn't dry. The tall stones we were standing near blocked some of the wind. Our jackets quieted to a flutter.

"Come closer," she commanded. Then, "listen."

As the wind blew in between the stones, its pitch changed. First, higher. Another gust of wind came through, but from a slightly different direction and another note sounded, lower. The wind was strong, and the notes were faint. I wasn't sure I was really hearing anything. I looked at Josh. Could he hear it? He nodded, anticipating my question.

"You are, no doubt, familiar with Stonehenge in Amesbury. The Ring of Brodgar here is at least as old, built around 2500-2000 BCE. The word 'henge' actually refers to the ring around it, the ditch, not the stones. The henge here was most likely constructed before the stones were put into place.

"Many theories exist about the Ring's construction. It may have been a temple or part of a temple complex. The nearby village of Skara Brae, also from the Neolithic period, may once have been inhabited by a group of priests or magi who came here to communicate with the heavens. Acoustics may have had something to do with the Ring's original purpose."

"Like it was a giant prehistoric stone flute?" Zia asked.

"Perhaps," said Dr. Calleo. Another blast of wind, another note. "Originally more stones stood here, sixty instead of the current twenty-six. The full complement of stones would not have entirely closed off the circle, but it would have made it sound very different inside from outside."

"I count twenty-seven stones," Josh said.

Dr. Calleo's head jerked toward Josh. Her eyes were wide open, as if he had caught her in a lie. She smoothed the scarf at her throat. "Oh, yes. You are correct. Twenty-seven. Yes."

"Maybe it was just a giant circular wind block," Aranka said, "a good place to rest in a gale."

"Perhaps," Dr. Calleo said, "but would you go to such extremes to build a shelter from the wind?"

I looked around. Most of the stones were gray, but one appeared more beige than the others. I would have named it ostrich plume if someone asked me. Or ziggurat.

"Most of the stones came from a local quarry, about five miles away. Since each one weighs approximately two tons, the effort involved in moving them would be substantial."

"But they're not all from the same place," I said.

"You are noticing the pale one over there," Dr. Calleo said. "Yes, that one especially has puzzled many people, including archaeoacoustologists, those who study sound in ancient places."

"I doubt they ran out of local stone," Neith said, looking around at the rocky landscape.

"Maybe it makes a different sound than the others," Zia offered. "If you strike it or speak into it or the wind whistles past it."

"Perhaps," Dr. Calleo said.

"What happened to the other stones? The missing ones?" Fintan asked. "Who would take a stone from this place?"

"Two mysteries then," Dr. Calleo said. "The mystery of the foreign stone and the mystery of the missing stones. Perhaps one of you will figure it out and solve an ancient puzzle. You have an hour to explore," she said. "Meet back at the land rovers at three o'clock exactly."

Josh, Neith, Zia, and I wandered toward the beige stone.

Neith said, "This area would have been pretty remote until not that long ago. I wonder how long people other than locals even knew about this circle."

I looked at Zia, eyeing the circle. "So, do you want to sing?" I asked.

"I am curious about the sound in here," she replied.

She opened her mouth, but I could hardly hear her above the wind. She stopped and shook her head. So this wasn't like the dome in St. Hildegard's Church.

Josh's eyes suddenly lit up. He took his votive out of his pocket and held it next to his ear. His votive was in shape of a lion.

"Listening for its roar?" I asked.

He ignored me and pressed his ear to the beige stone. Then to his votive again. He looked at us.

"I doubt you'll be able to hear this, but my votive and this stone share exactly the same frequency. It's like they're humming, very quietly, and sounding the exact same note." The stones were very similar in color too.

I handed him mine. He listened.

"Nope," he said. "Different pitch. I'm going to stay here and look around a little more. Mind if I hold onto this for now?" he raised my little stone pig.

"Remember to give it back," I said.

Zia pointed at a grassy mound in the distance. "Let's check that out," she said and Neith and I headed off with her.

§

The mound had a small entrance way. A sign to the right of the entrance explained that the mound, Maeshowe, was a burial chamber, although all the human remains had been removed long ago. Vikings had broken into the chamber in the mid-1100s and left some runic graffiti behind.

I crouched down and crawled in. It was about four feet tall at its highest point and about ten feet in diameter. Enough light came in from the doorway for me to see. The interior was all precisely cut slabs, neatly fitted together. I turned around and stuck my head out. "Come on in," I said to Zia and Neith.

We sat down in the middle of the stone floor. It was so quiet. All sound from outside was blocked. I settled into the silence, enjoying the absence of the wind. Zia got out a flashlight and shone it around.

"Amazing the precision with which people cut these stones," she said. "This place is over five thousand years old and it's perfectly constructed."

"Hey!" said Neith, "There's Viking graffiti." He pushed Zia's arm gently so her flashlight focused one of the sidewalls. It was covered with scratches shaped like tree branches, crosses, and hooks.

"Runes," Neith exclaimed, standing up. Zia handed him the flashlight. "Cool!"

"What's it say?" Zia asked, getting to her feet. I stood up too.

Neith ran his fingers along the lines. "It's a bunch of statements, maybe unrelated to one another. Some of it seems to be regular old graffiti. 'Ingigerth is the most beautiful of all women.' 'Ingebjork the fair widow was here with Erlingr.'

"Great," I said. "We came all this way to see stuff I can see in the bathroom at school. Did they leave any phone numbers?"

Neith laughed. "A couple inscriptions are more interesting: 'In the circle a great treasure is hidden in plain sight. The one who returns this treasure to its home will gain great reward.' And this, 'A hole is here that shows the blood. This was carved by Engelheidrunfrigg.'"

"That shows the blood?" I asked.

"Great treasure?" Zia added.

"That's what it says," Neith replied. "Runes are pretty easy once you get the hang of them."

"But what does it mean?" I said.

Neith and Zia both shrugged.

"We'd better go," Zia said. "You know Dr. Calleo and time."

§

We rode back to the airstrip, saying nothing. I wanted to talk about the inscription and anything else we may have found out during our free time, but I wasn't keen to bring anything up with our driver and Grigori professors within earshot. Better to wait until we were on the plane.

This time, Aranka and Fintan were told to board the plane the professors were on. We boarded our jet, took off our rain gear, and settled in for whatever leg of our journey was next.

The plane jerked and bounced as we gained altitude. I looked out the window and saw the stone circle grow smaller and smaller. I thought I saw a long white rectangle attached to a white square—a truck and trailer?—move along the single track road that now looked like a smoke gray worm beneath us. If we had stayed the night, we would have seen the headlines the next day in the local paper: *Beige Monolith Mysteriously Vanishes from Brodgar Circle*.

§

"Okay, spill," Zia said, as we huddled close on the plane. The steward was busy in the back clearing up after our refreshments. Rukmini and Argyros were talking to the pilot. It seemed safe to discuss our findings.

Miyako and Dilani had gone to see the ruins of Skara Brae, the nearby village, during our free time. Josh had stayed at the Circle.

Josh said, "A sign was posted nearby indicating that it was rare for a henge—you know, the ditch—to have a stone circle inside of it. More often, there's just a ditch, or just a stone circle, not both, like here. Even Stonehenge is different. It has a ditch, but at a greater distance from the stones. At Brodgar, the ditch is definitely close to the stones, related to the stones."

Dilani offered, "Maybe something at Brodgar made whoever built it think a huge ditch all the way around it would be a good idea."

"You mean, someone dug the ditch to make sure whatever is inside of the ditch would be safe from whoever doesn't want to have to cross a ditch to get to them," I said.

"Would that really work?" Neith asked.

"Would for me," I replied. "I wouldn't want to swim or take my chances just to get closer to the stones. I would be happy to stay on the outside and look in. I'm glad the water's been drained, or whatever made the ditch pretty much dry."

"What did you find out at the village?" Zia asked Miyako and Dilani.

"Skara Brae was abandoned suddenly about 2000 BCE. No one knows why," Miyako said.

Neith spoke up about our discovery. "Maybe it had something to do with the inscription we found." He repeated it.

"A great treasure is hidden in the circle in plain sight," Josh said.

"I didn't see anything in the circle," I said. "Just the stones."

Josh said, "Maybe the treasure is in the stones, or is the stones, or one of them. You saw how my votive and that beige one seemed to have some connection."

"That reminds me," I replied. "Can I have my votive back?" Josh handed it to me.

"What was that about showing blood?" Miyako asked.

"There's a hole that shows the blood," Neith said.

"The ditch is a hole," Zia said.

"But what does it show?" Dilani asked.

"It would show who is afraid to cross it." I said. "Who is afraid of water, I mean besides me?" I asked.

"Angels and demons can't live in water. So Nephilim wouldn't like it either," Dilani said.

"Maybe a ditch full of water would demonstrate the presence of Nephil blood," offered Josh, "and keep Nephilim out of the Circle, but why? What's the treasure? If it's the stones, or a stone, why would that be treasure and who would hide it? And from whom?"

"And how would someone return it to get a great reward?" Neith asked.

"I did notice one more thing," Josh said. There was a divot in the beige stone."

"A hole?" Neith asked, like he wanted to make sure he understood.

"I suppose so," Josh said. "But the strange thing is, my votive fit into it. Not precisely, not tightly, but the size was right. Like someone could have carved my votive from a piece of that stone. And when I stuck it in, I heard something. This will sound weird, but it sounded a little like a lion's roar."

I said, "Did you find a stone my votive fit into?"

"No," Josh said. "Nothing for your votive there."

"Who was Engelheidrunfrigg?" Zia asked Neith. "The Viking who wrote the inscription," she explained to the others.

"I don't know, but her name means 'the one who has seen hidden angels.'"

We were quiet.

"You know," said Dilani, "we really should talk with Fintan and Aranka about all this stuff. Their lives may be in danger too. Plus, maybe they know things that could help us."

I was skeptical, not only because Aranka had been so close to Xanthe and both of them were close with Fintan, but also because at this very moment they were with our professors on the second plane in our little entourage. I mentioned this to the others and added, "Who knows what they're talking about. Maybe they've been separated out to see what they know. Maybe to see what they know about what we know."

Dilani shook her head. "We really should include them. They're in the same situation we are, and we should get all the help we can."

"But we need to make sure it's really help," I retorted.

"Too late," Dilani replied. "Just before we boarded, Fintan and Aranka said they wanted to talk with us. They said they had information they thought we might find interesting. Ms. Rukmini was standing right there, so I couldn't ask them anything, but I told them we would all get together at our next stop."

The steward came back to us. "You all should get a little sleep before our next adventure. I'm dimming the cabin lights now."

I asked Josh just before the lights went out, "Can I see your votive, or hold it for a while? I just want to think about something."

He shrugged and handed it over. I put it close to my nose and inhaled as deeply as I could. I wasn't sure what, if anything would happen, and nothing did, at first, except for my nostrils filling with the overwhelming scents of buttercup and clover pollen and ancient rock dust. The lights went out, and I fell into a deep sleep.

I was standing in an open field staring at a large tower, wide at the base and progressively narrower as it reached toward heaven. The top blocked the sun from view, just enough so I could see that the bricks of the building gleamed golden yellow. The yellow reminded me of sunflowers—brilliant yellow heads turning toward the sun. I could hear people laboring, calling out to one another in a language, which I knew I couldn't speak, and yet was somehow familiar. Two oxen strained in their yoke, pulling a heavy cart loaded with stone and brick. I could hear their grunts and the wheels of the cart squeal and moan against the rocky ground as they pulled, a man shouting at them in that same language. The sun was hot, and I felt deep gratitude, almost joy, to be standing in the shade provided by the tower. Or was my feeling of joy a result of hearing the sound of the unknown, yet familiar language, as I heard a group of women speaking to one another to my left?

Suddenly, darkness passed overhead, as if a huge bird was flying over and blocking the sun. The air became cool, and I could see the tower clearly without the glare of the sun, its stones the color of the odd-one-out in the stone circle at Brodgar, the one I had called 'ziggurat.'

The shadow passed and the sunlight resumed, burning hot and bright. Then another passing of the great winged bird. Was it a bird? It stopped atop the tower, its great wings unfurled, opalescent feathery surface glistening even with the sun behind it. A great hush fell as the temperature dropped again. Someone in the crowd began to speak, in a plaintive tone, then others joined in. I could almost make out their entreaty . . .

§

I awoke as a ding sounded, and the flight steward's voice said, "Time to prepare for our descent."

I responded in my head, *our descent into what?*

§

We made two more stops on our way to Dubai. At both, we stayed on the planes. At both, a van pulled up to the jet the professors, Fintan, and Aranka were on. Two men got out and loaded a wooden crate onto the plane, about the size of a refrigerator both times, onto the plane, then drove away.

Finally, the pilot announced, "Our next destination is Dubai. Prepare for landing."

Okay, Babel. Show us what you've got.

41

1866

Samya Stricken

Before returning to the manor where the Peerless had assembled, Samya allowed herself one more look at the notes she had copied from Brother Josef's notebook in the monastery. She had already sent the specimens, the mummified Elioud children, on ahead by courier, but the notes she wanted to deliver herself. With these notes detailing the possibility of recessive traits amongst the Elioud and the possibility of illness amongst the Nephilim, she now had everything she needed to make her demands known to the Peerless.

All along she had been keeping track of what the Peerless sent her to obtain. She had not just mindlessly handed things over to them. She was building her case, her store of knowledge that would guarantee that they would meet her demands.

First, she had read the manuscript she had obtained from the Malmesbury Abbey in England. Since she had also been assigned to pose as one of the sisters directly under St. Hildegard's authority when the abbess still lived, Samya was familiar with the *Lingua Ignota*. So she was able to translate the text and knew why it was so important to the Peerless to get hold of this document. The Book of Noah held the key to the survival of the Peerless. The information contained within it, combined with the last thing she saw the demented Noah do, made sense to her.

Noah's last action had puzzled her before she read the letter his great-grandfather had written to him. Just before the original language that everyone knew and spoke and understood was taken away by the Enemy, Noah started giving his little carvings to anyone who would take one. Not to her, not to the Peerless—who saw them only as worthless trinkets. But to anyone Noah could persuade to accept one, he gave them. "Protect this stone," he said to those into whose hands he tucked a miniscule pony or giraffe or dog. "The Tower will not be finished. The stones will be dispersed. Carry this with you." The people had been dispersed, taking Noah's stones, and clues to the original language, with them.

The information in the Book of Noah meant the Peerless could get the immortality they wanted, and Noah's rock carvings would help them in this endeavor.

Now, she held in Brother Josef's notes the proof that the Peerless needed the Elioud, those they had discarded in the past, to accomplish their goal.

She rehearsed her address as she made her way. She would start by telling them that she knew they were sick, that they had begun to disintegrate, that their bodies were rotting internally. She thought she might even reveal that Gadreel had asked her to concoct some scent with which she might mask the fecal odor he had started to omit. She knew the antimony they consumed, that her own mother had mixed into cosmetics for Nephilim, was no longer working to counter the pulling apart of their two natures.

Every scrap of information she collected for the Peerless should have raised her value in their eyes, but not once did they show her the respect she deserved. True, over time, she had received enough elixir that she had even developed wings, but why shouldn't she have them? Wasn't she actually superior to Nephilim since she seemed to have no problem with disincoherence, while their disintegration grew worse?

She would tell them she knew they needed her more than ever and that she would give them the manuscript only if they regarded her as equal with them and stopped using her as a mere errand-runner.

Samya was shown into the manor's dining hall where the Peerless were drinking the manor's prize claret, fortified with antimony, of course. Rather than bowing, as she always had, she unfurled her wings and held the chest containing the copied notes in front of her, where they could see, but not reach it.

"I now possess the information you seek concerning the Elioud. I understand the Book of Noah and the significance of the votives," she said, her voice possessing a strength she had not heard before. The sound of it made her smile.

"But before I give this information to you," she continued, "I demand a reward, the reward I deserve."

She watched as the eyes of the Peerless widened, then narrowed. Gadreel and Vadim stood.

Vadim snorted. "You dare to demand?"

"You know about the little stones," Gadreel imitated her, and laughed. He looked around the table. "She knows about the old Merely's little stones." He shook his head, then turned to her. "You do not know about the large stones, the Babel stones. As usual, you confuse the insignificant for the important."

"The large stones?" Samya began, curious now, but her voice was shaky.

"You think you deserve to know, to be further rewarded? After your impudence?" Vadim snarled.

Samya bowed out of habit but despised herself for doing it.

"I suppose she would like more elixir," Gadreel sneered. He and Vadim looked at each other and laughed. "Have you figured out the elixir as well?" he asked Samya as if speaking to a precocious child.

She raised her head and replied quietly, "Nephil blood."

The Peerless broke into laughter.

"We would never give you our own blood!" Vadim snorted.

"It is Elioud blood," Gadreel said, suddenly somber. "The blood of your children." He broke out in a cackle again. "What a terrible mother you are, to not know it was they, and others like them, who have been keeping you alive all this time, who helped you sprout the pathetic wings of which you are so proud."

She spied Gadreel nodding almost imperceptibly to someone behind her. She gasped as she felt strong arms grab both of her wings where they joined at her shoulder blades and where their roots went deep to intertwine with her lungs. A large hand holding a damp cloth covered her nose and mouth and everything went dark.

Samya awoke, a seering pain stabbing her back and piercing her lungs. She did not know where she was and couldn't lift her head. She inhaled and smelled the cedar boughs above her and the loamy soil beneath her. She was grateful she could breathe although her lungs felt on fire. She already knew her wings were gone.

She swore if she survived she would do what she could to repay the Peerless for what they had done.

And then, for the first time Samya could remember since she had seen the little drowned Nephil in the glade, she experienced a feeling that both broke her heart and made her want to live. The feeling was pity, perhaps even compassion. Not for the young Nephil any longer, but for the Elioud.

42

Kaia

Limestone and Clay

Muggy heat blasted us as we exited the jet. Thankfully it was only a few meters to the Lincoln Navigators waiting for us on the airstrip, but I was still soaked with sweat and my hair was plastered to my head as I got into a car. I noticed the readout on the driver's control panel: 113 degrees Fahrenheit.

As we sped toward Dubai, heat radiated from the sand and asphalt and caused everything near the ground to shift and blur, like the city was built on a foundation of vapor. From the city's center, the Burj Kahlifa, our destination, pierced the sky. The tower dwarfed all other buildings, like a sunflower had blossomed in a garden of geraniums. Yet it was more aggressive than any flower, with its sharp angles and edges. What it looked exactly like was the formation Miyako had shown us in the chemistry lab, a stibnite sample, with crystal daggers and needles jutting out of a silver base, one sticking out much higher than the rest. "Stibnite. Beautiful, isn't it?" Miyako had marveled. "The most important source of antimony."

So, here we were, zooming toward a city of stibnite with an elegant silver needle, glistening like a ray of antimony, thrusting up from its center.

His eyes focused on the Burj Kahlifa, Neith turned his lightest shade of pale yet.

"Will you be all right?" I whispered.

He gave the smallest of nods. "I will. I won't look out the windows, and it's not like that thing has an outdoor balcony."

"Actually, it has three observation decks, at floors 124, 125, and 148, but only one outdoor deck," Josh said. I shot Josh my that's-not-helpful face.

"It's better that he knows now, don't you think?" Josh retorted. "He can prepare if he knows. At least you can't go up to the top. There's a radio antenna up there, but no observation deck."

"I'll survive," Neith said.

We pulled up in front of the building.

The driver informed us, "Your hotel is located on the thirty-ninth floor."

"That's not so high up," Dilani said in Neith's direction.

He wiped his upper lip with a hanky.

We hurried into the building's glass and steel lobby and waited in its hushed coolness for our group to assemble. The professors were conferring with the security man at the front desk. Josh scanned the area out front of the building. He elbowed me in the waist and nodded toward the driveway we had come in from. I spotted it right away. I tapped Dilani's shoulder. She put her hand on Neith's arm.

"Same kind of van we've seen at all our stops, right?" I said. They nodded. The vehicle drove slowly past without stopping.

"They must be going around to a loading dock," Zia said.

"I wonder if they're picking something up or dropping something off," Josh said.

"It's time to find out," I said. "Let's meet tonight, as soon as they announce lights out."

"I'll let Fintan and Aranka know," said Dilani.

Dr. Calleo appeared and gathered us to go up to the Armani Hotel.

As we got off the elevator, Dilani gestured toward her backpack. "My votive is so warm I can feel it through my bag."

"Mine too. Something here is activating it, something more powerful than our touch."

She nodded. "Maybe tonight the mystery gets solved."

"I hope so, I think."

We met in the alcove that housed the ice machine on our floor. Aranka and Fintan weren't there.

"I couldn't find them," Dilani said.

I was relieved. I didn't trust them after they had spent so much time on the flights with the professors.

"We should go ahead without them," I said.

"Okay," Dilani agreed. "We can fill them in later."

We'll see, I thought.

"Look," Neith said quietly, pointing at the logo on the machine. "Skyvolt. Glacial Ice For Your Refreshment." A vending machine with bottles of carbonated and still Skyvolt water stood next to the ice dispenser.

"In case we didn't already know the Grigoris have their fingerprints all over this place and every other place we've been," Josh said.

"Okay," I whispered. "We need to know why they've brought us here three days before the constellation is supposed to line up."

"Especially when I overheard the professors say we're here for two days," Josh said.

"We also need to know why we're here, as in, why us? What do we have to do with whatever they're up to?" I said. My mouth was getting dry from whispering. I wished I had some money for a Skyvolt.

"Let's see if we can find out where the van went and what it was doing," I said, although I had no idea how we could.

"The building must have a service corridor or service level. Maybe a bunch of them since the building is so large," Zia said. "Let's try the elevator and see if we can find something."

We got on the elevator and prayed no one would catch us snooping if we had to try a lot of floors.

"Remember the elevators will have security cameras so we can't spend too much time trying different buttons," I said.

"Or maybe we can," Miyako responded. "What would be more normal than a bunch of kids goofing around in the elevator in the world's tallest building? Don't sweat it. As long as we don't look like we're trying to get somewhere in particular, we'll be fine."

Maybe.

We stared at the panel in the elevator. Several buttons had an asterisk after the floor number. Maybe those buttons would open doors into the service area. Dilani moved her hand in a circle, choosing a button at random and clicked on it. 66*. The elevator glided into motion, but instead of just going vertically to the sixty-sixth floor, it added a little horizontal movement backwards. We all gave each other a 'did you feel that?' look. The doors behind us opened onto a beige cinder block wall with 66 stenciled in black on it. A couple of large carts heaped with laundry stood nearby.

"What just happened?" Neith asked.

"The service areas must be inside the building, in an inner core. The rooms with the windows and the gorgeous views are on the outside ring. It's quite clever," Zia said.

"But why not just have the rear doors open to the rear?" I asked. "Why the extra movement?"

"I'm not sure I understand your question," Josh said.

"I mean, what is the elevator going past to get to the service corridor? The outer ring is where people live and work and look out the windows, and some floors have a service corridor. But we just felt the elevator move through some space to get there. What is the elevator passing when it moves horizontally?"

"Let's try another floor and see if it happens again," Dilani suggested. We watched as she randomly selected another. 39*. The elevator swooshed forward, then swiftly down, then backwards again. It opened to a similar beige hallway. The chalky smell of clay and limestone hit me. I saw a couple of bags marked "cement" propped against the wall.

Miyako said, "Kaia's right. The elevator is passing over the top of something or through some space to get to the inner service areas on these floors. I wonder what we're gliding over."

"Or under," Neith added.

"Where do the asterisk floors start?" Josh asked.

"At the ground level." I said, pointing at the elevator panel. "Then they seem to occur every dozen or so floors, all the way to the top. See, 163*."

"That's not actually the top," Neith said. "There are another forty-six levels past the top story. They're not called 'stories' because they're only for maintenance." He paused. "Know your enemy," he said quietly.

"There aren't any buttons for those floors." Zia said. "I wonder how people get up there."

We stood in silence for a moment.

"Maybe the space between the regular corridor and the service corridor has something to do with how you get to the maintenance floors," I offered. "They can't possibly get to them from outside the building."

Neith sighed. "Actually," he said, "people wash the windows up there. They dangle from ropes." He turned pale. "The windows on the lower floors have moving platforms, but the spire and top floors are handled by specialists who work on super skyscrapers."

"We all have our gifts, I guess," I said. I wanted to get off the topic of aerial exposure at high altitudes for Neith's sake.

Zia said, "Let's go to the top asterisk and see if we can figure out anything when we're up there. Maybe if we listen closely we'll be able to hear something when we go through that extra space."

Suddenly I got an idea. "Who's got their votives on them?" Ever since Josh had that experience in Orkney, I carried mine around in my pocket. I brought mine out.

Dilani and Josh got theirs out too.

I said, "Dilani and I noticed that our votives are much warmer since we arrived in this building. They glow brighter too." Everyone nodded as the carved details and scratched lines lit up slightly. I looked at Josh. He said, "There's a frequency here mine is responding to, like it did in Orkney. I can hear yours all humming as well."

"Zia, when you said, 'listen,' it made me wonder if the votives respond differently depending on where we are in the building. Push the button. Let's listen and watch when we get to 163*."

The elevator accelerated and brought us swiftly up to the 163rd floor. I held my breath as it next made its now-familiar horizontal glide toward the service corridor. Sure enough, the votives momentarily glowed brighter as we passed through the space between the outer hall and the service corridor. Josh's eyes lit up and he nodded.

"It's a little louder there," he said.

The door opened to the usual beige and cinder block scene. This time, though, against the wall was a cart holding masonry tools—trowels, buckets, a level, and a hammer.

I jumped off the elevator and motioned to the others to join me.

Dilani looked alarmed. "What are you doing?"

"Something's going on here," I said. "Come on!"

No one else came. I think they were trying to decide whether to leave me behind or yank me back onto the elevator. The door started to close, and Josh stuck his hand out to make them open again. "Okay," he said, stepping out into the hallway, followed by the others. "What are you thinking?"

"There was cement in the corridor on the thirty-ninth floor. I thought that was random laundry on the sixty-sixth floor, but now I think I saw work gloves and drop cloths. They're building something in here somewhere."

"They could be redecorating or renovating," Zia said. "A building this big is probably always under some kind of repair or renovation."

I shook my head. "This building is too new, and who redecorates with masonry, especially when every public area we've seen is glass and chrome? They're making something out of bricks and cement."

We were quiet for a moment. Suddenly we heard a quiet *ding* and the sound of the elevator swooshing away from us. Neith's eyes got big. "Uh-oh. We're stuck."

"We're not stuck," Dilani said, "We just have to push the button and wait for the elevator to come back."

"Which gives us time," I said, "to see if we can see what's in the space between the elevator door and the side that opens onto the public halls."

"How?" Neith asked.

"We just have to pry the elevator door open and we should be able to see what's across there, right?" I asked, looking from person to person to make sure I wasn't saying something completely crazy.

"I'm pretty sure they have safety features in place so people can't open the door and fall into the elevator shaft if the elevator isn't there," Josh said.

We were quiet again.

"So, if someone is building something inside this building, using bricks and mortar . . ." I tried.

"Or stones," Dilani said. "What if they're using stones too? I'm not sure what I'm getting at, but, isn't it weird that the votives are lighting up like we've never seen before?"

"And the frequencies are more intense," Josh said.

"The votives are stones, right? Small, carved stones," Dilani said.

I nodded.

"And remember how Josh noticed his reacted to another stone?"

I nodded again.

"What if it's other stones the votives are responding to?"

"Could the votives be useful in a building project?" Zia asked.

"Maybe they could be decorations," Dilani offered. "They're pretty small. It would take a lot of them to build anything of any size."

"Dr. Calleo said there are thousands of them, and they've been found all over the world," I said.

The *ding* signaling an arriving elevator stopped our conversation.

"Someone's coming!" I exclaimed. I grabbed Dilani by the hand and we all ran.

Unfortunately, Dilani, Josh and I ran one way and Neith, Zia, and Miyako went the other.

The hallway we were in was a dead end. There were no doorways except one at the end of the hallway. It was a plain, windowless, metal door, painted brick red, with a stainless steel doorknob and a small panel, about the size of a cell phone, the same color as the door, but its texture was different—glossy.

Josh tried the doorknob. Nothing.

I wanted to see what was on the little panel and had to get up on my tiptoes to look directly at it.

But when I did, it came to life. It went black, then made a flash of white light, like it was taking a picture. Then I realized: not a regular picture, the kind of picture the eye doctor took when I was having my retina examined.

I blinked to clear away the residual glare. "Holy cow," I started, turning toward Josh and Dilani and pointing at the panel. "That's a retina scanner."

We heard a click and the door swung open.

"That's a door opener," they said.

I was glad my weird retinas were good for something. We heard the voices of people turning into the corridor behind us and hurried into a dark and airless space. It wasn't large. We could tell by the way we could hear our own breathing and the sound coming back to us like it didn't have far to travel.

"Airlock?" Dilani asked.

A fan started above us and a breeze blew through holes in the floor. After about ten seconds it stopped.

"Decontamination chamber," Josh said. "But why?"

The wall to the left of us slid away, and we could see a small vestibule. The vestibule opened onto another area we couldn't yet see, but we could see that it was well-lit. I peeked around the corner. What I saw made my heart stop. Then soar.

43

Oil Paint and Tears

K iran was standing in front of us. Behind him was a large easel that held a canvas, a painting by Monet I know I had seen in the Art Institute of Chicago. On the last field trip we had taken there from school, right before the summer vacation, it had been replaced with a sign that said "Removed for Conservation." Next to that easel was another one, with a half-finished copy of the painting. Kiran was holding a paintbrush.

Our eyes met. Before I could call out, he glanced up toward the corner of the ceiling. My eyes followed his gaze, and I saw the large camera mounted there, pointed into the area where Kiran was working. I dropped my eyes to his feet and noticed the long chain that connected the shackles around his right foot to a ring in the wall. My eyes welled with tears, both from joy and the pain of seeing him held captive.

Then Kiran sang out—yes, *sang* out, "Stop! Don't come any closer!" and "I can't believe you came! You found me!"

He sounded like an English version of the operas my parents used to listen to, where a big musical number with a lot of music and a lot of people singing on top of each other has come to an end and one of the characters goes on singing, all by himself, not a song, but words with notes that go higher and lower. It always seemed strange to me when a person sang like that when he or she could have just spoken.

"Why are you singing?" My voice came out like a quiet sigh. I was afraid that any sound I made would be picked up by some Grigori listening somewhere, and the jig would be up, and Josh, Dilani, and I would be captured, and who knows what they would do to Kiran. But I had to ask.

"I'm singing, because they don't listen in here, they watch." More sing-songy words, a random tune, but it actually sounded kind of nice, his voice pleasant, innocent, especially in such a depressing environment. "They're watching me on a monitor, but they can't see where you're standing. They can tell by my face that I'm singing, so I hope they think I'm singing to myself, like I often do, and not talking to you." He sang the *you* in two syllables, like *you-oo*, bringing the line to a lovely melodic closure. It made me want to sing back, my speaking voice sounding rather plain.

"Why don't they listen?" I said, but it actually came out more like a chant, like Kiran and I were playing a children's game called Pretend We're In An Opera. I almost giggled. Kiran smiled.

"They don't like my singing!"

"But it's so nice," I sang back, meaning it.

"Thank you, but Nephilim can't take it. Too melodious for them, too harmonious."

I shrugged.

"They deal in discord. Harmony and melody reminds them on a cellular level of heaven. Somehow it resonates in them in a way they find unbearable."

"Why do they let you sing if they can't stand it?" I was giving it full diva soprano treatment now. Josh nudged me in the ribs. "Don't get carried away," he said. We don't have much time." He glanced nervously behind us to make sure no one was coming.

"I told them it makes my work better. And they want me to do excellent work." He sighed.

"How are you?" I asked quietly, finally getting to the important part.

"I'm okay," Kiran said. I could tell he was fighting tears. "They told me I was lucky because I had a gift more valuable to them than my blood. I'm one of their forgers. I make them money."

"More valuable than your blood?" I repeated.

"That's what they're doing with the other Elioud," he sang, but with anguish in his voice. "Do you know what I'm talking about, Elioud?"

We nodded. I sang, "You, me, the others, we're Elioud."

He paused and breathed so he could keep a peaceful look on his face as he continued, "Some of the other students have been brought here too. They're not as lucky as me. The Grigoris are harvesting Elioud blood. They think it will keep them from disintegrating. They also use . . ."

I couldn't keep myself from interrupting, "Antimony! They use antimony to keep their angelic and human natures from pulling apart from each other."

"They must think Elioud blood is better. They take it from the Elioud they have imprisoned through there," he motioned with his head toward a doorway at the end of the room, "and give it to the ones they call the Peerless. The Peerless inject it and use antimony only when they're running low on Elioud blood." We looked at the door. Above was written *Nuscantur ut moriantur.* I would have to ask Neith what it meant.

"The ones in charge here talk in front of me. They think because I'm chained there's no risk. Who would I tell?" He blinked back tears. "They told me they would let me copy paintings instead of having my blood extracted. If I refused, they would make me watch as they extracted all the blood from two Elioud, two deaths for my one refusal." He was having a hard time keeping up the charade of singing to himself.

He forced his face to look calm as he continued. "The Elioud die eventually, but if they took all their blood they would die instantly. At least this way we all stay alive and hope someone will come to rescue us. And here you are." He smiled.

"I am so sorry," I said. "We can't rescue you yet. We'll come back for you as soon as we can figure out how to get you out of here." I looked at Josh and Dilani who were starting to sweat from nervousness.

"We have to go before they find us here. We'll come back and get you and the rest out of here. I promise. You are not alone. It won't be long."

Josh and Dilani nodded and waved. Josh put his arm around me as we ducked back into the vestibule next to the decontamination chamber.

"We've got to get out now. Whoever was behind us in the hall must be coming. We'll figure this out. We will," he said rubbing my back reassuringly. "Plus, now we know they don't like good singing."

"That only helps some of us," I said, laughing slightly as I brushed my tears away. "I've heard you sing," I said to Josh. "No Nephilim repellent there. So, how do we get out of here without going back into the hallway?"

"You're not going to like this," Dilani said, "but remember that breeze when we came in here?"

"Yeah," said Josh.

"I bet it came from here." She pointed at a large panel in the wall next to the decontamination chamber. "It's an air vent and right now it's our best way out."

"Oh boy," said Josh.

A sliver of light shone into the glassed entry area. Someone was coming in.

"Ready?" Dilani asked.

"Ready." Josh and I said together.

She pulled the panel off the wall and added, "I'm guessing we have about thirty seconds until the vent runs out of air."

"Tick-tock," I said, and jumped feet first into the vent.

44

Smelly Feet and Pomegranates

M y feet knocked loose a large grate and I spilled out with a thud into a hallway after an exhilarating ride through the air vent. It had been completely dark until the end when what felt like an enclosed metal luge track tilted from straight up and down to diagonal, leading to the screen I had just burst through. Josh and Dilani landed in the hallway right after me. When they hit the floor they both started laughing hysterically, giddy with relief.

"We are so lucky the access panel to the air generator wasn't open when we came through and we landed out here instead of in some bone crushing generator," Dilani said, still giggling.

Josh was suddenly somber. "What?" he asked. "Bone crushing generator?"

"I don't know if it would crush our bones exactly," she said, "but something makes the air come up into the decontamination chamber. It must have been closed when we came through. I was counting on it," she said when she saw that Josh realized he just had a close encounter with his own mortality.

"We're fine. Right?" she said, looking at me, eyebrows raised in a "what's the big deal?" look.

"Let's find the elevator and head back to the hotel. If Zia, Miyako, and Neith are all right, I'm sure they headed back there," I said.

It turned out that our indoor luge experience had only dropped us down a few floors to 112. We were able to find an elevator, but the one we got on served only floors 100-149 and the lobby. We would have to go all the way down to the lobby again to get on an elevator that would take us back to our floor.

When the elevator doors opened at the lobby level, we were greeted by the sound of Zia's voice, accompanied by a piano played by a man in a tuxedo with slicked back black hair and mustache. Zia had changed, somehow, into a glittery, silver, floor-length evening gown. She was singing "Defying Gravity," from the musical *Wicked*. Neith was sitting in a lounge chair near the piano, with a red drink in a large snifter, bobbing his head appreciatively as she sang. I sniffed. Neith's drink was a Shirley Temple. The grenadine smelled like it was made from real pomegranates. Miyako was sitting next to Neith, pouring liquids of various colors from elegant little crystal cordial glasses into a hurricane, watching bubbles rise and their colors swirl as she poured. A large dish of salty sesame snacks that smelled like feet sat on a table next to her.

Zia caught our eyes. We sat down in the nearest group of empty chairs and waited for her to finish the song. As it came to an end, lounge patrons burst into applause, and Zia said into her microphone, "I'm going to take a little break now, but I'll be back soon."

She took Neith by the elbow and they came over to where we were sitting. Miyako followed closely behind.

"You're okay!" Dilani said.

"You're singing in the lounge at the Burj Kahlifa," Josh said.

"Cool, right?" Neith said.

"But how . . . ?" I said.

"It was pretty great," Neith said. "After we realized we lost you guys, we got stuck at a dead end with a locked metal door. A man with a maintenance uniform came up to us and asked what we were looking for. Then Zia sang a line from an old song, 'Someone to watch over me.'"

"Why?" asked Josh.

"I panicked," Zia said. "It's like a nervous tic for me. When I get nervous, the first things that come to mind are old song lyrics, things I used to sing when I was little in talent shows to make my grandparents happy."

"It gets better," Neith chirped. "The man asked, 'Do you know 'Somewhere Over the Rainbow,' honey?'"

"Which I do," Zia said. "Another talent show classic. I started to sing it."

Neith continued, "The man gave us this huge smile and said, 'you're late. Come this way.' He led us down here, gave Zia the gown to change into and said, 'you're on in five.' She's been singing everything she knows from Broadway musicals. The crowd loves it." He gestured with his thumb toward a huge glass jar that was full of money. "Tips. And free drinks," he said, holding up his big red beverage and swirling it around. "Delicious."

"You got lucky," Josh said. "We've got stuff to tell you, but you've got fans to entertain, and we don't want to get caught out past the curfew."

"Suit yourself," Neith said. "We'll be up after another set."

§

At breakfast, we looked around for Fintan and Aranka. There was no sign of them, and no mention of their absence. I thought of the area where Kiran was being held. Could they have been taken to the Elioud holding area? I suddenly felt guilty we hadn't gone looking for them before. I decided to hope they were still okay.

After breakfast, Dr. Calleo announced that we would take a tour of the building.

"We are aware, however," she said with a frown, "that some of you have already done some exploring on your own." My hands went cold, and I fought the urge to wrinkle my forehead. Maybe they were talking about Fintan and Aranka.

But Zia spoke up, "I'm sorry, Dr. Calleo, the urge to perform was simply too great. When I got the offer to sing in the lounge, I felt I couldn't say no."

What was she doing? Trying to throw Dr. Calleo off? Taking one for the team? Seeing what Dr. Calleo knew?

Dr. Calleo flashed a cold, empty smile at Zia. "We are aware of your need to use your considerable talent. So Dr. Grigori and I are releasing you from the program."

Zia looked stunned. "But, Dr. Calleo, I just . . . I never meant to . . ."

"You misunderstand, Zia," Dr. Calleo said. "This is not punishment. We have been contacted by Pietro Muttati, vocal director of La Scala in Milan. We are releasing you to begin training for their chorus immediately."

Zia looked even more stunned.

"But, the program . . .?" she said.

"The program has done its work for you," Dr. Grigori said in his oaky voice. "I promise our Young Scholars that we will help them fulfill their potential, and you have. It is time for you to greet your destiny."

"Thank you so much," Zia said, tearing up. "This is my dream. I can't believe you are doing this for me, especially since neither you nor Dr. Calleo have ever listened to me sing."

Zia looked at Neith, then the rest of us. Neith and Dilani were smiling, but tears welled in their eyes too. I wondered if this were some kind of Grigori trick, and how we would do without Zia in our efforts to figure out the puzzle we were caught up in. Maybe I should have just been happy for her instead of feeling like she was abandoning us when we needed her most.

"A limo is waiting. Say goodbye and get your things," Dr. Calleo said.

Zia wiped her eyes, and then hugged Miyako, Neith, Dilani, Josh, then me. She whispered in my ear, "Don't trust them and remember the power of harmony."

She pulled away from me and said in a playful voice, "Kaia, don't wrinkle your forehead—your aunt was right. It makes you look ancient."

A GYSP security brute appeared, apparently to usher Zia from the room.

Zia turned to leave, but then turned back and said quickly and quietly to Neith, but loudly enough that I could hear, "I'm just sorry I never got to sing for you at the top of this tower. My voice could carry forever from up there."

The goon took Zia by the elbow and they left the room.

I looked at Neith. He looked at me and shrugged his shoulders.

We were given a fifteen-minute break before our tour began. We huddled over the Belgian waffle station.

I told Neith, Josh, Miyako, and Dilani what Zia had whispered to me, then asked Neith, "What was that about singing for you at the top of this building? That would be impossible for you, right? You couldn't stand it with your fear of heights."

"Yeah," he said. "It makes no sense."

"That must be why she said it, to get our attention," Dilani said. "She wanted to emphasize what she said next—that her voice would carry forever from up there."

"Huh," I said, and then to Josh, "You said this building has a radio antenna on top."

He nodded and asked, "So, who is trying to communicate what?"

"That's what we need to find out." I paused. "Remember the power of harmony," I said, repeating Zia's message.

I thought about Kiran's words. "The Grigori deal in disharmony," he had said. I thought about our time in the church and the terribly discordant noise Zia had made when the dome's space was interrupted by the ladder. I thought about how we were now in the world's tallest radio communications building. But I had no idea what it meant.

Then I remembered to ask Neith about the words above the door where Kiran was being held: *Nuscantur ut moriantur.* I wrote the words down on a piece of paper and handed it to him. "What does this mean?"

He looked stricken. "Where did you see this?"

"Why? What does it mean?"

"They are born in order to die."

We needed to figure this out. Fast.

45

Munster and Mustard on Rye

After breakfast, we were given a tour of the building. At least, we were shown highlights of the lower one hundred forty-nine floors. The upper floors, the ones designated 'for maintenance' were off limits "for safety reasons." I wondered if the tour was meant to keep us busy while our GYSP profs were up to something else. Still no sign of Aranka and Fintan. I kept my eyes peeled for any sign of why there would be extra space between the service corridors and the regular, public ones, or how to access it, but couldn't see anything that helped.

When the tour was over, we came back to the hotel floor and for a break before lunch. I walked with Dilani to our rooms.

"I have something to show you," she said, a huge grin on her face.

We sat down on her bed. She reached into the pocket of her pullover and gently lifted out a white rat. She cupped it in her hands. It looked back at her with its little red eyes, whiskers twitching and sniffing in her direction.

"Adorable, right?" she said.

It was kind of cute, if I didn't look at its beady red eyes or hairless ratty tail, which hung down behind the perch Dilani had made with her hands. "He's an albino *rattus rattus*. I named him Bruce. I found him in the elevator."

"The elevator?" Wouldn't more people than Dilani notice a rat riding the elevators in the world's tallest building?

"When I got on, I felt something brush against my foot. I looked down, and there he was. Everyone else was turned toward the door and watching all the floor numbers whizzing by."

262

"But what's Bruce doing in the Burj Khalifa?"

"Probably a pet who got loose or was let go. People buy pet rats and then don't feel like taking care of them anymore. They just release them. Sad." She brought Bruce up to her face. "But Bruce is a survivor. Aren't you, Bruce?"

Bruce sniffed some more and twitched his whiskers.

"Don't rats carry diseases?" I asked. "Should you be holding him like that?"

"Look at how clear his eyes are and how thick his fur is. He looks very healthy and he's definitely well-fed," Dilani said. She rubbed him behind his little flappy ears. "Wait a second." She looked closer. "He wasn't a pet." She held him up in front of my face and smoothed his fur back so I could see the matching pink bald patches behind each ear. "He's been experimented on. Those smooth spots are where electrodes get attached."

"Electrodes?" I gasped, suddenly feeling very protective of Bruce. "What did people do to him?"

"Whatever it was, I don't think it was painful, like shocks," Dilani replied. "He looks too healthy. And he doesn't seem anxious. Maybe they were trying to scan his brain waves." She looked Bruce in the eyes, I guess reading Bruce for a sign that she was right. "Anxious rats are super skinny, and Bruce is fine. Either he got free very recently or he's already figured out a new food source."

"Speaking of food," I said, my stomach gurgling, "it's almost lunch-time. What are you going to do with Bruce?"

"I'll make him a little nest," she said, looking around her room. "If he knows he's safe here, he'll stay, even without a cage. I can bring him some food from lunch."

She set Bruce down on the bed and pointed toward the gift basket of toiletries on her dresser. "That will work nicely, and it's got all that crinkly paper in the bottom."

Bruce looked up at her, then at the door to the room. Then he took off like a shot.

"No! Bruce!" Dilani yelled.

But Bruce had already squeezed himself through the tiny gap underneath the door. The last little bit of his weird bald tail wriggled from view.

"C'mon!" Dilani said. She yanked the door open, and we saw Bruce heading down the hallway.

"Maybe you should just let him go!" I called after Dilani, who had already followed the little white blur running along the hallway baseboards.

"Got to catch him!" Dilani called. "He's got the flash drive!"

Dilani ran down the hall, turned the corner, and stopped abruptly at
the end of the corridor. She appeared to be staring at a blank wall. I caught
up with her and panted, "He's got the flash drive? The SPREE flash drive?
Are you sure?"

"I put it on the bed so I wouldn't forget to put it in my pocket after I
changed my clothes. Rats are attracted to shiny things. We've got to get it
back."

I couldn't believe it. We needed that flash drive. It held the only proof
we had of the existence of the SPREE sanctuaries and the list of rescued
Elioud. I looked back down the hallway from where we stood. No sign of a
white rat with a small silver thumb drive.

"He's gone," I said.

"He went this way," Dilani said, pointing at the baseboard. "Through
here. Look."

I had no idea what she was looking at. She crouched down and motioned to me to follow.

"See?" She pointed at a faint brown oily stripe that ran along the baseboard. "It ends right here." She was right. The light brown trail came to a
stop right where she was pointing.

"Rats use the same route over and over again and the oil on their fur
leaves a mark. Bruce went under here," she said, digging her finger into the
carpet's pile where it met the end of the rat run. "Yup." She used both hands
to push the carpet down and exposed a hole about the size of a quarter. "He
went through here."

"But through here to what? It's just a wall. This doesn't go anywhere.
Remember our tour? The ends of the hallways are just the interior of the
supporting structure. Behind here are mammoth steel beams and concrete."

"Bruce went somewhere," Dilani said. "And he's been using this run
long enough to build up a trail." She paused and looked lost in thought.
Then she nodded. "This hole leads to food."

I sniffed. I didn't want to be compared to a rat, but I could smell food
too. Stinky cheese with Dijon mustard on rye bread.

I stood up. "Too bad we can't follow him." I imagined Bruce threading
his boney little way along a gap between the interior wall and the concrete
and steel buttresses that made this skyscraper possible.

"I think we can," Dilani said. "I think the space is bigger than we realize." She tapped the wall on either side of Bruce's escape hatch. "Listen
closely," she said.

She tap-tap-tapped. It sounded hollow compared with the wall that
was closer to the last doors on the corridor.

"Rats are very attuned to sound, and very attuned to ways that lead to food," she said. "There's a passageway behind this wall. We just have to figure out how to get to it."

I stood back from the wall and took another look. It looked solid. I leaned up against it, putting my shoulder into it. Dilani joined me. For just a second we hesitated, as if we were afraid it would swivel like a false book-shelf in an old movie and we would find ourselves in a cobwebbed secret passageway. When nothing happened, we pushed harder. No such luck. I turned to my right, to the wall that formed a ninety-degree angle to the one we were trying to move, and that's when I saw it—another retina scanner. I did the honors.

A panel in the wall slid to the side, and we entered a windowless, ce-ment corridor lit overhead by fluorescent lights. It led off to our left. Hushed sounds, mechanical and spoken, and the sandwich smell wafted from far along the passageway and down from above us.

The votive in my pocket had become very warm. I looked at Dilani. She nodded and mouthed, "Mine too." Even though I wanted to see what it was doing, I left it concealed, in part because it seemed like it might be too warm to touch with my bare hands.

Dilani and I joined hands and we headed toward the sounds.

We walked for about five minutes and came to a cage-like elevator. No floor buttons, just a lever.

"Let's go," Dilani said.

We got into the lift.

"Bruce!" Dilani exclaimed. There he was, his back end pressed into one corner. His whiskery snout lifted at the sound of his name. The flash drive hung from his mouth. Dilani scooped Bruce up and nuzzled him to her cheek. "You waited for us!"

"I'll just take that flash drive," I said, not convinced that Bruce hadn't just preferred to take the lift rather than climb the walls to get to food. I grabbed the little silver tablet from between Bruce's teeth and tucked it into my jeans pocket.

"We have to go up," Dilani said. "We've got the flash drive back, but we need to see what's up there, don't we?"

I nodded. "Now's our chance," I said.

"For the SPREE," she said.

I pushed the lever into the "up" position and the lift creaked to a start and made a whirring sound as it lifted us up, up, up. I looked at Dilani, who was smiling at Bruce. Bruce twitched his whiskers. The lift was dark, then bright as we passed a bare light bulb, then dark, then light. Points of white light streamed vertically over Bruce's red eyes.

"The communications level," I whispered. "We've gone up far enough that we must be close. This must be how you get up to those floors."

The sounds we had heard earlier became more distinct: voices giving orders, the tap of metal on stone, and ropes pulled through squeaky pulleys.

The lift came to a stop. Ahead of us about fifteen feet was a plain concrete wall. To our right was another wall. To our left, a cinder block wall extended just far enough to keep us from seeing whatever was happening in the large, well-lit space beyond. Against this wall was a table with a tray of sandwiches, some soda cans, and a bowl of chips. Dilani went up to the table, took a half a sandwich, broke off a corner, and gave it to Bruce.

"Ready?" I mouthed to Dilani. She nodded and stuck Bruce and what remained of the sandwich in her hoodie pocket.

We stuck our heads beyond the edge of the wall. We both gasped at once and yanked our heads back.

"Is that . . .?" Dilani whispered.

"It looks like . . . ," I stammered, "a ziggurat, like a Tower of Babel."

Dilani started to giggle. I poked her. "Stop it," I whispered. "What's so funny?"

"Bizarre, don't you think? We're in this ultra-modern place and at the top of it there's a top secret project to make an ancient pile of stones? I don't get it."

I didn't get it either. My forehead was puckered big time.

We poked our heads around again. I pointed to a large crate a few yards from where we stood. It had "Orkney" stamped on the side. We would both be able to get a better view from behind it. We scuttled over to the crate and crouched down.

The massive stone structure stood about six stories tall, and clearly was unfinished. The stones on the top were jagged, uneven, as if there were supposed to be more, but the workers hadn't gotten to it or the architect's plans ran out. The building was constructed from stones of different shapes and sizes, although there were gaps here and there, like someone was working on a giant 3-D puzzle. The ones on the lower level were the largest, huge rectangular blocks. The stones were different shades of goldish brown, similar to the odd stone in the Ring of Brodgar. I reached my hand up over the top of the crate we were huddled next to and felt around. The lid was off. I poked my head up and peered inside. Empty.

I turned my gaze to the workers. Men and women in business suits, with clipboards and tablets were giving orders to others who wore work gear and boots. Some ladders were tilted into place against the stone next to pulleys and ropes with baskets from which workers several stories up hoisted stones and maneuvered them into place. Voices were hushed and serious, like solving this jigsaw puzzle would save the world.

Or destroy it. I saw that Dr. Grigori was one of the suits. He handed his tablet off to another suit and walked over to a large flat screen monitor and studied it. I pointed him out to Dilani who nodded and pointed to another suit, a woman, and mouthed, "Dr. Calleo." She was right.

"Let's go closer," I whispered. Dilani pointed at another crate, and we scurried over and ducked down behind it. My heart was pounding so hard I could feel it in my feet.

Two workers dragged a crate from off to our right up to the base of the tower, where a suit was checking something on her tablet. One worker used a crow bar to pry off the crate's lid. They both reached in and hauled out a stone the size of a schnauzer. The suit motioned to an empty space about second story high. The workers set down the stone. One of them got a ladder and the other brought a pulley, rope, and basket. The worker on ladder duty climbed to the gap, while the other worker hoisted the rock in the basket up to his level. The worker on the ladder hauled the stone out of the basket. It must have taken a lot of strength for him to lift the stone into place. He pushed it so its outside edge was flush with the other stones around it. He started down the ladder, but the suit came over and started yelling, "No, no! That's not right. Remove it!"

Dilani and I looked at each other. It looked fine to us.

The worker hustled back up to where he had placed the stone, while the other worker grabbed a ladder and leaned it against the wall so the offending stone was in between them. Pulling long flat implements that looked like industrial spatulas from their tool belts, they worked at prying the stone loose again. Working together, they turned the stone around, looked down at the suit, who nodded, then wedged it into place. They looked at the suit one more time, who motioned for them to come down. I couldn't see what difference it made.

Dilani whispered, "I still can't tell what this is all about, can you?" I shook my head no, then looked around for another safe place we could watch from that was closer by.

"We need to go now!" Dilani said urgently while she poked me in the side.

"Ouch!" I said, trying to keep my voice down. Then I saw what had gotten Dilani's attention. Two workers were coming toward the crate we were hiding behind. I pointed at a crate off to our right, a little closer to the tower. We sprinted to it and ducked down along its side so the workers who were now opening the crate where we had been wouldn't be able to see us. Another suit with a tablet came over and the process we had just witnessed began again. The gesture of the suit indicated that this stone was going up to the fourth story. I looked at the tower. I could see at least ten more gaps and there were probably some on the other sides of the tower I couldn't. But several teams were working and they seemed to be making good time. I looked over at the crate that was now empty. It was marked "Florence." Florence, Italy, was one of the stops we had made, where a van had loaded something onto the professors' plane.

"What did you say they were doing?" I whispered to Dilani. She shrugged like she didn't know what I meant. I tried to be clearer. "When we first saw this tower, what did you say?"

"I said, they're making an ancient pile of stones."

"That's it! That's exactly what they're doing. But it's not an ancient pile of stones, it's a pile of ancient stones. Particular ancient stones. Certain stones."

Dilani nodded. "Certain stones they've collected from different places: Orkney, Florence, and Paris, and . . ."

We both looked back at the tower.

She said aloud what we both realized. "That's not any old ziggurat, and it's not *a* tower of Babel. It's *The* Tower of Babel. They're rebuilding the Tower of Babel, with the actual stones. They must have been dispersed all over the world. The Grigoris have been collecting them and are putting them back together."

"And in two days, the constellation that appeared over Babel on the Plains of Shinar is going to happen again here," I said.

"They're trying to get the Tower reconstructed by that time."

"But why?"

We turned toward the Tower.

"Remember what happened when we put the ladder into the dome at St. Hildegard's Church?" Dilani asked.

"Disharmony," I replied, thinking of how Zia's gorgeous voice had turned to a terrible, ear-shattering shriek.

"This tower, the Burj Khalifa, I mean, is a gigantic radio antenna," Dilani said.

I nodded. "And?"

"And they must be planning some kind of broadcast, some kind of disharmonious noise that they can beam around the world, that will somehow make use of the fact that the completed Tower of Babel will be in place under the stars where they were aligned were when the Tower was originally abandoned."

"A noise worse than what we heard in the church would be terrible. Painful," I said.

"Maybe even destructive," Dilani elaborated. "Discordant sound, on that kind of scale, would shatter eardrums, bring human activity to a halt." She paused and her eyes went wide. "That's why they had me study the mantis shrimps!"

"What? Why?"

"Mantis shrimp use sound waves to stun or even kill their prey. They strike at the speed of a bullet leaving a gun. The waves they create make bubbles that implode with such a huge force between themselves and their dinner, dinner doesn't know what hit it. It's called 'cavitation.'"

"Wouldn't the force of the bubbles hurt the shrimp too?" I asked, trying to picture super fast shrimp striking at whatever shrimp eat.

"It would, but their shells are so tough people are studying their cellular structure to see if they can use it to make better body armor for combat troops."

I thought about it.

"I'm not sure the cavitation part makes sense. If shrimp cavitate, or however you say it, then they do it under water. Wouldn't that make a difference? Radio waves go through air, right?"

"Yeah," said Dilani, and sighed.

"Plus, I still don't know why the Grigori would want to destroy things on a massive scale, no matter what method they would use," I said. "What do they get out of destroying a lot of stuff? If they want to take over the world, who wants a world where everything is broken?"

Dilani shook her head. "I don't know," she said quietly, then added, "We should get out of here."

I nodded, but we both still stared at the Tower. A suit yelled for a light to be moved, and some workers adjusted one of the tall lights that shone on the base of the Tower. As the light's position was changed, it raked across one of the blocks at our eye level, bringing the texture on the block into relief. I nudged Dilani, who indicated that she could see it too. On the upper left hand corner of the block was what looked like two squiggles or symbols, too ornate to be random scratches. I looked at the other stones around it where the lighting exposed the surface detail. Each of them showed two symbols.

"Any idea what those mean?" I asked.

"None," she replied. "If it's a language, Neith would know. Maybe we can bring him up here. We'd better go."

"Yeah." I looked around to see what might be the safest way back to the lift. I heard Dilani squeak. "Bruce!" Her hoodie pocket was flat against her stomach and her hands were empty. She pointed toward the Tower. "He's gone inside!"

"This time he's on his own," I whispered sternly. I added in a softer tone, seeing Dilani's worried face, "He'll be fine. He's a survivor. You said so yourself."

"Uh-oh," she said, looking past me. I turned and saw what she had noticed. Two workers were coming for this crate, and they blocked the most direct route to the lift. Other workers had moved several of the other crates so the one we were crouching behind was the last I could see that provided any cover. I looked toward the Tower, then at Dilani. "You're positive Bruce went in there?" She nodded.

"Okay, we follow Bruce again. But this is the last time," I said.

A suit yelled for another light to be moved and got the attention of all the workers in our vicinity, except for the two who were about to reach our crate. "One-two-three, go!" I mouthed and we both ran toward the Tower. We veered off to the right along its base, hoping we wouldn't run into any workers or supervisors as we turned a corner. Just past the corner we saw a small, low opening, barely tall and wide enough for us each to crawl through. We scrambled in.

I thought the Tower would be dark inside, but the soft warm glow of flickering oil lamps filled the space. The lamps were perched on stone shelves that protruded from the walls every ten feet or so, and seemed to be situated at all levels. The interior of the Tower was open, a big golden-lighted cavern. The stone walls hushed the sounds from outside. We had the place to ourselves. We stood up and walked toward the center. We could see all the way up to the open space at the top, where the harsh artificial light coming from outside the Tower made it look like we stood below an abnormally white sky.

"Bruce," Dilani whispered, but the sound of her voice reverberated through the space. I held my breath. We had nowhere to hide. I hoped no one outside heard. "Sorry," Dilani mouthed. I nodded. She scanned along the base of the walls. I examined higher up.

Unlike on the exterior, many of the stones on the interior had small niches carved into them. Some were empty, but several of them held smaller stones, stones that looked familiar. I walked over to one of the blocks for a closer look and knew instantly why. The small stones were votives.

The ones I was standing in front of all seemed to be fish of some kind. The details were different, but the general shapes and sizes were the same. I looked at the stone next to the fish collection. Other sea animals. Starfish, seahorses, octopi, anemones, some things I couldn't identify but had flippers, gills, or suckers that seemed to put them in a sea creature category. I walked around the room. Each large area held a collection of votives that were all of a similar kind: horses, cows, dogs, cats. The niches of some areas were filled, like the set was complete. Some areas had open niches. I kept walking and looking. Birds were next. Chickens, gulls, raptors, other winged things. Then pigs. The pig section had an empty niche. I took out my votive, lifted it to the niche and slid it in. It fit perfectly. It glowed momentarily and as its light dimmed I heard a soft sound, like a word was being whispered. The sound reverberated in the Tower, but the sound was so soft and sweet I wasn't afraid it would get anyone's attention. I wanted to hear it again. I took my votive out and slid it in again. The sound repeated.

I looked at Dilani, who had already taken her votive out. I could see her standing by the horses. She located an empty niche and slid hers into place. Another sweet and soft sound filled the air, but it was different from the one the pig had made.

Dilani took her votive out and came over to me. She was smiling. "It reminds me of a toy I loved as a child. It was a colorful plastic circle with a farmer in the middle and pictures of different animals. When you pointed the arrow at a picture and pulled the string, a voice said, 'What sound does the pig make?' and a little oinking noise would come out of the speaker."

"You think we're inside a giant 'See and Say' toy?"

"Yes," she answered. "Putting the votives in place seems to release some kind of sound."

Suddenly we both heard voices coming toward the entry door we had crawled through. We froze and I heard a voice, maybe Dr. Calleo's, say, "Construction is almost complete. A few more votives and we will be ready to move forward with the plan."

"Are the pronouncers prepared?" a deep, male voice responded.

"I believe we have identified one with the proper amount of devolution," the higher voice replied.

Dilani spotted Bruce, who had appeared at our feet and looked up at us. "Let's hope he knows another way out," I whispered as quietly as I could.

Dilani bent down toward him, but Bruce started running along the base of the wall and we followed as quickly as we were able. Sure enough, Bruce led us to another opening, the same size and shape as the first. We were on the other side of the Tower and had a clear shot to a lift. I didn't know if it was the same as the lift we came up on, but it didn't matter. Bruce sprinted ahead and waited for us.

Dilani made it, but I was still out in the open, when I heard a deep voice.

"Stop right there. This area is off limits."

I froze, my back to whoever had caught me. Then I thought my fear was making me hallucinate. Aunt Alina rushed toward me from the elevator. With swift, expert movements, she pulled a turban towel over my hair, smeared a mud mask on my face, slapped cucumber slices on my eyes, and pulled me swiftly toward her by my elbow.

"Aunt Alina," I gasped, spitting out a little mud from the corner of my mouth.

"Principessa!" she replied loudly, grabbing my hand and squeezing hard. "I wondered where you had moseyed off to. You know you're due for your dermabrasion before the fashion show."

To the person behind me she vowed, "This will not happen again. The principessa is still on Milan time and must have sleep-walked away from the spa."

She pushed me ahead of her toward the elevator. I got on board and took the cucumbers off my eyes while she pushed the down lever. The elevator lurched to a start and I hugged her hard.

"I can't believe . . ." I began.

"There's no time, I'm afraid, honey cakes," she said. "You're safe for now, just keep on going."

"But how . . . ?"

The elevator stopped and the door opened.

"Go back to your rooms. You'll figure out what to do next. We probably won't see each other again. Remember, you're never alone." She squeezed my hand, touched Dilani on the cheek and stepped into the hall. As she went she sang, "Guardian angels, God will send thee, all through the night . . ."

I stared at Dilani. I realized I left my votive behind. But it was getting my aunt back, and just as suddenly losing her again, that made me start to cry.

Then I heard it. Dr. Grigori's voice, now steely and menacing, and calling in the direction Aunt Alina had gone. His words chilled me to my core: "Samya. This ends now."

46

Sandalwood and Decomposing Diapers

B ack in Dilani's room we explained to Neith, Josh, and Miyako what we had just experienced.

"You're sure he called her 'Samya'?" Neith asked. "Like the person in your dream who saved the Nephilim?"

I nodded, swallowing the lump in my throat. "It can't be a coincidence," I muttered, "but I don't know how she can be the same person unless . . ."

"Unless?" Josh prompted gently.

"Unless the Nephilim helped her stay alive somehow," I said.

"With antimony?" Miyako offered. "But it would have killed her a long time ago. No one could take that much and survive."

"Blood," said Josh. "Elioud blood. Has to be. A reward for helping them."

"Until now, when she helped us instead," Dilani said quietly and touched my hand.

I wanted to sit there forever, with Dilani's hand warm on mine, with actual friends who were with me in this. But Neith broke the silence.

"The 'one with the proper amount of devolution'—I think that's me. While you've been off finding the Tower of Babel, Dr. Eder has been making me read lists of words."

"As in vocabulary lists?" Miyako asked.

"I think so," Neith responded. "I couldn't recognize most of the words. Since I couldn't understand what I was saying, it was more like putting together strings of sounds. Dr. Eder said he was perfecting my pronunciation, but when I asked, 'of what?' he just said, 'Keep going.' He's starting to smell really bad, by the way."

I had noticed. Although his choice of cover up scent was different from Xanthe's, the rot was getting stronger.

"What does that have to do with 'devolution'?" I asked. "I don't even know what 'devolution' means."

"Remember those larynxes in the Div School bell tower?"

It would be hard to forget the display of bi-sectioned heads.

Neith continued. "I was studying not only how languages developed, but how the human capacity for speech developed. This work would be important for piecing together a map of human communication over time."

"But," Dilani interjected, "we don't have examples of human larynxes over time. Larynxes are tissue. They decompose. We have skull and skeletal remains of earlier hominids, but we don't have tissue samples to compare—." She froze. "Cheese and pepperoni. We do too. We have mummified remains . . . or, rather, the Grigoris do . . . but they're not old enough . . . only a couple of thousand years . . ."

"You're talking about the mummified babies," Josh said, trying to coach Dilani into speaking in complete sentences. "And adults, too, for that matter, like the Gerasene Demoniac mummy."

Dilani nodded, but then shook her head. "But none of the mummies is old enough to indicate what happened on an evolutionary scale. You would have to look back much further for that kind of information."

"Maybe we're making the wrong comparison. Try to think like a Grigori," Josh said, frowning, like the idea of it was disgusting.

He started again. "They're Peerless. Humans are Merely. Peerless are the best. Anything different from them is lesser. They're the perfect blend of angelic and human. Humans have no angelic genetic makeup, so are worthless. The Elioud, us and others like us, are somewhere in between. Some of us are closer to being half and half—the perfect mix, and could pass for Nephilim, like Xanthe apparently did."

At least for a while, I thought, recalling the scorch marks where her portrait had hung amongst the Nephilim in their gallery of hyper-centenarians in the Div School Bell Tower.

"But some of us are further away," Josh continued.

"Go on," Dilani said, looking like she was getting the idea.

"So," Josh said, "angels don't evolve, right? Over time, they wouldn't change. That's one of their attributes. They're not affected by time and circumstance like humans are."

Dilani broke in excitedly, "But humans have evolved over time. And different creatures with different amounts of human make-up would show different amounts of change."

"And this has to do with larynxes how?" I asked.

Neith spoke up. "What we know—Dilani, correct me if I have this wrong—is that the difference between apes and humans, larynx-wise, is that our larynx sits lower in our throats than it does in apes, with whom we share a lot of genetic material."

"And that's why we can talk and apes can't?" I asked.

"It's more complicated than that," Dilani said, "but yes, that may have something to do with it."

"Okay," said Neith. "I'm thinking that if angels didn't evolve, or don't evolve, but humans do, then to speak a particular language in a particular way, you need a particular kind of larynx, or one in a particular place."

Dilani nodded and added, "And the evolutionary scale the Grigoris are interested in may not be the kind anthropologists measure, say from *australopithicus* to *homo sapiens*, but what angelologists measure, that is, from Watcher, through Nephilim, to Elioud, to human."

"You mean, someone with a higher angel content, if that's what we can call it, would pronounce words differently than someone more human, because of where their larynx is," I said.

Neith and Dilani nodded together.

"It might not make a huge difference," Neith said, "but if someone knew what to listen for, they could probably tell. And if the language, or word, was for some purpose in particular, you would want someone who can speak it perfectly to do the speaking."

"Like saying 'Open sesame' in just the right way would make the passage way open, but someone with a lisp couldn't do it."

Neith smiled. "Yes. 'Open thethame' wouldn't work."

"It's a shibboleth," Josh said. Neith nodded. I drew a blank. Josh explained. "It's from a story in the Bible. Jephthah was a commander of the army of Gilead, fighting against Ephraim. Some Ephraimites tried to fit in with the Gileadites so they could escape, but the Gileadites told every fugitive they met to say the word 'shibboleth.' Ephraimites couldn't make the 'sh' sound and said 'sibboleth,' so they were found out. Neith would pass the Grigoris' 'shibboleth' test, but they themselves can't."

"What does 'shibboleth' mean, anyway?" I asked.

"It comes from the word for 'flowing stream.' It shows up in Psalm 69:2, in the word for 'flood.'"

"Interesting that a water word would be used, don't you think? Angels can't be in water, but humans can, or at least do better there," I mused. "But we don't know if they're interested in a specific word or phrase, do we?

Neith shook his head. "Only that the Grigoris are very interested in the sound of my voice."

"So what's 'devolution'?" I asked.

"It's what the Grigoris call 'evolution' for becoming more human." Josh said somberly. "It's an insult. You're more devolved if you're more human."

"And you think Neith is more human?" I asked.

"I think the Grigoris think so," Neith answered before Josh could. "They're trying to get me to say certain words. And if that's what they're doing, it's because they think if I say them, something important will happen."

"Or something bad. For humans, at least," Josh said.

Neith spoke quietly. "They must think I've got the right larynx to pronounce something properly to achieve the right effect. But I don't know what, or why."

Suddenly, pieces of the puzzle started coming together. I said, "They're looking for the word Jesus used to send the demons out of the Gerasene Demoniac. Jesus set the man free from the demons, but he also set the demons free of the man, releasing them from their human enclosure. Did you recognize any of the words?"

"Yes," Neith said. "I'm certain of at least three of them."

"Oh?" said Josh.

"'Noah', 'antimony', and 'book', like Rowan LePlage had said them from the 'Book of Noah.' He knew those three words." Neith pronounced them. They sounded like random syllables to me.

"Hey!" Dilani said. "Say them again. And watch Bruce."

Dilani had set Bruce down on the bed. Our backpacks and my art history book were lying in the middle.

Neith said the three words. Bruce went and sat on the book of paintings.

"Which one means 'book'?" she asked Neith.

"This one," Neith said, and pronounced the word again.

"Wait a second," Dilani said. She put Bruce in her lap, then let go of him. "Okay, say it now," she said to Neith.

He repeated the word. Bruce sat up on his hind legs, sniffed, then scurried over to the art book. He sniffed its binding then sat down in the middle of its front cover, blocking out the picture of "The Presentation in the Temple" by Ambrogio Lorenzetti.

We all stared at Bruce.

"Try it again," Josh said. "Start him somewhere else, though, and say some different words too. Maybe he just likes how that book smells."

Dilani carried Bruce to the easy chair by the window. "Okay," she said. "Try it."

Neith spoke distinctly and slowly. He said in English, "Peanut butter, swiss cheese, pool cue, Leaning Tower of Pisa," and then the word he thought was "book." Bruce ran quickly from the chair to the little desk on the wall opposite the bed, climbed up one of the desk's leg and sat down on his haunches on top of the desk.

"So much for that," Josh sighed. "I'm a little relieved."

"I'm not," Dilani said gravely. She went over to the desk, picked Bruce up, and then picked up what had been between Bruce and the surface of the desk: *Dubai Today! A Guidebook to Our City [English Edition].*

"That's too weird," said Miyako.

We sat in silence for a moment. Dilani stroked the back of Bruce's head.

"It can't be, but what if it is . . ." Neith said.

"What?" I asked.

"What if all of the words are from 'the Book of Noah'?" Neith said. "Rowan LePlage said the original would have been written before the flood, right?"

Everyone nodded.

"Babel supposedly happened after Noah and the great flood and the ark, and all that, right?" Neith looked at Josh.

Josh nodded. "According to the Bible, Noah was still alive at the time of Babel. But yes, the order in Genesis is Creation, Watchers, Flood, Noah and his family repopulate the earth, Tower of Babel; which means diversity of languages comes after the flood."

"So, the Book of Noah could have been written in the original, universal language, just like Rowan LaPlage said," Neith offered.

"And Dr. Eder is coaching you in the original language," Josh said, skepticism in his voice.

"I know it sounds ridiculous," Neith said, "but what if it's true? We know that the Grigoris found the Book of Noah. They must have got their hands on a translation, maybe the one in Hildegard's language. They have either figured out the original language, or at least a bunch of words in it. If it is the original language, wouldn't animals also know it? If it came from a time before a universal disharmony, before the diversity of human languages and enmity between humans and animals?" He looked at Dilani. "So, Bruce could know the word for 'book.'"

"But books in ancient times weren't like ours." I said. "Wouldn't their books be tablets or scrolls, not paperbacks or hardcovers like we have?"

"True," Dilani sighed. She sounded disappointed in her protégé rat. She looked at the art book in the middle of the bed. "You are a genius!" she exclaimed and kissed Bruce on his whiskery cheek. "Look!" she said to the rest of us and pointed at the cover. "That's what Bruce was sitting on! The painting has an old woman holding a scroll. He knew it!"

Sure enough.

Josh picked up the Dubai Guide. "The cover is a picture of a clay tablet from their museum of antiquities."

"I wonder what other words Bruce knows, or rather, I wish I knew the meaning of any of the other words Dr. Eder made me practice, and we could try them out on Bruce," said Neith.

"I wonder," Dilani said, her chin tilting up and her eyes looking off in wonderment as she considered. "Try this." She got her horse-shaped votive out of her hoodie pocket and set it on the bed. "Do you know the word for horse?"

"No idea," said Neith.

I spoke up. "I'll try." I tried to remember the soft sighing sound I had heard in the Tower when Dilani had put her votive in the niche. I remembered it sounded like a horse's mane riffled by the wind. I made the sound as well as I could remember it. Bruce leapt off Dilani's lap, went to the votive and sniffed at it.

"How . . . ?" Josh and Neith said together.

I shrugged. "I think Neith has some more words to learn. And we need to figure out why the Grigoris want him to. What were you looking at when you were doing this vocabulary drill?" I asked Neith.

"He gave me a list of words, written in our alphabet, so I was just sounding out syllables."

"What did he have? Did he have a list that looked the same as yours?" I asked.

"I wasn't close enough, but I could see that his page had three columns. I think his page had my list in one of the columns, probably a list next to it in the original script, and then a list of meanings."

"You have an idea about the original script, don't you?" Josh asked Neith.

"I think it's the same as what Rowan LaPlage had."

"Wow," said Dilani. "Did it look like this?" She scribbled some lines with the hotel pen and paper pad she found on the nightstand and held them up. She had written what we had seen on the Tower.

"Yeah, something like that," Neith responded.

Dilani said, "Then I think words were written on the Tower in the original language, and also in some other ancient languages."

"It would be like a giant 3-D Rosetta Stone," Josh said. "The Rosetta Stone had two languages people knew and a third that no one knew. Since the words written in the first two languages meant the same thing, they figured the third set might too, and they could use clues from the first two to figure out the third."

"But why would someone write all over the building, or on each of its building blocks?" I asked.

"It's a giant puzzle!" Josh exclaimed. "If you were taking a building apart, how would you put it together again and know you had all the right pieces in the right place?"

"I would mark the pieces. I would number them," I responded.

Neith spoke next. "But many ancient languages used letters for numbers. Like A equals one, B equals two. Maybe that's what they did. And if they knew the original language was falling into disuse, they might mark each stone with a couple of languages, to be sure that someone would be able to reassemble it someday. If we could get another look at the Tower, we could—"

Suddenly I could smell the particular odor of Dr. Eder, rotting diapers under a strong dose of sandalwood.

I thought about shoving everyone but Dilani ahead of me into the closet, since no one but Dilani was supposed to be in her room. But I couldn't react before we heard the door lock click open. Dilani stuffed Bruce in her pocket. Dr. Eder strode in.

He spoke. "Your blatant disregard of the rules has saved me the effort of knocking on another door. This part of the trip has reached its conclusion. You have fifteen minutes to pack your things for departure."

"Departure?" I asked. I felt relieved he hadn't said 'Extraction,' but confused about why we would leave now. If the Grigoris needed Neith for something having to do with the original language, wouldn't we stay here by the Tower? Wouldn't they want us, or Neith at least, to be here for the big broadcast or whatever they were planning in two days?

Dr. Eder's eyes looked steel gray. "You have figured out so much already, I am sure you can discern where we go next." He looked at each one of us, his left eyebrow raised. "Which one of you will say it?"

I did. "Iceland."

"Fifteen minutes," he repeated. And then, "You can stop wondering about Fintan and Aranka."

I could hear us all suddenly hold our breaths. He said, "Fintan turned out to be of more use as a subject of medical experimentation than as a student."

Dilani and Josh gasped.

"And," Dr Eder said, extending a canvas bag toward Neith, "here is your final larynx for study."

Neith shuddered and Dr. Eder put the bag on the floor in front of him. To me Dr. Eder said, "Your dreams have the power to cross realms from present to past. Aranka's dreams reveal the future. We couldn't have her spoil the surprise for you."

He paused and said, "Security guards are outside this door. Don't even think about trying to escape."

The door made a faint hiss as he closed it behind him.

47

Love and Anger

"That's where we should be landing," Neith said, pointing out the jet's window at the landing strips of Reykjavik Airport in Iceland, as we hurtled past with no change in altitude.

"We must be headed to another private airstrip," Josh said. "Don't know why our trip to Iceland would be any different from the others."

"But it is," said Dr. Grigori from his seat near the front of the plane.

Neith, Dilani, Josh, Miyako, and I, plus Dr. Grigori and Dr. Calleo were together in the cabin, along with two well-armed Grigori goons. We were prisoners. We weren't in handcuffs but we didn't need to be. Where would we go, even if we made a run for it once the plane landed? Everywhere outside of Reykjavik was sparsely populated and it's not like any of us were equipped for long-term survival outdoors. Plus, we had heard as we boarded the plane over the pilot's radio a warning that a gale was on its way.

Still, a glimmer of hope burbled inside me. The part of me that wanted answers was about to be gratified. It made no sense, I know, but I took some smidgeon of pleasure thinking that I might die, but just before I went lights out, I would think, "Oh! Now I get it," or, "That's what this was for."

We already knew we were getting close to the SPREE sanctuary that had sent the distress video, although we didn't know whether or not any Elioud were still there. We were also certain that Iceland was where the Watchers were imprisoned.

"This trip is different," Dr. Grigori repeated. He looked like a contented cat deciding what to do with the wounded animals he had trapped between his paws. "We are landing at the Zozzaezsk Airstrip, built by the

Russians and officially closed at the end of the Second World War. Neith, explain for your less logophilistic companions why the name of the airstrip is significant."

Neith sounded defeated. "The letter seta, equal to zed or zee in English, was abolished by official act of Icelandic parliament in 1973. It had fallen out of use, with a few exceptions—some older people's names, the name of a school and the title of one of the newspapers. The airport's abbreviation would be all setas, ZZZ, making it officially non-existent."

"However, Dr. Grigori said, "As you will soon see, still very much in operation."

"Dr. Grigori, what are we doing here?" I asked, trying to strike a tone of mild curiosity, heavy on indifference.

He wet his skinny lips with his pointy little tongue. "You are the Young Scholars we have most carefully groomed, the ones with the abilities that, in the end, have proven most valuable to us for this mission. You tell me what you are doing here. Let us see if your education has been successful."

We were quiet. Only the hum of the plane's engines accompanied our thought. I wondered how much to say. I looked at the others, silently asking their permission to start. I got a small nod from each.

"You're taking us to release the Watchers. The place they have been held captive is on this island and you want them released. You think we have the ability to do that for you and for some reason we would be willing to do that, even though it sounds like a very bad idea."

"Very good," said Dr. Grigori. "Except for your assessment. You have learned by now that judgment is a relative task. One group's 'bad' is another's 'life-giving.'"

I tried to keep a neutral face. "Why do you think we'll help you?"

"We know you. When provided the opportunity and the correct circumstances, each of you will put yourselves above the others, despite your little group's superficial feelings of camaraderie."

I felt my eyebrows rise. The others looked surprised as well.

"Don't be surprised. Zia also had this characteristic of self-interest. She could not keep details of your extracurricular adventures, your little explorations into what we might be up to, to herself when given the choice to give us information or forfeit the one thing she wanted most in life. What is the expression? She 'sang like a bird'?"

"You tortured her!" Neith cried in alarm. "She wouldn't just tell you that!"

"True, it took effort to get information from her. When we finished, we did promise to reward her for her troubles. And we are keeping our word. She is perfecting her sound, working with an exacting vocal coach, although she is not in Milan. The final performance in her short career will be, shall we say, earth-shattering."

"Why do you want to hurt us?" Neith asked. He looked into his lap as he spoke. I'm sure he was trying to keep back tears.

"Your feelings are not our concern," Dr. Grigori said calmly. "But why should we not take advantage of your weaknesses if you offer them to us? How you respond is your concern, perhaps even your choice. For example, Neith has allowed himself to feel affection for Zia and now he suffers the consequences of those feelings. Feelings are a waste of time, a distraction. In the end it is your actions that define you."

"But wasn't it the Watchers' feelings that got all this started?" Josh said. "They felt attracted to human women and desired life with them on earth. If they hadn't followed their feelings, they would have stayed in their place, everything would have been fine, and, actually, you wouldn't exist."

Josh stopped, probably realizing that none of us would. Without the Watchers and their rebellion, there would be no Nephilim, and no Elioud.

Dr. Grigori looked at Josh, cocking his head, a look of mock pity on his face. "Yes, is that not the irony? Something you label as evil, the cause of many very bad things in the world, results in good as well. You do think your own existence is good, do you not?"

"Of course," Josh said. "But that's the wonder, right? That even out of something bad, something good can arise? Isn't that the great point of resurrection, of grace, whatever you want to call it? That doesn't mean setting the Watchers loose is a good idea."

"I return to my earlier point. The Watchers' actions were what defined them. Perhaps your action, in setting them free, can vindicate them. After all, if the end of the story is that they stay imprisoned because beings on one side label their actions as 'evil,' then history will judge them so. But if, on the other hand, they are set free, overturning the sentence originally placed on them, would that not prove the original judgment was false?"

"That doesn't necessarily follow," Josh said.

"In the end, it is your actions, not your feelings that will be judged. And you will, when the moment of decision comes, take action to help us."

A chime sounded, indicating we were about to land.

"Our final journey," said Dr. Calleo.

48

Ash and Angels' Fear

We got into the two silver Porsche Cayennes that were waiting when we stepped off the jet and zoomed off along a smooth paved road toward an ice-covered mountain in the distance. Between that mountain and us was another mountain, smaller than the icy one, dark brown, the color of dried acorns, and craggy. A wreath of smog hovered over it like the halo on a saint who had gone off the rails. Deep green moss-covered rocks covered the ground on either side of the road.

"The volcanic ash that has periodically covered this part of the island makes for rich soil," Dr. Calleo said, like we may as well enjoy the scenery as we traveled. She gestured out the window on our right hand side, "See the steam? Hot springs. Iceland is covered with them. Most of the energy humans produce here is geothermal, derived from hot water that courses underground. Fortunately they have not figured out how to transport this energy efficiently off the island. Such a discovery could make an unfortunate dent in the use of fossil fuels by neighboring countries."

I tried to tune her out and think about what Dr. Grigori had said about why we would help. He said they knew that each of us, under the right circumstances, would put ourselves above the others. I felt my face redden as I realized what this meant. They knew about my refusal to share my antimony with Dilani. Maybe they knew I had lied to her about not having enough. I felt ashamed.

Then again, what had the others done? Each of them also must have done something that made Dr. Grigori so cocky. I started thinking about Josh and how he was always so sure that he was right, how his opinion counted for more than the rest of ours. How Miyako seemed like she enjoyed that we had all been dependent on her for the antimony she got us from the lab. How Neith always made me ask for an explanation of whatever fancy word he used, as if he liked watching my confusion while I tried to figure out what he was talking about. How he always preferred Zia to the rest of us. I bet his little secret had something to do with her. Dilani showed more compassion to her rat, or any animal, than she ever did to any of her actual friends.

I shook my head. *Snap out of it!* I thought. *This is exactly what they want you to do! They are hoping to divide us, turn us again each other.* I looked at sweet Neith, so gentle, and so sad over Zia's departure, and even more sad thinking she had suffered, and how he always just wanted what was best for her. Josh was so funny and thoughtful and smart. Why shouldn't his opinions count for more when they were so often right? Miyako always watched out for us, and I'm sure giving antimony away could get her in big trouble. And Dilani had stuck with me the whole time, when her animals probably were kinder to her than any of us, including me, had been. I blinked back a tear and resolved not to give into the temptation to put myself first.

The road under us had turned to crushed red gravel, but we still rocketed along, a plume of dust rising behind us. The smell of gravel always made me carsick. If I had to throw up would they stop? Could I make a run for it? Where would I go?

The landscape around us looked more like moonscape. The mossy green rocks had given way to dusty carmine, the color of dried blood. Ahead of us the mountain appeared closer, but between it and us was desolate, hard-packed earth. I focused on looking out the front window and pretended the bounces and jerks of the drive came from being on an amusement park ride instead of inside a speeding vehicle taking us to a hoard of evil angels. Tower of Terror had nothing on us. *Breathe in, breathe out*, I thought. At least no water was in sight.

When we got closer to the brown and desolate-looking mountain with its grimy halo, we slowed, and I could see that it wasn't deserted at all. Workers emptied buckets of silvery rocks into steel ore cars on a rail. Smoke belched from a stack. An iron contraption emptied large containers of the silvery rocks onto a pile. Workers scurried over to the pile as soon as the container was emptied and filled their buckets, then loaded another car.

"Our newest and most efficient antimony mine," Dr. Grigori beamed, nodding in the direction of the mountain.

Beyond the mountain of antimony, I thought, recalling the Book of Noah. That's where the Watchers are imprisoned.

Dr. Grigori went on, "Recently opened and already producing a sizable yield. Do not look too closely at the workers. You will not like what you see. Antimony burns the skin of beings not suited to its consumption." He tutt-tutted. "Look at you—so concerned, but you would not trade places with them voluntarily. If we had no other plans for you, I would give you the opportunity to test my assertion. Their families are grateful for the small income they receive. You are grateful for the product. All but Neith cannot survive without it. A small price: discomfort for workers with no other options. Great advantage for us. You feel superior in your judgment of me, but in your secret thoughts you agree."

I saw a pink face, marked with scars like overblown roses, look up from behind a bucket as we rolled past. The driver hit the accelerator and we left the antimony mine behind.

After about thirty more minutes the hard packed red landscape and gravel road ended abruptly. Our vehicles stopped right at the edge of an immense rock fall. The driver opened our doors and we stepped out onto stones the size of loaves of bread. Ahead of us, the stones got bigger: the size of end-tables, then sofas, then boulders taller than any of us. The SUVs shifted into reverse and roared off, leaving us teetering on the rocks. The wind howled. I turned the collar up on my thin jacket and hugged my elbows.

We stood there keeping our balance and shivering against the blowing wind for only a minute when a huge slate gray vehicle with oversized tires crunched up next to us on the rocks. 'Landrover Defender' was emblazoned across its grill. Although it looked powerful, I wasn't sure the Defender would live up to its name if we did what the Grigoris wanted us to and released the Watchers. What would the Watchers do if they got out? Toast us to a crisp in our not-so-tough-after-all truck? A tank couldn't keep us safe if these rebel angels lived up to their reputation.

"Super Jeep," Josh said. "I wondered how we would get over these rocks."

The driver got out and propped a stepladder next to the vehicle's side doors. The tires on the jeep were about five feet high. One of the goons motioned us to get in and the jeep started to roll over the rocks. I thought of the Mars Rover and hoped we wouldn't flip over if we hit a rock at the wrong angle. Who would find us out here? Then again, how had the Super Jeep arrived so soon after we had been dropped off? Maybe abandonment wasn't what I needed to be afraid of.

The Jeep lurched and bumped its way over a large hill of brick red boulders. When we reached the top I inhaled sharply. In front of us was a valley of boulders that led to a huge field of ice and snow, a glacier that stretched as far as I could see. The top of it formed a clear demarcation with the sky. The world might end right at the top of it, except that I could see the peak of the mountain we aimed for poking up behind its silver-white expanse.

The Jeep picked and growled its way across the boulders and burped to a stop outside a small wooden shack perched at the edge of the ice field. A guard ushered us out and a tall man with broad shoulders and thick blond hair came out of the shack. The temperature here was much colder than where we got off the plane, just above freezing. The man motioned us to come into the shack. The warmth of the building made me feel a little better, but the snowmobile suits hanging on a rack did not.

"Put these on," Dr. Calleo said. "Gunter will assist you."

The blond brute who must be Gunter looked at each of us and handed us black snowmobile suits, boots, gloves, and helmets, and motioned for us to put them on. Dr. Calleo and Dr. Girgori went to a closet at the back of the shack and pulled out two sleek black leather suits that fitted them perfectly.

"Hurry up," Dr. Calleo said, when she saw me staring at them.

Gunter led us outside where another vehicle had pulled up with a fleet of snowmobiles. Each was driven by a black-leather outfitted driver wearing a black helmet and reflective goggles so we couldn't see a face. The drivers revved the snowmobile engines and Gunter escorted each of us to a snow-mobile and indicated that we should get on and hold onto the driver. He gestured to me to put my helmet on. I did and pulled the face shield down.

Being inside the helmet made me feel better. Its thick padding quieted the roar of the snowmobiles and made me feel safer, although I wished I had more than a Grigori-employed stranger to hang onto for security. Gunter waved his arm down like he was signaling the beginning of a race, and we roared off toward the summit of the icy hill. Rivulets of water ran beneath us. The glacier must be melting. The combination of speed, ice, and flowing water about six inches deep made my stomach lurch and my head feel a little woozy. I repeated to myself, "Never alone" as I clung tighter to the stranger speeding me toward certain danger.

When we reached the crest of the hill, I noticed that the ice had be-come solid. The glacier field stretched out ahead of us about another half mile, then was interrupted by a large crater, about one hundred yards in diameter. Thin strands of steam rose from its dark maw. So this is what a volcano encased in ice looked like. I breathed a sigh of relief when I realized the volcano must be dormant since the ice around it was completely frozen. Despite the wisps of steam, the magma in the middle must be fairly recessed and calm not to be heating up any of the ice we were zooming across.

We reached the lip of the crater. The driver reached around and plucked me off the back of the snowmobile. I pulled off my helmet. The sun had come out and the glare off the ice was blinding. I squinted, shielded my eyes with my hand and saw that everyone else was also standing beside their snowmobiles. Suddenly, the snowmobiles all revved and reversed, then spun around and roared off in the direction from which we had come, leaving the four of us alone with Dr. Calleo and Dr. Grigori. Apparently they didn't think we would need a return trip any time soon.

The snowmobile roar reduced to a drone, like a small squadron of bees in retreat, then silence. Then I realized it wasn't silent at all. I thought I heard the roar of air in my own ears, like when you put earplugs in and your own breath sounds as loud as thunder. But it wasn't my breath; it was coming from outside of me. My first instinct was to put my helmet back on and regain the muffled quiet. Instead I listened and heard a deep rumble and grinding, and below that, the strangest sound I had ever heard, a keening and moaning, mournful, yet beautiful, haunting in its sadness.

"Can you hear it?" Dr. Grigori asked. "Better yet, can you decipher it?"

"Magma?" I responded, choosing to ignore the deeper and more disturbing sound. I wished I could keep the question mark out of my voice as if sounding certain would give me the strength I lacked.

"Yes," he said. "Magma is the source of the rumble and hiss. As it heats, one also hears a roar that will increase until the sound is masked by the earthquake that will most likely accompany the eruption. But whether one will hear the roar of the volcano or the roar of the Watchers when they are freed is a better question in our particular circumstance."

"What's the whining sound?" Josh asked, an edge to his voice. It was almost a sneer. I wanted to cheer him on when he continued, "Is that your precious Watchers? Are they crying?"

"You be the judge," Dr. Grigori replied. "Could be the Watchers. But, perhaps it is coming from over there." He pointed past the crater's far rim and we saw it, a small wooden hut. "The new location of SPREE's Iceland sanctuary. We decided to relocate its residents here once we found them. Our way of honoring these young Elioud who will be amongst the very first to see the Watchers released."

"The sound is definitely coming from the crater. It's the Watchers." I said, pleased with myself.

Dr. Grigori frowned. "So it is. But not for long."

"You still haven't explained why we should or would help you, let alone how," Dilani said.

"Give me the rat," Dr. Calleo said and stuck out her gloved hand toward Dilani.

"What rat?" Dilani said, unconvincingly.

"He will smother inside your snowmobile suit. Give him to me."

Dilani undid one of the snaps and reached into her suit. "What are you going to do to him?" she asked, I think stalling for time.

"I am not going to do anything," Dr. Calleo said calmly. "I am giving you a choice. Go into the crater, and I will bring your little friend along. Do not go into the crater and you both freeze out here. Your choice."

Dilani looked like she was thinking. I thought too. The presence of Bruce didn't really make any difference, did it? We would all freeze if left out here by ourselves, rat or no rat. But Bruce had proved useful in the past. Maybe bringing him along was a good idea.

"Okay," she said, and handed Bruce to Dr. Calleo, who put him in her pocket. "I'm sure we all want to see what's down there anyway." Dilani sounded almost jocular, like we were all just on an unusual field trip.

"That's the best they can do?" Josh whispered to me. "Get down there or the rat turns into a popsicle?"

I stifled a giggle. It did seem lame.

"At least we know the volcano isn't active," I said quietly. "There's only the faintest whiff of sulfur. If this volcano were about to erupt, the smell of rotten eggs would have choked us all the moment we got off the plane." The sulfur smell was tempered by the odor of rock, soil, must, and moss. Okay, one thing not to be afraid of.

"It is time to make our descent," Dr. Grigori said.

The wind picked up and I started to shiver. Maybe going into the crater would provide some relief, at least until the snowmobiles came back or we figured out what to do next to get us out of this situation.

Dr. Grigori led the way to a ladder that poked the capped ends of its side rails just above the lip of the crater.

"Single file," he said and pointed at Josh. "You first."

"Neith, you can go last," Dilani said loudly, as if daring Dr. Grigori to contradict her. "That way we'll all be just below you, rooting for you."

"It should be fine," Neith said, a slight quaver in his voice. "I'll be facing a wall, so I won't be able to tell the height I'm at."

"Dr. Grigori," I said suddenly, "What's to prevent other people from discovering where we are? Don't tourists here love these sorts of adventures—snowmobile on a glacier, climb into a volcano—that sort of thing? What makes you so sure someone won't come upon us while we're in here?"

"Very astute, Kaia," he said. "However, there are two reasons no one will discover, or rescue you. First, most Super Jeeps aren't so well equipped to handle the terrain we have crossed to get here. The second, Neith can guess."

Neith rolled his eyes. "Whatever the name of this glacier and volcano are, they have a lot of setas in them."

"Correct," said Dr. Grigori. "No longer on the map. Where we now stand is merely a speck on one of the largest ice fields in Europe, formerly known as Zeszerbrezz. Descend," he repeated, pointing at Josh, who dutifully started down the ladder.

We inched downward. The ladder felt secure enough, but I was nervous trying to find the rungs with my bulky snow boots and big puffy mitts on my hands. Thankfully, about fifty steps down, we reached a large rocky shelf. A railing had even been installed along the edge so we could look down to where the next rock shelf jutted out. Another ladder connected the level we currently stood on with the one below. The bright sun shone down into the crater and illuminated the hole. I could see that the crater walls narrowed in, like we were climbing into a funnel made of red rock. It was definitely warmer inside. Dr. Grigori and Dr. Calleo removed their gloves and undid the zippers on their snowsuits and nodded to us to do the same.

"How far down do we go?" Miyako asked.

"Three more levels," Dr. Calleo said. "We must keep going so we do not lose the light."

Dr. Grigori motioned to Josh, who made the next descent, then helped each of us off the ladder at the next level. The mossy smell was stronger, and the air was more humid. I could hear water dripping. The rungs were more slippery. The moaning sound was louder, more urgent. I felt a little sorry for whatever was making such a mournful sound.

Miyako started to talk, actually babble a bit. "Good thing the volcano isn't active. Volcanic gas is heavier than the air we breathe. It would force the oxygen out of the air around us, and we would suffocate."

"You're not making us feel better," Josh said, but he put a hand on her back. "It's going to be okay," he said.

I wasn't so sure.

Our descent to the third level was the longest. The walls had become quite narrow, with not much space around us, maybe about five feet. I tried to remember what we had learned about volcanoes in science class. Were we in the throat of the volcano, the part where the ash, then lava spews out?

When we reached the bottom of the third ladder, the space opened to a much wider chamber, with a low ceiling and a wide, firm floor. Small torches were affixed to the walls and they burned a smoky light that flickered and made our shadows lengthen, then shorten, then lengthen again. It looked like strange black expanding and shrinking creatures were dancing all around us. I could hear the Watchers' keening, a hissing, the drip of water onto rock, a low rumble and the whoosh of the torch flames. The gale brewing above us outside the volcano was completely shut out. I was reminded of the burial chamber on Orkney and how only the sound of my own heartbeat and breathing were perceptible, as if the outside world didn't exist.

I allowed myself a deep breath through my nostrils. I thought if this was going to be my last experience, I should experience it fully. The combination of scents was incredible: the tang of sulfur, the comfort of moss, the heady vapor of gas from the torches on the walls, the smell of ice crystals that must be passing above the volcano, and then a scent so beautiful I let myself fall into it, I focused on it, let it fill me: the scent of sunshine, the first snowfall, the first crocuses signaling spring, summer rain breaking open a heat wave, a bushel of just picked apples. I ached to know what it was, and everything around me went black.

§

The Watchers wailed as the Archangels walled them off inside the stone chamber. Their multi-colored wings, covered with eyes, that had glowed with opalescence and gold, were folded down behind them. They covered their faces with their lissome hands. Heavy chains affixed to shackles clinked as their shoulders shook with their weeping.

Then, as the last stone was put into place, the sobbing stopped instantly. They looked up as one and their eyes changed appearance from reddened and teary to cold, blue steel. "Let us take an oath," said Shemihazah, their leader. "We will be freed before the judgment. Our offspring will come to our rescue. Then we shall have vengeance. We shall destroy and build once again on the ashes of ruined humanity. The Enemy shall regret that he chose them over us, denied us our right to use the pathetic, weak Merely to our benefit." The Watchers reached their hands toward the center of the circle they formed. Their chains prevented them from touching one another, but they said in unison, "I swear," and the sound reverberated through the chamber like the sound of an earthquake, but nothing moved.

The four Archangels looked down into the tunnel of stone that led to the Watchers' prison. Michael stretched his hand toward the tunnel and flames leapt high within the mountain, filling the passageway to the prison's entrance. There was no scent, no ash, just heat.

"The Watchers are contained," Michael said. The other three nodded solemnly.

Gabriel spoke, "You wish to say more."

"I do not question the plan of the Almighty," Michael intoned. "But yes," he hesitated. "I want to add, 'for now.'"

The mountain rumbled beneath them and the Archangels took flight.

§

"Kaia! Kaia!" Josh repeated, as he held my hand and dabbed at my forehead. "Are you okay? You left us for a moment."

"I just felt a little faint," I lied. I hoped I hadn't been out for too long. I didn't want to answer any questions about whether I had been dreaming and how the scents had set me off. "It's claustrophobic down here," I said. I hoped it wouldn't happen again, especially if I were on a ladder or hanging out over some magma chasm.

"Time to get to work," Dr. Grigori said. "You know why we have come."

"You want us to release the Watchers," Josh said, "although we don't know why you need our help, or what you expect us to do that you can't do by yourselves, unless . . ."

"Unless?" Dr. Calleo said.

"Unless this is some kind of suicide mission and you think we're expendable," Josh finished.

"You are far from expendable," Dr. Grigori said, "at least to us. And we believe the Great Ones will reward you for coming to their aid. If you refuse or fail, we will find others who will complete the task. But it will be so much easier, and certainly less painful for you if you simply cooperate. Then a reward, rather than wrath, may come to you. Why should it not after you have done all the work?" He was practically purring.

"The Watchers are enclosed in a cavern of stone, below us, correct?" I said, stalling for time.

"Yes," Dr. Calleo said. Her face glowed with anticipation.

"And you need a way to get through this rock." I said. "Why can't you just blast through it? You're into mining after all. Surely you know how to blast through even really hard rock." I paused, thinking. "Would the Watchers get hurt?"

"Do you think rock projectiles would hurt the Great Ones?" Dr. Grigori screeched. "Repent of your blasphemy!"

"Sheesh," I said, trying to sound casual, but his weird high-pitched voice frightened me.

I tried again. "No, it's you, and we, who would get hurt. Our bodies would suffer from a blast."

Dr. Grigori nodded. "Correct. If we blast through the rock while we are in the vicinity, we will be hurt."

"So, what's the plan?" Dilani asked.

"Patience," Dr. Grigori said, the deep, soothing quality back in his voice. "It is gratifying to watch you, our students, put the pieces together yourselves."

"You want to keep the Great Ones waiting?" Josh mocked.

"Silence!" Dr. Grigori hissed at him. But then his brow furrowed. He seemed confused. Josh was right. We heard a rumble from below. Surely the Watchers wouldn't wait forever. They must have sensed that a chance for escape was close.

"I pray for the Great Ones' forbearance. It will demonstrate your worthiness if you can figure this out yourselves. But, yes, we must not keep them waiting." He opened his palm to Dr. Calleo. She nodded and put Bruce onto his hand. Bruce sniffed at him, then sat up on his haunches and rubbed his whiskers, as if wanting to get rid of the smell. Dr. Grigori closed his large hand around Bruce so only his head protruded. The rat's eyes bulged.

"Think faster," he said.

"It has something to do with the Tower of Babel," I said. "The one you've reconstructed in the Burj Khalifa."

"Go on," Dr. Grigori drawled.

"You're going to broadcast something from there . . ." I stopped. I gulped and raised my hands to my mouth before I could stop myself. The pieces were coming into place, like a giant puzzle, a giant, three-dimensional architectural jigsaw puzzle. I stuffed my hands in my pockets and breathed in deeply before I spoke, trying to stay calm. The mix of moss and sulfur scents made me gag a little.

"The Tower. That's what the Tower is for. And," I breathed again, "and Zia. That's what Zia is for. That's why you have her. Discord."

"All that time you wasted thinking of yourself as inferior," Dr. Grigori said. He made a tutting sound. "You had the power to reason all along. Perhaps you just preferred to think of yourself as incapable. Laziness. Fortunately you have the opportunity to repent of that now. A second chance. You love second chances, do you not?"

My face bloomed red with shame. I blinked back tears and steadied my voice.

"You're going to broadcast Zia's voice, but turn its beauty to discord. You're going to broadcast a horrible noise using the Tower of Babel in the Burj Khalifa as the transmitter."

Josh nodded and continued, "The noise will disrupt all radio and broadcast communications, interrupt cellphone service, wifi. You'll cause chaos."

"For precisely six hours," Dr. Calleo said, "Exactly the period of time we need to distract the rest of the world from what we are actually interested in accomplishing, while everyone panics."

"Meanwhile," I said, "with all eyes, or ears, focused on Dubai and the aftermath of disharmony, we go into the volcano and free the Watchers. But you don't think it's going to take us six hours to accomplish that, do you?"

Dr. Calleo shook her head. "Of course not. We have no interest in being here that long. We are, however, convinced that six hours will prevent any military response once people become aware of the Watchers' release."

I continued, "But there's still the problem of getting through the rock to get to the Watchers."

"Cavitation!" Dilani said. "The Watchers are in a rock chamber, surrounded by ice, and you want to use cavitation to break through. You're going to use sound waves through the ice to pulverize the rock and let them out of the chamber."

"Very good, Dilani," Dr. Grigori smiled.

"But if the sound waves you broadcast are that strong, strong enough to affect the thick ice layer all the way over here, they are also powerful enough to destroy everything surrounded by water in any form. You could start tsunamis on every coast in the world. And then what will you have? You, or the Watchers, will have nothing to rule over, no one to take revenge on. You'll preside over ruins."

"Just when you were showing such promise," he clicked his tongue and shook his head. He looked at Josh. "Can you help?"

"You won't destroy everything. You will focus some of the sound. You'll harness some Zia's noise and aim it here. Am I right?"

"Well done."

"You'll do it with some help," Josh said.

"We have been waiting centuries for this moment," Dr. Calleo sighed. "We have been trapped. The Peerless have had to act as if we have less angelic blood than we do, pass for Merely even, although we can never truly pass as inferior." She stroked her blond hair with her hand and straightened her shoulders. She seemed to have grown six inches since we came down here.

"An army of Peerless is ready to unfurl their glorious wings at my command. They will take to the skies and use their wings to direct some of the sound waves here. The rocky chamber will be opened." She looked at Josh and me. "You could have joined us, if your beloved SPREE rescuers had not deformed you with that terrible surgery. Your wings would have been your glory, had you not been butchered by those SPREE barbarians."

Josh and I looked at each other. We were Peerless? A sharp pain like a jolt of electricity ran through my scars.

"Imbeciles!" Dr. Calleo scoffed. "You are not Peerless. But your particular genetic makeup gave you one of our most exquisite features, lost through mutilation."

I suddenly knew why Xanthe's portrait and ashes had been removed from the bell tower. "Some of us get very close to Peerless, though, don't we? You thought Xanthe was one of you. You gathered her ashes. You hung her portrait. Then you discovered she wasn't 'pure' enough. She had passed for one of you and you couldn't stand it."

Dr. Grigori's eyes flashed. I caught a whiff of charcoal and burnt toast—anger. He took a deep breath and regained his composure. "I assure you, we would have set her to different tasks had we exposed her earlier."

"There's a flaw in your plan," Dilani said. "The cavitation could activate the volcano. The magma will liquefy, the glacier will melt. The Watchers, and we, and you, and everyone within a hundred mile radius will suffocate or drown."

Dr. Grigori looked impressed.

"Drowning is the real danger, isn't it?" Dilani paused, then nodded as the implications became clear to her, and to me. "That's why none of us likes water, why some of us, like Kaia, are positively afraid of it. Angels can't survive in water. They were never meant to inhabit watery realms."

"And the Watchers are still chained," Josh said. "Even if their stone cavern is blasted open, they're still in chains, unbreakable chains that will keep them from escape. Water will pour into the cavern around them, and they will face the most terrifying death they can imagine. Judgment Day will come early for them. And you will have brought it on. In the cosmic scheme of things, your extinction will be justified as well. Even by the Watchers' standards. You think they would forgive you for that? The other Peerless would fly away, leave you for dead, and they, not you, would be the most powerful beings in the world."

"No Peerless can last forever." Dr. Grigori said. "Even with our antimony mining and harvesting of Elioud. Elioud blood is becoming too feeble, watered down through further intermixing with Merelys. I hate the smell of Elioud blood, but sometimes it is unavoidable."

His nose wrinkled in disgust as he said this and my nostrils flared with rage. I tried to stay calm as I asked, "And how does releasing the Watchers help you survive? How do they make up for your 'feeble Elioud blood'?"

"Why, the Watchers will created more Peerless, of course," he sneered. "And this time, we can be selective in breeding and concern ourselves exclusively with the only legitimate use for Elioud—our preservation. This is why the Watchers must be released and the timing of the cavitation of the rock and their release from their chains must be impeccable."

"Why do you think Zia will help you?" I asked. "She's a strong person. She would go through hell to keep you from hurting anyone else. We know her."

"You love her," Dr. Grigori said. The cloying sweetness in his voice made me gag. "And she loves you. And that is why she will help. She knows we will kill you if she does not. She would do anything if she thought it would save your life. Love is a terrible motivator, so useless in the end."

He raised Bruce up in front of us and then clamped his other hand hard over Bruce's head. I heard bones snap.

"No!" Dilani screamed.

Dr. Grigori opened his hand. Bruce lay lifeless, his neck at too sharp an angle to his little body.

Dilani flew at Dr. Grigori and started pounding his chest. Dr. Grigori calmly dropped Bruce to the rock floor, then grabbed Dilani by her raised fists.

"Anger is another matter. Anger is a powerful and effective motivator." He folded her arms down behind her and spun her around so she faced us.

"What would you do out of anger?" Dr. Grigori asked. "You have seen that Dilani would attack me because I killed a rat, an animal most humans would rather see dead. What would you do if any of you did something that caused pain one of you?"

Dilani stopped crying. A shadow crossed her face.

"For instance," Dr. Grigori said, "What if Dilani had given information that had sent some of your friends in the program home early? Well, as you know, not 'home.' We needed something to call it, and 'extraction' or 'extinction' would have caused alarm."

Neith said, "What are you talking about?"

"What would you do if you found out that it was Dilani who chose you to stay and others to leave? What would you do if you knew we left many of the choices up to her? The good news is you mean something to her. She chose you. The bad news is she did not choose people you grew close to, people you each cared about."

"I didn't know," Dilani said, tears welling in her eyes. "I just thought I got to pick my friends. I didn't know what would happen to the others." Her face was crumpled in surprise. "I didn't know. You have to believe me."

Miyako charged at Dilani. Josh and I pulled her back. "She didn't know," Josh said. "She thought she was doing the right thing." Miyako relaxed and dropped her head to her chest. She sniffled. I let go of Miyako and scooped up Bruce. I rubbed his head.

"I'm so sorry, Dilani," I said. She nodded sadly.

"Me too. So very sorry."

"Here," Neith said. He took a folded handkerchief out of his pocket and reached out for Bruce. He wrapped the dead rat in the white cloth.

"I know why you need us, or me at least," he said. "I'm the only one who can help you with the final piece." He looked at Dr. Grigori and Dr. Calleo. "The universal language, right? That's the only thing that will break the chains that bind the Watchers. That's why you collected votives and put them in the reconstructed Tower to hear the sounds. That's why you collected manuscripts and looked for the Book of Noah. That's why you killed to get it translated."

"At last," huffed Dr. Calleo. "I was beginning to think we would need all six hours. Of course it is the language."

"You thought about using the antimony acid, fluoroantimonic acid," Miyako said. "I found the cylinder in the lab, but it's not strong enough. It can't break the chains. Only the power of the spoken word can do it, saying exactly the right word, exactly the right way."

"And what is the word?" Dr. Calleo asked, as if conducting a final oral exam.

"The word Jesus said when he released the demons from the Gerasene demoniac," I said. "Jesus said the word that releases demons. It doesn't matter what they're bound by—a person, a chain. What matters is the word and saying it just the right way."

The rumbling beneath us got louder.

Neith said, "And I'm the only one perfectly formed, or deformed, you would say, who can say the right word perfectly, just like a human would say it, a human living at the time of Jesus." He smiled. "And if I refuse?"

"The Tower is ready, Zia is prepared, the Peerless are ready to take flight. With or without you, the cavitation happens, the magma explodes, the rock crumbles, the glacier melts. If you do not release the Watchers, we all die. For nothing."

"Or maybe your 'for nothing' saves the world, at least for now. It all depends on how you look at it, right?" I said. "Isn't that one of your precious lessons?"

"Neith will do it," Dr. Calleo said calmly. "And soon. At precisely the right time. He can say the word, even from here, and it will be enough. The chains will be broken. The rock will be opened. The Watchers will be freed.

We will be taken up with them, and their gratitude for your cooperation will bring you glory as well. Why choose death and oblivion when you can have glory?"

"As a reward," Dr. Grigori said to Neith, "your friends can leave right now. The snowmobiles will come here to pick them up by the time they reach the top of the ladder. They will have enough time to make it far enough away to survive the volcano's eruption. I am sure the Great Ones will be merciful at the judgment, in recognition for the roles they have played in the release."

The rumble below us turned into a roar, the Watchers' keening into a whine.

"I'll do it," Neith said. "But my friends are staying here, with me."

We looked at each other. My first thought was thanks, but no thanks; I would be happy to hop on a snowmobile and get as far away from here as possible.

"The choice is theirs," Dr. Grigori said. "If they are willing to stay and watch, so be it."

After a little hesitation, we each said okay.

"Never alone," Neith said. "Stronger together," he said, and we knew he had a plan.

"One more thing. Guarantee that the SPREE sanctuary by the top of the crater is empty," Neith said.

"You already know it is empty," Dr. Grigori said.

"You wouldn't waste Elioud blood," Neith replied. "Just in case your plan to release the Watchers failed, or you need more time . . ."

"Or fresh recruits for the GYSP," I added.

"Any more requests?" Dr. Calleo snapped. "We have only ten minutes before the fullness of time."

"Yes," Neith said. "We need to be with the Watchers in the chamber. You were mistaken when you said it would work from up here. The acoustics won't be right, and it won't work. Isn't that right, Josh?"

Josh nodded, although the look on his face showed he had no idea what Neith was up to.

"That is impossible," Dr. Calleo said. "We know there is a tiny fissure in the wall of the cavern through which the sound of the Great Ones is heard, but there is no time to find it in order for you to get in."

"Bruce could have found it," Dilani sniffed.

"Yes," sighed Neith. "If only we had Bruce. To think Dr. Grigori is to blame for our not being able to carry out the plan after all." Dr. Grigori looked stricken. A hiss rose from beneath our feet. Dr. Girgori looked down at the floor in alarm. Had the Watchers heard? He went pale.

Neith looked down at the shrouded rat in his hands. "If only there were something we could do. When you're so close to getting the one thing in the world that you want, and what stands between achieving glory and bliss, and utter blame and disaster is a dead rat. I really don't know what to say at a time like this."

"Try this!" Dr. Grigori screamed, and then made a sound like wind blowing through pine needles, a breath, then a rattle, just enough to set a branch chattering and to cause a loose cone to drop. He doubled over after doing it and rested his hands on his knees while he panted.

"No, that's not quite it. I'm sure you're close, but you'll never have it quite right."

Dr. Grigori held his hands toward Neith in supplication. "Please." The 's' came out as a hiss.

"No," Josh said, a look of recognition in his eyes. "It's not your word to say, so you can't do it," he spoke in Dr. Grigori's direction. "Only angels have the power to say it correctly, angels of goodness. Kaia?"

I started, surprised. "But I'm not . . ."

"No," he said. "You're not. But the conditions in here are just right, if you choose."

And I suddenly knew what he was talking about. I could choose to make contact. To use the anamnesis Dr. Grigori said was one of my gifts, to make an angel present, to open myself to the possibility of an angel speaking through me, maybe even my guardian angel, through a waking dream.

I let every other sound fall away. I listened to the beating of my own heart. I let the drip, drip, drip of the water running down the wall be my focus and my heart got in sync. I sought and found that scent of cleanness and purity and let it fill me. I fell backwards into warm, comfortable darkness. I closed my eyes and felt filled with light—light that I knew came from an Archangel, Raphael, the Healer. He spoke the word. It sounded like wind over water, just enough wind to make a starling's flight rise, to cause it to wheel and double back in delight. A feeling of awe, then deep peace washed over me.

I blinked my eyes open.

Bruce stirred, whiskers first. Then sat up.

"The word of life," said Josh quietly. "The angels know it, because they were there when the Author of Life spoke it over the void. They aren't allowed to speak it often and the power isn't in the speaker, unless the speaker is the Creator of Life. No wonder the Grigoris can't get it quite right."

Dilani laughed in delight. Neith extended Bruce on the handkerchief toward her, like Bruce was riding a little rat chariot. She took it and lowered it to the ground. "Go on," she said. Bruce took off. Miyako grabbed a lamp from the wall and we followed, leaving Dr. Grigori and Dr. Calleo at the base of the ladder. I looked back, and saw Dr. Calleo check her watch.

Bruce led us down a passageway that got narrower and darker. Soon we were on hands and knees. I hoped Bruce hadn't just decided to save his own ratty skin. It was getting very hard to see with just one little lamp. The smell of stinkweed and match-heads was making my eyes water and my breath come out in hiccups.

"We must be in a vent that's become mostly sealed up. That would explain the texture and smell. I'm sure steam used to shoot out of here prior to previous eruptions," Miyako said.

"What's the plan, Neith?" Dilani asked. "You're not actually going to release them."

"Of course not," he said. "Miyako, tell them. I saw you siphon the gas before the snowmobiles left."

She smiled and pulled a flask from her jacket pocket.

"What's that for?" I asked impatiently.

"It's risky, but we need to make the volcano explode before the cavitation starts and we lose our advantage," Miyako replied.

I couldn't see any advantage to being in a volcano when it explodes, whether it happened now or a little while from now.

"We want to make the volcano erupt before they are expecting it, beat them to it so we have a time advantage. Catch them off guard. When the volcano erupts it will cause a major flood of glacial ice melt."

I definitely couldn't see any benefit over the Grigori plan.

"The water will stream into the chamber where we and the Watchers will be. They only get saved if Neith releases them with the word. If they're still bound, they drown."

"And us?" I asked, my heart palpitating and my breathing turning shallow.

"We will be fine," Miyako said. "Right, Neith?"

He nodded. "We will. I learned more than one word from the Grigoris."

"We need to get busy activating that volcano. Cavitation isn't the only way. We can also use a major source of heat, get it close enough to the core, and it will set off a reaction. The volcano will do the rest."

"Greek fire!" Josh exclaimed. "But, where do we get Greek fire?"

"Gasoline—check," Miyako shook the flask, "sodium nitrate—active ingredient in Neith's asthma medication—check," she said as Neith handed her his inhaler, "and antimony. Hand it over." We emptied our stashes into Miyako's open palm.

"The Watchers' chamber is right above the core. I'll make the fire when we're in their chamber. It won't take much. We have to get moving now. Only five minutes before cavitation begins."

We turned a corner and saw a blaze of light. It was emanating from a crack where the floor met the wall of the tunnel. We crawled faster and found the hole. Dazzling light shone through it. Neith was closest and covered his eyes.

"It's too bright!" he said. "I can't see."

"Don't use your eyes," I said, "Use your nose!" I had closed my eyes and for the first time could smell something other than the guts of the volcano. It was the most intense combination of beauty and ugliness I had ever encountered: rose petals and vomit, peach blossoms and rotting meat, fresh rainfall and road kill, baby's forehead and feces, hope and fear. I could smell the source of the light, so I didn't have to see it. But I felt something run over my hands and opened my eyes. It was Bruce heading the other direction. I scooped him up and put him in my pocket.

"You're sticking with us," I said.

"I can't smell it," Neith said. "I don't know what you're talking about."

I looked toward the light and was surprised that, although it was dazzling, I could see it. Dilani, Josh, and Miyako were fine too.

"We must have enough of the golden reflector in our eyes," Dilani said. "That extra layer on our retina. Neith doesn't have it, or enough of it."

"Let me go ahead," I said to Neith. "I'll guide you in. You can keep your eyes closed."

He squished himself as close to the wall as possible and I squeezed past. The light coming through the hole was intense and the sound grew louder the closer I came. It sounded like crystals shattering, but in different notes, like the keys on a piano were made of glass and that pressing a key caused it to break, but thousands at a time. And each breaking glass caused a color to release.

The hole was just large enough to let us squeeze through. Anyone with shoulders broader than Josh's would get stuck. I put my feet in first, put my arms as close to my sides as possible and shimmied through. The light felt thick around me, like I had jumped into cloud vapor. I moved away from the hole and guided Neith through, then Josh, then Dilani. I looked around, expecting to see the Watchers, but couldn't. They must be farther away, or hidden somehow. I looked at Dilani. Her eyes were completely golden. Josh's too.

"Weird," said Dilani.

"I know," I said. It looked freakish, but it must be how we could keep our eyes open and see with all the light.

"Where are they?" I asked.

Josh replied. "They're here, but we can't see them. It would be too much for us to take, even with our extra retinal protection. They would have to transmute into another form to allow us to see them."

"Will you do that?" I asked into the vaporous light.

"You possess not the courage, nor the stamina, nor the fortitude," a voice that hissed like a snake said, close to my ear.

"We're here to help," said Neith.

Were we? I still didn't understand the plan.

"You need us," said Neith. "You need me, my voice. The word, and my voice to say it. I demand you show yourselves. In a way I can see too."

The hissing changed to deep, moist breathing. Consideration.

"Better hurry," Dilani whispered. "They may be immortal, but our time is running out."

"Theirs too if the volcano blows before we're ready," Josh said.

A crack sizzled through the air and the hair on the back of my neck stood up, like lightening was about to strike. The vaporous light dissipated, and the chamber became dimmer. Soft light in all the colors of the rainbow sparkled and twinkled. I watched as Neith uncovered his eyes, then I followed his gaze.

Nine children huddled against the wall. They were barefoot and clothed with rags. Heavy shackles weighed down their arms. They scratched at their skinny arms and their chains clanked. Their eyes were in shadow with deep circles underneath. Their dark hair hung in dirty clumps. I could see their distended bellies push against their filthy robes.

"Help us," the smallest pleaded in a faint voice.

"Don't fall for it," I said. "They want us to pity them. This is a guise to manipulate us. They don't trust that manipulation isn't necessary to receive help." I looked hard at Neith. There was no way Neith really wanted to let them go.

I looked at Josh. He had cocked his head, listening. "Zia's warming up," he said. The broadcast of sound waves must have started from the Burj Kahlifa.

"Decision time," I said.

"Please," begged another. A chorus of "please, we suffer so," came up from the children.

"Show yourselves as you would appear if you and we were free," I said. "Quickly."

The smallest, evidently the leader, raised his arms. The shackles and chains remained, but their bodies grew in stature—fourteen, fifteen feet high, their musculature immense and firm, their eyes large and sparkling with light. The filthy rags disappeared and were replaced by resplendent light robes. Wings appeared, folded against their backs, the edges, tops, and tips visible. Myriad eyes blinked from iridescent bands in the full spectrum of the rainbow. Their hair and skin shone.

The leader, now the tallest, spoke, but as he opened his mouth, his tongue, like a serpents, first licked his lips. "Now! Release us now and we will have mercy on you. Do it now!"

Neith tugged on Josh's sleeve. "Tell me when," he said.

I looked at Josh. He must be able to hear before the rest of us the sound waves strengthening, beginning to reverberate back toward the Burj Kahlifa. Soon they would start to affect the glacial ice. Josh nodded to Miyako, who squatted on the floor, covering something with her jacket. I could smell gas fumes. She gave Josh a thumbs up. Josh said to Neith, "It's time."

Neith spoke first to us, "Do not be afraid. We are never alone. The water is the water of life. Take shelter under their wings, trust the power of the word, and do not be afraid."

Then he turned his face to me and said, "Kaia, you have to say the word. No human can say it properly. It has only been used by the Almighty and the angels." He spoke a syllable, but nothing happened.

I took the word Neith had uttered, listened to it reverberate through my body. Then I opened my mouth. The sound that came forth was the sound of a mother's breathing a lullaby over her baby, a bird enveloping its young, a father lifting his newborn, the release of air from a cloud as the rain ends and the molecules of moisture refract light into a rainbow.

We ran to take cover under the Watchers' wings when the explosion cracked open the world around us, the waters rushed in, and everything went black.

§

I saw my adoptive parents reaching down to me through warm turquoise water. Light streamed down in shafts from above, and the water turned all the greens and blues of the universe. They smiled. Their reach was a greeting, not an attempt to own or even guide. An acknowledgment. Pride, knowing, peace. They withdrew, the colors deepened, the shafts of light twinkled, then diminished, then disappeared. I wasn't afraid. I was ready for whatever came next. I inhaled deeply to greet the next moment. The sound of laughter and small crystalline bells surrounded me and lifted me. My own heartbeat sounded like joy.

§

The cold shocked me into panting, straining to get my breath.

"She's all right," I heard a woman's voice say. I could make out the sounds of rumbling thunder and whizzing rockets overhead, and water below, underneath the hard plank I was lying on, slapping against the side of something—a boat, I thought. I was on a boat. The smell of saltwater and rotten eggs filled my nostrils. I coughed.

"She's fine," another voice, a man's said. "That makes five. I don't see anyone else."

I turned my head and coughed again. I saw Josh smiling back at me. I returned the smile and looked to the other side. Dilani was there, her eyes closed, but she was breathing. I could see her chest rise and fall.

"Neith?" I said, coughing again.

"Here," came the reply. "I'm here."

"Miyako?"

"Yes," she said. "I'm all right."

I tried to sit up.

"Save your strength," said a woman wearing bright orange waterproofs. "We've got a bit of a trip until we get out of the volcano's flood zone. Rest until we get back to shore, then you can tell us all about your adventures. We want to hear how you happened to be in one of the volcano's branch pipes, the only way you could have been blasted out by flood water, rather than fire."

A man spoke. "You could not be luckier with your timing. We had just experienced a break in all communications. When the volcano erupted, suddenly communications were restored."

I smiled. Zia knew. Somehow she knew she could stop.

I thought I heard a rat squeak as I shut my eyes and fell back to sleep.

§

The crew from the rescue ship had left us in the waiting room of the hospital in Reykjavik. A doctor was due to come in, so we spoke quickly.

"What was the word?" Josh asked Neith. "It wasn't the word of release, was it?"

"No," he said. "They should still be chained. And it's possible they drowned. I do know the release word. It was the one word Eder drilled me on that Eder could hardly stand. It must mean *be free, be released*, or something like that. But the Watchers can't stand the thought of actual freedom.

Their own freedom of movement, being released from the chains, yes, but actual, true freedom, they can't."

"But wasn't their whole thing about exerting their free will?" I asked. "Choosing not to do what they were made for and choosing their own path instead?"

"That's the thing," Josh said. "They refuse to believe the freest free is found in doing precisely what you were made for. Trusting that the Creator got it right and choosing to follow your purpose." Josh turned to me. "So what word did you say?"

"A word of restraint," I replied.

"What?" Dilani asked.

"The word that restrains the waters. God used it at creation to separate the waters from the waters, making the oceans from some, and storing waters above the sky, at least the way the myth describes it. God used it again when Moses and the Israelites crossed the Red Sea on dry land. God spoke to the waters and made them stand still until the Israelites got through safely."

"But how did you know it?"

"Neith knew it but is too human to be able to pronounce it. It was on the list from the Grigoris, from the Book of Noah, right?"

Neith nodded and said, "Noah had heard it. He heard it breathed over the waters when finally the rain stopped. It had to have been one of the words the Grigoris drilled me on. I chose the one that sounded like the opposite of *release* and hoped it meant *restraint*. Kaia could say it perfectly." He smiled at me, then added, "Under the Watchers' wings and with the word restraining the flood water around us a pocket of air would be formed, and as long as we held onto one another, I thought we had a chance. I knew we were still in for a watery ride, but that we might survive. The blast caused by Miyako's Greek fire would be strong enough to get us to sea and away from the explosion, as long as the Watchers didn't grab onto us to try to protect us."

"Which, of course, they didn't do because they were thinking of themselves," I said.

"And they were depending on the strength of their wings to protect them through the blast. Then they would just fly away when released," Dilani said. "Angels' wings have the same cellular structure as the mantis shrimp. That was the other thing the Grigoris wanted me to compare. They wanted to make sure the wings of the Watchers could withstand the blast.

Neith said, "The Watchers must have drowned. They weren't protected by the word that restrained the water from around us. The restraint of the water went out of the volcano with us and left them there for the water and lava to do their work.

"They may have survived," Josh said cautiously. "Enoch said they are supposed to remain captive until the Great Judgment. The important thing is that they didn't get released."

"So, what happened to Drs. Calleo and Grigori?" I asked.

"Dead, maybe," Dilani said. "They didn't get into the chamber with us, and they weren't expecting the volcanic eruption when it came, so they would still have been in the path of the volcano's explosion. No Watchers flew out to shelter them. Depends if their army of other Peerless showed up a little early to help them."

The others looked relieved, but I knew there was no way Dr. Grigori wouldn't have an escape plan for himself.

The doctor came in and looked pleased to see us talking.

"This is a good sign," she said. "You look well enough that we can start with some basic information, like your names, ages, and country of origin. And then we'll get on to what you were doing on a volcano that isn't supposed to exist."

She smiled. Her eyes lit up and I thought I saw a flash of Elioud gold in them.

"Then we'll take a tour. There's a sanctuary I think you will be interested in seeing. Some children there want to meet you."

I wanted to meet the Elioud children, others like me, like us. I wanted to assure them we were all safe now. But I knew the assurance wouldn't be real until we knew for sure that the Watchers were dead. The others would have to go rescue Kiran and the rest in Dubai. I needed to go back to the Div School for one final encounter with Dr. Grigori.

Acknowledgments

This novel began with a prompt: write about a scar you have. I'm grateful to Laura Oliver, Anne Brooks, and the writing group Anne gathered to be prompted and mentored by Laura: Reid Buckley, Sherry Cormier, Amanda Gibson, Mary Luck Stanley, Nancy Jo Steetle, and Roberta Watts, who read and improved many pieces that became chapters of this novel. My gratitude goes also to Dr. Andrei Orlov who introduced me to 1 Enoch and Dr. Deirdre Dempsey, co-director with Dr. Orlov of my dissertation on the gospel of Matthew and 1 Enoch. Thanks to Jamie McLaughlin, Rich Pagano, Eileen Tess Johnston, and Joseph Pagano, who read the whole manuscript, and to Ellie Pagano who read an early draft. Their questions and suggestions made Antimony much better. Andy Richter answered my science questions. Joel Richter read an early draft and helped with website design. Jill Brickey Wilson once liberated a lab rat named Bruce, and Lydia Brauer helped me imagine the character of Dr. Grigori. Thanks also to the great people of Wipf & Stock. Above all, I am grateful to Joe for his enthusiasm for this work of fiction and even more for the real-life adventure of being partners.